UNDER THE PAINTED EYES

UNDER THE PAINTED EYES

A Story of Nepal

• *The Gurkha King* • *The Great Mountains Weep*
• *The Rising Mist*

FERD MAHLER

SINCE 1901

MOTILAL BANARSIDASS
PUBLISHING HOUSE

Reprint: Delhi, ***2026***
First Edition: Delhi, 1999

Also available at:
MOTILAL BANARSIDASS PUBLISHING HOUSE

- 4637/20, F-2, Hari Sadan, First Floor, Ansari Road, Darya Ganj Delhi–110 002 *Tel.*: (+91-11) 4559 7999
- 1st Floor, 1/2 Rathnavilas Road, Basvanagudi, Next to Pai Vista Convention Hall, South End Circle, Bengaluru–560004 (India) *Tel.*: +91-80-41275911

ISBN: 978-93-5971-307-6 (Hardcover)
ISBN: 978-93-5971-217-8 (Paperback)

Printed & Published by
Rajendra P Jain *for*
Motilal Banarsidass Publishing House
A-44, Naraina Industrial Area, Phase I, New Delhi–110 028 (INDIA)
Email: naraina@mlbd.in Website: www.mlbd.in
Tel.: (+91-11) 4751 1592

FOR THE MEMORY OF
MY MUCH LOVED WIFE
Elwyn Mahler

Preface

The three novels in this book relate to happenings in Nepal from the nation's beginning when the Gurkha King fought and took the Valley of Nepal in the 1760, through the tragedies and the rise of the Rana dynasty in the nineteenth century, to modern times. They are essentially historical novels, perhaps more so than some others of that genre because they are as much novels of events and places as they are of characters. I have adopted this approach because I found Nepal's culture so rich, its history so fascinating, and its successful fight for democracy of recent times so commendable. Whilst there are many books on mountaineering in the Himalayas there is a dearth of novels about Nepal. Until Nepal has more of its own authors, I hope that these three novels—set in its towns and villages and on the plains of the Terai and on the border with Tibet—will, in a modest way, add a little to Nepal's cultural record. I also hope that they will help to serve the already wide interest in Nepal and add to the growing number of tourists visiting that country. Finally I would like to point out that I have attempted to write a book that is concerned with human values and these are intended to offer some challenge to the reader.

Acknowledgments

I wish to thank many people who have helped me in writing this book. Foremost amongst them are my Nepalese friends and colleagues from whom I learnt much about their country's fascinating history and rich culture. There are those who have read drafts of the book, particularly Mr Pramod Adhikari and Mr Krishna Hamal. There is the Australian National Book Council for their technical suggestions and editor Patricia Munro for her much appreciated assistance and advice. My thanks also go to my family, particularly my late wife, for their comments and encouragement.

Contents

PREFACE		vii
ACKNOWLEDGMENTS		ix
BOOK ONE	: THE GURKHA KING	1-156
BOOK TWO	: THE GREAT MOUNTAINS WEEP	157-278
BOOK THREE	: THE RISING MIST	279-402
APPENDICES		403-426
ONE	: FACT AND FICTION	405
TWO	: WAR WITH THE BRITISH	407
THREE	: THE RANA CENTURY	413

'They are the all seeing eyes of the Adi Buddha,' the old priest said.
'What is that under the eyes, like a large question mark?' Hume asked.
'It is the ancient symbol indicating Dharma. The duteous way to happiness, you could say,' the priest told him.
'What way is that?' Hume asked.
The old priest shrugged, 'That, we must decide for ourselves.'

THE GURKHA KING

One

It was a July evening of the year 1764, when the British East India Company's Indiaman, "Winchester", came to moorings in the Hoogley. Calcutta gave its welcome with Fort William's big guns booming out a salute, and the men-of-war "Kent", "Tiger", and "Cumberland" signalled their greetings. Native craft dotted the river's wide brown waters, plying between the larger ships and the shore and along the Hoogley. Ashore were the trading factories, administrative buildings, houses and cantonments and, further along, yellow sands, coconut palms, native housing.

Hume Clarke, in his mid-twenties, was on deck and watched the sun setting in a curdled mass of red and gold amongst the grey monsoon clouds. He was ready to go ashore. His sea-chest was locked and brought up on deck. He had packed things the Company Headquarters in Leadenhall St, London, said he would need. He had presents for his brother and a compass and maps which he never needed, as it turned out, and his late father's pistol, a matchlock from Pistoia in Italy, which had been in the family for generations, a valuable piece and still in good working order. And, sadly, he had his father's will and the papers relating to the family estate in Hollybrook, Kent. His father had been Sir Roger Clarke, Fourth Baronet, who had farmed the estate and represented the Borough in the Parliament at Westminster.

Hume heard oars lapping the water and looked to see a boat glide out of the dusk and secure longside. They lowered his sea-chest, and he made his farewells to the "Winchester". They were farewells he was not sorry to make after five long months at sea; one hundred and fifty eight days since leaving Spithead, often tossed and buffeted by the winds and waves, a passenger with little to do, cooped up much of the time in a small, damp and dark cabin. It was not that he regretted the voyage, with the novelty of shipboard life and the crew's company, the varied beauty of the ever-changing sea, and now, here was India. Here was his brother.

Ashore, tied up at the sea-gate at Fort William, Hume found Alexander waiting for him. He grasped his brother, held him at arm's length to get a good look at him, and then they embraced with all the affection they felt for each other.

Alexander's chaise was waiting and the syce whipped the pony along the cobbled road into town. Hume never forgot his first meeting with India. The night was hot, humid, altogether beyond his expectations. The air was heavy with new odours for him: spices, dank smells from the nearby jungle, oil fumes from the lamps, cow-dung burning in the cooking fires, and animals. The bazaars were open, offering rice, vegetables, bright cottons, tropical fruits and silks for sale. There were precious stones and jewellery, spices, betel nuts and hashish. There were also brass castings of the gods, gods which Hume was to come to know well. The syce picked his way through the crowds of Hindus and Moslems, sepoys in uniform, Buddhist monks in their yellow robes, the British soldiers, cripples, beggars. Cows wandered by, and an occasional elephant. It was altogether a new world for Hume, one that excited him, fascinated him.

On past the town, past the maidan and the cantonments, they reached Alexander's bungalow which was one in a line for unmarried officers. A servant took Hume's sea-chest, and the syce drove off to the stable. Hume caught the sweet scent of jasmine as he walked with his brother through the garden to the door.

Out of the night, in the bungalow, and over a Trinidad rum and cool coconut milk, the brothers took a long look at each other. Hume saw that Alexander had changed little since his home leave three years back. But no one would take them for brothers, he thought. Alexander was the shorter man, leaner, clean-shaven with short black hair and his uniform neat. He sat stiffly in his chair rather worried-looking. Hume was the larger man, larger than most men, bearded and with fair hair which he let grow long and tied at the back in a knot. He was much more relaxed. He was dressed plainly in a black cocked-hat, knee breeches, a grey cut-away coat and a short waistcoat, all being devoid of any of the fashionable ornaments of the day, the spangles and embroidery.

Hume noticed Alexander's insignia. 'Let me congratulate you on your captaincy, Alex. You well deserve it, 'he said. Alexander Clarke had done a lot in his ten years in India. He fought under Robert Clive against the Nawabs and the French in the Decan. He came north with Clive to Calcutta to retake the town and Fort William from the Nawab. Later he distinguished himself at the Battle of Plassey.

Hume pointed to his sea-chest. 'There are things for you, Alex,' he said, his voice a baritone and with a suggestion of both farmer and gentleman. 'There's an Italian watch and chain from me and a silver crucifix from Father O'Connor.'

Alexander thanked him.

'And there are papers about the title and estate, Alex. They're yours now of course, with father dead. Let me congratulate you again.'

Alexander's face saddened. 'God, I hadn't wanted them so soon. It shocked me, father's death.'

'I can tell you it shocked us all in Hollybrook.'

'He's buried with mother now.'

'Yes, in the churchyard.'

'Father O'Connor still has the parish and he often asks about you Alex, 'Hume said. 'Still worries about you living in a heathen country, as he calls it.'

'I know, 'Alexander replied. 'He writes sometimes. I write saying I am still trying to be a good Christian. That's true enough.'

They sat in silence for some time, until Alexander asked for other news from home, happier news. Hume had much to tell him and they talked on well into the night. He spoke of relatives and friends, their tenant farmers, and happenings in Hollybrook village.

Hume rose early next morning to look around and get his bearings. Crudely built his brother's bungalow might be, but he saw its charm with its sun-dried bricks limed white and terracotta roof. Inside, it was sparse but clean, with Indian tiles on the floors and just the essential table, chairs, cupboards and beds. The windows were open to catch any cool breeze and covered with netting to keep insects out. In the garden, Hume recognised the jasmine and hibiscus, but the palms and other tropical plants were new to him. He could hear a regiment already at drill on the nearby maidan. He joined Alexander and they made a breakfast of scotch oats and goat's milk, bread and Indian tea.

Alexander had a worried glance for his brother. 'I hate to tell you, Hume. So soon too. But I must leave you to look after yourself, for some days it seems. I must apologise. They've got extra duties for me.'

Hume was disappointed, but assured him he would manage.

'We're busy with our planning. A fight's coming up, Hume. No doubt about it. Mir Kasim's out in Bihar with his army. He doesn't like us. We sacked him and got Mir Jaffar back as nawab. The Nawab of Oudh has joined forces with him. They've got around fifty thousand together.

'That's a great force,' Hume said.

'Right enough, Hume. But we're better soldiers, better trained, and much better led. We've got our thousand British and six thousand or so Indian sepoys. We'll make a match for them. Colonel Carnac has most of them out in Bihar. Cheeky fellows, Mir Kasim and the Oudh Nawab.'

As Alexander went off to take up his new duties, he apologised again to his brother.

Alone now, Hume set out to see something of Calcutta. Before long, passing a bungalow not far from Alexander's, he met a young man not yet middle-aged, a small man with a tan complexion and a pleasant face with its smooth skin and high cheek bones and dark, almond-shaped eyes. He was dressed in a tunic and white trousers with a cummerbund around the waist and an oval-shaped, black and white topi cap. He introduced himself as Puskar Maske, and, smiling a welcome, invited Hume into his bungalow for tea.

'I think you are Mr Hume Clarke, the brother of Captain Clarke,' he said. 'My servant told me that. I am glad you are accepting my invitation. I am friendly with the British, but I must apologise for the weakness in my English.'

'No, you speak English well,' Hume told him.

A broad smile lit up Puskar Maske's face. 'Thank you. I have learnt it here. I have been here on a task for my King, who is Jaya Malla. I am a Newar from the Valley of Nepal, which is far to the north in the very shadow of great white mountains. Would you like me to tell you about it?'

During tea Puskar Maske talked at considerable length. He spoke of his valley's three ancient kingdoms of Kathmandu, Lalitpatan, and Bhaktapur, and of their Malla kings. He spoke of the great white mountains there, the fields and rivers, the fertile farms. He told Hume of the great temples, the pagodas, the important festivals both Hindu and Buddhist, and the gods and goddesses. The afternoon was drawing to a close when Hume at last rose to take his leave.

'What shall I call you, Mr Clarke, how do I address you?' Puskar Maske asked as Hume was going. 'Is it sahib, like they say here, or something else? I am a Shestra and I am Sri Puskar Maske in my valley. But you need not use the Sri.'

'You can call me Hume.'

'But that is your Christian name. It would be informal. And the British are usually very formal I think,' Puskar Maske said with a broad smile.

'Not always, Puskar Maske. Hume will do.'

'Well I have a suggestion, Hume,' Puskar Maske said. 'You are new here and I have been here a year. I have a chaise and pony. I would like to show you something of Calcutta.'

'Thank you,' Hume accepted. He had already decided that he liked the look of Puskar Maske. He liked his unassuming self-confidence and the broad smile often on his face. And he liked the way he wore his jaunty topi cap, wore it most of the time apparently, indoors as well as out, Hume noticed.'

During the next week or so, Hume saw a lot of Calcutta with Puskar Maske. Alexander arranged that they visit Fort William and then the maidan, where they watched a regiment at drill. Visits into the town pleased Hume; the vibrant life excited him. One day they drove out to Dum Dum, past the mansions of senior Company people and rich Indian merchants to stop at Governor Robert Clive's great house. Clive was in England for a while and Vansitart had taken over as governor; but a caretaker showed them through some of the rooms, showed them the great luxury, the Italian furniture, French chandeliers, Indian marble and Persian carpets, and then over the extensive gardens.

Leaving Dum Dum, Puskar Maske said, 'I once talked with your governor, Hume. My King sent me here for that. I must tell you that my valley is in trouble. The Gurkha King threatens us.'

'The Gurkha King?' Hume queried.

'He is Prithvi Narayan Shah, the King of Gurkha, who is a great warrior and has already taken several princedoms in our mountains. Now he wants my valley and has blockaded it. My King sent me to get British help against him.'

'Will they help?' Hume asked.

Puskar Maske shook his head. 'One day perhaps, not now.'

One evening when Alexander returned to his bungalow, he poured drinks, and looked worriedly at Hume. 'Couldn't tell you earlier, Hume. Only had Governor Vansitart's approval to-day. Major Munro will take over from Colonel Carnac out in Bihar and command our forces at Patna. I'm to go with him on his staff. Governor Vansitart wants action. It's a great opportunity for me, Hume. We'll thrash Mir Kasim, and the Nawab of Oudh with him, and we'll get all of Bengal, Bihar and, later, Oudh. And more. They have the Mogul from Delhi, Shah Alam, with them. We'll take him too. We'll get much of India. You'll have to do without me for a while, Hume.'

He looked at Hume again, concerned about his reaction.

Hume did not hesitate. 'No Alex, I won't do without you, not after I haven't seen you for so long. I've come a long way to visit you. I'll go with the army too.'

'Come with us you say?' Alexander looked dubious. 'God, there'll be a big battle. You're not a soldier, Hume.'

'That may be, Alex. But I insist. I've decided to go.'

Alexander sat there for a while, thinking. He saw Hume was firm on the idea and would have his way. So he agreed. 'Right, then. It will be an experience for you. I'll arrange it. I'll attach you to Surgeon O'Neal.'

When Hume next met Puskar Maske, he found he knew that Major Munro was relieving Carnac and that Alexander and Hume were going with him.

'It will happen soon, Hume,' he predicted. 'It will be a greater battle than Plassey. The British will have a great victory. Of that I have no doubt at all.'

'You seem sure,' Hume said, with the fifty thousand soldiers in mind.

'The British always win, Hume. I have learnt of their victories against the Indians and the French. I know they have much of Bengal. And they will take Bihar and Oudh.' Puskar Maske looked concerned.

'It worries you?' Hume asked.

'It does and it does not, Hume. I was thinking that it would bring the British to the very door of my own country. To Makwanpur just to our south.'

'You don't want the British so close.'

'It is not at all easy, Hume. I am afraid that one day the British will cast their eyes with envy on my Valley of Nepal and want to take it. They will want the trade with Tibet and China which can pass through there. But at the same time, Hume, we need the British as friends. I told you the Gurkha King blockades us. We want British help against the Gurkhas. The Gurkha King is a man without mercy.'

'But they are not ready to help.'

'Not yet, it seems. It is sad for us. There is nothing more I can do here, so I shall go back to my country and I shall miss your company, Hume.' Then, brightening up, he said, 'But there is something else I want to do. I want to see your British army in action against Mir Kasim and the Nawab of Oudh. That would be of much interest to me and to my King. I pass through Bihar on the way back to my valley and I might have the opportunity.'

Discarding his cut-away coat, vest and cocked hat, Hume had himself fitted out with the uniform and accessories of an ensign, less the insignia. He drew a sword and ammunition for his Pistoia pistol from ordnance;

and Alexander found a horse for him from the reserves of the 3rd Cavalry.

The evening before their departure, there was a farewell function at the Governor's house, a grand affair which was held at dusk in the great reception room, spilling over to the lawns that led down to the river. Oil flares positioned around the grounds lit the warm evening, and a regimental band played. Officers were in the scarlet of the infantry, the blue and gold of the light cavalry, the green of the rifle companies, and officials wore their honours and medals. The Indian guests were heavily jewelled. The few British womenfolk, wives and daughters, wore their silks and laces, and the Indian women their colourful saris. Guests who had heard Hume was going with Major Munro wished him well. And he met Governor Vansitart, who spoke of the important battle coming up, the possibility of casualties, and his pleasure to know Hume was going with Surgeon O'Neal.

But back in the bungalow, Alexander's mood was serious and he showed concern as he spoke. 'I don't want to alarm you, Hume. Not at all. But I must point out there will be risks for us. I could be killed. Or you, God forbid.'

'God forbid,' Hume repeated, meaning it.

'Come,' Alexander said. 'I'll show you something.' Taking Hume's arm, he led him into his bedroom, turned up the lamp, unlocked a cupboard and took out an iron safe. He unlocked this and laid its contents on the table. Hume had not expected it. A great deal of wealth was there: gold, precious stones, silver, coinage. Alexander handed Hume one of the gold bars, it had a Nawab of Bengal's stamp on it. Then he took up a pendant with a beautiful stone, a huge ruby of a deep burning red, blood red, surrounded by great diamonds. 'Look at it, Hume,' he said. 'Isn't it magnificent? I got it after Plassey, from the Nawab's treasury at Murshidabad. Shuja-ud-daula's treasury.'

Hume saw he was proud of it.

Alexander felt he had to explain. 'Wealth comes, Hume. Trading, commissions, rewards, and the rest. I've been ten years in India. I've fought here.'

Of course Hume knew the East India Company was a trader, a great trader; and everyone knew that some of its senior officials had made fortunes for themselves, Governor Clive particularly. But the wealth there surprised him. Alexander must have noticed Hume's surprise. 'We also trade on our own account here, Hume. Officers and officials, most of us,' he explained.

Then Alexander took an envelope from the safe and looked thoughtfully at Hume for some moments before he said, 'My will, Hume. It would all go to you. The ruby pendant. All of it.'

'Let us pray it doesn't, Alex.'

Hume picked up the ruby pendant, held it under the light of the lamp and watched the flames burning in the great red stone, the surrounding diamonds sparkling. It was old, undoubtedly old, he thought. He wondered about its past. What had it seen in the Nawab's court, many nawab's courts, the great stone on the breasts of their womenfolk through the centuries? He wondered about its future, and, true, he had doubts about that. But he said, 'No, I am sure you will marry one day, Alex. The ruby pendant will surely go to a fortunate lady.'

Two

It was late August when Major Munro marched out from Calcutta for the Company's encampment near Patna, some three hundred miles to the north-east. He rode ahead with his staff; the reinforcements for the 3rd Cavalry followed, then the field surgery unit, with a line of supply wagons making up the rear. Quite a gathering and a regimental pipe and drum band saw them off.

They made their way along the west bank of the Hoogley, past the old French town of Chanderagore and to the north of Plassey. With monsoon rains still flooding the fields, they often had to make wide detours and at night bivouac on high ground. Hume spent time with Surgeon O'Neal, learning of the field surgery's work. But he also had Alexander's company, often riding with him in the van of the detachment. He usually had his tent pitched near his at night.

They made better progress in the broad Valley of the Ganges, which pleased Major Munro who was anxious to get to Patna and take control. Hume noticed that the Major kept much to himself, riding alone by day and having his tent pitched apart at night. He seldom saw him engage in conversation. When he spoke, it was to issue orders to be passed on by his staff.

Alexander explained, 'Major Munro has a great responsibility on his shoulders. He's a worried man. I would be in his situation. His new command's a difficult one.'

Hume remembered that Mir Kasim and the Nawab of Oudh had some fifty thousand troops against the Company's thousand British and six thousand sepoys. 'We're greatly outnumbered. That's worrying him, Alex?'

'No, not only the numbers.'

'There's something else then?'

'You haven't heard, Hume? There's trouble with some of our sepoys. Unrest. Refused duty some of them. Won't leave their quarters. A few have deserted. Mutiny, Hume. Carnac reported to Fort William that they're too unreliable for battle at present. That's one reason he's being relieved.'

Alexander explained that the unrest started a year back with the

British troops, because Fort William had not paid their prize money due after they took Patna. Some rebelled, and they were paid and things quietened down. Then the Indian sepoys, in their turn, wanted their prize money. They were given a little, but not enough.

Hume saw the unfairness of it. 'Calcutta ought to pay up,' he said.

Alexander shrugged. 'Not the problem now. Major Munro must cope. And on the eve of battle. He'll enforce discipline.'

The encampment near Patna was along the Ganges to the south of the town. The fields were covered with long lines of tents, stables, ammunition dumps and stores, the light artillery and rows of cannon. Soldiers were busy looking to the stores, servicing their weapons and tending the horses and preparing for or returning from training sorties out in the countryside. The maidan was in constant use by regiments at drill. It was a busy place, well organised. But Hume saw some sepoys with sour faces and heard murmurings of discontent.

One evening, work finished, Hume was sitting outside his tent when a sepoy in the uniform of the Bengal Native Infantry came up to him. 'Mr Clarke,' he said. 'Do you know me?'

Hume was taken aback. The officers lines were strictly off-limits to the native soldiers. Then he recognised the voice. 'Puskar Maske!' he exclaimed. 'What are you doing here?'

Puskar Maske laughed. 'Do I give you a surprise, Hume? As you see, I am now fighting with the British.' He indicated his uniform.

'Yes, I see you in uniform.' Hume was sure he should not be wearing it. 'Tell me. How did this come about?'

'It is because I am fighting with the British,' Puskar Maske repeated.

He stood smiling, looking pleased with himself, but Hume felt uneasy. He knew there had been no time for Puskar Maske to be properly enlisted In any case he would hardly be acceptable, and wearing the king's uniform unlawfully was serious. 'You owe me an explanation,' Hume said.

Puskar Maske did not share Hume's concern, apparently oblivious of any offence he was committing. 'I was going back to my valley,' he said, 'when not far from here I met a jemidar I knew in Calcutta. I must not say his name. He told me that a sepoy had deserted. Now I am that sepoy. I have become Haiji Ahmed, number 5912.' He touched the identification disk hanging round his neck. 'It cost me a little gold.'

'An impostor,' Hume said.

Puskar Maske did not understand the word, or ignored it. Hume remembered that in Calcutta he had said he wanted to see the British forces in action against the Mir Kasim and the Nawab of Oudh, to report to his king. Well let him see British power in action, he decided. Let him tell his king about it. It might prove useful to the Company in the future.

'You'll have a close view of the action, Puskar Maske. Perhaps too close.'

'I think it would be most useful for me, Hume. I know the battle will be a great one.'

'You say that?'

'I say it because the forces of the Mir Kasim and the Nawab of Oudh are many. I have seen them.'

'Where?'

'Not so far from here. It was near the village of Phulwari, a few days ago.'

'They were encamped there.'

'No, they were on the march. They were on their way to Buxar. I took a place beside their path and watched. I can tell you it is an immense force. Their column went for many miles. They have sixty thousand or even more than that. They have more than fifty thousand on foot, a thousand horse, fifty cannon, three hundred camels, many elephants. It was a fine sight. I saw the princes and generals and the jewelled harnesses of their horses, the rich howdahs on the elephants, the flags and banners, their regimental colours, the buglers and drummers. Teams of buffalo were drawing the wagons with the great cannon and hundreds of supply carts. After all that came the merchants with their bazaars, the priests and the saddhus, the astrologers and the magicians and the camp-followers.'

'You say sixty thousand!' It was even more than Hume had heard.

'Very many. Many more than we have in the Valley of Nepal. Many more than the Gurkha King has.'

Puskar Maske left to return to his adopted regiment. Hume's excitement rose. News of the enemy on the march sharpened the idea of battle for him. Then Alexander told Hume they would march on Buxar in two days. 'Major Munro won't stay his hand,' he said. 'We're ready. Discipline is better, and he intends to do more about that. We know the ringleaders causing the unrest. There are twenty nine of them. They'll be court-martialled immediately. This afternoon. They're guilty. Everyone of them is guilty.'

Hume questioned that. 'Isn't it prejudging them, Alex?'

'I'm not on the court martial. I know some of them. A nasty business.'

'And the punishment?'

Alexander shrugged. 'Execution. Major Munro will make an example of them.'

'Execution? Can they justify it?'

'It's necessary.'

That afternoon the court martial found the twenty nine sepoys guilty. Major Munro confirmed their execution. The verdict and punishment were promulgated widely. The next morning, groups of the doomed men were to be executed before different regiments, eight to be executed on the nearby maidan. A gloom fell over the encampment that evening, and Hume noticed British as well as Indian soldiers downcast and subdued while they obeyed orders, concentrating on their duties. Perhaps it is necessary he thought, but he turned in that night regretting the next day.

Towards morning Hume awoke to someone in his tent and reached for his pistol. The intruder whispered urgently, 'Don't be alarmed, Mr Clarke. I come for your help. A mistake has been made.'

Wide awake now Hume jumped to his feet. There was light enough in the tent for him to make out the intruder's uniform. It was a jemidar, a shawl wrapped around his face.

'You do not know me, Sahib.'

'No,' Hume replied.

'I come to speak for someone you do know. He is Puskar Maske. Is he your friend?'

'Yes, he is my friend.'

'I said there has been a mistake.'

'Tell me, jemidar. Who are you?'

'That does not matter. Your friend Puskar Maske is in trouble. He will be executed tomorrow with the sepoy ringleaders.'

Hume was shocked. 'You say executed with the sepoy ringleaders. How can that be? He's not a mutineer. He's a Newar from the Valley of Nepal.'

'He has told me that and I believe him. But here he is a sepoy. He is Haiji Ahmed who is one of the ringleaders. That is, he took Haiji Ahmed's place. He was Haiji Ahmed this afternoon at the court martial.'

'He must have explained to the court.'

'I do not know, Sahib. Perhaps he had no opportunity. There were many charged and there was little time. If he did explain, it was not accepted.'

Fully alerted, Hume realised he would have to act quickly to save

Puskar Maske. He thought of waking Alexander and having him intercede, or, to save time, going directly to Major Munro. Apparently Puskar Maske had no proof of identity with him. But they would take his own word for it, Hume thought. He would see to that.

Then the jemidar was saying, 'Puskar Maske is here, Sahib. He is waiting outside your tent. I arranged for the sentries to let me have him.'

'Bring him in then.'

The jemidar waited till he saw Hume recognise Puskar Maske; then he left and disappeared into the night.

Puskar Maske grasped Hume's hand. Hume noticed the tremor and returned a friendly pressure. He lit the lamp to see a different Puskar Maske, not so self-assured now, his brown face pale, his eyes showing alarm. Puskar Maske's voice quivered. 'Thank you, Hume. I offer you my deepest thanks. It is unfortunate that I must impose on you.'

'You've had a bad experience.'

'I have been very unlucky.'

'You told the court martial who you were?'

'I tried to. It was too hard.'

'You have no papers with you?'

'They are in Patna with my belongings.'

'You were able to escape tonight?'

'The jemidar I knew heard of my trouble. He came with others to help me.'

'They'll find Haiji Ahmed gone. They'll come looking for you,' Hume warned.

'That may be, but they will know he deserted some days ago.'

'They'll count. The number will be short.'

'I think the jemidar and his colleagues will look after that.'

No doubt he is right, Hume thought. 'You're a lucky man to be out of custody.'

Puskar Maske smiled grimly. 'I can tell you, Hume, it always pays to carry a little gold.'

They sat in the tent thinking over what could be done. Puskar Maske's sepoy's uniform had to go, so Hume gave him clothing to wear until he could get back the Newar garments he had left in Patna. Hume urged him to leave the encampment immediately and continue on his way back to Kathmandu. But Puskar Maske's self assurance was returning. In spite of his ordeal, he still wanted to see the British in action. He said it was his duty. His country had much to learn from the British. His King wanted them as an ally. Eventually Hume was persuaded and they considered how it could be arranged. They agreed that Puskar Maske would collect his papers and the Newar clothing he had left at Patna, after which Hume would arrange with Surgeon O'Neal for him to come to Buxar with the field surgery.

Next morning Alexander explained that he himself had a duty to attend the executions, a duty he found painful, but that Hume was under no obligation to go. True, Hume was not a man to watch executions, and back in London, where public hangings were common, he had always avoided them. But here he decided to go, telling himself that after all he was acting as a Company officer and he did not want to show weakness, or what might be regarded as weakness. So he went to the maidan and joined a group on a rise a little way from the river.

There he found that eight cannon had been placed in the centre of the parade ground in line, their muzzles pointing towards the Ganges. Each gun was manned by an Indian crew with a jemidar at the breach and a British ensign in charge. A British regiment of foot was lined along one side of the maidan and native regiments along the other two sides. The lieutenant in charge stood alone in the centre of the field. Eight sepoy ringleaders were marched out and placed before him, most of them dejected, with faces downcast and shoulders hunched. Only two were upright and defiant.

The lieutenant read out their charges, the court martial verdict and their punishment; and one by one, they were stripped of any medals, their insignia, their buttons. Then at the lieutenant's signal soldiers from each gun came at the double to take the condemned men. Hume saw them strip away the clothing from each sepoy to expose a brown body to the waist, and he was surprised at the smallness of them, their seeming frailty. He saw each sepoy lashed to a cannon with the iron muzzle biting into the small of his back and his face towards the holy river.

The whole company was hushed, watching in silence as the lieutenant gave his order. The first cannon fired with a great roar and belched its smoke. Hume winced at the brutality as the smoke cleared a little and he saw the broken body. Then some moments later the second cannon fired, then the third fired, and on to the eighth. As the last sepoy died, his body broken, the watching regiments, both Indian and British, broke their silence to show their disapproval, by a murmur at first which grew to a loud rumble. Then it stopped and there was silence again; and through the smoky haze hanging over the parade ground Hume saw that no one, not a single soldier, broke ranks. The lesson had been learnt, he thought, a terrible lesson. Major Munro had enforced discipline.

As Hume walked slowly away from the parade ground he was tense, his mind's eye still seeing it all: the brightly coloured uniforms of the regiments, the blue smoke of the guns and the red of the lieutenant's tunic, blood-red. He again thought of the frailty of the sepoy's bodies and the iron muzzles of the cannon, and he shuddered. As he approached his tent he looked away over the fields, still lush from the monsoon rains, and he bent over and took handfuls of the long green grass and threw them off to relieve his tension.

Back in his tent Hume found Puskar Maske waiting for him. 'Yes, you are indeed a lucky man, Puskar Maske,' he told him again.

'You will have my thanks, Hume, always,' Puskar Maske replied.

On the 23rd of October they fought the Battle of Buxar. The evening before, Hume and Puskar Maske had gone with the field surgery to a position on a wooded hill, out from the army's left flank. At dawn Hume could see the Indian force over a stream two miles off—a great host—away behind it was the town of Buxar. He could make out their regiments of foot, the cannon, the grenadiers and camel companies, the cavalry and elephants. And he heard the sounds from that army, the drums, bugles, the horses, elephants trumpeting, and a hum of a multitude of distant voices. The morning sunlight played on the Indian force and their weapons glistened.

From the field surgery Hume overlooked the Company's force waiting. The infantry regiments were formed in compact squares, the cavalry deployed out on the flanks, the batteries of cannon already in line. On a hill out past the right flank he could see Major Munro's command post. Alexander was there with the Major and his staff, but too far off for Hume to make his brother out.

As Hume watched, dust rose in front of the Indian force. A group of horsemen had come out from their lines, their horses pranced about, exercising, then reformed into position. The horsemen approached slowly at first, at a slow canter, then suddenly they charged with their horses at a gallop, yelling and flashing their sabres. While still out of range, they stopped, wheeled around and withdrew. They charged again and withdrew.

'They're just at play,' Surgeon O'Neal remarked. 'Not an opening skirmish even. They are Rohillas though, Afghans, who are outstanding horsemen and courageous. They'll attack soon with a vengeance.'

They did. Less than half-an-hour later, two hundred or more of the Indian cavalry, including Rohillas, came out from the Indian force. They crossed a bridge over the stream, approached to within a thousand yards of the British lines and regrouped. Then they charged, galloping madly. Their attack was vicious. There were casualties.

Hume and Puskar Maske and others from the surgery hurried down to the field. They searched through the dust and smoke—ignoring the dead, seeking the wounded. The walking wounded they directed to the field surgery tents; others they carried to the rear.

The fighting intensified. The cavalry charges continued. The cannon on each side roared and the British regiments of foot and the musketry regiments came into action. Soon many dead lay on the field, and many fell wounded. Hume worked desperately. He lost all sense of time, all sense of the battle, its ebb and flow and tactics. Hume saw only the wounded, their cut bodies, the bleeding, and heard only their cries, their pleas as he had to choose between those to save and those to leave lying on the ground.

Then Rohilla cavalry broke through on Hume's part of the field and fighting surrounded him. He was amongst the full force and fury of the battle. Through the billowing dust and smoke and the stench of burnt powder came the glaring eyes of the horses, their snorting nostrils and the heavy pounding of their hooves. There were the clash of weapons and yelling of the attackers. Then the screams of those cut. The reality of it was brutal beyond imagination.

Fully aroused, Hume saw a Rohilla horseman come at him with his sabre raised to slash. When he was almost on him Hume aimed his Italian pistol and fired and hit. The Rohilla fell back in the saddle; as he dropped to the ground his horse lurched off. Hume grasped the dead Rohilla's sabre and cut the next attacker.

Looking back on it later, Hume realised he had lost all self-control then. He had joined in the slaughter fully and unreservedly, losing all fear of being killed and killing. He had slashed and cut at the flesh around him. He slew those who came at him. He never tired. Gave no mercy. He did this—later it puzzled him—not against any personal enemy, not as a soldier with a duty, not even to save his own life, because he could have withdrawn with no loss of honour to care for the wounded. Only when the Rohillas left that part of the field did he go to the rear, to the many wounded there.

The battle raged throughout the morning. Mir Kasim and the Nawab sent wave after wave to attack, and the British cannon and the cavalry took a heavy toll. Towards noon, however, the Indian attacks lost their vigour and became less frequent. Surgeon O'Neal called Hume and

Puskar Maske back to the field surgery, which was now congested. There they had news from a wounded senior officer that the fighting would stop soon, that the Indian force had suffered greatly. A little after mid-day the fighting ceased and they could see it was getting ready to withdraw. The Company's force regrouped.

But the battle was not finished. In the afternoon the Nawab sent a large detachment across a bridge over the river: five thousand foot soldiers or more. The Nawab's engineers destroyed the bridge to deny them, their own men, a way back, leaving them to fight a rearguard action whilst the main Indian force retreated. They had to fight or surrender, there was no escape. The Company attacked, its cavalry moved amongst them, then the regiments of foot. The carnage was great that afternoon and by dusk many of the five thousand Indian soldiers lay dead or wounded on the field.

'It's a truly bloody action,' Surgeon O'Neal said. 'Perhaps the bloodiest of all the Company's victories.'

Hume was relaxed next morning. The intense excitement, the great tension of the day before had gone. Already the battle was starting to seem unreal, even the images of those mutilated were fading. Hume felt safe now, relieved to have survived, and exhilarated to think that the battle was won. He had a message from Alexander praising the Company's force and thanking him for the part he had played. Alexander regretted that he could not join his brother for some time. The army would pursue the Nawab across into Oudh and possibly on to Benares. Alexander was to go, of course. He suggested Hume should wait in Patna for his return, and referred him to the Company's agent who operated a trading factory there.

Hume went with Puskar Maske into Patna, where the agent was generous with his hospitality, providing accommodation for them. Then within days, late one evening Hume had a message from the agent asking him to come to the factory as soon as possible. Hume found him in his office leaning over his desk with an open letter in front of him.

'It's from Major Munro,' he told Hume, speaking softly. 'It concerns you, Mr Clarke.'

Hume's interest quickened. 'My brother's returning to Patna?' he asked.

'No, not that. I'm afraid it's not good news.'

'He's wounded then?'

The agent's eyes avoided Hume. Then Hume looked at the letter on the desk, the light from the lamp flickering on it.

'Is he dead?' The words came softly.

'Yes, he is dead, Mr Clarke.' The agent turned up the lamp and handed the letter to Hume, then got up from his desk and walked over to stand near the window.

Hume's hand trembled as he held the letter. It was very brief. Major Munro wrote that Alexander had taken a small cavalry detachment to scout far out on the army's flank. A detachment from the Nawab's force attacked unexpectedly and Alexander and his men were killed. Major Munro went on to commend Alexander's valour, his devotion, and to offer his sincerest condolences.

Hume refolded the letter carefully, replaced it in its envelope and found himself squeezing the broken wax, as if to seal it up again. He sat in silence until the agent came over to him. Placing a sympathetic hand on his shoulder, he suggested they dine together. But Hume declined. He wanted to be alone to think, to try to come to some understanding of his brother's death.

He left the factory office and went through the yard and along to the Ganges, where he walked slowly along the river bank. It was warm and the wide, dark waters glistened in the starlight. But there was no beauty there for Hume that night. They were long hours for him, the saddest of hours. Memories of Alexander flooded back, memories of their young life in Hollybrook, in the family home, on their father's estate with the tenant farmers, the village playing field, attending Mass at the village church, then Alexander leaving for India. So many memories. One memory in particular came back to Hume that night. Once during Alexander's home-leave they had gone into Hollybrook village, to a fair with stalls, acrobats, jugglers and a gypsy fortune teller. He had persuaded Alexander to go to her tent where she sat at a table with a crystal globe, and as they entered she beckoned to Hume to sit opposite her. He remembered it well. She peered into his face and then into the crystal. 'What do you want to know?' she asked.

'My future,' Hume replied.

'Both good and bad?'

'Yes,' he told her, undaunted.

'For a start, I see a black-haired lady.'

Hume laughed at that. 'A black-haired lady,' he mocked. 'And I'll marry her, you'll see.'

'She is beautiful and you will marry her,' the gypsy replied. 'Her hair is blacker than mine.' She ran her hand through her own hair.

'And what else?' Hume asked.

'I can see a strange land, a strange people.' She looked again into the crystal. 'You are not alone there, but you are the only one.'

Alexander cut in. 'What do you mean by that, gypsy? Is it a riddle?'

'No, I spoke what I saw.'

'What else did you see?' Hume asked.

The gypsy traced a path around the crystal with her finger and, without looking up, replied. 'There is much dark there. Much dark all around. It is here and here.' She dabbed at the crystal. 'It is as dark as I have ever seen. It is death, young man. Many deaths.'

Annoyed now, Alexander interrupted again. 'Take care gypsy. Don't try to frighten my brother. Do you see his death? I'll have you run out of the village.'

'No, not his death,' she replied. 'He will see great changes, but he will live a long life. It is others who will die.'

Hume got up from the table for Alexander to take his turn, reluctantly with Hume persuading him. 'Come gypsy,' Alexander said, wanting to get it over, 'What do you see for me?'

As the gypsy looked into the crystal she frowned and shook her head. Watching Alexander, her eyes narrowed. 'There is a short time there,' she said, 'Then nothing. I shall say no more to you.'

By the Ganges that night, Hume remembered that Alexander had shown his annoyance with the gypsy, tossed her a few coins and hurried out of her tent.

Soon after Hume had news of his brother's death, Puskar Maske invited him to visit the Valley of Nepal. 'You could accompany me when I return to my country,' he suggested. 'You would be welcome there, Hume. I assure you of that. My King, Jaya Malla, would welcome you. So would my Newar people.'

Hume had not expected this, but without any hesitation he decided he would accept. The adventure of visiting that remote valley in the very shadow of great white mountains attracted him. And now that Alexander was dead, there was little to keep him in Calcutta. 'Yes, I would be delighted to visit your valley, Puskar Maske,' he said. 'I accept your invitation with pleasure.'

'I must point out that entering the Valley of Nepal could be dangerous, Hume. Breaking the Gurkha King's blockade might be difficult,' Puskar Maske warned. 'But I know of little-used tracks to follow. You should come for at least three months. No Britisher has ever come to the Valley of Nepal and almost no Europeans.'

'Almost?' Hume queried.

'There are Capuchin priests there. Father Michaelangelo and others. I know them well, because I sometimes go to their church. I can tell you that I am a Christian as well as a Hindu.'

That surprised Hume, but he made no comment on it.

'First I must to go to Calcutta to attend to Alexander's affairs with the East India Company,' he told Puskar Maske. 'I will do it with all haste. You could wait in Patna for my return.'

In Calcutta, when Hume called on Governor Vansitart and John Spencer, who was a member of the Fort William Council, they offered their condolences on Alexander's death; and their praise of him was unstinting. They were interested in Hume's intended visit to the Valley of Nepal.

'No doubt you are aware of the possible dangers, Sir Hume Clarke,' Governor Vansitart cautioned. 'You will have that title now. The people there are a war-like lot and you will be on your own and far from any Company help. But please do not let that put you off. I am sure it will be an adventure for you.'

John Spencer spoke of Puskar Maske. 'He came to us from his king, Jaya Malla, begging us to send an army against this Gurkha King who is threatening their valley. And I must say he spoke of generous trade concessions for us, and also trade routes to both Tibet and China. We could not offer help then. But now, with Buxar won, it might not be long before the Company will send help. Would you represent the Company to Jaya Malla, Sir Hume Clarke? I shall let you have a letter to him.'

Hume agreed.

Hume spent the next few days in Calcutta sorting out Alexander's affairs. It was a sad duty and the bungalow was an empty place for him now. He wrote to the estate manager at Hollybrook with news of Alexander's death, asking him to arrange with the local notary for the will to be processed and for action to be started for the title to come to him. He also wrote of his intended journey to the Valley of Nepal.

That done, Hume had Alexander's safe opened and he took out the gold, the precious stones, the silver and coins, and the ruby pendant which Alexander had got from Shuja-ud-daula's treasury after the Battle of Plassey. He took the gold bar by bar to judge its weight. It was considerable, but Hume decided to take it also, recalling Puskar Maske's remark that it was always wise to carry gold.

For a long time he stood at the window, watching the huge blood-red ruby aflame in the sunlight and the great diamonds sparkling around it. 'Alexander was very proud of it,' he said to himself, 'I shall keep it with me.' The rest of Adam's things he left with the Company for safe-keeping.

Back in Patna, Puskar Maske was waiting for Hume. He suggested they leave the following day; it was a Sunday. 'It is a propitious day for starting a journey, Hume,' he said. 'That is important.'

The Company's agent provided them with horses, muskets and provisions, and wished them both a safe journey to the Valley of Nepal, and for Hume a safe return.

Three

Hume and Puskar Maske rode northwards following the Gandaki River and then across to Sagauli, a pleasant enough journey in spite of the heat and humidity. The countryside was green from the monsoon rains; the peasants were at work on their farms, tending their paddy and working their buffalos. Puskar Maske willingly helped Hume to practise his Newari. They rode on and a few days later reached the village of Roxaul. There they camped beside the stream that bordered Bihar. Puskar Maske was light-hearted, pleased to be approaching his own country.

'I am nearly home, Hume,' he said, laughing happily. 'We leave Bihar and India tomorrow. Look across. That is Makwanpur.' He gestured out across the stream. 'And beyond Makwanpur, high in the mountains, is my homeland. It is the Valley of Nepal.'

'How far off?' Hume asked.

'Ninety miles perhaps. But a long ninety miles, Hume. Difficult miles, we cross the Chauria Hills and then the flat Terai and the duns. We climb high up in the Mahabharat mountains, and then on the other side below us is the Valley of Nepal. We must be cautious, Hume. The Gurkha King controls Makwanpur and most of our route to the valley.'

Next day they reached the top of the Chauria hills, and Puskar Maske called a halt to rest the horses. He walked off through an opening in the trees to a little temple, which was crudely built in stone and almost lost in the undergrowth.

'It is a temple for the God Ganesh, Hume,' Puskar Maske explained when he came back. 'I worshipped there, made puja. I have asked Ganesh for a safe journey for us. Ganesh is a god of wisdom and success. Many need his help. He is a son of the great Lord Shiva. Have you heard of him, Hume? The elephant-headed god.'

Hume had not. 'Why elephant-headed?' he asked.

'It is said Hume that once long ago the great God Lord Shiva came home to his beautiful wife, Parbati, and found a young boy barring his way to her. Furious, he cut off the boy's head. Then full of remorse when he was told the boy was his own son, he sent his servants into the forest to cut the head off the first animal they saw that was sleeping with its head to the north. This happened to be a young white elephant. Lord Shiva fixed the elephant head on his son's body and the child lived to be Ganesh.'

Hume laughed. 'Do they believe that?' he asked.

Puskar Maske shrugged. 'Many believe it—be it myth or fact—and you can make what you will of it, Hume. Ganesh is a widely worshipped god and much loved. It is fact, perhaps. Who knows?'

They rode down to a village. 'It is safe here,' Puskar Maske said. 'They are Tharu people. I have met them before. It is a poor village, but they are friends.'

The village headman welcomed them. He bowed low and joining his hands in a long namaste he invited them into his hut. Puskar Maske spoke at length with him, then turned to Hume. 'There are things the headman will do for us. He will give us provisions and two porters for our journey, and care for the horses until your return, all for a small payment. He tells me that the monsoon rains are finished but the deadly miasmas are still on the duns. They are the white vapours that come up from the ground and bring the aul, Hume. People they touch will get fever and tremble, and soon die. The headman will also sacrifice a goat to Ganesh to protect us against the aul.'

That afternoon the villagers gathered around a large flat-topped stone which held a kalash water jug and was adorned with red sindar powder and flowers. A priest held a goat with its legs bound; and the villagers watched in silence as he took his long knife and slit its throat, carefully so as to let the blood spurt in a stream into the kalash and over the stone. When the goat was dead, the priest cut off its head and placed it on the stone, to a loud murmur of approval from the people.

Killing animals was not new to Hume. He had seen many a farmer back in Hollybrook slaughter a sheep or pig, although not as skilfully as here, and occasionally he had slaughtered one himself. It was the attitude of the villagers and also Puskar Maske that impressed him: the reverence, the awe in which they held it all. 'Do you believe the sacrifice will help?' he asked.

'The miasmas do not bring death to the Tharu people,' Puskar Maske replied. 'The gods protect them from the aul.'

But Hume doubted this. 'Why not cover your body to keep the vapours off when you cross the duns?' he suggested. 'We should try it. The headman could ask the women to make us coverings of straw.'

The goat's body was prepared for eating. Villagers held it over a charcoal fire to burn off the hair, washed it and cut it into small pieces.

They cooked it in a large cauldron with spices, and then Hume and Puskar Maske dined on goat and rice that evening.

Next day, in coverings of rice straw roughly woven by the village women, they crossed the duns, keeping to the high ground and avoiding the thick elephant grass and swamps, wherever possible. Their muskets were loaded and ready against the tigers, leopards, and elephants that abounded here. They crossed the duns safely and neither Puskar Maske nor Hume nor the porters suffered any bad effects. Puskar Maske put it down to the sacrifice to Ganesh, and Hume to the straw coverings.

Across the duns, the Mahabharats lay before them. A maze of mountains and valleys extended far to the east and west, and northwards to the great Himalayan massifs. They began their climb up the steep slopes, avoiding the villages and towns, and particularly the garhies, the forts, controlled by the Gurkha King. They picked their way over the rocky ground, seeking secure footholds, careful of the rock-falls. Late that day they climbed the steepest slope of all up the Chandragiri Mountain, the Mountain of the Moon. For thousands of feet they climbed, up the zigzagging tracks, around the great boulders, up rough wooden ladders and over the rock-falls, until after dark at last they reached the mountain top. Here Hume and Puskar Maske rested for the night, hidden in a thicket near a clearing. The two porters hid in the forest.

Hume woke early on the mountain next morning. The sky was blue, the air cold and crisp. Patches of snow lay on the clearing and flowers were in bloom, yellow primroses and blue irises. Rhododendrons grew amongst the oaks and sal trees of the surrounding forest.

But something else was on the clearing as Puskar Maske indicated, smiling grimly. There were about forty Gurkhas, well armed with flint-lock muskets, talawars and kukhries and a small cannon or two. Their uniforms were in good condition. They wore blue jackets, and their tightly rolled turbans of dark cloth had brass badges and small chains indicating their rank. From an elite regiment, Hume thought. The Gurkhas had lit a fire and some were cooking breakfast of rice and sinki and tea. Two were skinning a leopard they had caught in the forest, their knives cutting carefully, not to spoil the pelt. Some were sitting around chatting and joking with each other. Others cleaned their muskets, pointing them to practice their aim. To Hume they seemed to be in a happy mood, glad to be in their mountains.

'Prithvi Shah is there!' Puskar Maske exclaimed, alarmed. 'It is certainly the Gurkha King.'

The Gurkha King stood in the centre of the clearing. His tunic was richly brocaded, his turban had jewels, gold badges and a plume. The hilt of his talawar and the kukhri in his cummerbund were encrusted with precious stones. He was a tall man, Aryan-looking and black-bearded. Even from where he was hiding, Hume noticed his face was stern, his eyes dark and hard.

Hume learnt later that Prithvi Shah was a descendent of Rajputs who, some two centuries ago, had fought bravely against the Moguls and then, when they were defeated, fled from India to the Himalayan foothills to escape Akbar the Great. One of these Rajputs, Drabigar Shah, founded the tiny princedom of Gurkha around the Hanumanbanjang Mountain about eighty miles to the west of the Valley of Nepal; and Prithvi Shah was the eleventh of that line.

For years he had watched the British taking India piece by piece, and his great mission in life was to stop them coming to his mountains. He was determined to build a mountain nation strong enough to defend itself. To this end he had added to his dominion—by war or diplomacy—some of the Baisi and Chaubisi princedoms in the basins of the Gandak and Kali Rivers; the Kingdom of Makwanpur on the Indian border; and the town of Nawakot just to the north of the Valley of Nepal, which he made his second capital. Now that the British had come to the very border of his mountains, his time was running out. He had to expand his dominion quickly. He had to take the Valley of Nepal which was by far the richest and most populous part in all the mountains.

Prithvi Shah beckoned to two of his officers, 'One is his brother, Surpratap,' Puskar Maske said softly. 'I know that from the red scar on his face and the sunken eyelid closing over the empty socket. The other is a Thapa perhaps.' The two officers hurried over to the far side of the clearing where, near an oak tree, five people were crouching on the ground huddled together—two men, a woman and two no more than boys.

'They are Newars from the valley. Blockade breakers of course,' Puskar Maske said, the fear in his voice obvious. 'Their punishment is death. Surpratap is telling them that, I should think.'

Surpratap called several of his sepoys, who bound the five by their arms and legs. The boys struggled, the woman looked about helplessly. The sight enraged Hume. He felt for his pistol and clutched it tightly, his body stiffening, ready to rise from the thicket to help. But Puskar Maske held him back. And without further ado, the soldiers hanged the men, the woman and the boys from the boughs of the oak tree, their legs and arms twitching till eventually they dangled there lifeless.

When the Gurkhas left, Hume and Puskar Maske came out from the thicket. Puskar Maske led the way through the forest to a rocky outcrop on the edge of Mount Chandragiri. Seating himself on a ledge, he beckoned to Hume to sit beside him. Below them, nearly four thousand feet below, the Valley of Nepal stretched away to the north.

It was still early morning and the floor of the valley was under a blanket of thick white mist. Puskar Maske waved towards the protruding tops of the surrounding mountains and went on to name Champa Devi, Shivpuri, Pulchowki, Nagarjun and others as well as Chandragiri. 'They have guarded the valley, Hume,' he said. 'For centuries they have kept intruders out. They have let us live, us Newars, in our own ways, with our kings and government, our worship of the gods, our works of art.'

But Hume's attention was elsewhere. He was gazing further to the north, transfixed. There, rising high in the air above the surrounding mountains and seeming so close, were the immense white peaks of the Himalayas, the roof of the world. They were truly massive as they reached up into the morning sky, which was now a deep blue. Their eastern faces gleamed white in the morning sunlight and their western sides, still with a little of the night, were tinged with purple.

Puskar Maske pointed to some of the great white peaks. 'There is Langtang Lirung,' he said. 'And Dorje Lakpa, Jugal, the Ganesh Himal.'

Hume was satiated with the splendour of the mountains, trying to absorb even more of their glory. Then by some quirk of the atmosphere the sun's rays splashed red on the snow and ice of one of the great peaks.

'It is Ganesh's Himal,' Puskar Maske said. 'The red of a sacrifice. This is a fine omen. It augurs well for your visit, Hume.'

They sat until the mist had cleared from the floor of the valley leaving only a few lingering wisps. Then far below they could see the fields stretching away, some green with crops, some golden and ready for the harvest, and others tilled black, ready for another sowing. The valley's main rivers, the Bagmati and the Vishnumati, wound their way from the north, their waters flowing down out of the valley through Makwanpur and into India, to merge with the holy Ganges. Towards the centre of the valley, away from the surrounding mountains, were the ancient towns of Kathmandu, Lalitpatan and Bhaktapur, the capitals of the valley's three kingdoms. Their buildings of burnt brick and terracotta tiles clustered together within their walls. The golden roofs of their palaces and temples and tall pagodas glistened in the sunlight. And closer, was the smaller town of Kirtipur, perched high on its hill and behind the strong walls that had long defended it against the Gurkha King.

Puskar Maske pointed a little to the west of Kathmandu towards the ancient Swayambhunath, which was the great Chaitya of the Adi Buddha, the Self Born Lord, and represented the very womb of creation. To the north of Kathmandu, on the bank of the Bagmati, was the Pashupatinath which was Lord Shiva's temple, a most holy of Hindu places. To the north-east was the ancient Bodnath temple which was the largest of all, a great white stupa favoured by pilgrims from Tibet.

After a time Hume and Puskar Maske continued with the porters on the last few miles of their journey. They made their descent down Chandragiri into the valley. They passed the hill of the town of Kirtipur, went through the farm lands, past the villages, and they crossed the Vishnumati. They arrived at the walls of Kathmandu.

Four

Puskar Maske and Hume and the porters whom they had brought from the Terai walked around the ancient walls and through the gate at the south-eastern corner of the town. Recognising Puskar Maske, the guards welcomed him back, joined their hands in a namaste and let them pass.

Immediately Hume was the object of much interest. People in the streets stared and crowds gathered around him. Hume looked back at the Newar people, their black hair and brown skin and dark almond-shaped eyes. Men wore tunics and dhotis or white trousers, and their Newar caps. Women wore saris, and the young children wore little more than loincloths. Sadly, the boys reminded Hume of those the Gurkha King had handed from the oak tree on Mount Chandragiri.

Laughing excitedly, some pointed Hume out to others. They commented on his appearance, which was natural enough. His large build and fair hair, and his cocked-hat and grey cut-away coat were strange to them. A few were fearful, but most were just curious. The more venturous came close and held out their hands to touch him. Children ran after him, calling out to him. When Puskar Maske discouraged all this, Hume saw he was immediately obeyed.

Hume and Puskar Maske came to a large building with a curved roof and wide eaves, which Hume took to be a temple. Puskar Maske led into a small room saying, 'It is a rest house for pilgrims, Hume. It is called "Kashtamandap" in Sanskrit, and gave Kathmandu its name. It is said that long ago it was built from the wood of a single tree, by the Tree of Paradise when it came here disguised as a man.'

Puskar Maske went to the palace to report Hume's arrival and came back with an older man whom he introduced as General Josi. For a long time the general stood looking at Hume, no doubt the first Britisher he had seen. At first Hume thought he saw hostility in General Josi's face rather than welcome, but before long the general joined his hands in a namaste and, with Puskar Maske interpreting, said, 'I welcome you, Sir Hume Clarke. It is an honour for me to have you in my country.'

'Your arrival in Kathmandu pleases King Jaya Malla greatly, Hume,' Puskar Maske said. 'Very soon he wants to welcome you at the palace. He is giving you a house. I do not know how it compares with those in your own country, but I hope it will be to your liking. I shall take you there and also arrange a servant for you.'

Hume thanked him, saying, 'The King is generous. I am sure the house will be suitable.'

Still studying Hume, General Josi said, 'I am to tell you Jaya Malla has said you may come and go where you wish in Kathmandu and the surrounding fields. The temples and our festivals will be open you. Even though you are a Christian, you may attend our sacrifices. The Raj Guru and the lamas will agree to that.'

'My thanks again, General,' Hume replied. 'Your welcome pleases me.'

Hume's house was in Makhan Tole in a narrow cobbled street. Like the other houses, it was of brick with a tile roof, abutting on its neighbours, three storeys high. Its facade was richly decorated with fine old woodcarvings of fish and gryphons, and a peacock which Hume learnt later was the vehicle of the God Kumar. Its windows had wooden shutters and a verandah overhung the street. At the back, it opened to a courtyard. Hume walked inside. The ceilings were low with dark wooden beams and he had to watch his height. From the street a heavy door opened to a lower room, which was used by servants and often to house a fowl or goat awaiting slaughter, or to shelter a cow. The floor was of pressed earth. A large fireplace was for cooking and winter warmth. A nearly vertical ladder led up to the second floor which, Puskar Maske explained, womenfolk and children usually used. Another ladder led to the top floor. Hume made his quarters on the top floor which was comfortable enough he thought, although not at all to be compared with the family home in Hollybrook. His room, like the rest of the house sparsely furnished, had a bed, a table and chairs, and a cupboard.

Hume stowed away his belongings. He found a safe place for the gold bars he had brought with him. With a kukhri he scraped the mortar from several bricks in the wall of the room and found a cavity behind them. There was space enough for the gold and he replaced the bricks carefully.

The next few days Hume spent looking around Kathmandu, alone or in Puskar Maske's company. The November days were cool and, after the morning mist lifted, sunny. He would walk along the narrow streets in the shadow of the encroaching houses, stop at a market square and sit for a while enjoying the warm sunlight. The market was busy with merchants and farmers selling their wares. It was full of colour with merchants and farmers selling their wares. It was full of colour with sunlight playing on yellow oranges, red chillies, green vegetables, garlic and onions. There was also buffalo meat, goat and fish from the mountain streams.

One afternoon walking with Puskar Maske to the Durbar Square, suddenly without warning Hume found himself in the very heart of Kathmandu—as he came to think of it—amongst a profusion of ancient buildings, the gems of Newar art. There was the ancient Hanuman Palace with its Monkey God Gate, said to keep out evil spirits, witches and smallpox. An image of Hanuman shaded under a parasol stood to the left of the gate, and guarding the gate were statues of the Lion God Narish and two great hounds. The roofs of temples for Lord Shiva and his wife Parbati and many other gods curved gracefully and their gilt and copper sparkled. There was the tall temple for Taleju, who was the Goddess of War and the patron deity of Kathmandu. And throughout all in the Durbar Square that sunny afternoon was a bird-like twittering as the breeze fanned the little brass leaves hanging from the eaves of the pagodas.

Hume spent a lot of time there. He looked at the image of the Kalo Bhairab, the Black Bhairab, the Bhairab of Death, a fearsome image with its great black body, its eyes glaring red from their surrounding whites, its great fangs protruding from a snarling mouth. A chaplet of human skulls surrounded its head and a string of skulls hung around its neck. The hands of its six arms clutched a sword, Lord Shiva's trident and batches of severed heads, and its feet trod heavily on an image of a naked man. How well it portrayed the idea of wrath and terror, Hume thought.

Puskar Maske stopped at a temple. 'This is the Kumari Ghar, Hume. It is the home of a living goddess, a little girl who is a reincarnation of the Goddess Kumari who is also the Goddess Taleju.' He pointed to a window. 'You can see the little Kumari looking out sometimes. She lives with two little boys who are her attendants. She is a lovely little goddess. Beautiful and dressed in gorgeous robes.'

'A living goddess?' Hume queried.

'Yes, Hume,' Puskar Maske asserted. 'Once the Goddess Taleju came to Jaya Malla in a dream and admonished him for looking at her with lustful eyes, saying she would never appear before him again. But she told the king that if he selected a young Newar girl, she would live in her body and that she was to be worshipped as the Goddess Kumari. Jaya Malla did this and gave her a temple, a chariot, attendants and a grant of land which brought her an ample income.'

'When a Kumari reaches puberty,' Puskar Maske continued, 'she is no longer possessed and returns to her family. A successor is selected. To make sure she would have the courage to cope with the Kumari's duties, she is put in a room of a temple which is darkened and the floors covered with the newly severed heads of buffalo sacrificed at the Festival of Durga Puja. The little girl selected must show no fear.'

'A severe test for girls so young,' Hume said.

'It is necessary, Hume,' Puskar Maske replied.

When Puskar Maske called for Hume to take him to the palace, he spoke of Jaya Malla. 'I must tell you, Hume, that Jaya Malla can be arrogant and cruel, also capricious. He is not a popular king. Brave no doubt, but not popular.'

Hume learnt that Jaya Malla had earned the enmity of many in the valley. He had increased taxes on rich and poor. To pay his Nagar mercenaries, whom he had brought from India as much for his own protection as for the defence of the valley, he had taken ornaments and gold from the Pashupatinath, to the annoyance of the Brahmans including the Raj Guru, and from the Swayambhunath, to the annoyance of the lamas. Perhaps his greatest cruelty, and indiscretion, was his treatment of his general, Ram Thapa, who lost to the Gurkhas at Nawakot. Jaya Malla had his Nagar mercenaries flay Ram Thapa alive and murder his supporters. This was greatly resented, not only by those in Kathmandu but throughout the valley.

At the palace, Hume and Puskar Maske joined General Josi and went into the first courtyard with its fine old carvings of wooden monsters supporting the roofs. They followed an officer of the royal guard through a maze of small courts to a flight of stairs and along a corridor lit by oil lamps of red earthenware moulded in the shape of peacocks and placed along the bottom of the walls. The officer admitted them through a heavy oaken door to the audience chamber, a low-beamed room, wood-panelled and dimly lit by brass oil lamps.

Jaya Malla was already in audience, seated on a chair with white cushions. He was a stocky man, black-bearded and heavily browed, with a red tika mark was on his forehead and he was dressed in the blue and gold uniform of a Newar general. A large gilded image of Lord Vishnu and two soldiers of the royal guard with talawars in hand stood nearby.

A white robed Capuchin and two ladies were standing before Jaya countries known as Portugal,' Puskar Maske whispered to Hume. 'I know him well. I told you I am a Christian, a member of the Capuchins' church. The older lady is the Lady Bachhla who is a cousin of the king and a lady of great influence at court. The young lady is Maneka, her attendant. They, too, go to Father Michaelangelo's church.'

'Please forgive me, Sire,' Hume heard Father Michaelangelo saying, his voice high-pitched and faltering. 'I've been told that my church has to pay a tax of twenty tolas in gold to the Court Treasury.' He was a small thin man with dark hair and a sharp, pale face. Hume was pleased to find his Newari had improved enough to make something of the conversation.

'True,' Jaya Malla replied, his black eyes glaring at the priest. 'In gold.'

'I do not object to the tax, Sire,' the Capuchin replied, feeling for the beads at his waist.

'That is fortunate for you, priest.'

'I would say again, Sire, I have no objection to the tax. It is necessary.'

'Your complaint then?'

'I come to say it will be hard for us to pay. Impossible. We are a poor order. We have little. Only the house in Wontu Tole which your great generosity gave us, our clothes and just a few utensils. That is all.'

'Make your followers pay.'

'They too are poor, and few. Three hundred, no more.'

'There is treasure in the house I gave you to use as a temple. The golden cup I hear of.'

'It is our chalice. It is sacred. We use it in the sacrifice of the Mass.'

Jaya Malla waved a hand disparagingly. 'Your bloodless sacrifice. Is that all? There are other golden objects.'

'The monstrance is brass, not gold.'

'You have other wealth.'

'We do not, Sire'

Jaya Malla frowned at the Capuchin. 'The Gurkhas threaten us, priest. We have need for gold.'

'That I know, Sire.'

The Lady Bachhla interceded. 'They are truly poor, Sire. The Capuchins have no treasure.'

Jaya Malla stared at her, frowning again. Abruptly, he changed his approach. 'You commune with the Gurkhas, priest. That is treachery. You journeyed to Nawakot,' he said.

'I have been to Nawakot. That is true, Sire.' Father Michaelangelo's face was tense, the bones pushing on the skin. 'We Capuchins have medical skills. I took my herbs to Prithvi Shah.'

'I know. To my enemy.'

'Yes, Sire.'

'Without my permission.'

'The Pradhans of Lalitpatan asked me to go.'

Hume saw him wince. The priest had not intended to say that, he thought.

'The Pradhans!' Jaya Malla's voice was harsh, a growl. 'So you are in league with traitors. You also brought your herbs to the Gurkha, Surpratap, to heal the wound on his face.'

'We try to be merciful, the Capuchins.'

'You show mercy to my foes.'

'To all people, Sire.'

'You would make a poor general. A poor minister.'

'I am neither.'

But Jaya Malla's mood changed, and he laughed. 'I could make you, such a merciful man as you are, my executioner. Would you like that? Or I could banish you to India. You and the other priest. And banish your followers.'

'You could, Sire.'

'This time, I shall overlook your fault. But take care, priest,' Jaya Malla warned. 'You will pay the tax. In gold.'

With that Jaya Malla dismissed the three of them, the Capuchin, Bachhla, to whom he gave no opportunity to intervene again, and her attendant, Maneka.

As they left the room Hume noticed Maneka turn and glance quickly in his direction. Totally unexpectedly he felt a sudden surge of pleasure at that glance, momentary as it was. He was delighted and he looked back at her, at her soft olive face, her dark almond-shaped eyes, the tika mark on her forehead. Her glossy black hair was gathered up at the top of her head and fixed with a gold ornament. Her sari was of a light blue silk, and her cholo, a short blouse of white muslin, exposed the bare skin of her waist. She wore gold earrings and bangles set with turquoise. As Hume sat in the audience chamber after she had gone, his pulse quickened, the image of her lingering.

Even with his twenty five years Hume had never actually fallen in love. True, he had the acquaintance of young women and liked most of them, a liking often returned. Many a time he had frolicked with the daughters of the tenant farmers on his father's estate, and more than a few had been pleased to sleep with him out in the fields on a warm summer's night. And he was often a sought-after escort for young ladies from Hollybrook village and neighbouring estates. But watching Maneka as she left, in that moment Hume had his first fleeting encounter with love.

Hume's attention was brought back to the matters in hand as the officer of the King's guard led in a small man wearing a black topi cap, to stand before Jaya Malla. 'It is the Dewar, Hume. He is Ari Lawat,' Puskar Maske said in a low voice. 'He is the treasurer, the collector of taxes. We shall have to wait our turn.'

Jaya Malla moved irritably in his chair. 'The Nagar mercenaries I have brought from India want their pay,' he said bluntly.

'There is some delay, Sire,' the Dewar replied anxiously.

'I punish failure, Dewar,' Jaya Malla threatened.

'It is not my fault, Sire.'

'Is it not?'

'Taxes are hard to collect, Sire.'

Jaya Malla brushed this aside, growling, 'The executioner's sword is also hard, Dewar.'

Then Hume heard Jaya Malla saying to the Dewar, 'There is treasure hidden in the valley. Much of it. You will find it. Sri Puskar Maske will help you.'

The Dewar looked surprised, but said, 'You are right, Sire. Yes, there is much treasure. Buried in ancient times. That is well known.'

'There is much wealth underground.'

'That is true. It has long been spoken of. It is said the Nagas guard it, and that only a King may take it.' The Nagas were the Snake Gods that had lived in the valley since mythical times.

'There is treasure underneath the temples, buried in long forgotten vaults.'

'That is true,' the Dewar agreed again.

'And treasure is here, under my palace.' Jaya Malla enthused. 'Here under the foundations of Mohar Chok. Patrap Malla put it there a hundred years ago.'

'I have heard, Sire.'

'And more. There was Patrap Malla's Tola-dan. He and his family were weighed in gold. Where is that treasure now?'

'I shall make a search,' the Dewar promised.

'You will, and Sri Puskar Maske will help you. You will find it, Dewar. Look first near the village of Tolu. Dig holes in the ground.

Check with the court astrologers where to dig. They will know.'

Jaya Malla dismissed the Dewar. He got up from his chair and came to join Hume and General Josi and Puskar Maske. For some moments he looked at Hume, then, with a polite namaste, he greeted him. 'I am pleased, pleased indeed, to welcome you to my Kingdom, Sir Hume Clarke. Sri Puskar Maske has told me of you. You saved his life. He has nothing but friendship for you. He told me that your brother died in battle. So brave a soldier. Please accept my condolences.'

With his arrogance gone, affable almost, Jaya Malla was a different person from that giving audience to the Capuchin and the Dewar.

'We are privileged to have you here,' Jaya Malla said. 'I have read the letter you brought from your Governor Vansitart. I welcome you as a representative of your great East India Company. We shall do all we can to make your stay a pleasant one. I hope the house is to your liking and that Sri Puskar Maske is attending to your needs.'

'I thank you for your welcome and for the house,' Hume replied. 'And I will say it is I who is privileged to be in Kathmandu.'

'Your army is a great one from all accounts,' Jaya Malla said. 'We are not entirely isolated in our valley. I have heard of your Company's victories against the Nawabs in the south of India, at Calcutta and Plassey. Sri Puskar Maske has told me about the battle at Buxar.'

'And you will have heard something of the threat to our valley, Sir Hume Clarke.' Jaya Malla continued, frowning. 'You will have heard of the Gurkha King, Prithvi Shah. He is in our surrounding mountains; he has taken many of our outer villages and imposed his blockade. And he is waiting to attack and take all. He is an evil King. The bodies of Newars he has killed hang rotting at the passes to the valley. Some years back, he murdered my general, Jayant Rana, cruelly, had the skin torn from his body, had him flayed alive. And Prithvi Shah is no friend of the British.' He turned to General Josi. 'That is so, General?'

'Indeed it is, Sire. Prithvi Shah is no friend of the British. And he is a tyrant, a cruel tyrant.'

'I have fought the Gurkha King for many years,' Jaya Malla continued. 'I am fighting him now. I have sent a force to retake the fort at Naldum which the Gurkhas have occupied. That is important. Naldum controls our pass to the north-east. We will take it back and resume trade with Tibet.'

Hume's thoughts again went back to the morning on Mount Chandragiri, to the struggling of the two boys and the helplessness of the woman, to their bodies hanging from the oak tree. His anger rose.

the woman, to their bodies hanging from the oak tree. His anger rose.

Jaya Malla lent forward in his chair and spoke in a confidential tone to Hume. 'You heard my talk with the Dewar and the Capuchin, Sir Hume Clarke. I am raising gold to pay for the defence of the valley. We have treasure here. I defeated the Gurkhas when they first attacked Kirtipur, and I shall do so again. My cousins at Lalitpatan and Bhaktapur will help. I shall organise that.' Then, looking straight into Hume's face, he said, 'I want British help to defeat the Gurkhas, an army from your great East India Company. Will one come?'

Hume did not take long to reply. 'I shall do my best to get help for you. I saw the Gurkha King's work on Mount Chandragiri. It angered me greatly.'

Jaya Malla was pleased at this.

'But the people in your valley,' Hume continued. 'From Bhaktapur and Lalitpatan as well as Kathmandu, from the three kingdoms, could surely raise a force to defeat the Gurkha King.'

Jaya Malla turned to General Josi. 'I shall send a deputation to my cousins in Bhaktapur and Lalitpatan. You and Sri Puskar Maske will go. You will tell them of my intention to defend the valley, and you will seek their support.' He hesitated and looked at Hume. 'And it would please me if Sir Hume Clarke would accompany you. If he would speak to my cousins about British help against the Gurkha King,'

Hume agreed.

'And after that,' Jaya Malla said, 'I shall send a letter to the Governor in Calcutta seeking his support and telling him how determined we are to defend the valley. And, of course, tell him of the generous trading concessions I would grant him.'

Five

Hume would sometimes go outside the town walls, out into the countryside to the villages. It was coming on to winter, but the days were still pleasant after the morning mists had risen, the sunshine warm, the sky a cloudless blue, and the great Himalayan massifs close in the cool clear air.

The harvest was almost finished and the fields were full of the colours of the last of the golden paddy still to be harvested, the green of the vegetable plantings, the vivid yellow of early mustard in flower, and trees still with their Autumn tones. Wherever there were hard surfaces, in the village squares, the courtyards and cobbled ways, unhusked rice lay awaiting threshing, and the early onions and garlic and bright red chillies were spread out to dry in the sun.

One day Hume noticed people in the villages with small clay bowls. They placed them in rows by the roadsides and at the windows and doorways, and on the roofs of their houses. Then they filled them with oil and put little black wicks in them ready for lighting. There were many images of a goddess who held a conch shell and was adorned with flowers and gems and coloured stones. On enquiring, Hume learnt that people were preparing for the Dipawali, the Festival of Lights, and that the goddess was Laxmi the beautiful wife of Vishnu, the Goddess of Wealth and Good Fortune.

When Hume returned to Kathmandu he found Puskar Maske waiting at his house in Makhan Tole, smiling broadly, his topi cap at an angle. He had with him a servant who carried a basket filled with small clay bowls, a pot of oil and a bunch of black wicks.

'They are for the Dipawali, Hume,' Puskar Maske greeted. 'Everyone will have them. I have taken the liberty of bringing some for your house. The lights will be everywhere, around all the houses, in the market squares, along the streets, on the temples. And with your permission my servant will set them out on your house.'

Hume had no objection, being happy to participate.

'At this time everyone worships the Goddess Laxmi,' Puskar Maske explained. 'You will like her. We all adore her. And she brings good fortune.'

Leaving the servant to the lights, Hume led Puskar Maske up the ladder to his quarters on the top floor. He opened the wooden shutters on the window to let in what light there was from the narrow street outside, then he called down below to his own servant to bring up two bowls of raksi, the popular rice spirit, from the pot-full he had bought in a village that morning and which the peasant had already delivered. They saluted each other and drank.

'You'll be busy with the tasks Jaya Malla gave you,' Hume said. 'When will the deputation go to Bhaktapur and Lalitpatan? Have you started your search for treasure?'

'Both will have to wait, Hume. Business is not done during the Dipawali. Not for five days. Gambling, yes. You will see many people gambling in the streets. It is allowed then. But serious business is not done. That is the custom.'

'You worship Laxmi for five days?'

'There is more to the Dipawali, Hume,' Puskar Maske said and went on to explain. He looked at Hume for some moments when he spoke of the fifth day, and Hume long remembered his hint of a smile. 'It is the Bah Tiki. On that day every man or boy is blessed by his sister,' he said. 'It is important. A sister's blessing is necessary for a propitious year ahead. In return for the blessing, the sister receives a Bah Tiki present. If someone has no sister, then a female relative or friend may give the blessing.'

Hume had his servant refill their bowls with raksi. Then before he left, Puskar Maske made arrangements to return Hume's hospitality. 'You are invited to my house on the fifth day of the Dipawali, Hume,' he said. 'I and my family and a friend would be honoured if you came. It is a special occasion.'

During the days that followed Hume saw much of the Dipawali Festival. He went into the streets at night to enjoy the spectacle of the lights. He gave small coins to the children who came around singing. On the first day he saw people put out dishes of delicacies for the crows, to find favour with them because they were Yama's messengers from the Underworld. On the second day, all dogs, even the despised strays, the pariahs, were treated well. And on the third day people worshiped their cows. They bathed them, painted their horns and tails red and yellow and anointed their heads with vermilion powder. Many cows had flowers and sweets to eat. Hume's servant set up a tiny statue of Laxmi in his house and decorated it with flowers, and, just in case—amused at what he was doing—Hume left the door open to admit the goddess should she come to bless his wealth, the gold he had brought to Kathmandu and the beautiful ruby pendant.

Then on the afternoon of the fifth day, Hume went to Puskar Maske's house near Anson Tole. They sat and talked, and drank several bowls of raksi before Puskar Maske suggested they join the women and children in the courtyard. 'As I mentioned,' he said, 'today is the Bah Tika, the brother blessing. It is a pleasant ceremony. Something I think you will like to see.' He continued, a little anxiously. 'I must tell you it is not usual to have a stranger witness it. And you are still a stranger, Hume. The Brahman, who is our family priest, will officiate and will have no objection. But my womenfolk will be uncertain of you. You will find them shy.'

On their entering the courtyard, the three women there had their saris drawn up to their eyes and gave Hume a timid welcome. But Puskar Maske's children, his two sons and their sister, obviously curious, came up and welcomed him with their namastes. Puskar Maske led to seats on one side of the courtyard. Hume's arrival was the sign for the ceremony to start, and he watched the white-robed Brahman priest, his headgear a shining gilt, put in place an image of the elephant-headed God Ganesh, a kalash of holy water, a pot of oil and a lighted brass lamp. The priest knelt and began a low-pitched chant that was to continue throughout the proceedings.

'Ganesh is worshipped,' Puskar Maske said quietly, 'and it is a sacred flame burning. The priest will seek blessings for all of us. He will beseech Yama not to take us to his Underworld during the coming year. Our new year has just started, Hume.'

Hume saw one of Puskar Maske's sons come and sit on a brightly coloured cloth. His sister followed and, taking oil from the pot and holy water from the kalash, she sprinkled them to form a circle around her brother.

'It casts a spell,' Puskar Maske said. 'Evil spirits and the messengers of death cannot pass into the circle.'

A serving maid placed little clay lamps in a ring around the boy and lit them, then stood to one side, burning incense. Another brought handfuls of sweets, nuts and flowers and gave them to the sister, who offered them to her brother, kneeling before him in the haze of the burning incense and the glow of the lamps. Then she lent close to her brother, drew a line of yellow powder down his forehead with her finger and dabbed it with dots of different colours.

'It is the Bah Tika blessing,' Puskar Maske said.

Now the sister was praying. 'It is the invocation,' Puskar Maske whispered to Hume. 'She is saying that by marking her brother's forehead she is planting a thorn bush at Yama's door, keeping Yama in his Underworld, and so making death impossible for her brother. She is asking that, as Yama is immortal, so might her brother be. She asks that her brother's life be long, that his body be as hard as a walnut but that his heart be soft as butter.'

Puskar Maske's other son received his blessing from his sister. Then Puskar Maske got up from his seat. 'It is my turn now,' he said. 'I have no sister here. It is a cousin who will give me my blessing. She will act as my sister.'

The circle of lamps glowed. Red, blue and white petals now lay thick on the ground. The scent of the incense had spread and strengthened and it was heady now. There was the priest's endless chanting and Hume sat there absorbed, almost hypnotised perhaps.

Puskar Maske, his blessing received, his forehead coloured below his jaunty topi cap, returned to his seat and sat in silence for some minutes before he turned and looked at Hume. 'I shall make a suggestion,' he said uncertainly. 'Refuse, if you wish. I would not take offence. May I speak?'

'Yes, of course.'

'Why not yourself, Hume? Why not receive a blessing?'

Hume had not expected it. 'Would it be fitting?' he asked, startled. 'As you said, I am a stranger here.'

'But a valued one. It can do you no harm, and it might protect you.'

'But I have no sister.'

'That does not matter. There is someone here who will act as your sister. I have spoken to her.'

Puskar Maske pointed to the three women sitting with his children. 'One is my second wife, one is my cousin. The third, the youngest of them, will give you your blessing. You have seen her before.'

'Have I?' Hume looked over at her, still with her sari pulled up to her eyes.

'Remember the audience with Jaya Malla? The Capuchin and the lady Bachhla. She is Maneka, Bachhla's attendant.'

Hume found himself sitting in the circle of glowing lamps, burning incense and the priest chanting. He was acutely aware of Maneka as she sprinkled the oil and water around him, of the rustling of her sari and her closeness. She came and knelt opposite him in the circle and offered him the sweets and nuts. She had lowered her sari from her face, and

Hume well remembered her, her soft eyes, her shapely features and her glistening black hair.

She lent close as she marked his forehead with the coloured powder. He met her gaze, and shyly she returned his smile. Keeping her face low, her eyes downcast, she prayed to Yama, reciting the invocation. Then the blessing given, she stood and, looking down at Hume, smiled again, quickly, before pulling her sari up to her eyes again and going to join the other women.

After the ceremony, Puskar Maske and Hume joined the womenfolk and children and the priest for a meal of sweet rice cakes and tea. Hume thanked Maneka for her blessing. Remembering that Puskar Maske had said it was customary to give a Bhai Tika present, he promised her one.

'It is very nice of you to offer me a present. But it is really not necessary,' she said shyly and went to join the other women.

But Hume could see she was pleased. He had in mind the ruby pendant that Alexander had taken from the Nawab's treasury after the Battle of Plassey. Before he left that afternoon, he drew Puskar Maske aside and asked about Maneka, and if she were a cousin of his or another relative.

'No, she is not a relative,' he told Hume. 'A family friend, you might say. Her mother was a Newar. You might remember that Jaya Malla spoke of his General Jayant Rana. Jayant Rana was a Gurkha and was once one of Prithvi Shah's own generals. But he deserted, came over to us, and was in command of Jaya Malla's army when the Gurkhas defeated it at Belcot. Prithvi Shah captured him and had his revenge. He followed Jaya Malla's example and ordered that he be flayed alive. Maneka is Jayant Rana's daughter. She was a child when the Gurkha King murdered her father.'

'Do you find her beautiful?' Puskar Maske asked, as Hume left to return to his house.

'Exceedingly so,' Hume said.

Six

Soon after the Dipawali Festival, when Hume went with General Josi and Puskar Maske on Jaya Malla's deputation to his cousin, Tej Narsinha Malla in Lalitpatan, he had changed to the dress of the valley: to the tunic and white trousers, a waist-band and black and white topi cap. The early mist had cleared and the sun was warming the cold morning as they walked across the fields, and Hume glanced northwards to the towering Himalayas white with winter snow. He looked above the terraced hillsides, up on the mountains surrounding the valley, and here and there he could see the smoke of the Gurkhas' fires.

They went up the gently rising ground, through the town gate and along the narrow streets to Lalitpatan's Durbar Square. Here Hume stopped to gaze at another profusion of pagodas and palaces, the tall columns and images of the gods, all a blaze of colour. The sunlight sparkled on the gilt, the copper, the bronze, the old red brick, the woodcarvings. To one side of the square, a market was crowded with people buying the peasants' produce, or resting and enjoying the sunlight. There were officials, priests and monks, people from the nearby hills carrying bundles of firewood on their backs and lamas from the high valleys or from Tibet in their maroon robes and cloth boots.

They made their way to the palace gate with its fine carvings and lion guardians of stone. The Captain of the Guard escorted them along the corridors to where they were to meet Tej Narsinha Malla. They waited in a wood-paneled room under low ceilings with aged wooden beams, its windows opening to the Durbar Square. A large oil lamp burnt at the far end, its light flickered on a large gilded image of Lord Shiva: on his three faces, wings and chaplet of skulls. Of his six arms, two held his wife, Parbati, in an eternal act of copulation.

'The Pradhans, the King's ministers, will come. He has the six of them,' Puskar Maske said. 'They have the power here, Hume, not the King. They are the true rulers of Lalitpatan. They are both king-makers and king-destroyers. Once they took Rajya Malla, one of Jaya Malla's brothers, for their King, then they blinded him. Did it so clumsily that he died soon after. Once they drove Jaya Malla himself from Lalitpatan. Another time, they chose Viswajit Malla then accused him, falsely I am sure, of adultery with one of their wives, and murdered him as he was entering the Temple of Taleju. His queen was watching from the palace.'

Puskar Maske turned to the window. 'From this window perhaps. She cursed the Pradhans and the people of Lalitpatan, so that their voices might fail and their troubles be terrible. And later they gave the throne to Dalmardan Shah, a brother of the Gurkha King, but soon drove him from Lalitpatan and put Tej Narsinha Malla in his place.' Puskar Maske sat shaking his head doubtfully.

Tej Narsinha Malla came into the room, wearing the blue and gold uniform of a general and followed by the six Pradhans. Each of the Pradhans wore a padded tunic of dark brown cloth and a brown Newar topi cap. They were all past middle-age, all similar in appearance, their faces thin and their black eyes keen. They took their seats at the table, and sat, dour faced, their seldom-blinking eyes fixed on Hume. No doubt they found his large size and fair complexion strange. But Hume saw more to it than that; their hostility was barely disguised and there was no sign of welcome on their faces.

Tej Narsinha Malla said softly, 'We welcome Sir Hume Clarke from the British Company. We hope he has a pleasant stay in our valley. He should feel free to visit my Kingdom as he wishes. I have discussed this with my ministers and they agree.' He turned towards one of the Pradhans. 'That is so, Kalidas?'

'It is, Sire,' Kalidas replied. But Hume noticed he still gave him no sign of welcome.

The General handed Narsinha Malla Jaya Malla's letter, which he read cursorily then passed to the Pradhans. 'What does my cousin want of me?' he asked.

It was Hume who replied. 'Your support, Sire. Support against the Gurkha King. Surely you know your valley is blockaded and will soon come under attack. Your people suffer death at the Gurkha King's hand. Your children and womenfolk included.'

Narsinha Malla looked towards the Pradhans sitting there. 'My cousin wants our support,' he said.

'It is a matter to consider carefully, Sire. Jaya Malla has been no friend of ours,' Kalidas replied, after quietly consulting the others.

'It is to protect your valley, your town here,' Hume said, not concealing his growing impatience. 'The Gurkha King watches even now. Bides his time, I should think. The valley must fight. Fight or its fate is surely sealed.'

Another of the Pradhans, Bhinkhuar, spoke, 'Perhaps that is true. But we need help from your British army. We have heard of its many victories in India. Your army is much greater than Prithvi Shah's, so it will have little trouble in defeating him. When the Gurkhas are defeated, trade will resume. We will help defend the valley when the British come. We will grant the British Company generous concessions. We will reward it liberally.'

Hume spoke bluntly, 'It is your valley. It is you who must defend it. I shall do all I can to get British help. But don't depend on it. Prepare to defend yourselves.'

The talk continued in this vein until Tej Narsinha Malla invited the three of them to stay a while to enjoy his hospitality. Kalidas signalled to an attendant standing near the image of Lord Shiva, who left the room and returned shortly with servants carrying platters of roast venison and buffalo meat, vegetables and garlic. Servants followed with pots of the rice beer, chan. During the meal the Pradhans questioned Hume about the Company's army, asking about its weapons and particularly the cannon, the soldier's dress, and their training. Apart from this, there was little conversation. It was late afternoon when the meal was finished and General Josi took his leave.

Since coming to Kathmandu, Hume had not called on the Capuchin priests, or they on him. So the next afternoon, a Sunday as it happened, he called at their house in Wontu Tole. A young priest introduced himself as Father Matteo; he seemed pleased Hume had called and invited him into the house, which was similar to Hume's own. The priests had made their living quarters on the ground floor. As Hume looked around he realised that they were indeed poor, with only the meanest necessities: crude furniture of rough wood, bedding in a corner, an old iron pan on the hearth, a few platters and bowls on a shelf and clay pots holding their stock of food.

Hume found Father Matteo a cheerful young man about his own age, stout and rounded in his white habit, with curly black hair and a fresh face. He talked freely. He told Hume he had attended a Capuchins' missionary college in Rome. He had been in Kathmandu for two years and liked his work and the Newar people. He was proud of his church with its congregation of about three hundred.

'Father Michaelangelo will return soon,' he said. 'He's been wondering if you'd come. He thought you might not because you are English, and a Protestant no doubt.'

'I am of the Catholic faith, of your Church of Rome.'

Father Matteo nodded his approval. 'That is good.'

'As for being English, I assure you I have nothing against the Portuguese. It is many years since the troubles between our two countries.'

'I'm not Portuguese,' Father Matteo said. 'Father Michaelangelo is. I am Italian. I am a Donelli, Alfredo Donelli. My family is well known in Italy. When I became a Capuchin I took the name of Matteo for our blessed founder, Matteo di Bassi. It was he who had the good Pope Clement allow us to have hoods on our habits.' He touched the hood hanging down his back.

Father Michaelangelo returned and joined them. Hume remembered him from Jaya Malla's audience and thought that, close-up, his face seemed even paler and his bones sharper. A worried man, Hume thought. The priest welcomed Hume hesitantly. When Hume remarked that he had been surprised to hear they were in Kathmandu, he explained, 'No, I assure you Christian priests are not new to the valley, Sir Hume Clarke. The Jesuit, Joao Cabral, passed through here as much as one hundred and fifty years ago. We Capuchins first visited here fifty years ago. I am pleased to learn you are of our their faith. I invite you to dine with us on our dal and rice tonight. You are welcome to the Benediction of the Blessed Sacrament in our church later.'

The Capuchins' church was on the second floor of their house, and Hume climbed up the ladder and sat at the back waiting for the people to arrive. The little wooden altar was whitened with a wash of lime, with brass candle-sticks on each side, the candle's glow falling on the brass door to the little tabernacle and the vases of flowers. The monstrance, its rays shining in the candlelight, which Hume noticed was certainly of brass not gold, already displayed the Host. On a stand before the altar the usual little red lamp was burning.

The rest of the room, lit dimly, contrasted with the bright altar. The old beams in the ceiling hung low, and around the rough brick walls the Stations of the Cross were roughly carved in wood and only dabbed with paint. Little paintings of Christ, the Christ of the Sacred Heart, and the Madonna hung in the corners near the altar. At the back of the room was the image of a saint Hume took to be Saint Francis. A dozen wooden benches served as pews.

Newar men and women and a few children came and took their places and started to toll their rosaries. Hume watched for Maneka, his Bhai Tika sister, wondering if she would come that evening. He was not disappointed. The church was almost full when an elderly lady in a brown sari with heavy gold ornaments came up into the room and took her place in front near the altar. It was Bachhla.

Maneka followed and sat beside her. Hume could see Maneka clearly in the candlelight from the altar, her finely featured face, her glossy black hair again done up on top in Newar fashion. She wore a brightly patterned sari and golden earrings and bangles. Father Michaelangelo conducted the service while Father Matteo assisted. The room filled with the sweet aroma of incense burning in the censer. The congregation worshipped the Host. Father Matteo sprinkled the holy water, there was the Tantum Ergo and a small choir sang. All bowed their heads low as Father Michaelangelo held the monstrance high to give the blessing.

But Hume had paid more attention to Maneka than to the Benediction Service, watching her from his seat at the back. When the service finished, she and Bachhla were the first to leave, and others followed. When Hume's turn came to descend the ladder, the two were already out in the street, on their way back to the palace.

Outside the Capuchin's house, Hume spoke to Father Matteo while he farewelled his congregation. He hoped Hume enjoyed the service. 'The Lady Bachhla was there,' he said, pleased. 'Many who attend our church are from the lower castes or slaves. But some are from the high castes. The Lady Bachhla is a cousin of the king and a lady of great influence at the Hanuman Palace. She will become a Christian soon.'

'And her attendant, Maneka?' Hume asked. 'Does she come to your church often?'

'Regularly,' Father Matteo replied. 'I often talk to her. She is a devout and sincere young lady.'

Seven

Hume rode across the fields with General Josi and Puskar Maske on Jaya Malla's deputation to Ranjit Malla in Bhaktapur. The town was well placed to defend itself, being built on high ground and strongly walled. They passed through the gate with no trouble and went to the town centre along streets wider than in Kathmandu and with a well-kept appearance. In Bhaktapur Durbar Square, again Hume was surprised at the profusion of temples and pagodas, tall columns and images of the gods.

They dismounted and entered the palace through the Mula Chok, the great door of heavy bronze with its exquisite castings of Kali and Tantric gods and goddesses, shining in the cool sunlight. Legendary monsters of the land and sea decorated its flame-shaped tympanum.

'It's a masterpiece,' Hume pronounced.

'The people of Bhaktapur have long been proud of it,' Puskar Maske said.

At the palace, an officer of the king's guard led them through the labyrinth of little courts to Ranjit Malla. The room was richly furnished and had large gilded images of Lord Shiva and Vishnu; it was well lit by oil lamps and streams of sunlight from the windows which opened to the Bhaktapur's Durbar Square. With only a priest in attendance, Ranjit Malla, an old man, was seated on an elaborately carved chair and dressed, not in military uniform like his cousin kings, but simply, in a padded tunic and cotton breeches. He seated the three on chairs drawn up close to him.

He took Jaya Malla's letter from General Josi which he opened and, holding it in his hand but not reading it, sat for some moments looking at Hume. 'I extend my welcome to you, Sir Hume Clarke,' he said. 'I understand you come from the British Company in Calcutta. I have heard of it. I see you are indeed a large man. I wonder if all British people are of your large size.'

Hume told him they were not.

'You are European, I am told,' Ranjit Malla said. 'We already have Europeans in Bhaktapur, two of them, Father Fransesco and his assistant. They are darker than you, black-haired, and they have been here a long time. They are priests of your Christian Church. I have supported these priests because they are my friends, and I am their friend. You must meet them one day.' He paused for some moments, reflecting. 'I remember when they first came here. A long time ago, now. They were agents of the Black Bhairab. We all saw that because they dressed in black and they had long black tails from their necks down their backs.'

Hume had seen Capuchins in England in their black habits. As for the tails, he thought Ranjit Malla must mean their pointed hoods, which they would drop down their backs away from their heads.

'We all feared them,' Ranjit Malla continued with a startled look. 'But what could we do? Agents of the Bhairab are not to be crossed. People avoided them, and walked away from them in the streets. Few dared to speak to them.' Ranjit Malla sat smiling to himself. 'But I thought it might not be the priests themselves, just a spell they were under, the black they were wearing and the black tails. So I called them here to the palace and gave each of them a garment of white cloth, white cloth woven here in Bhaktapur. I made them take off the black and put on the white. They objected, I remember, and even wrote to their Pope about it. But I insisted and they obeyed me. Have you seen them in their white?'

Hume told him he had seen them in Kathmandu.

'Since then they have not been agents of the Black Bhairab, and they have a following here. I do not mind that. And I am a friend of their Pope. I wrote to him once.'

Hume was growing impatient, wanting to get down to the business of the deputation. 'Sire,' he said. 'I suggest you read Jaya Malla's letter. It is important.'

'It is, Sir Hume Clarke,' Ranjit Malla agreed, but looked at the letter so quickly that he could not have made anything of it. 'I know that Jaya Malla is fighting the Gurkha King even now at Naldum. I am not sure I agree with that. What does my cousin want of me?'

'Your support, Sire, against Prithvi Shah, the Gurkha King. The letter also says that the British army is likely to come and help us,' General Josi said, looking to Hume for confirmation.

'I remember Prithvi Shah well,' Ranjit Malla said. 'He was my guest here in Bhaktapur once. When he was a young man, he stayed for three years nearly. We liked him and treated him well. He learnt much from us. You might say we educated him here.'

'It is a different matter now, Sire,' General Josi intervened.

'Yes, he was our friend,' Ranjit Malla went on, ignoring the general.

'He was also a friend of my son, Bir Narshina. They spent much time together. Prithvi Shah was sad indeed when my illegitimate sons murdered Bir Narshina. I was told he showed great anger, that he swore vengeance against the murderers.'

The general went to interrupt again, but Ranjit Malla waived him aside. 'Yes, it was the Satbahalyas, my illegitimate sons, the seven of them, who murdered Bir Narshina. They were jealous of his right to the throne. They are still troublesome, those sons, hard to control in my old age.'

General Josi, no longer checking his impatience, said in a loud voice, 'You know well enough of the Gurkha threat, Sire. Has Jaya Malla your support to repel a Gurkha attack?'

Ranjit Malla thought for some moments. 'Do you believe, Sir Hume Clarke, that Prithvi Shah will attack?'

'It is most likely, Sire.'

'But would he attack Bhaktapur?'

'He wants all the valley,' General Josi asserted. 'Has Jaya Malla your support to defend it?'

Ranjit Malla sat upright in his chair and there was a touch of annoyance in his voice when he replied, 'It is not for my cousin to ask that, General. I am the senior king. It is I who would defend the valley. You know full well I am of the senior line. Yaksha Malla saw to that.' He looked at Hume, 'It was three hundred years ago, Sir Hume Clarke, when Yaksha Malla divided the valley amongst his children. His eldest son got Bhaktapur. It was he who founded my senior dynasty.'

'Of course, Sire, we respect that,' General Josi replied.

'Now, General,' Ranjit Malla went on, 'I suggest you raise this matter of the Gurkha King with my seven sons. They are expecting you, all of you. The priest will take you to them. Talk to them about the problem my cousin in Kathmandu has and see what they say. Show them Jaya Malla's letter.' He handed the letter back to General Josi.

They took their leave of Ranjit Malla and followed the priest through the corridors. 'Ranjit Malla is old,' Puskar Maske told Hume. 'He has lost interest in the affairs of his Kingdom. His concerns now are with the gods, and he prepares for Yama's messenger from the Underworld. His sons are the real rulers of Bhaktapur; and it is said they are in league with Prithvi Shah, that they have an undertaking with him which will let them continue to rule and keep their revenues.'

They found the seven illegitimate sons waiting in one of the larger courts of the Palace. Each joined his hands in a namaste and welcomed them affably, particularly Hume as a foreigner, their manner contrasting with that of the sombre Pradhans at Lalitpatan.

General Josi gave them Jaya Malla's letter, and each in turn read it carefully, taking his time. When the last had finished, they consulted, speaking too softly for Hume to hear; but from the movement of their heads Hume understood that they were all in agreement.

One of them asked General Josi, 'What has our father told you General? Is it that he himself should decide on the defence of the valley? That he is senior to his cousins in Kathmandu and Lalitpatan?'

'He said that.'

'That is also our view. But we can also say Bhaktapur will assist Jaya Malla against the Gurkhas if the British come. Yes, we would do that.'

'When the British come,' Hume repeated. 'I am new to your valley, but I see it has strength. United you could defeat the Gurkha King. Stop his blockade. Stop his murder of your people, your children and womenfolk. You say if the British come.'

The Satbahalyas looked at each other. 'Yes, it is what we say,' one said. 'There is no more to be said on the matter.'

Then one of them clapped his hands and servants came into the room with large pots of raksi and bowls for each of them. The servants poured the raksi, filling the bowls to the brim. It was strong liquor. That afternoon the conversation with Ranjit Malla's sons never flagged. They spoke no more about the defence of the valley or British help; instead they put many questions to Hume about England, about Calcutta, and about the East India Company's army. He answered as best he could, but it was difficult for him because the Satbahalyas knew little about the world outside their valley, and it was all strange to them. Whilst they talked the servants kept the bowls filled with the raksi, until finally General Josi called a halt, saying he wanted to be back in Kathmandu before nightfall. They took their leave and left Ranjit Malla's sons continuing to enjoy the liquor.

It was Christmas Day when Hume next attended the Capuchins' church, which women of the congregation had decorated with more flowers than usual. Newar tradesmen had built a crib with wooden images of the Virgin Mother, the Christ Child, St Joseph and the farm animals. Hume took with him the ruby pendant, which he intended to give Maneka as her Bhai Tiki present, thinking that Christmas Day would be appropriate. This time he sat not at the back of the church but near the entrance, so he would not be delayed leaving after the service.

As he hoped, Maneka attended and she gave him a warm smile as she took her place beside Bachhla. That day Hume was the first to leave, to wait for her in front of the Capuchins' house. Bachhla came out with Maneka and they returned his greeting. But that was all. Bachhla looked at him coldly, waved her hand to indicate he should not approach them, then quickly ushered Maneka off, back along the street towards the palace.

Hume wondered about Bachhla's attitude. Although still new to Kathmandu and not yet familiar with the customs, he resented it. When he met Puskar Maske again, he told him of his difficulty with Bachhla, how she had treated him. He also told Puskar Maske he had a Bhai Tika present for Maneka, the ruby pendant he thought she would like.

'You must expect such treatment, Hume,' Puskar Maske told him. 'They are ladies of the court. Bachhla is a noble lady of the first rank, Jaya Malla's cousin and close to him. Maneka, I told you before, is the daughter of Jayant Rana who was an important general before Prithvi Shah had him murdered. He was a high caste Gurkha, a Thakuri wearing the sacred thread.'

And I am English, Hume thought, a baronet now my brother is dead, with an estate in Hollybrook. But he did not say this.

'You will learn our customs here,' Puskar Maske continued. 'People of the higher castes, as I am, guard their womenfolk jealously. And most others do, the Jyapu peasants and Kuma potters. But there are concubines to be had and slave girls. We take them into our houses. Many of us do. General Josi does, as well as our ministers, senior officials and military officers do. Ranjit Malla's sons in Bhaktapur have many maids. Some poor families are glad of this for their daughters and the payment they ask is not large.'

Hume thought that Puskar Maske might have explained the reason for Bachhla's attitude without telling him this. He wondered if Puskar Maske was hinting that he, too, should take a concubine or slave girl into his house, that it would be acceptable for him to do so.

But then Puskar Maske said, 'I shall arrange for you to meet Maneka, Hume. I shall invite the both of you to my house so you can give her the Bhai Tika present.'

That pleased Hume. He showed Puskar Maske the ruby pendant. 'Is it suitable?' he asked

Puskar Maske examined the stone in the light from the window. 'It is suitable. It is magnificent. I am certain she would be very pleased with it.'

Then, surprising himself and perhaps Puskar Maske too, Hume said, 'I should like you to tell me something, Puskar Maske. I would like to know if Maneka is betrothed. Is she promised in marriage? I've heard Newar women are often married young.'

Puskar Maske looked at Hume for some moments. Then, hiding a smile, replied. 'Yes, she is married, Hume.'

'She is,' Hume exclaimed. He was crest-fallen, unable to hide his emotion.

'Are you that interested, Hume?' Puskar Maske was smiling now. 'Yes she is married. She is married to a bel fruit.'

'What are you saying? To a fruit?' Hume asked, puzzled.

'To a bel fruit. A pomegranate, I think you call it.'

Hume was not prone to anger, but he was angry now. 'That is no answer,' he said sharply. 'What I asked is important to me. It was no answer you gave. Don't make fun of me, Puskar Maske. Take care. You're trying to provoke me. I'll not have it.'

Puskar Maske now showed his concern. 'Forgive me, Hume. Accept my apologies. I was thoughtless. I have taken advantage of you because you do not know our customs. What I say is true. It is a custom here, a Newar custom, for girls aged six to ten or thereabouts, before puberty anyhow, to be married to a bel fruit. It is, of course, symbolic. Young girls, usually a group of them, are dressed nicely in red and yellow saris, with jewels and other ornaments, perhaps a porcupine spike in their hair for luck. They look like little brides. Each girl has a bel fruit, a perfectly formed fruit that her parents have selected especially. On an auspicious day chosen by the astrologers, a priest performs the ceremony. Many guests attend. A red canopy is placed over the altar and the priest invokes the gods to favour each girl in her married life. Each girl has her bel fruit beside her and her parents give her to the fruit in marriage. After the ceremony the guests are treated to a feast. It is all very pleasant, Hume. And the bel fruit the girl might keep or offer it to the God Ganesh, or sometimes throw it in a sacred river.'

'Maneka is not married, then?'

'Yes she is, but to the fruit.'

Hume relaxed. He did not hide his relief. 'It's a strange custom you have,' he said.

'For you it is strange. I can understand that. But for us, for our womenfolk, it has a great advantage. Here in the valley we believe that a marriage can take place only once in a lifetime. The bel fruit represents a god, often Narayan or Vishnu, and for all her life the girl remains married to that god. True, she will have an earthly husband. Later her parents will arrange it for her. But he will only represent the god. Even if her earthly husband dies, she will never be widowed. She need never burn on her husband's funeral pyre as a sati because she will remain married to the god.'

'Maneka's mother was a Newar,' Puskar Maske continued. 'As a young girl Maneka was married to a bel fruit. No, Maneka has no earthly husband, Hume. She is not betrothed. Her father was a Thakuri and they do not marry their daughters young.'

When Hume went to Puskar Maske's house he found Maneka already there. Her two soldiers from the palace guard were stationed in the street outside. Welcoming Hume, Puskar Maske explained, 'I have to tell you that my womenfolk and children are away from the house visiting. And I myself must leave you. I have been summoned to the palace and I cannot refuse. I have asked the servants to bring tea for you. Please accept my apologies.'

Maneka gave a start as if to object. But she did not, and Puskar Maske left.

For some moments Hume watched Maneka sitting there, her dark eyes looking back at him over the hem of her sari which she had pulled up to her face. Again he thrilled at the closeness of her. 'Thank you for coming, Maneka,' he said. 'I have been looking forward very much to meeting you again.'

She moved her head to acknowledge this, then after some moments, Hume saw she lost a little of her shyness, and wanted to talk. 'The ladies in your own country,' she asked, 'are they like you, with fair hair and skin, or have they black hair like mine and are darker?'

'Some are dark,' Hume told her. 'Most are fairer. Only a few are as beautiful as you, Maneka.'

She turned her gaze away for some moments, then looked back at Hume, her face showing her pleasure. 'It is pleasant for you to say that. It pleases me.'

'I have watched you at the Capuchins' church.' Hume told her.

'Yes, I know. I have seen you.'

'You have become a Christian.'

'I have. I attend church regularly. Father Matteo tells me I will make a good Catholic. He told me you came from England.'

'You talk of me with Father Matteo?'

'We all talk about you in Kathmandu. Everyone does. It is natural. You are from a far-off country, so different from my own I think.'

'Yes, different, many customs are different.'

'Our customs can be difficult for us.' She hesitated. 'I ought not be here with you now, with Sri Puskar Maske and his family away. I had not known.'

'You regret you came then?'

'I do not. But if others knew they would object. Object strongly, I think.'

Hume took the ruby pendant from his pocket and handed it to her. 'It is for you, Maneka' he said. 'It is the Bhai Tika present I promised in return for your blessing. Do you like it?'

She looked closely at the great red ruby. 'I do. It is beautiful.'

'Would you like to wear it?'

'Yes, I shall do so now.' She drew the sari away from her face with a shy smile. He watched as she took the pendant's chain and with a little trouble made it secure around her neck. The pendant rested on her breast, the ruby glowing red against the whiteness of her cholo blouse, the diamonds sparkling, and as she adjusted it in place she smiled at Hume again, warmly this time.

'Do you give such presents to ladies in your own country?' she asked.

'We give them presents. This ruby is of a rare quality.'

'Yes, I have not seen one like it.' Then lowering her eyes away from Hume, she said, 'I do like it. I thank you for offering it to me. But I will not take it.'

'You don't want it?' Hume was concerned.

'I could not take it from you. I would not be allowed.'

Hume persisted. 'Take it. Keep it for only you to see.'

Maneka thought for some moments, but refused. Then with a worried expression darkening her face, she asked, 'Could you tell me if your British army will come to our valley? Will it come and help us against the Gurkha King?'

'Perhaps.' Hume told her. 'I shall do what I can.' Remembering that the Gurkha King had her father flayed alive, he asked, 'Tell me, Maneka, does the Gurkha King have a special worry for you?'

'Yes, I fear him. I have reason to.' Then she pulled her sari up to her face again, rose and made to leave. As they walked towards the door Hume took her hand. At first she started to withdraw it but did not, letting it rest in his.

'We could meet again,' Hume suggested.

She did not object. 'Perhaps. It might be.'

'Would you like that?' Hume asked.

'I think I would not be allowed to meet you. I do not know.'

Maneka rejoined her escort and went back to Jaya Malla's palace, and Hume returned to his house.

That night Hume walked through the streets of Kathmandu and outside the town walls. The night was cold with winter in the Valley of Nepal, and in the distance the ice and rock of the great Himalayan peaks were a faint blue-white reaching up into the black night sky. Maneka was very much in Hume's thoughts, her gentle manner, her soft smile, and the touch of intimacy when he took her hand. He felt in his pocket for the ruby pendant, which he would now keep with him, and regretted her refusing it.

Then the difficulties came to mind, their greatly different cultures, their countries so far apart and the attitude of Jaya Malla's court, no doubt opposition from Jaya Malla himself. Perhaps Maneka would not want to meet him again, even if she were allowed to do so. But his spirits rose as he thought of her half-promise to see him again, and other signs of her interest in him.

Looking towards the valley's surrounding mountains, Hume could see the red glow of the Gurkha's fires and he thought of their coming attack. Again he thought of Maneka. Knowing of her fear of the Gurkha King, more than ever now he was determined to help defend the valley.

Eight

When Hume went with General Josi and Puskar Maske to the Hanuman Palace to report on the deputations to Lalitpatan and Bhaktapur, they found Jaya Malla with the Raj Guru and the shaven-headed old priest, Vajracrya, from the Swayambhunath. Hume was not at all pleased with what he had found on the delegations. It was obvious that little was being done to defend the valley and he was doubtful about the support for Jaya Malla.

'I am afraid, Sire,' he told Jaya Malla, 'that there is much complacency amongst your cousins. Both the Pradhans and the Satbahalyas say they would help defend the valley, but only if the British come. There is complacency, much complacency.'

'And treachery, no doubt,' Jaya Malla added. 'The Pradhans are my enemies of old. They are certainly not to be trusted.' His face darkened and he glared as he turned to the Raj Guru. 'You have heard. What do you say to me?'

'I am but a priest, Sire, not versed in these matters,' the Raj Guru replied. 'It is you who will decide. It is I who ask the gods for their support.'

With a hint of a smile, Puskar Maske whispered, 'Some Brahmans in the valley would welcome Prithvi Shah, Hume.'

Then the old priest Vajracrya stood up and addressed Jaya Malla. 'I wish to speak to you, Sire. I and the many who worship the Buddha, people in Kathmandu and elsewhere in the valley, want the Gurkha King's defeat. We must defend the valley, with or without British help. It is the wish of Lord Buddha.'

'The priest fears the Gurkha King,' Puskar Maske said quietly. 'The Malla kings have treated the Buddhists well. For centuries Hindus and Buddhists have lived together happily in our valley, Hume. They have worshipped together sometimes, and attended each other's festivals. The priest fears Prithvi Shah would favour the Hindu people at the expense of the Buddhists.'

For some moments Jaya Malla sat thinking, looking at the Raj Guru and the old priest, from one to the other. Then, without saying more, he got up and dismissed those present.

As Hume left the palace, the old priest Vajracrya came up and invited him to visit the Swayambhunath. Hume accepted readily. He had often looked out from Kathmandu to the great Buddhist temple, the chaitya on its high hill rising above the valley two miles to the south-west. It was truly ancient, its building started more than two thousand years ago. It stood out clearly as they approached. Its gabh, the massive white hemisphere, was one hundred feet wide and fifty feet high. On top of this, its toran, the square, gilded tower, rose high, and on each of its four sides were great painted eyes, half-closed, watching out in all directions over the valley. The eyes looked down on Hume and the priest as they approached.

'They are the all-seeing eyes of the Adi Buddha,' the old priest said.

'What is that under the eyes, like a large red question mark?' asked Hume.

'It is the ancient symbol indicating dharma. The duteous way to happiness, you could say,' the priest told him.

'What way is that?' Hume asked.

The old priest shrugged. 'That, we must all decide for ourselves.'

High above the toran—Hume saw it closely now—was the conical canopy, its gilded rings glittering in the winter sunlight. They climbed the hill, up the steep steps and past the tremendous Vajra, which was the cast thunderbolt representing the power of the Buddha's all-knowing mind: power over even Indra the King of Heaven. They walked around the great gabh and past the images of the five Divine Buddhas, which were the Adi Buddha's creations and the governors of the past, the present and the future. They passed the many prayer wheels holding their paper prayers, each with the sacred phrase, "Om Mani Padme Hum".

'The words address Buddha, Dharma and Sangha, our Trinity, and you might translate them as, "Hail the Jewel of the Lotus",' the old priest told Hume. 'It is a benediction of peace.'

They walked amongst the many small sub-chaityas, images of gods, the stone lingams which were the phallic symbols of creation, and the sacred flames burning in the urns. They entered a vihar, with a large gilded image of the Buddha near the door, dimly lit by small lamps, and smoke from the burning incense heavy in the air. Through the haze, Hume made out images of the Buddhist gods, a great prayer wheel, flowers, coloured tapestries and red carpets, and then the officiating priests in their richly embroidered vestments and mitre hats. To one side, a row of shaven-headed monks in wine-coloured robes tolled their beads and sang a low-pitched chant to the throbbing of drums and an occasional blast from a long Tibetan trumpet. Worshippers sprinkled their offerings of rice and red sindar powder.

Leaving the vihar, Hume went with the priest to the nearby Temple of Saraswati the Goddess of Learning. Here, too, people were worshipping, making their offerings, and receiving from the temple priests a blessing, a tika mark on their foreheads and flowers in their hair.

'It's a Hindu temple,' Hume remarked.

'It is,' the priest replied. 'We Buddhists also worship here. Saraswati is also Mukhseddar, a wife of Manjusri the Mortal Buddha who created the Valley of Nepal. The footsteps of Manjusri are there and those of the Divine Buddhas. There is much worship in common in the valley, both Hindu and Buddhist.'

They returned to the gabh of the Swayambhunath and sat on a stone bench which overlooked the valley. The priest stretched out an arm from his robe to take in much of the scene, the towns and villages, the fields, to the surrounding mountains. 'Once it was all a lake,' he told Hume. 'It was at the beginning of time. It was the Nag Hrad, the abode of the Nagas, the Snake Gods whose king was Karkot Raja. Then one day in the dim past, a lotus flower appeared on the surface of the lake's waters. It appeared below where we sit now, a beautiful flower perfect in all respects. Eventually a sacred flame of dazzling brilliance sprang from the lotus. Holy men came to worship the flame, some from the north, from across the great white mountains.' The priest pointed to the Himalayan peaks which were clear in the northern sky. 'And some holy men came from the south.'

'And they saw,' the priest continued, 'that the flame was the Adi Buddha, the Self Created One, the Supreme God called Swayambhu. Then the Divine Buddhas came and worshipped it, and the Mortal Buddhas came. And it is said that Brahma, Vishnu and Shiva, the great Hindu gods, also came in the guise of deer. Eventually Manjusri came from Mount Sirsha in far-off northern China and worshipped the flame as Swayambhu. Manjusri came with his two wives, Burdar who is also Lachmi, and Mukhseddar who is also Saraswati as I have told you. Manjusri had with him his disciples and followers of all ranks. Amongst them the Raja Dharmakar.'

'Manjusri created the Valley of Nepal,' the priest continued. 'The Buddha revealed to him that he should do so, that he should drain the waters of the lake to make a place for people to live. At that, with great strides Manjusri moved along the tops of all the mountains surrounding the valley, and placed his wife Burdar on Mount Champa Devi and his wife Mukhseddar on Mount Pulchowk. On his second circuit, the Buddha told him of the place to draw the waters away. On his third circuit, Manjusri took his great talawar and slashed through the mountains at that place, which is to the south of the valley, to cut a deep ravine. Today it is known as the Chowbar Gorge or the Place of the Cut. The waters rushed from the lake, and the valley was formed.'

'And the Nagas, the Snake Gods who lived in the lake?' Hume asked the old priest.

'Most were swept from the valley as the waters drained away, but some stayed. Their King, Karkot Raja, stayed, and Manjusri gave him power over the treasures of the valley. It is said that he is still here and lives with his great treasure in the black water of a deep pond in the Bagmati, at Taudah near the Place of the Cut.'

'Manjusri walked through the valley he had created,' the old priest explained. 'He saw it was beautiful; and he built the hill where we are today around the sacred lotus and protected it with masonry. Near the centre of the valley he found the root of the lotus beside an ever-flowing spring of clear water. He knew this was the home of a deity, and as he worshipped there a goddess appeared to him. It was Gayeshwar, the Glorious Concealed One, who is also Durga the powerful mother of all the gods. Manjusri built a shrine to Gayeshwar over the lotus root in the form of a yoni, the female symbol. He also planted trees which, today, are the grove of Pashupati.' The old priest pointed towards them, out past the town of Kathmandu. 'Manjusri built a house for himself and his wives on Mount Manjusri. His followers settled in the new valley which was called "Naipala", the "Cherished of the Gods", and he made Dharmakar the King. At last with all that done, he returned with his two wives to China and became a Mortal Buddha.'

'It is indeed a beautiful valley,' Hume said, looking out again from the Swayambhunath over the fields to the great mountains. 'My thanks to you for bringing me here and for your account of the valley's creation. It is a pleasant legend.' As the afternoon was passing, he rose and made to leave.

But the priest detained him, placing a hand on his shoulder and pointing to the town of Kirtipur, a few miles to the south of the Swayambhunath, which Hume had looked on from Mount Chandragiri the day he came to the valley.

'It is Kirtipur, the City of Fame, that the Gurkha King will first attack,' the priest said. 'He will come there again, even though twice he has failed. It is Kirtipur he wants, as a base inside the valley to go on and take the three kingdoms.'

Hume looked over to the town on its hill some three hundred feet above the valley floor. He could see access to it was difficult, up along a steep winding road or up a few rough and narrow paths. Kirtipur's walls were high and strong and the gates few; and behind the walls the outer houses and other buildings presented tall defending faces of solid brick. Kirtipur would be hard to take, impossible almost without great cannon, no doubt of that, he thought.

'And the people of Kirtipur are brave,' the priest continued. 'True, the first time the Gurkha King attacked, they had help from Jaya Malla, from the three kingdoms. That was nearly seven years ago now. It was a pitched battle then, on the plains below the hill. I watched from here. Jaya Malla routed the Gurkhas. Many were slaughtered, their General Kalu Pandey was killed, and Prithvi Shah himself escaped death only narrowly. It was a long time, seven years, before the Gurkhas returned.'

'They returned only a short time ago for their second attack. This time, the people of Kirtipur had no help from the valley and had to fight alone. The Gurkhas planned to scale the walls and fight inside the town, and Surpratap, the Gurkha King's brother, led them. But it was Kirtipur's walls that won that day. Surpratap was on a ladder on top of a wall when an arrow struck his face and pierced his eye; it left the great scar on him. After that there was much confusion amongst the Gurkhas and they retreated.' For some moments the priest looked out at Kirtipur, then turned to Hume. 'But it will be different the next time the Gurkhas come. Prithvi Shah has learnt. The slaughter will be terrible. The Gurkhas will show no mercy. Kirtipur will need much support.'

'From a united Valley of Nepal,' Hume said, doubtfully.

The old priest moved his head slowly. 'Either from that or with the help of the British army. Can you tell me? Will the British army come?'

'It is possible,' Hume replied. 'We shall see.'

Back in his house late that night, Hume awoke to a knocking on the door below. Leaping out of bed, he took the pistol he kept ready and peered through the latticed window down to the street. Two soldiers in uniform were standing there.

Hume's servant climbed quickly up the ladder. 'They say they are from the royal guard, master. They say it is you they want.'

Hume looked down at them again. Their uniform was in fact of the royal guard. He went down and spoke through the closed door.

'What are you doing here at this late hour? Be off unless you have good reason,' he said, not pleased at being disturbed.

'Jaya Malla has sent us,' one replied. 'He apologises for the late hour. He asks you to come to the palace now.'

'Why at this time?' Hume asked.

'We do not know,' came the reply.

Hume followed them along the dark streets which were deserted now except for the occasional cow. A gong struck twelve garhies, which, as time was measured in the valley, meant it was past mid-night and only five hours left till the dawn with light enough to count the tiles on the roofs of the houses. They reached the Durbar Square and made their way amongst its many temples, now black shapes except where the cold starlight touched an open space or a gilded roof. The great pagoda of Taleju loomed up against the sky. They passed the image of the Black Bhairab, now almost lost in the blackness of the night.

An officer of the royal guard was waiting at the Monkey God Gate. He had a lamp burning and led Hume through the maze of the palace courts, along a corridor, towards an open door with a dim light showing in the room beyond. Hume entered and found Jaya Malla seated at a table with a young soldier in uniform. He had the insignia of a jemidar.

Jaya Malla rose, joined his hands in a namaste and welcomed Hume. He dismissed the officer of the guard and asked Hume to sit with him at the table. 'I have broken your sleep, Sir Hume Clarke,' he said. 'You must forgive me for that. But there are things we must do late at night in Kathmandu, away from eyes that spy for the Gurkha King. You will know by now, Sir Hume Clarke, that there are some in my kingdom who are against me. They would like to see the Gurkha King come to the valley.'

Hume looked first at the jemidar, and then at the paper and quill and pot of ink he had on the table.

'You wonder why you are here, at this time?' Jaya Malla asked.

'I do, Sire.'

Jaya Malla pointed to the writing materials. 'I wish to write to your Company in Calcutta. I will ask your governor for help from his army without delay. I will tell him how generous my trading concessions for him would be. But I have no experience in writing to your Company. You must advise me.'

'Yes, of course,' Hume offered to draft a letter in English. He set about the task willingly, explaining what he was writing. He wrote about the Gurkha King's blockade and his ever-present threat to the valley. He told how Jaya Malla had long defended the valley, mentioning the force he now had fighting near the Naldum fort. He stressed—perhaps more than he should, he thought—the strength of the Gurkhas and Jaya Malla's need for help from a British force. He wrote that the Company would find a friend in Jaya Malla; and of the generous concessions Jaya Malla would give the Company, not only for trade within the valley but also for trade on to Tibet and China. It would be trade in many items: gold and silver, grain and salt, copper and other metals, cloth, precious stones, conch shells, yak tails, to mention some.

Hume continued the letter to give the Company information about the route from Patna over the Terai and up into the valley, and the local supplies a Company army could expect. He emphasised the need for care when crossing the duns to avoid the miasmas that brought the aul with its fever and death.

Jaya Malla showed his pleasure. 'I should like to add to it,' he said. 'I will express my gratitude for your presence in Kathmandu. Shall I ask the Company to extend your stay with us? Sri Puskar Maske told me your intention was to visit us for three months only. That time is nearly gone. It will be necessary for you to stay longer, Sir Hume Clarke, until your British army and I defeat the Gurkha King. I hope you will agree. It would please me greatly.'

He spoke politely, but Hume noticed the hint of a threat in his voice. 'It is I who will decide whether I stay longer in the Valley of Nepal. Not the Company,' Hume told him. 'I'll think over what you ask. If you wish me to suggest it to the Company in your letter, that is a matter for you.'

'The Company's governor. Who is he now?' Jaya Malla asked.

'Robert Clive by the time the letter gets to Calcutta. It should be addressed to him.'

'We will also offer him part of the treasure we find in the valley.' Jaya Malla thought this important.

'It would help,' Hume agreed.

'The jemidar will take the letter to Patna,' Jaya Malla said. 'He will find a way through the Gurkha King's blockade. He knows the country well, the little-used tracks, and he is one I can trust.' Jaya Malla dismissed the jemidar with instructions to be ready to depart within the week.

'And now to your own affairs, Sir Hume Clarke,' Jaya Malla said, the two of them alone in the room. 'Your help has pleased me greatly. I trust your house in Makhan Tole is satisfactory?'

Hume assured him it was.

'And your other arrangements. Is our food to your liking? Your servant satisfactory? I understand that Sri Puskar Maske and others are hospitable.'

'I have no complaints, Sire.'

'Our weather is cold now, Sir Hume Clarke. It will not last. Soon you will enjoy our spring and then our warm summer.'

Jaya Malla thought for a while. 'You will need to occupy yourself. You will need an income whilst you are here. I will make a jagir grant to you. There is land across the Dhobi Khola, not far from the village of Deo Patan. The peasant Dongal is the tenant there. I will grant it to you with half the grain that Dongal crops.'

Hume said the offer was generous. He would consider it if he decided to stay longer.

Jaya Malla sat studying Hume for some moments before he went on. 'There is another matter I will speak of. The servant whom Sri Puskar Maske found for you. It is a man, I understand? Not a woman?'

'That is so, Sire.'

Jaya Malla looked knowingly. 'You have no woman in your house then. No slave girl, even?'

'No, my servant is a man,' Hume told him, wondering what Jaya Malla would propose.

'But you need not live alone here in Kathmandu. Few of us do. It is not natural for a young man like you. I will not permit it. I could send you someone you can take into your house to keep you company. She is most attractive, and she will please you. I assure you of that.'

He wants to send me a concubine, Hume thought, recalling Puskar Maske's talk of concubinage in the valley. But he objected, 'Whether or not I take someone into my house is a matter for me to decide, Sire. It is not for you. I would ask you not to meddle in my affairs.'

Jaya Malla shrugged. 'As you say, Sir Hume Clarke. But we shall see.'

Nine

Hume went to the Capuchins' church hoping Maneka would attend the service. Father Matteo was waiting at the front of his house and came up to Hume saying, 'I suggest that today you do not leave with the congregation after I say Mass but wait in the church. There is someone who wants to talk to you. A surprise for you, perhaps.'

Hume took his seat near the back of the church and, as usual, waited for Maneka and Bachhla to arrive. People climbed up the ladder and soon the church was full, but, to his disappointment, there was no sign of either of them. When the service had finished and the congregation gone, Father Matteo tidied up the altar and climbed down the ladder. Hume waited, as the priest had suggested.

After some time he heard movement on the floor below and then someone climbing up the ladder. It was indeed a surprise for Hume. Maneka had come into the church, not with Bachhla this time but alone. She glanced at Hume, then sat in her usual place, looking towards the altar with her rosary beads in her hand. For some moments Hume watched her, the golden ornament in her black hair, the light blue sari she had worn at Jaya Malla's audience when he had first seen her. He sat beside her on the seat Bachhla usually took.

Close to her now, Hume could hear Maneka's breathing quicken. 'I am delighted be with you again, Maneka. It is a most pleasant surprise,' he told her.

'I wanted to see you,' she said. 'It worried me.'

'Worried?' Hume queried.

'I thought I offended you.'

'By not taking the ruby pendant, the Bhai Tiki present?'

'Yes, that is so.'

Hume took the pendant, which he had kept in his pocket, and held it out to her with the great red ruby glowing in the light of the candles which still burnt on the altar. She took it and fixed it around her neck.

'I shall think of you wearing it,' Hume said.

'No, I will not be able to wear it, not at the palace. I would not be allowed to wear a present from you. They are very strict. I shall need to keep the ruby hidden. Usually men are not allowed to even look at the ladies of the court.'

'I look at you, Maneka,' Hume reminded her.

She smiled. 'In church. Yes, I know. People must know. Jaya Malla must know. It surprises me.'

'I shall go to the palace. Talk to Jaya Malla. Tell him of my present to you.'

'Please do not do that,' she said. 'Jaya Malla would have me locked in my room. Send me away from Kathmandu perhaps. Please do not do that.'

Hume controlled his annoyance. 'Not yet then, Maneka.'

Maneka thanked him and shyly placed her hand in his. 'There is the Gurkha King. Tell me, will the British army come?'

Hume lent towards her and placed his arm around her shoulder. 'I believe it will come, Maneka. But whatever happens, I shall ensure your safety.'

Maneka took Hume's hand and pressed it. As she rose to go she tightened her sari around her to hide the ruby pendant. Hume followed her down the ladder and out into the street, and watched her set off for the palace with her two escorts.

Some mornings Hume would walk with his servant to the market near Makham Tole, where he liked to look over the peasants' produce: the winter vegetables, rice, goat and buffalo meat, the stacks of bright yellow oranges and flowers. He would mingle with people making their purchases, and talk with some, sitting for a while to enjoy the winter sunshine. One morning not long after his nocturnal meeting with Jaya Malla, he chanced to see the Dewar, Ari Lawat, there. The Dewar, knowing who Hume was, greeted him with a friendly namaste and said he was waiting for Puskar Maske; that they would be going on Jaya Malla's business that day.

It was not long before Puskar Maske joined them. 'Again, we are going to search for treasure for Jaya Malla,' he told Hume.

'What success have you had so far?' Hume asked. He hoped to hear that some treasure had been found for spending on the defence of the valley.

'Our search yielded treasure, Hume. But only once. Treasure is hard to find,' Puskar Maske said.

'You found something,' Hume encouraged.

'Yes, at Tolu. Jaya Malla suggested Tolu. He said we should consult the Court Astrologer and dig there first. So we did that and we had ten peasants digging in many places. At last we found the site of an old temple, so ancient that only its foundations were left. It was a long forgotten temple, of what god no one remembered. It was Kali, perhaps.'

'Not Kali,' the Dewar objected. 'It was the Goddess Basundhara or Annapurna, some more benign god, because a spring of clear water spouted from the digging.'

'He fears Kali's vengeance for desecrating the temple, or what is left of it,' Puskar Maske said with an amused smile.

'That is so. It is sensible to fear her,' the Dewar asserted.

'Far underground we found an old vault,' Puskar Maske said. 'The treasure was there. We found many coins of gilt copper, worth half a lakh of rupees. There were little images, also in gilt copper. Some of Vishnu, some of Lord Shiva, some of Kali.'

'And some of Basundhara, I should think,' the Dewar said.

Hume had doubted that any treasure at all would be found. 'It would please Jaya Malla,' he said.

'Yes,' Puskar Maske answered. 'He will use the coins to pay the Nagar mercenaries for a few weeks. But he needs much more.'

'Jaya Malla is no longer pleased, I hear,' the Dewar said. 'Not after his visit to the Pashupatinath. He went there yesterday to seek treasure himself. I had warned him against it. It has been said there is gold and silver there, but it is Lord Shiva's and it would be dangerous to take it. The Raj Guru agreed with me. He also warned Jaya Malla.'

This surprised Puskar Maske. 'He went to the Pashupatinath?'

'He did. One of the temple priests told me of it. It was disastrous for him.'

The Pashupatinath, Lord Shiva's great temple as Pashupati the Lord of the Animals, was one of the most sacred of places. The great two-tiered temple was on a hill above the bank of the Bagmati, with gilded roofs and a silver-plated facade. It had a great stone lingam representing Lord Shiva's phallus and a gilded image of a huge bull many times life-size. Smaller temples were nearby; small pagodas and many lingams were on the surrounding hills and the river banks. There were many memorial shrines with their own lingams and stone bulls. Below the temple along the river banks were the burning ghats, the Arya Ghat where the bodies of the valley's kings were burnt, and where at times their wives met their deaths as satis in the flames. The burning ghats for the nobles were next, and further along those for the lower castes. Near the burning ghats were the dhamsalas where the dying came to await death. They would wash in the river, then wait for Yama to take their spirits to the Underworld, for their bodies to be burnt and the holy waters to take away their ashes. The Pashupatinath portrayed Lord Shiva as the god of both reproduction and destruction.

'I was told that Jaya Malla arrived at the Pashupatinath,' the Dewar continued, 'and found the Raj Guru already there and waiting for him. Again the Raj Guru advised him against taking Lord Shiva's treasure, to not even seek it, reminding him of Shiva's wrath. But again Jaya Malla ignored him and demanded the key to the treasure vault.'

'I have heard of the treasure there,' Puskar Maske said.

'Jaya Malla called together some of the temple priests. He had them get their torches flaming well and ordered the Raj Guru to show the way,' the Dewar said. 'They walked hesitatingly through the dark corridors to the vaults. Jaya Malla himself turned the key in the door of the vault where the treasure was thought to be. At first the old door, which is of heavy iron and rusty with age, would not open. I should think this would have been a warning from Lord Shiva—warning enough. But Jaya Malla had the priests push, and eventually the door did open. They entered the vault, the priests holding up their torches to see through the blackness. I am told gold was there, great quantities of it. Gold bars in high piles, coinage covering the floor, and silver. It all shone through the blackness, glittering under the flames of the priests' torches.'

'It is true then? Treasure is there?' Puskar Maske asked.

'So the priest told me. But something else was also there. Its great coils were wrapped around the gold and silver. Through the torch light they saw the Snake God. It was Basuki Naga. The great snake was protecting Shiva's treasure.'

'Is it true?' Puskar Maske asked, wanting confirmation. 'It was Basuki Naga?'

'The priest told me that,' the Dewar assured him. 'He said it was without doubt Basuki Naga guarding Shiva's treasure. The Snake God lifted its great crested head. It glared at Jaya Malla with its eyes flashing sparks through the darkness and its hoods raised. The great body reared high, ready to strike.'

'At the King?'

'Yes. But Jaya Malla did not wait for that. He left the vault quickly and the priests hurried after him. The Raj Guru managed to pull the old door closed and Jaya Malla locked it again with the key. The temple priest told me the treasure is still there. No one will take it.'

'It does not augur well for Jaya Malla,' Puskar Maske said. 'He has angered both Shiva and a Snake God. He will need to placate them.'

'That is true,' the Dewar agreed. 'And to-day we must not anger the Karkot Raja. We must take care.'

Puskar Maske turned to Hume. 'We are going to visit the Karkot Raja at the Taudah Pond where he lives, to seek treasure from him.' The scepticism on Puskar Maske's face was obvious. 'Jaya Malla has ordered it. You could come with us if you wish, Hume. The Taudah Pond is near the Chowbar Gorge in the Bagmati near the Place of the Cut, only a few hour's walk from here.'

Hume accepted the invitation. He remembered the old priest Vajracryas's account that day at the Swayambhunath, of how Manjusri cut through the mountains to drain the lake, which was the Nag Hrad, the home of the Snake Gods, letting the waters flow out to create the Valley of Nepal. Manjusri had allowed the Karkot Raja to stay and gave him powers over the treasures of the valley.

'There is evidence of the Karkot Raja's great wealth,' the Dewar said. 'Once, his wife, the Karkot Rani, suffered eye strain, and in the guise of a Brahman priest Karkot Raja came up out of the pond and sought an eye-healer in a nearby village. He blindfolded the eye-healer and took him down to his palace at the bottom of the pond. The eye-healer cured the Karkot Rani and was taken back up to his village. He was given valuable gifts of gold and jewels for healing the Karkot Rani's eyes. The eye-healer spoke much of Karkot Raja's wealth, of the stacks of gold bars, the gold and silver coins, and the palace with floors of gold, its walls encrusted with jewels of all descriptions, and of the jewelled thrones.'

'So much treasure,' Puskar Maske said, dubiously.

'Yes,' the Dewar said. 'It is said that once the demon king, Danasur, stole Indra's great wealth and Karkot Raja regained it for him. He kept a fourth of it as a reward. That would account for much of his treasure.'

Hume wondered if the Dewar was serious about Karkot Raja's palace and his treasure. 'How will you meet this Karkot Raja?' he asked, with the practicalities in mind. 'If he's in his palace at the bottom of the deep pond.'

Puskar Maske shrugged but the Dewar pointed to a group of peasants, ten or more, standing nearby. 'They are waiting to come with us. They will call up the Karkot Raja so we can speak with him.'

They went out of Kathmandu, past the junction of the Bagmati and the Vishnumati Rivers, to the east of Kirtipur, and past Chowbar village and on the track towards Mount Chandragiri. They walked downwards—the Dewar looking back to make sure the peasants were following—

through the oaks and chinaberry trees, which were already promising spring with touches of their purple flowers, till they reached the river. They stopped to rest at Jala Binayak. Nearby was a pagoda, not with the image of a god but with a great stone, a monolithic boulder, garlanded with flowers and crowned with stone cobras. In the eaves of the pagoda were images of people in various creative acts of love.

'The stone represents nature's great lingam,' Puskar Maske explained. 'People come from Chowbar and the surrounding district to make offerings to it. It is said to foster their fertility.'

They left Binayak and made their way beside the river, along the rocky tracks and up and down the high banks, until they reached the Taudah Pond. The water was still and dark, away from the river's flow, down between steep banks with overhanging shrubbery blocking the sunlight. Puskar Maske, the Dewar and Hume stood beside the pond peering into its black depths. Hume, with much scepticism, pictured the great snakes, the Karkot Raja and his Rani, down below in their bejewelled palace, with their gold and other treasure as the Dewar had described. Hume noticed that the peasants the Dewar had brought were gathered together, talking excitedly amongst themselves, pointing down into the water.

'It is the peasants who will call the Karkot Raja up from his pond,' the Dewar explained. 'I have arranged for them to do that. When the Snake God comes we shall tell him of Jaya Malla's needs. He will make a contribution.' The Dewar noticed Puskar Maske's doubtful smile. 'There is a possibility,' he said.

'We have a day for the Snake Gods called Naga Panchami,' Puskar Maske said to Hume. 'If neglected or annoyed in any way, they can be dangerous. Bring death or disease. Attack foundations and make houses fall down. But worshipped properly, they can bring wealth and protect treasure, so people are pleased to keep a little snake in their moneybox. And they control the valley's waters, Hume. In time of drought peasants come here to the Taudah Pond and call on Karkot Raja to bring rain.'

The Dewar signalled to the peasants and they began their chanting, not for rain this time but for gold and other treasure. Hume seated himself on a boulder and looked down into the pond. Now and then the water would ripple and they all would look expectantly. But each time it was only a fish breaking the surface, or a falling leaf. And so the afternoon drew on. For a long time the peasants' supplications continued. But at length they stopped their chanting. There was no response from Karkot Raja.

By now the nearby hills were in shadow and Puskar Maske suggested it was time to leave. Hume looked at the Dewar's face for signs of disappointment, but saw only resignation. He is satisfied he tried, Hume thought, he had not really expected the Karkot Raja to come. Hume was sure Puskar Maske had not.

They left the Taudah Pond to the Karkot Raja and his Rani and the coming night, and climbed up the river bank to the track which would lead them back to Kathmandu. The Dewar dismissed the peasants, who went their own ways to their farms.

Hume stopped and gazed out at the Himalayas, the great white peaks now touched with reds and purples from what was left of the setting sun. His gaze was broken when they heard people approaching. Puskar Maske beckoned to Hume, and the three of them stood back in the bushes at the side of the track. Three men came out of the dusk. Two were priests, Hume saw, as he watched them go by, and the third man was old, obviously of low caste, dressed only in a loincloth and barefoot. He walked between the other two, dejected, his eyes downcast, not seeing the things about him, his hands bound. He is drugged, Hume thought. Hume noticed the tension in Puskar Maske and the Dewar, their eyes fixed on the three as they passed; then their heads turned to watch them along the track until the dusk claimed them again.

'The two are Tantrics,' Puskar Maske said, and the Dewar agreed.

'They will be going to Pharfing and down to Dakshin Kali,' the Dewar said.

Puskar Maske looked at Hume. 'I am not sure I should speak to you of them. But I shall. The old man they will offer as a sacrifice at Dakshin Kali—a human sacrifice. There is no doubt of it. It is done sometimes at Kali's temple. Only at night.'

'Is it allowed?' Hume asked, surprised. He pictured the ceremonial slaying of the old man and felt a surge of pity for him.

'It is done,' Puskar Maske replied. 'Many do not condone it. I do not. The Dewar does not. We believe that the sacrifice of animals, the he-goats, the cocks and buffalo, is enough to please the gods, to appease them if necessary. But it is done.'

It was after nightfall when they returned to Kathmandu. The Dewar left them and entered the palace to report to Jaya Malla on the lack of response from the Karkot Raja. It was a report he could not have been pleased to make, fearing Jaya Malla's temper.

Near the Military Council Chambers of the Kot, Hume and Puskar Maske saw a group of men standing talking in the darkness, and a large number of men about the parade ground. Puskar Maske went to investigate and Hume joined him. General Josi was there, as well as General Vamsi, who was a most important soldier, and other senior officers. The parade ground was crowded with soldiers, the largest gathering Hume had seen since coming to the valley.

He learnt that Jaya Malla's force had suffered a bad defeat. The Gurkha King had sent reinforcements to Naldum at night, from the south-west which was the direction of Kathmandu. Mistaking these Gurkhas for their own soldiers, Jaya Malla's men had welcomed them and admitted them to the fort. The Gurkhas wreaked havoc that night, and Jaya Malla's soldiers not slaughtered were in the parade ground of the Kot.

'Has Jaya Malla been given the news?' Puskar Maske asked of General Josi.

'He has. His rage is terrible.'

'And your own position, General?' he asked.

'Safe, I think. I was not at Naldum. But there will be changes. Punishments, no doubt.'

Puskar Maske spoke to Hume. 'It is a serious loss for us. The Gurkha threat looms even closer now. They will be on us soon. The loss at Naldum is indeed a disaster.'

'It is Poush, the unlucky month of Poush,' General Vamsi said. 'It is always an ill-omened month. Jaya Malla should have known it, should have remembered it.'

Puskar Maske was more hopeful. 'Maybe, General. But Poush will finish soon. The holy month of Magh is coming, and after that the spring with better fortune for us. Let us hope for that.'

Ten

One day in the month of Magh, Hume met Father Matteo who was returning from a visit to the house of one of the Capuchins' flock. 'It is Basant Panchami,' he told Hume. 'It heralds spring. People in the valley believe that the Goddess Saraswati visits Kathmandu today, and she is adored. She is the daughter of Shiva and his wife Parbati. She is a lovely goddess, kindly and scholarly. She dresses in pure white robes and holds a book and a harp and her vehicle is a swan. She is the sister of the elephant-headed Ganesh.'

As they spoke a wedding procession appeared at the end of the road. People drew back to give right of way to the band of musicians playing their pipes, beating drums loudly and clashing large brass cymbals. Next a priest carried a kalsa, which was a small model of a temple decorated with blue and yellow cloth and little brass bells that tinkled. Then a score or more people came marching along, dressed in their best, who were relatives or friends of the bride.

The bride came last in a silver-coloured palanquin carried by four young men and attended by two little girls who, every now and then, sprinkled flower petals on the road. People waved to the bride and came back onto the road to get a better look. She did not respond, but sat upright in her flowing wedding dress of red silk, looking straight ahead, her eyes downcast modestly behind her red veil. People watched until the procession passed then turned a corner, and the sound of the band died away.

'There are many weddings during Magh,' Father Matteo said, 'And today is thought to be the most propitious day of all for them, because Saraswati comes. Saraswati has a shrine near the Swayambhunath; and people say she is also Mukhseddara, a wife of Manjusri who created the Valley of Nepal. Many people go to her shrine today. Would you like to come with me?'

Father Matteo and Hume joined the crowd of people walking across the fields to the Swayambhunath, people of all ages, all castes, Buddhist and Hindu. Under the All Seeing Eyes of the Adi Buddha painted on the toran, they mounted the many steps to the great gabh. Hume and Father Matteo found Saraswati's image surrounded by a mass of offerings, of flowers of many colours, sweet-cakes, rice and balls of unspun cotton.

'The goddess fasts today,' Father Matteo said. 'Later she will need the food they offer her. And people ask her to bless the cotton so they will be more skilled when they take it back to their houses to spin.'

Men carried a large roll of cloth on a litter, which was decorated as a little temple. 'It represents the carpet which Saraswati spreads out for Shiva. People believe she will bless it, so it will make good garments,' the priest told Hume.

'It is pleasant, their worship of Saraswati,' Hume remarked.

Father Matteo agreed, but added, 'I would prefer them to be worshipping the Blessed Virgin though, the Holy Mother. It is my hope they will one day.'

Near Saraswati was an image, roughly cut in stone, of her brother Ganesh, elephant-headed, one-tusked, four-armed, pot-bellied and dressed in a brown cloth. Here, too, people were worshipping and making offerings of vegetables and rice, eggs and flowers. Lamps were lit and incense was burning. People brought he-goats and cocks and gave them to the priests who had long knives. Hume and Father Matteo watched as a priest cut a goat's throat and let its blood spurt near the stone Ganesh. He cut off the head and placed it on a clay dish, put a lighted wick on top and, bowing, offered it to Ganesh. Some people there prayed telling Ganesh of their needs, whilst others discussed the ritual and the priest's technique.

Father Matteo looked at the dish with the goat's head, its eyes glazed, under the lighted wick. 'They're sacrificing to Ganesh on behalf of Saraswati. The gentle Saraswati doesn't like blood sacrifices. So Ganesh accepts them for her.'

Returning to his house in Makhan Tole that afternoon, Hume found his servant waiting outside in the street. The servant, greatly concerned, ran up to him and stood wide-eyed, unable to speak for some moments.

'It is not my fault, master,' he stammered. 'He said I had to let them into your house.'

'Who said it? Who is there?' Hume demanded.

'The officer from the palace. The officer with the lady and her two maids.'

'In my house?'

'They are there.'

Hume remembered that night at the palace when they wrote to the East India Company in Calcutta. So Jaya Malla has sent me company after all, he thought, annoyed, one of his concubines from the palace and her maids no doubt.

Hume admitted to himself that before he had met Maneka he might well have welcomed such an intrusion, but not now. He hurried into his house, and there waiting for him were an officer of the royal guard and the three women. The officer saluted, then, taken aback by Hume's show of annoyance, stood in silence. Two of the women, the maids Hume thought, were sitting near the hearth and they watched him anxiously.

Hume turned to the third woman, a lady of the court he realised from her dress. She lowered the sari from her face and looked at him. Hume looked back, amazed. His pulse quickened. For moments he refused to believe that it was Maneka. This time she had no smile for him, her dark eyes glared, and she had only anger in her face.

As the officer of the guard spoke he grinned, 'My orders were to bring the lady to your house with her maids and possessions. Orders from Jaya Malla himself.'

Looking again at Maneka, Hume realised she had not come willingly. That was obvious—her anger made that clear. But he also saw her sadness, and tears glistening in her eyes. His own anger subsided, and, in its place, he felt a surge of pity for her. He made a step towards her, but she backed away, pulling her sari more tightly around her body, as if to protect herself. He moved towards her again. 'You have nothing to fear, Maneka,' he told her. But she backed away still further and went and stood beside the maids near the hearth.

The officer of the guard, impatient to go, pointed to several boxes. 'They are the lady Maneka's. I have carried out Jaya Malla's orders. May I take my leave?'

Hume consented. The officer left him with Maneka and her maids; he wondered how to cope. Maneka made no move, standing there apprehensively, her dark eyes watching him.

'I will go to Jaya Malla,' Hume said to her. 'I will have this stopped. Return you to the palace.'

But Maneka made no answer.

'I will go to Jaya Malla,' Hume repeated. But again she had no answer.

Even as he spoke, Hume realised it was not what he wanted. He did not want to return her to the palace. Looking at her, he felt the full force of his affection for her. He wanted to keep her with him. He could care for her. He thought of her fear of the Gurkha King who had flayed her father, of his vengeance against her, perhaps. He would protect her from that, to the very end if it became necessary.

'You have nothing to fear from me, Maneka,' Hume told her again.

'You have already harmed me,' she replied. You have brought disgrace on me. You have done this, the two of you.'

'The two of you?' Hume repeated.

'Yes,' she replied and Hume could see the tears running down her cheeks.

He stepped towards her to console her, his arm extended to touch her. But she backed away quickly and said, 'You must not touch me. Keep away from me.'

Maneka regained her composure a little, and turned to her maids and spoke with them. They moved the boxes towards the ladder, and Hume called his own servant from the courtyard and asked him to take them up to the floor above. The women followed and Hume went to his own quarters.

Next morning Hume rose early but stayed in his own quarters, looking down from the open window to the misty street below. He was wondering how best to approach Maneka. Then out of the mist he saw someone come and knock at the door. His servant said it was a messenger from Father Michaelangelo asking him to come to the Capuchins' house.

Father Michaelangelo was waiting at the door but offered Hume no friendly welcome. He ushered him into the house, to the table, and sat before him, blessing himself as though to avoid contamination. 'I hear you have taken the lady Maneka as your concubine. She is one of my flock. Your sin is grievous,' the priest said, his high-pitched voice raised almost to a scream; his distaste clearly visible.

Hume started to object but the priest stopped him. 'No don't interrupt me. I'll open your eyes to your sin, to the evil of it, the Holy Church's hatred of it. I'll tell you what lust and fornication lead to here in the Valley of Nepal. And I will warn you.'

Hume tried to object again. 'No, I will speak,' Father Michaelangelo continued. 'I have lived in the valley for many years. I know of the lust here. It pervades the valley with the stink of sin. It is the valley of sin. Even their gods lust. You have seen Shiva's great stone phalluses, the lingams near the Pashupatinath and elsewhere. Do you think I accept that, the evil slight against me and the Church? In her purity what can the Blessed Virgin think, the most holy Mother? I say little about it to them. But each day I pray. I ask God the Father to smite those phalluses, to smash their stone into many pieces. I pray for the lust to cool, for the people here to come, pure and free of sin, to our Holy Church.'

'I can see your concern, Father,' Hume said and started to explain how Maneka came to his house.

The priest still would brook no interruption. 'Fornication itself is a deadly sin, my son, to be punished in the eternal fires of hell. Make no mistake about that. And here it is the door to even greater evil. There is the Tantric cult, the men who worship with human skulls. They perform their rituals in their Tantric temples, heinous rituals, seated on the corpse of a person whose throat they have slit and whose blood they have spilt in a sacrifice to Kali or their secret gods. Viler even are the men of the left-hand way, debauched perverts, rapists, murderers. In their secret rituals, they swallow forbidden meats and much liquor. They will capture a young virgin or entice her to their temple in some way. They rape her, cut her throat, then let her blood spurt as a sacrifice to their gods of lust.'

Hume recalled passing the Tantrics on the way back from Karkot Raja's Taudah Pond and witnessing the old man they were taking to sacrifice at Dakshin Kali. The Capuchins' account horrified him. 'Are you sure of what you say, Father?' he asked. 'It is a terrible charge to make.'

'Fornication leads to it. Evil as those Tantrics are, fornication itself is equally hated by God. I warn you. You lead yourself and Maneka to Hell. True there is no blame on her, not yet. She can have no wish to be your concubine. I told you she is of our flock, devoted, a good Catholic already. You must not corrupt her. You must rid yourself of her, send her from your house.'

'It's not my doing, Father,' Hume said. 'Her coming to my house was a complete surprise to me. Jaya Malla sent her.'

The Capuchin shook his head sorrowfully. 'Don't add to your sins, my son. Don't imitate the Prince of Lies. I know of your designs on her. I have seen your lecherous eyes on her in my church. Jaya Malla, as bad as he is, wouldn't send her unless you had asked it of him.'

Hume denied it. But Father Michaelangelo ignored him, saying again that Maneka must leave his house.

'Where would she go?' Hume asked, confident she had nowhere to go.

'To our Catholic community in Bettiah, in India not far from Patna. They would accept her gladly. She could enter the convent there, become a nun perhaps.'

It surprised Hume. He had not thought of that. 'You would let her risk the Gurkhas' blockade? Be killed perhaps?' he asked.

'Better to die at Gurkha hands than to live in sin with you. Now I will warn you, Sir Hume Clarke. You risk excommunication, my son. Rid yourself of her or I will deny you our Holy Church.' With that the Capuchin dismissed Hume, pointing to the door for him to go.

When Hume left, he did not return to his own house but went to visit Puskar Maske. He was a friend he could trust, he thought, who would know the valley's customs and give him good advice.

Puskar Maske had already heard that Jaya Malla had sent Maneka to Hume's house. 'Such news travels quickly in Kathmandu, Hume,' he said. 'We were all surprised.'

'And I, too,' Hume assured him.

'You did not expect her then? Had you not arranged it with Jaya Malla?' Puskar Maske asked looking doubtful.

'Not at all. True, Jaya Malla suggested he'd send me female company. A concubine, I thought. I refused. That was all.'

'Jaya Malla has acted with indiscretion,' Puskar Maske said, frowning. 'Maneka is a high-ranking lady, not one of the court concubines. Her father was an important general, a high caste Gurkha. Jaya Malla will offend many by this act, his queen, Bachhla and other ladies of the Court, as well as ministers and generals and their wives.'

'But why Maneka?'

'To make sure you stay longer in Kathmandu, Hume. After our defeat at Naldum, Jaya Malla needs you more than ever. Even more now, he needs your influence with Calcutta, needs help from a British Army. He knows Maneka attracts you. He has informers in many places.'

'What am I to do, Puskar Maske? Maneka hasn't come willingly. She is greatly offended, and insulted and angry. She will have nothing of me.'

'Are you sure, Hume?' Puskar Maske asked. 'She has affection for you. I, too, have seen that. My second wife has told me so. Maneka has spoken of you to other women. Yes, she has affection for you.'

'Not now, I would think.'

Puskar Maske shrugged. 'Why not take things quietly for a while? She has little option but to remain in your house, at least for a time. Her relatives—she has few in Kathmandu—would not take her in and suffer Jaya Malla's ire. Why not be nice to her. Wait a while and see what happens. I believe she will come to you eventually.'

That same day Father Matteo called on Hume, and they walked to the Durbar Square and sat near the image of the Black Bhairab. Father Matteo came quickly to the point. 'Let me ask you Hume, have you great affection for Maneka? Would you say you are in love with her?'

Hume certainly did not deny it.

'She has great interest in you, the priest said. She talks with me at times and I discerned it, although of course she never said as much. And I hear remarks to that effect from women of our congregation. They talk. The maids know these things and talk. I heard Maneka was your Bhai Tika sister. I know of your meeting with her at Puskar Maske's house. I have noticed her glances at you in our church. She is a noble lady and was under strict discipline at the court. She would not risk such things unless she had affection for you.'

Hume accepted this.

Father Matteo pointed towards the Black Bhairab and said, 'No one dares to speak an untruth here. It is widely believed the Bhairab would take offence, become angered and vent his anger on anyone who was untruthful.' The priest searched Hume's face. 'I'm sure Maneka believes you arranged with Jaya Malla to get her. Tell me, did you do so? Was it your doing?'

Father Matteo accepted Hume's assurance it was not so. 'You will have to marry Maneka,' he said. 'You have no option. Come to our church where I shall marry you in the grace of Christ. If you wish, I will talk to Maneka and arrange it for you.'

Hume agreed.

Not long after his discussion with Father Matteo, Hume noticed a change in Maneka. It happened suddenly. Her face lost its tension and in its place her shy smile returned. She started organising her maids in work around his house, sending one of them to the markets with his own servant. Maneka now took an interest in the preparation of meals, which improved greatly. And she dressed in particularly bright saris and wore her best jewellery.

One morning as she sat in the courtyard at the back of the house combing her hair, she smiled up at Hume as he approached. The suddenness of her changed attitude towards him surprised Hume, and delighted him. Then he realised that Father Matteo might have talked to her, and he asked her if he had.

'He has,' she said. 'Please forgive me. He has told me of Jaya Malla's treachery, his great insult to my honour, and to my dead father. I had thought it was you, that you had asked him to send me to your house. But I find it was not so. You must forgive me.'

'Did Father Matteo suggest we should marry in his church, Maneka?' Hume asked her.

'Yes,' she answered, looking away from him.

Hume decided he would not delay. He took her hand. 'I love you, Maneka. The first time we met I started to love you. I want you to be my wife. Will you marry me, Maneka?'

She turned towards him. 'Yes,' she replied, softly.

Hume put his arm around her shoulders and they sat there in silence. He could feel the beat of her heart, the warmth of her body, and was relaxed and content. Eventually Maneka drew away and Hume let her go. But for the rest of the day in the house the two stayed close, delighting in each other's company.

That evening after the servants had gone to bed, Hume and Maneka sat before the hearth enjoying the warmth of the fire. Maneka cast a worried glance at Hume. 'I am fearful now,' she said.

'Tell me, Maneka, what troubles you?' Hume asked, hoping the matter was not serious.

'I have been thinking,' she said, and hesitated. 'Is it my honour you want to save? Would you marry me because of that? You know I must stay in your house. I have nowhere else to go.'

'It is not that, Maneka.'

'What else? Do you really want me to be your wife forever? My country is so different from yours. Our ways are so different in so many things, I think.'

'Yes, I do. It's because I love you,' Hume told her.

'But you say that just to please me.'

Hume thought for a few moments. 'I will tell you something that might not please you, Maneka. Whether we are married or not, it is you I want. I would keep you in my house because I love you,' he said again.

Maneka gave a little smile as she looked back at Hume. 'You would keep me in your house? Have me live with you in disgrace?'

'I would hope you would eventually be my wife. That you would come with me to my estate in Hollybrook, when we can leave the valley.'

Maneka smiled warmly now. 'It is nice for you to say that. But would I be able to be like an English wife? I would need to learn your language. The ways there would be new to me. Would people there accept me? You would have to teach me.'

'Certainly I would do that,' Hume assured her. 'Now tell me. Are you sure you really want to marry me?

Maneka did not hesitate. 'I am sure,' she said. ' And I would go with you even to a land so strange to me.'

Hume put his arm around her to draw her close to him.

When Puskar Maske called at Hume's house Maneka had a needle-woman making white saris for her two maids and herself, for the wedding in the Capuchins' church.

'The Capuchins' wedding is different,' Puskar Maske commented.

Hume agreed, remembering the wedding procession he had seen in the street with Father Matteo.

'I remember Bachhla's wedding, about fifteen years ago now,' Puskar Maske said, glancing at Maneka who was busy with the saris. 'There was a great procession. Thousands lined the streets to watch. Nearly a whole regiment of foot soldiers marched, and I remember General Josi was in command of it. The band had many instruments: large and small cymbals, pipes and many types of drums, and even sarangi fiddles.'

Maneka turned from the needle-woman to listen.

'All of Kathmandu throbbed with the loud music,' Puskar Maske continued. 'And there were wagons with sweetmeats and other delicacies. The Kelsa was a large model of Taleju's Temple decorated with flowers and coloured cloth. Bachhla sat in a silver palanquin, which was carried by soldiers, splendid in her red bridal robe and veil and jewellery. Slave girls scattered flowers about her. Her husband followed in his own palanquin. At the end of the procession there were more than twenty elephants with howdahs of gold and silver and other colours. Jaya Malla rode in the first howdah and his relatives in the others.' Puskar Maske glanced at Maneka again.

'Would you like such a wedding, Maneka?' Hume asked her.

She put down the white sari and smiled at him. 'I would have liked it once. As a girl I used to dream of such a wedding.'

'Could we have one now for Maneka?' Hume asked Puskar Maske.

'Perhaps, Hume. I think Jaya Malla would be generous with you.'

But Maneka was shaking her head, disagreeing. 'No, I do not want a grand wedding,' she told Hume. 'I want to be married to you in the Capuchins' church.'

During the following days people prepared for the wedding. The needle-woman finished Maneka's white sari and her bridal veil, and then the white saris for her two maids who were to be her attendants. Bachhla and other ladies from the court and Puskar Maske's two wives got ready their best saris and jewellery. Hume's servant cleaned the church and Father Matteo polished the little, brass tabernacle door and the gold chalice till they shone. Puskar Maske had the altar limed white again. The day before the wedding, women from the congregation filled the church with flowers and Hume bought bouquets at the markets for Maneka and her maids.

On the morning of the wedding, the mist rose and the sun warmed the streets. Hume was accompanied by Puskar Maske carrying the wedding ring, and Maneka, beautiful in her white sari and a veil over her black hair, was accompanied by her two maids as they all walked the short distance to the Capuchins' church. A crowd of well-wishers made way for them to let them enter. Inside the church, Hume looked approvingly at the profusion of fresh flowers, the polished brass and the golden chalice gleaming under the candlelight. The church was full. Many of the Capuchins' congregation were there and Hume recognised others: the Raj Guru, the old priest Vajracrya, General Josi, the Dewar, ladies from the court who were friends of Maneka, and Puskar Maske's wives and children.

Father Michaelangelo said Mass and Father Matteo assisted. Maneka rose and stood in front of the altar to receive Holy Communion, glancing at Hume to ensure he followed and stood beside her. Then others in the congregation went forward to receive the Host.

When Father Matteo was ready to conduct the wedding ceremony he beckoned to Hume to come and stand before him; Puskar Maske joined him at his side. Father Matteo beckoned again and Maneka, followed by her two maids, rose and stood before the priest. The congregation was hushed now, watching. Hume looked tenderly at Maneka as quietly but firmly she took her wedding vows. Hume himself spoke loudly, confidently. Father Matteo looked towards the congregation, raised his arms high above his head and pronounced them man and wife. Then Puskar Maske handed Hume the wedding ring and he slipped it on Maneka's finger, lifted her veil and kissed her.

Outside the Capuchins' house many well-wishers congratulated Hume and Maneka. Hume thanked Puskar Maske. He thanked Maneka's two maids and his own servant and gave each a silver coin. To the Capuchin priests, he gave two tolas in gold.

Jaya Malla gave them a wedding feast at the royal palace, in the Nasal Chowk; he was well satisfied with the part he had played in bringing the marriage about. Many of Kathmandu's nobles, ministers and senior soldiers and their wives attended. Hume accepted Jaya Malla's congratulations well enough, but Maneka, still resenting the King's treatment of her, accepted them coolly, in contrast to her happiness and warmth throughout the day. The sun was in the afternoon sky and the shadows were lengthening in the palace courtyard when Hume and Maneka left and walked home as man and wife.

Eleven

Hume recalled the time Jaya Malla had sent Maneka to him as a concubine and she had stood there angry and sad. It was so different now. He took Maneka in his arms and held her close. 'My dreams have come true. You are my wife,' he told her.

'And you are my husband,' she said softly.

'Your maids and my servant can have a holiday. I shall send them to their homes. The house will be ours today. Would you like that, Maneka?'

She smiled in agreement, a shy smile. 'I will make tea for you,' she said.

'Can you do that, Maneka?' he asked, teasing her.

'Of course, and more. The ladies in the palace learn much from their maids.'

Hume took wood from the courtyard and built the fire up until the flames leapt high to warm the coming night. Maneka brought him tea, and sweet rice cakes from their store. With Maneka in Hume's arms, time passed quickly for them that evening, almost unnoticed. Hume thought that Maneka would no longer sleep on the second floor with her maids, where as Puskar Maske had told him the womenfolk usually slept. He decided she would always share his own quarters, the bed of padded quilts and warm coverlets. He wanted her close to him each night.

The last of the dusk gave way and night set in. Eventually Hume rose and found a lamp and lit it. Rousing Maneka, he held the lamp to light her way up the ladders.

In Hume's quarters on the third floor, Maneka looked away as Hume took off her sari and her choli and undressed her. She was too shy to look at him as he held her close; so shy when he laid her on the bed and looked down at her. 'I will be very gentle with you, Maneka,' he promised.

She turned her face away to avoid his gaze.

Hume undressed and lay beside her. He drew her close to him and could feel the tension in her body against his and her heart pounding in her breast. Slowly, tenderly, he caressed her, for a long time, until at last she relaxed a little. Then he turned Maneka towards him. 'I love you, Maneka. I will always love you,' he said.

Maneka did not reply. But her black eyes looked back up at him through the darkness. Full of desire now, Hume made love to Maneka. He felt her responding to him, tentatively at first then eagerly, till finally her passion was as great as his as they consummated their marriage.

Modest, yes, but Maneka was to become a passionate wife to Hume. Although shy with him, she was proud to be married. When she went out from the house she put vermilion powder in her hair to denote her married status and wore a tilahani necklace of glass beads with a golden tube as a pendant. She continued to wear much jewellery, selecting each day pieces she thought would go well with her saris: her gold bracelets, a necklace, earrings and silver anklets which tinkled pleasantly as she walked. Sometimes she would wear the ruby pendant Hume had given her.

About that time a sati was burnt on the ghats near the Pashupatinath. It horrified Hume. He knew of the cruel practice, how wives and sometimes concubines were burnt alive with the husband's corpse. A widow would be dressed in her best, adorned with jewellery and flowers, put in a decorated palanquin and carried to the funeral pyre to be placed amongst the wood beside her husband's corpse. The fire would be lit and the flames would rise around her, engulfing her as the spectators watched. And a band would play or drums be beaten to drown her screams. Sati was performed, Puskar Maske had explained, shaking his head doubtfully, because some believed that a wife's spirit would go with her husband's to the Underworld, and that later she would be reincarnated on this earth with him. Hume was thankful Maneka would never be a sati.

Gradually Maneka lost some of her shyness, and she kept only some of the obeisance of Newar wives towards their husbands. Hume put this down to her idea of how an English wife would act. She set about managing the household and, with no mother-in-law to control her, had much of her own way and was happy about it.

She had her maids find the best supplies at the markets, the choicest cuts of buffalo or goat, and sometimes venison and wild boar. And they always came back with the best rice and vegetables fresh from the fields. Maneka knew of a peasant, Musa, and arranged for him to bring ample bundles of wood for the fire in the hearth to burn well through the cold nights. She asked Hume to engage workers to repair the earthen floor with a mixture of clay and cow dung to give it a hard surface again and be free of dust. And carpenters made new furniture, cupboards, and tables and chairs.

At one end of the ground-floor room Maneka set up a little altar, where she placed images of the Blessed Virgin and her Holy Son and a painting of Christ of the Sacred Heart like the one in the Capuchins'church. She always kept fresh flowers on the altar and had candles burning there. As the weeks went by, Maneka and Hume grew even happier in their newly married life.

Full spring came in the Valley of Nepal, pleasant weather, balmy days, and Hume and Maneka went to visit the farm near Deo Patan village, which Jaya Malla had given him under a jagir grant. Outside the walls of Kathmandu the oaks and chestnut trees were dressed in their young foliage, the chinaberry trees still had purple blossoms, wild flowers filled the fields and rhododendrons were in flower higher on the mountain slopes.

They walked through the fertile farmlands, where the peasant farmers were busy harvesting the winter wheat and the sweet potato crop. Some were already preparing fields for the coming rice sowing. They came to the peasant Dongol's house, which was set in the middle of the fields and circled by a grove of cherry trees now in bloom. Built of sun-dried brick, it was painted with pink earth, its roof thatched with straw, and vines grew from the eaves to provide ripe squash in the autumn months. An image of the God Ganesh was crudely painted on the lintel above the door.

Dongol and his wife bowed low and joined their hands in a long namaste to welcome Hume, their new landlord, and Maneka. Inside the house was poorer, Hume thought, than those of the tenant farmers on the Clarke estate in Hollybrook. The floor was earthen, hardened with cow dung and clay, and the heavy beams under the thatch were blackened with age and smoke.

The family lived in the half of the house towards the hearth. The other half was used for storage: rice from the last harvest was there, the wheat just harvested and a few vegetables, crude ploughs and hoes and other farm implements. A cow would shelter there in the cold weather, and an occasional goat awaiting slaughter for the table or at the altar of a god.

Dongol's wife made tea for them and offered sweet rice cakes with a conserve made from the last season's cherries.

'Your rice cakes are well made,' Maneka told her. 'And the cherries you serve with them are pleasant. Perhaps when this season's crop is ready you will show me how to make them.'

It pleased Dongol's wife, who said, a little embarrassed, 'I would be honoured to do that. Would you take a pot of last season's cherries when you leave? I will show you.'

While they were talking, Dongal took Hume to look around the farm. The fields were brown with wheat stubble and the cherry trees promised a good crop. 'You should sow all the fields with rice this year,' Hume told him, thinking of the need if the Gurkha King came to lay siege to Kathmandu. 'I will buy extra seed and hire peasants with their ploughs from nearby villages to help you.' After seeing more of the farm, he told Dongol, 'I would like you to plant the edges of fields for a larger harvest of squash in the autumn. And I will stock the farm with several young gelded goats to grow and provide meat.'

Dongol made no objection to all this, and was pleased when Hume assured him he would still get half the harvest, large as it might be this time, under the terms of the jagir grant.

On their the way back to Kathmandu that evening, Hume would look back towards the Himalayas, their white peaks now catching tints of pink and purple as the sun sank lower in the sky. Closer in, the valley's surrounding mountains were a dark green in the dusk, and he saw distant smoke rising.

'The Naldum Garhi is in that direction. It is where they fought a little time ago,' Maneka said. 'I think the smoke is from the Gurkhas' fire.' She held back a little, looking at the smoke, and Hume turned and saw the worry on her face. She caught up with him to walk closely by his side, wanting the security he offered.

Back in the house that night, Maneka sat close by Hume in front of the fire which the servants had stacked well with wood. But she was still worried. 'Is it the Gurkhas, Maneka?' he asked.

'I fear the Gurkha King. He killed my father. The Gurkha King is cruel. True I have Gurkha cousins, but they are lost to me. All except one, my cousin Atal Thapa who is at the Naldum Garhi. He is the Gurkha sardar there. I have known him since I was a child. Once we would write to each other.'

'How did you do that?'

'Peasants would take our messages for a small payment.'

Hume had not asked Maneka about her Gurkha relatives, so he was surprised she had been in touch with her cousin. 'When will the Gurkhas come, Maneka?' he asked.

'I think Prithvi Shah will come when he is fully ready. He will want to be sure this time. But before the winter comes, I would say.'

Hume looked at Maneka as she sat there in the glow from the fire, without her jewellery now, her hair down and about her shoulders, her dark eyes softly returning his gaze. 'I love you, Maneka,' he said. 'You are very beautiful.'

'And I love you, my husband,' she told him.

Hume turned to the fire burning in the hearth and his thoughts went back to Hollybrook, to the Clarke family house. He pictured Maneka there, far from the Gurkhas and the dangers of the valley, assuming English ways, living the life of an English wife.

'One day we could go to England, Maneka,' he said. 'Live on my estate in Hollybrook.'

'I did tell you I would go with you,' she replied. 'If it is what you wish, my husband.'

On the night of the full moon in the month of Baisekhi, Hume and Maneka joined the people leaving Kathmandu and climbed the hill to the Swayambhunath for the celebration of Gautama Buddha's birthday. Everyone went, Hindus as well as Buddhists and most of the Capuchins' congregation. The great Chaitya was a glory of light that night. Its massive gabh gleamed white under the moonlight. Little butter lamps were burning everywhere, high on the golden spire, around the toran and on the walls, in the courtyards. Their yellow glow, thousands of points of light, outlined the great temple, silhouetting it against the dark blue of the sky. The all-seeing eyes of the Adi Buddha looked down from the toran on the crowds milling about the courtyards, about the many stupas, the smaller temples, the images of the Divine Buddhas and the Buddhist saints. Many people had come to watch, to worship, to pray for enlightenment as Buddhists have done throughout the ages. They stayed during the night to see, in the morning sunlight, the Swayambhunath dressed in a profusion of colour. Flags were flying and coloured bunting was everywhere; flowers adorned the courtyards, the temples and the many prayer wheels.

The old priest Vajracrya emerged from amongst the crowd. 'Would you meet a lama who has come from Tibet to see you?' he asked Hume. 'Come I will take you to him.' He led Hume and Maneka to a room in one of the vihars where the lama was waiting.

The lama greeted Hume and Maneka. 'I have a message for you,' he said. 'In Lhasa we have heard that a Britisher from Calcutta is in the valley. I have been sent to Kathmandu to ask a favour of you. I have to tell you we are short of coins in Tibet. We ourselves have no mint and no skills to use one. So we have to use little bags of gold dust, and also silver ingots which are heavy, of more than thirty Chinese ounces. These are too valuable for most of our exchanges.'

For more than two centuries, Tibet had bought coins from the Valley of Nepal, the Mahendramalla coins minted by the Malla kings at great profit—coins which were heavily debased with tin and copper and only half their weight being in silver. But now the Gurkha King's blockade had stopped that. Prithvi Shah had tried to sell his own coins to Tibet, but they were too pure and he would not debase them. The Tibetans would not use them. They would melt them down for their silver, sell them in China or India, or hoard them.

'We want coins like the old Malla coins.' the lama told Hume. 'I wish to ask if the British Company in Calcutta could mint such coins for us. It would be very profitable for them. Tibet would pay the Company a weight of silver equal to the weight of the debased coins, or gold to the same value.'

'I will make enquiries,' Hume promised.

'I thank you,' the lama said. 'The Tibetan lama at the Bodnath Temple knows of my request. I would be grateful if you could advise him of the outcome of your enquiries.'

But Hume was not to ask Calcutta to mint coins for Tibet. One day, needing money for purchases, he opened the cavity in the wall where he had hidden the gold he had brought to Kathmandu. 'Come and look, Maneka,' he called.

'It is good you have gold,' she said. 'It will be necessary if the Gurkha King comes. Gold will help buy his favour—perhaps his permission for me to leave the valley with you.'

Maneka stood thoughtfully, looking at the gold. She seemed undecided whether to speak further, but then said, 'You might need more gold. I think there is a way you could get more of it.' She hesitated for some moments, 'At the Swayambhunath, I listened to the lama from Lhasa. I had known Tibet needs coins. There is always talk at the palace amongst the ladies of the Court. We learn of many things. There is a way you could multiply your gold.'

'How, Maneka?'

'Why have the British mint the coins? Why not buy silver with your gold, have it minted here into coins, sell them to Tibet for gold?'

Hume shook his head doubtfully, 'Coins for Tibet? What would Jaya Malla do about that?'

'I believe he would agree. He would want part of the profit. He needs gold badly.'

'How would we get them to Tibet? It's a nice idea you have, Maneka. But there are difficulties.'

She persisted. 'There is a way. My cousin, Atal Thapa, the sardar at Naldum I told you of, could help. Lamas still come from Tibet to visit the Bodhnath. Prithvi Shah lets them. He does not want to offend their country. Their route is sometimes near the fort at Naldum. My cousin could arrange it.'

'You seem sure of that.'

'I am not sure, but I think it would be so. I am almost sure. I could send a message to him. Musa who brings our firewood would do that.'

Hume thought the matter over for some days, and eventually he agreed. He knew he would need help. Jaya Malla's cooperation had to be got, silver bought, the coins minted and sent to Tibet. So he involved Puskar Maske, being sure he could trust him and pleased that he, too, would profit from it. The peasant, Musa, took Maneka's message to Atal Thapa at Naldum; and it was only days before Atal Thapa replied, saying there would be a stone-throwing beside the Sangla River near the village of Nepaltar on Sithinakha Day. He would try to meet Hume there. Failing that, he would come to Hume's house in Makhan Tole.

'Will you go to Nepaltar village on Sithinakha Day to meet my cousin?' Maneka asked, when the message came from Atal Thapa.

'Yes, I will go,' Hume replied. But he saw her anxious look. 'You don't want me to go?'

'Would you rather he called here at your house?'

'No, I shall go. Your cousin suggested it. He'll be waiting there.'

'You would not rather he called here?' Maneka asked again.

'You don't think I'll be safe, Maneka?' Hume took her hand and held it.

'It is not that. If I thought there would be danger for you, I would ask you not to go.'

'What troubles you?'

'It is the stone throwing.'

'Why is that?'

She looked away from Hume to hide her face, embarrassed. 'It is the stone throwing,' she said again. 'It is shameful. It brings much shame on me. And in your eyes, my husband.'

Hume wondered at her objection, but told her he would go.

On the way to Nepaltar village, Puskar Maske told Hume something of Sithinakha Day. 'It celebrates Kumar's birthday, Hume,' he said. 'Kumar is a son of Lord Shiva and is the warrior God of War. Would you like to hear about his birth?'

Hume agreed and Puskar Maske continued. 'It was in very early times, Hume, when the demons had driven the gods from Heaven. So Agni the God of Fire disguised himself as a poor saddhu and went to tell Lord Shiva that only a son of his could get the gods their Heaven back. Unfortunately Agni timed his arrival badly.' Puskar Maske's face lit up in a broad grin. 'Impatient, he took it on himself to enter a room only to find Shiva bedded with Parbati, his beautiful newly married wife, and that he had interrupted their lovemaking. It mortified Agni and embarrassed Parbati. It enraged Shiva.'

'The great God rose,' Puskar Maske told Hume, 'and turned his third eye with terrible anger on Agni, ready to blast him to ashes with its glare. Agni thought quickly; he cupped his hands and held them out to Shiva as though begging for alms, and seeing this Parbati reminded her husband of the sin of harming a holy mendicant. True this stopped the great God blasting Agni, but in his rage Shiva ejected his semen into Agni's cupped hands; which Agni swallowed and quickly hurried off.'

Puskar Maske looked doubtful as he continued. 'It turned out, Hume, that the heat of Shiva's semen was so great that it burnt Agni's stomach and, even though he was God of Fire, he disgorged it into the womb of the holy Ganges as he passed. So Kumar was born. As the God of War, he fought the demons and restored the gods to their Heaven.'

When Hume and Puskar Maske arrived at Nepaltar, the festivities of earlier in the day had finished. 'People have already marched through the streets with Kumar's image,' Puskar Maske said. 'They have sacrificed goats and cocks, and feasted on their meat, and vegetables and rice and large pots of chan and raksi.'

The people of Nepaltar and nearby villages had now gathered by the Sangla River. Hume looked down at the flat, sandy river bank and the many rounded river stones. There was a lot of shouting and laughing as everyone waited for the stone throwing.

The women and children and the older men climbed up from the river bank and took up positions on the edge of the field near an altar of rock which was adorned with flowers and other offerings made to Kumar. The men, most of them young, stayed near the river and divided into two groups a hundred feet or so apart, and each group set about collecting the river stones and making heaps of them ready for use.

'It is an ancient custom, the stone throwing,' Puskar Maske told Hume. 'It is said that once the God Skadaswami came to a Malla king in a dream and suggested it. He told him it would make the young men of his kingdom loyal to him, that they would never rebel and would fight and defeat his enemies.'

'It's Jaya Malla who will need such loyalty now,' Hume remarked.

'He will. Word has gone around, and many villages will have a stone-throwing today.'

Hume noticed a small group of men standing on high ground a little apart from the other spectators and wondered if one were Atal Thapa. But Puskar Maske said, 'It is the sardar in charge, others are headmen from the villages. Those are the Brahman priests.'

The sardar signalled and the stone throwing commenced. To start, a few men from each opposing group took stones from their heaps, moved forward a little, and hurled them, cautiously, getting the range. More men came forward, steadied themselves, and hurled their stones. They retreated, and in their turn others on each side hurled the stones. Soon all in each group were joining in, taking up stones, dashing forward, hurling them at unprotected bodies.

Then the battle was on in earnest. Men were hit. Some fell and lay on the ground. Caution was abandoned as each group charged closer and stones rained through the air. The attackers yelled and the spectators urged them on. Some were hit badly and screamed and the fight rose to a furious pitch. Men lost their fear of being hit, and expressed hatred on their faces as they threw the stones to kill. More men fell bleeding, some with bones broken. Some must surely be dead, Hume thought. The fury of the fight surprised him, until he remembered the Battle of Buxar and the way he himself had fought.

At last the heaps of stones were depleted and the fighting eased. The sardar signalled to end the battle; only a few more stones were hurled, then it all stopped. The sardar went down to the river bank. There was no yelling now as the young men stood waiting and the spectators were hushed.

Puskar Maske looked into the crowd. 'I hope Atal Thapa will come to us now,' he said. 'He will certainly have recognised you Hume. He could come away with us and talk. We had better not wait any longer. I think it will not be pleasant for you now. Or for me. You know I attend the Capuchins'church.'

But Atal Thapa did not come—not then—and they waited. Hume watched the sardar picking his way amongst the stones beside the river, standing over the men lying there to examine each in turn. Finally he made his choice and beckoned to the priests, who came and lifted a young man to carry him up to the stone altar. As they passed, Hume looked at him, at his distorted bones, his bleeding, and his eyes which were wide and rolling in his frightened face.

'He is badly wounded,' Puskar Maske whispered. 'He would die in any case.'

'Is he to be sacrificed?' Hume asked, hardly believing it.

'He is,' Puskar Maske replied. 'It is the custom with the stone-throwing. Some of the wounded are sacrificed. He will be a sacrifice to Kali. I think Jaya Malla needs many sacrifices today because he must appease the goddess with much blood. He needs her favour when the Gurkhas come.'

As the priests laid the young man on the rock altar he was weak from his wounds with no struggling left in him. But he managed to turn his head towards the crowd as if in a mute appeal. The people, though, were silent, praying to Kali, asking her to accept the sacrifice. One of the priests lifted his knife and cut the young man's throat, carefully, a small incision, to let his blood flow slowly over the stone altar. As it drained away, convulsions shook his body. Then with strong thrusts of his knife the priest severed the young man's head, and placed it upright on the altar, its sightless eyes wide open and staring towards the river.

Soon the crowd dispersed and people left to return to their homes. Hume stood looking towards the altar with pity for the young man, still seeing the rolling of his eyes as he passed by. He thought of Maneka and understood her objection to the stone-throwing.

'He would have died in any case,' Puskar Maske repeated. 'It is better to be sacrificed. The gods come to love all those sacrificed to them, be they human or animal. They reward them. Their reincarnation is good. They will be reborn on this earth to a higher status, to a higher caste, to wealth perhaps.'

They were about to leave when Atal Thapa came and joined them, and, although dressed inconspicuously as a peasant, Hume saw his bearing was distinguished. He introduced himself. 'I trust my cousin, Maneka, keeps well,' he said. 'It is some time since I have visited her. It is the troubles we are having in the valley.'

Hume assured him she was well.

'I heard of Jaya Malla's treatment of her,' Atal Thapa said. 'His insult. His sending her to you as a concubine. An outrage. It would have been a gross indignity for her.' His face darkened in a scowl. 'Given the slightest chance, my sword will right that wrong. My sword in Jaya Malla's body.'

'She avoided that indignity,' Hume said.

'Yes, and I thank you for that, Sir Hume Clarke. I was glad to hear she became your wife. I approve of that.'

'Thank you for your approval. I am grateful for it,' Hume replied.

'I will let the coinage for Tibet pass by the Naldum Fort,' Atal Thapa said. 'There is a risk. But Maneka wants it. I will do it for her, my cousin. I would do it for no one else but her.'

'My thanks to you on Maneka's behalf,' Hume replied.

'Maneka might well need the gold when Prithvi Shah takes the Valley of Nepal,' Atal Thapa said. 'He still resents her father's betrayal, and I think he would have no love for the daughter. Gold will be her insurance. And Prithvi Shah will take the valley, Sir Hume Clarke. Have no doubt of that. Jaya Malla will need more than the sacrifice you saw here today. Very much more.'

Atal Thapa turned to Puskar Maske. 'Have you Jaya Malla's permission to mint the coins?'

Puskar Maske assured him it would come.

'You will need to do it in the greatest secrecy. My name must not be mentioned. Not at any time. That is important.'

'I realise that Atal Thapa,' Hume replied. 'You are putting your trust in me. I assure you I will respect it fully.'

'Then I shall tell the Tibetan lama at the Bodhnath,' Atal Thapa said. 'It is he who will arrange to transport the coins.'

Atal Thapa took his leave of them. 'My greetings for my cousin, Maneka,' he said. 'You are most fortunate, Sir Hume, to have her as a wife. The gods have favoured you.'

Back in Kathmandu, Jaya Malla agreed to the minting of the coins for Tibet on the condition that he share the profit.

'Again, you have served Jaya Malla well,' Puskar Maske said to Hume. 'The Dewar and I have found but little treasure. Jaya Malla badly needs the profit from the coins to pay his Nagar mercenaries who will help defend the valley.'

Hume was busy after Sithinakha Day. He kept a close watch on Dongol to ensure he sowed all the paddy fields. There was also the coinage for Tibet. The metal workshop in Kathmandu, where Hume went with Puskar Maske, was near the southern gate, an old building of burnt brick and tile abutting the inside of the town wall. It was dimly lit, dusty, full of fumes and the air was acrid. A score or more of smiths were at work, dressed in loin-cloths and cotton jackets. They squatted in little groups on the earthen floor, Newars of the Bare caste working on the gold and silver and Kamsakars on the alloys. Each group had its own tools, files, pincers and hammers, moulds and sand. Braziers were burning hot, glowing in the dimness, to melt the metal in little pots. Some men were at work on images of the gods, casting the pieces, filing them, joining them together. They gilded some of them, small images for households and larger ones for the temples.

The mint was set up at the far end of the workshop, and Puskar Maske and Hume made their way through the dust and fumes to the Bare silversmiths working under the eyes of two of Jaya Malla's guards. Hume had bought silver with half his gold. Progress had been good, and the finished Mahendramalla coins, which were piled on boards placed on the earthen floor, shone, ready to be packed in baskets and delivered to the Tibetan lama. Hume watched the smiths weighing the silver against the tin and copper, balancing them on a scale, then melting them together for an alloy of half silver and half inexpensive metal.

Puskar Maske took a handful of finished coins, enjoyed the feel of them, then let them fall back tinkling onto their heap. 'As good as pure silver,' he said, smiling. 'Even the Karkot Raja would not know the difference.' He looked at Jaya Malla's guards. 'And no Snake Gods can come and steal them. They will bring much profit, these coins. You will spend your share well, Hume.'

'And you, Puskar Maske. There is a share for you.'

Puskar Maske said thoughtfully, 'We face great changes in the valley, Hume.'

'It's always wise to have a little gold.' Hume replied. 'You said that once, at Patna I remember. It stood you well then. Saved you from a British cannon.'

'I have not forgotten, Hume. And the help you gave me.'

When Hume and Puskar Maske made the first delivery of coins to the Tibetan lama, the Dewar went with them to look to Jaya Malla's interest. A porter carried the coins in baskets on a pole across his shoulders in Newar fashion. They made their way early one morning through the mist, out the northern gate, across the fields, past the villages of Thamel and Ganeshwar and past Deo Patan to the Bodhnath, the largest of all the Buddhist temples in the valley.

As they approached the great Stupa, it loomed through the thinning mist, high above the fields, stark, bare of ornaments and with no gracefully curving eaves, no decorative carvings. The great grey hemisphere of its gabh, about ninety feet across, sat solidly on its massive tiered basement. Above the gabh from the square toran of ancient brick, the painted eyes of the Adi Buddha looked out sternly. Higher, its spire was sheaved in plates of copper gilt and topped by a gilded canopy and bell-shaped pinnacle.

A monk robed in dark red met them at the Bodhnath. 'The Tibetan lama knows of your coming,' he told them. 'He is waiting for you.'

Leaving the porter, they followed the monk inside the Tibetan lama's gonpa, to the pervasive aroma of the clarified butter burning in the sacred fires and the droning of monks at prayer. They passed through a chamber with its great painting of the wheel of life, the conch shells and large brass gong. The cymbals, a long trumpet, drums and other musical instruments were stacked beside a wall. These they also passed and walked along a dark corridor to the door of an inner room. The monk announced their arrival. They were in the presence of the Tibetan lama.

Hume looked around the room which was lit by oil lamps burning in their brass bowls, at the silver water jug with its peacock feathers and the thick carpets woven in reds and blues, the scrolls on the walls. A large gilded image of the Amitabha Buddha gleamed in the light from a sacred fire, and nearby was an image of the Buddhist Mother Goddess Tara, the White Tara with her lotus flowers and crown and the third eye on her forehead. At the far end of the room in his dark robe the Tibetan Lama sat fingering his beads, his head was shaven, his bronze thunderbolt and bell stood nearby. A monk was seated each side of him. He looked at each of the newcomers in turn, then beckoned to them to be seated.

'I am pleased you have brought the coins. I am pleased not to have to wait for the British to make them.' His voice was thin and soft. 'I am grateful to you, Sir Hume.'

'Yes, it would take much time to get them from Calcutta,' Hume replied.

The lama put his beads aside and pointed to a table stacked with Tibetan gold, then he turned to the monks and spoke to them. They left the chamber, and returned each carrying a heavy basket of coins. Another monk brought a scale which he placed beside the table.

Looking into a basket, the Tibetan Lama asked, 'Are they of the purity we asked, Sir Hume? Are they like those previously from the Malla kings?'

'They are half silver, the rest is only copper and tin,' Hume assured him. 'The required alloy. Like the coins from the valley before the blockade.'

The Tibetan lama lifted up a handful of the coins. 'That is satisfactory. We can make the exchange.' He beckoned to the monks, who took the scale and weighed the coins, then calculated and paid for them in gold and silver bullion, which they placed in the baskets. The exchange took time, and meanwhile the Tibetan lama had tea, thick with butter, served to them.

'We will need more coins like these in Tibet,' Sir Hume Clarke. 'We have a ready supply of gold to pay for them. And I look forward to when trade will be resumed in other things. There is salt for grain, and conch shells, wool, goats, turquoise, yak tails.'

'When we crush the Gurkha King, trade will come again then,' Puskar Maske told him.

The Tibetan lama shrugged. 'The Gurkha King will attack the valley soon. I have no love for him. I fear him. I prefer the Malla Kings'.

It was late morning when the monks finished weighing the coins and the exchange was completed. Hume and the others took their leave of the Tibetan lama and, with the porter's baskets now holding the Tibetan bullion, left the Bodhnath and slowly made their way back to Kathmandu.

Twelve

Summer in the Valley of Nepal brought the edge of the monsoon from far to the south, up from the Bay of Bengal and India. Its clouds were dark and heavy with rain, the days warm and humid. The Himalayan massifs lost some of their snow, exposing their great slabs of rock, the great precipices grey against the remaining white.

The valley's rivers ran high, charged with water from the melting snow, and the Bagmati roared through the deep gorge of the Cut down to India on its way to the Holy Ganges. The fields were a rich green now, with the young paddy quickly growing and the grass lush. The rains poured down cleaning the streets of Kathmandu, washing the temples, the eaves of the pagodas and the images of the gods, the roofs of the houses.

Some days Hume visited the metal workshop where smiths were minting more coins for Tibet, to check progress. The shelves at the entrance were lined with finished images of the gods and goddesses. Some were gilded and shining. The images of Lord Shiva, Vishnu, the Buddhas, Durga, Kali, Parbati, Saraswati, the mother goddesses, Tara, and the Tantric gods were all there and there were others. Hume bought a little gilded image of Ganesh the elephant-headed, pot-bellied God of Wisdom and Success, a fine casting of intricate workmanship.

Back in his house he gave it to Maneka. She held the image, looked into its gilded face and let her finger run along its little trunk. She shook her head at it reproachfully. 'He is only brass now,' she said. 'But he still means much to me. He is a kind god.'

'The God of Success,' Hume said, taking her in his arms and hugging her.

Maneka smiled to herself and looked from the image up at Hume. 'Yes, he brings good luck.'

When Maneka put the image of Ganesh on her altar beside the Blessed Virgin and the Christ of the Sacred Heart, its gilt shone in the candle light against the white of the altar cloth. They stood close together with Ganesh looking back at them.

'He's not out of place there,' Hume said.

Maneka did not reply but stayed close to Hume, sought his hand and held it.

During the days that followed, Hume noticed Maneka kneeling before the altar more often than usual, taking her rosary beads and praying. She made sure the flowers there were always fresh from the markets, and she kept the candles lit.

When Father Matteo came to visit he saw the image of Ganesh. 'You worship idols now,' he said to Hume, shaking his head.

'I'm afraid I worship very little,' Hume replied. 'No god of any faith.'

'Well, he's a pleasant god, Ganesh, most of the time,' the priest replied, ignoring Hume's remark. 'Father Michaelangelo wouldn't like him there. But why not? It is said he brings good luck in many ways. Did Maneka put him there?'

'Yes, she did.'

Father Matteo looked closely at Hume, his eyes smiling. 'Perhaps she has her reasons,' he said.

Then the priest talked of other matters. He had heard from his brother Capuchin, Father Fransesco in Bhaktapur, and had worrying news. 'Father Fransesco's parish covers Kirtipur,' he said. 'He has a few Christian converts there. He tells me the people of Kirtipur are preparing to defend their hill, preparing frantically. They're waiting for the Gurkha King to attack.'

'Do they expect it soon?'

'Very soon. Father Fransesco himself saw Gurkha soldiers in the villages near Kirtipur. In increasing numbers. He said that the people of Kirtipur carry stone and clay up from the valley to strengthen their walls, and that they carry up large boulders and place them on the walls ready to hurl down on invaders. Young men are taught to use the muskets, and they make large stocks of arrows for their bows. And men are taking up water and storing it in tanks and large pots in the town.'

'What hope does Father Fransesco believe they have?' Hume asked.

'None. None at all. Kirtipur might be well defended on its hill, with its stout walls and its people so brave. But Prithvi Shah will not fail this time. Father Fransesco is sure that Kirtipur alone and unaided has no hope.'

'Will the Valley Kingdoms help?'

Father Matteo shrugged. 'Last time, they gave no help. Father Fransesco tells me that the people of Kirtipur have approached the Pradhans at Lalitpatan and also Ranjit Malla's seven sons. But they got only vague promises, nothing more.'

'And Kathmandu? Jaya Malla?'

'Kirtipur is undecided whether or not to approach Jaya Malla. Last time the Gurkhas attacked, the people of Kirtipur sent a deputation to Jaya Malla seeking his help. You know what happened.'

Hume had heard. Then, Jaya Malla not only refused them help, he also had all in their deputation executed.

'Kirtipur has not forgotten.' Father Matteo said. 'They have no trust in Jaya Malla.'

About that time, Jaya Malla called Hume to the palace to say his jemidar had returned safely with a reply from the British East India Company; he gave it to Hume to read. 'Your letter has been well received in Calcutta,' Hume told Jaya Malla. 'The British show great interest. Governor Clive himself writes that he will send an army to support you against the Gurkha King. That is truly favourable. He also sends a message of friendship. He praises the part you have played in defending the valley. He sees a very profitable future for both the Company and yourself from the trading arrangements you offered.'

It delighted Jaya Malla. 'I will send my vakils down to Patna, to await the British, to advise them when they arrive,' he said. 'Please accept my deepest thanks, Sir Hume Clarke, for helping me to write to your Company.'

The jemidar also brought letters for Hume. He read that the Company had recovered Alexander's body and had buried it at Bettiah. It brought back the saddest of memories for him; and he dwelt for a long time on that day in Patna when he heard of his brother's death. 'When I leave the valley and return to India, I shall visit Alexander's grave,' he told himself. 'I'll put a tombstone there to remember him by.'

In a letter, addressed to Alexander from Humphries, the manager in Hollybrook, Hume read that all was well with the estate, and of news of neighbours and friends and the tenant farmers. There was also a copy of a London journal, ten months old but which Hume read with great interest.

Returning to his house that day, Hume found Maneka more than usually attentive and obviously wanting to please him. She had dressed in a sari she knew he particularly liked, had her black hair done up in Newar fashion held by a gold plate and wore her best bracelets and anklets, and the ruby pendant he had given her.

'I think you have news from Calcutta, my husband,' she said. 'And from your home in England.'

Hume was surprised she had heard so quickly.

'I know. My maid has been to the palace. It is good news, I think. The British will come and fight against the Gurkhas. And from England. Was that good news also?'

Hume told her he was pleased to receive it.

She pointed to the London journals and looked away from him. 'You have been thinking of your home in Hollybrook. It is calling you.'

'I read a journal. My mind went to my home for a while. That was all.'

'Do you want to go back there?' she asked.

'No, why do you say that?'

'I want to know. Are you content here in Kathmandu? Content with me as your wife?'

'I am, Maneka.' Hume assured her, taking her hand and putting it to his lips.

She grasped the sleeve of his jacket and with a gentle pressure led him to her altar at the end of the room before the little image of the God Ganesh there amongst the flowers and lighted candles. 'There is something I have to tell you,' she said, then hesitated, looking at the image of the Blessed Virgin and making the Sign of the Cross.

Hume guessed. 'Are you pregnant, Maneka? Will we have a child?'

'Yes,' she replied, and he saw the delight in her face. 'It pleases you?' she asked anxiously.

'It does. It pleases me greatly.'

'Are you sure of that?'

'Of course. Nothing could give me greater pleasure. I assure you of that Maneka.' He put his arm around her and drew her to him. 'I'm most grateful to you.'

Hume felt her relax in his embrace and they stood there for some time in silence. He pointed to Ganesh on the altar. 'Is this why you put him there?'

'He helps us. Helps a safe birth,' she told him. 'Women in the valley believe that Ganesh can ensure the birth of a healthy child.'

Hume laughed as he looked at the elephant-headed, potbellied god with one tusk. 'Not a child in his own image, I hope.'

'It will be a son who looks like you,' she assured him.

'Or a daughter as beautiful as you are,' he said happily.

That night Hume held Maneka tenderly, thinking of their child she was carrying. 'We will soon truly be a family,' he told himself, delighted at the thought.

Hume was with Dongol at the farm the day they planted the last of the paddy. Dongal and the other peasants Hume had engaged worked particularly hard, saying they must finish well before dusk. At last with the planting finished, they walked back to Dongol's house. He seemed preoccupied and kept looking at Hume, not speaking although Hume saw he wanted to tell him something.

'What is it, Dongal?' he asked after some time.

Dongol pointed to the sun, low near the horizon now, saying awkwardly, 'The night will come soon, master. You must leave now and be at your house before dark.'

'You want to get rid of me, Dongol?' Hume asked, laughing.

Dongol stammered. 'It is not that. Tonight we must take care. It is best to be indoors. That is necessary, to be safe. You would need to leave soon.'

'Why is that, Dongol?' Hume was curious to know what worried him.

'It is Ghanta Karna's night, master. This night, long ago, the demon Ghanta Karna died.'

Hume learnt from Dongol that Ghanta Karna was a demon, his body huge and horrible, immensely strong. He was evil and his red yes glared and the terrible fangs of his great black mouth dripped blood. Ghanta Karna roamed the land on his huge feet seeking people out.

He killed and ate children, he took wives away to his cave for his orgies of unmentionable horror and then ate their flesh. Ghanta Karna slew animals, poisoned crops and destroyed houses. And he cursed the gods, hated them, could not bear to hear even their names spoken. Of all the demons in the Valley of Nepal, Ghanta Karna was surely the most terrible.

'But you said Ghanta Karna's dead, Dongal,' Hume said. 'Why do you fear him now?'

'True he is dead,' Dongol replied, shaking his head as if to reassure himself as well as answer Hume. 'But he might return. And this night is favourable for evil things—witches and demons and people with the evil eye will roam tonight. They are Ghanta Karna's creatures. Indoors, we are safe from them. You must return home quickly. Beware. Hurry past the crossroads, master. The evil ones gather there.'

As Hume was leaving, he noticed Dongol's wife had a clump of long grass in one hand and a bowl of milk in the other. She would dip the grass in the bowl and dab the outer walls of the house as she walked around it. 'It is necessary tonight,' Dongal told Hume. 'The milk keeps away those with the evil eye.'

On the road back to Kathmandu that evening, Hume chanced to meet Puskar Maske, who had been to visit his own farm and check that his peasants had finished the rice sowing. He was hurrying, but stopped and waited for Hume to come up to him.

'We must not delay tonight, Puskar Maske,' Hume said in jest. 'I hear it's Ghanta Karna's night. The night witches and people with the evil eye are about.'

'So your peasant, Dongal, has told you.' Puskar Maske replied; his tone was serious. As they walked he spoke of Ghanta Karna. 'It was long ago, Hume,' he said. 'Soon after the valley was formed, perhaps. Even today Ghanta Karna is remembered as a thing of horror, a fearful thing, and the very thought of him coming back is dreaded. As well as hating people and committing despicable acts of obscenity against them, he hates the gods, blasphemes and refuses to hear even their names spoken. Ghanta Karna means Bell Ears, Hume. On each ear he wears a bell which jingles. He does that so he cannot hear the names of the gods.'

'He was killed because of Lord Vishnu,' Puskar Maske continued. 'Once Lord Vishnu, tiring of Ghanta Karna's evil, disguised himself as a little frog and sought Ghanta Karna out. He found him drunk on the blood of his victims, dancing and cavorting hideously, waving his arms and legs, and waving his monstrous genitals about with gleeful obscenity.'

'Vishnu, as the little frog,' Puskar Maske went on, 'stood before the demon, imitating his every action, making fun of him, looking up at the people who were watching, and showing his pleasure at their approval. Seeing this, Ghanta Karna's rage rose to a frenzy. His hands groping, his fangs snarling and yelling terrible oaths, he lunged at the frog trying to grasp him and squeeze him into nothing.'

'But he could not catch him. Each time the demon lunged, the little frog hopped quickly away, out of reach, still imitating the demon's grotesque movements. This went on for some time and so the demon's fury increased more and more. The frog led towards a well and jumped in. Ghanta Karna, stupid with rage, followed. So the demon was trapped. The people hurled stones down on him and dragged him up out of the well. They beat his repulsive body to its death. Then they burnt Ghanta Karna's corpse.' Puskar Maske showed his satisfaction. 'And and they cast his ashes to the waters of a holy river.'

By now Hume and Puskar Maske had arrived at where the paths to Deo Patan village and Kathmandu crossed. 'We must take care here,

Puskar Maske', Hume said teasingly, remembering Dongol's warning of the crossroads. 'We would be wise to watch out for Ghanta Karna here.'

'Have no fear of Ghanta Karna, Hume,' Puskar Maske said, although not very convincingly and with an embarrassed grin. 'Perhaps he is a myth from the past. If he did live once, he is dead now--long dead.'

'And the witches, the evil eyes, the demons?' Hume asked.

Puskar Maske thought before he replied. 'Maybe they are a different matter, Hume. Who can say they are not about and a danger to us? Yes, there are those with the evil eye. I have heard of those who wander through the night, floating with their feet above the ground, a forefinger pointing upwards and burning with a ghostly blue flame. I might have seen them.' He pointed to a large earthenware pot placed in the middle of the crossroads. 'But that will help keep them away from here.'

Hume looked at the pot dubiously, its top covered with flowers and on them a burning wick.

'It does help,' Puskar Maske assured him. 'It has flowers only on top. Inside, the pot is full of filth. Filth of the most detestable kind, the rotting bowels of buffalo, skins, human excreta. Demons and witches and those with the evil eye who come will find it there. They will eat the filth, delight in it. Full of it, satiated, they will not disturb people who pass.'

But Puskar Maske quickened his pace, hurrying on past the crossroads.

Thirteen

Winter came to the Valley of Nepal and the Gurkha King threatened Kirtipur. The old priest Vajracrya, who watched from the Swayambhunath, came to Kathmandu with the news that large numbers of Gurkhas had moved down from the mountains and now occupied the fields around Kirtipur's hill. They set up their headquarters near the village of Naikap, with Prithvi Shah himself and important generals including the scar-faced Surpratap.

He heard that the Gurkhas were trying to terrify the people of Kirtipur and were roaming under the town walls just out of range of Kirtipur's muskets. They yelled vile threats, threatened to behead the town's people, to castrate the men and rape the women. They promised to cause horrible disfigurement to the faces of all those who continued to resist.

Rumour was rife in Kathmandu and the astrologers were garrulous. Some said, 'The Gurkha King will surely take Kirtipur and then the rest of the valley. His vengeance will be terrible. Many will be slaughtered. The valley floor will shake and tremble causing great destruction.' Other astrologers predicted a Gurkha defeat; they had faith that the valley's gods would help.

The news from Kirtipur worried Maneka. But when Christmas came she set up a crib beside her altar with little painted images crudely carved in wood, of Mary and Joseph, the Christ Child in his manger and the farm animals; in it the three kings from the East came bearing gifts. Maneka decorated the altar with flowers and the glow of lighted candles. She spent much time before it praying, no doubt praying for the safety of her child who was to be born.

Hume accompanied Maneka to the Christmas service in the Capuchins' church. He took three tolas of gold from his stock for Father Michaelangelo, enough to pay the rest of Jaya Malla's tax with something left over for the priests. Again the church was decorated with flowers and candles and of course a crib.

'Many people are at your church this year,' he said to Father Matteo. 'There are more than usual.'

'Those in our flock come to church very often now,' Father Matteo replied. 'They worry, like everyone in Kathmandu. They hear of the vile threats the Gurkhas make to the people of Kirtipur. Many believe it will be their turn next.'

'No doubt they pray for Christ's protection,' Hume said.

'Of course they do. For the people of Kirtipur. For themselves. And more. I know many of them pray also to Shiva and Vishnu, to other Hindu gods, and to the Buddhas.'

'You don't object?

'I do not. It's true it saddens me. But I don't object. Much prayer is needed to keep the Gurkha King out of Kathmandu.'

The old priest Vajracrya brought further news from Kirtipur. 'It's not good,' he said sorrowfully. 'The people starve. Filth piles up in the streets mounds of refuse, and dead animals. There's a vile stench. Many are ill with fever; some die and corpses lie rotting because there is no wood for the funeral pyres. People come to the walls, the men, women, children, to look down from their hill at the Gurkha soldiers below, who are waiting there like vultures. It is truly a tragic town. But the people of Kirtipur, ill and hungry as they are, say they will fight street by street, from their forts and houses, even from the temples, from their Bhairab's great temple, Ganesh's Temple, the Buddhist's Chillandeo.'

During the following weeks, people in Kathmandu prayed. Many made sacrifices to the gods, to Shiva, Vishnu, and to the Buddhas. The Capuchins offered up Masses for the defeat of the Gurkha King and the safety of their flock.

'Kumar must come on his peacock high in the sky over the valley, master,' Hume's servant said. 'He must swoop down with all his might and utterly destroy the Gurkha army. And the Snake Gods must help. They must crush the Gurkhas in their coils and poison them with their fangs.'

But it seemed the gods were not answering. Late one evening towards the end of the Spring of 1766, Father Fransesco walked into Kathmandu with news that Kirtipur had fallen to the Gurkha King. He came a tired and dejected man, so sorrowful and dishevelled with blood soiling his white habit. He sat in silence for some time, his hands trembling as he tolled the beads at his waist. A crowd gathered around him.

'It is not God's will,' he said loudly, looking up at Hume and the others who listened. 'It cannot be. Kirtipur is Hell in all its vileness.' He stopped abruptly and blessed himself.

But after a time he regained enough composure to continue. 'Last night the Gurkhas entered Kirtipur,' he told them. 'A gate was opened.

The guards opened it on orders. Treacherous orders. What traitor gave them? No one from Kirtipur, I'd think. A Pradhan from Lalitpatan, perhaps. The Gurkhas' van crept up—stealthily through the night, up the winding road, then through the open gate.'

'Soon their main force came up, surged into the streets, clashing their weapons and yelling their blood-curdling "Ayo gurkha ayo gurkha !".' The priest blessed himself again, then said, 'Kirtipur defended bravely. But fighting in the streets was fierce that night. And many were slaughtered. The people of Kirtipur were weakened. Weakened from the long siege, starved, diseased. They gradually gave way, retreated to the strongholds of their forts and temples.'

There were murmurings from those listening to the priest. People moved in closer to him. Fear registered on most faces. One man called, 'I beseech the great gods. The great Lord Shiva. All the other gods. I pray for them to save us.' Another man looked over at Hume and called out, 'The British must come or we are doomed.'

'When morning came,' the priest told them, 'the Gurkha King called the people to Kirtipur's square. I went there with the others. A Gurkha general ordered: "Lay down your arms, men of Kirtipur. Come out of your forts and temples. Open up the other gates. I promise you no one will be harmed. There is an amnesty for all. Kirtipur is forgiven for resisting. It is forgiven for the arrow that pierced Surpratap's eye a year ago. It is forgiven for killing Kalu Pandey during our first attack".'

'After much discussion and with some doubt, the people of Kirtipur accepted the Gurkha general's promises,' the priest said. 'And they surrendered.'

'But how false those promises turned out to be,' the priest continued. 'This morning the Gurkhas occupied the forts and temples, manned the gates, patrolled the streets, and set up their government. Then came the terrible evil of the afternoon.' Father Fransesco blessed himself again; clutching his beads, he moved his lips in prayer. 'There was the stench of sin today.' He pointed to the blood stains on his habit. 'It is their blood—the blood of the men and boys of Kirtipur.'

They all listened as the priest went on. 'This afternoon the Gurkhas broke all their promises. Broke them all in the name of the Devil. Gurkha soldiers seized Kirtipur's ministers and generals, stripped them of their clothing to the waist and tied their hair in knots on top. They bound their arms to their bodies and their hands behind their backs. It was the square near Parbati's Temple the Gurkhas chose, a beautiful old temple built of purple brick. The Gurkha executioners were waiting there. One by one Kirtipur's ministers and generals were led in, made kneel and lean forward in the right position. Then a Gurkha would raise his talawar and slash down at a waiting neck and the head would fall, the blood spurting and the body lurching forward after it. Many people were beheaded there today.'

Yet again the Capuchin blessed himself, and stopped for many moments in prayer. 'But even worse was to come,' he told them, his hands agitated, fingering the cross at the end of his beads. 'The Gurkhas mustered all the men and boys of Kirtipur, those who were still alive. It was indeed a long, sad line which reached down and around the streets. Gurkhas soldiers waited in the square, a score or more this time with their sharp kukhries drawn from their sheaves. As each man and boy of Kirtipur was brought in, two Gurkhas seized him. One held him tightly. Another Gurkha cut at his face, disfigured him, cut away his nose and lips. They released him, let him walk away, his hands to his face trying to stem the bleeding.' The priest touched the bloodstains on his habit. 'Some of them I tried to console.'

'Were many disfigured?' Hume asked.

'Very many. The men, but also the boys no matter how young. Only the babes still in their mothers' arms were spared, and men in the bands who played wind instruments.'

'It is truly a great tragedy, Hume,' Puskar Maske said. 'For seven years, the brave people of Kirtipur held off the Gurkha King. It is a terrible end for them. Kirtipur will come to be known as Naskatapur, the Town of Cut Noses. It bodes badly for the rest of us. We are doomed, Hume. All of us in the valley.'

Fourteen

The next morning a sad line of people, a score of men and two little boys, came trudging slowly over the fields to Kathmandu. They came up to the town gate, bowing and joining their hands in timid namastes. Seeing their faces, the guards fell back and, without questioning them, let them enter. These were some of the men and boys from Kirtipur, their lips cut away and white teeth exposed. Their noses were gone and they had two dark holes for nostrils, the blood hardly yet dried. They had paid a terrible price for resisting the Gurkha King. Forever, their mutilated faces would be set in hideous skull-like grins.

The Gurkhas had sent them as a warning of what could be in store for Kathmandu. People stared at the noseless ones in horror, hardly believing. Many pitied them and wanted to help. A few shunned their advances, gave way to them in the narrow streets and walked away if they approached. News of their arrival spread quickly and ministers and generals came to look at them. That morning, staying together, the noseless ones roamed the streets of Kathmandu.

'We must help them,' Maneka told Hume although she was hardly able to hide her horror at the sight of them. 'It is the Gurkha King's worst crime. Cutting the faces of the boys is his greatest evil.'

Hume agreed. 'What do you suggest Maneka?'

'The two little boys came. I saw them. We could care for them until their mothers come for them. Till then let them live with us in your house'.

'Are you sure you want that Maneka?'

'I am sure. If they are not already being cared for, we must take them here.'

Hume went out to look for the two boys. He found that the Raj Guru had lodged the men from Kirtipur in the Temple of Wood, the dharmsala where he had waited the day he arrived in the valley, and had sent food to them. The two boys had already been put in the care of Kathmandu families.

The atrocity at Kirtipur struck fear into the people of Kathmandu, but to Hume's surprise life soon returned to normal, or almost so. Crowds filled the market squares again, people worshipped at the temples. Even yet, Hume saw that Jaya Malla was not preparing for the defence of the valley, and Maneka learnt from her friends that he spent much of his time at prayer. Hume had no doubt that he was waiting for the Company's army.

People did take some precautions. At night they made sure their doors were locked, pulled up the ladders between the floors of their houses and slept with their weapons at hand. Hume knew that, at bay on the top floor of his own house, Maneka and her maids would be safe, as long as the grain and water he had stored there lasted, and unless the Gurkhas set fire to the house or smoked them out. He could slay Gurkha soldiers, if they attacked, one by one as their heads came up the ladder from the floor below.

But their baby was about to be born. Maneka took to bed on the second floor of the house where her maids slept, so they could attend to her day and night. The ladies from the Court, particularly Bachhla, and Puskar Maske's second wife also attended. They encouraged Hume to stay away and leave Maneka to their experience.

Hume waited expectantly for several days but there was no sign of the birth. 'There are often delays,' Bachhla assured him. 'It is normal enough.'

But when Maneka's labour pains started and more time passed and no child came and she was weakening, Hume began to have doubts about it. He saw several other women come to the house, including midwives with good reputations in Kathmandu, who stayed a while and left. One of Maneka's maids told Hume that the ladies of the court had arranged for a goat to be sacrificed to Ganesh, and were praying to the god for the child to come. Bachhla asked the Capuchins to say a Mass for Maneka.

Then Bachhla came to Hume, agitated, tears in her eyes, her voice trembling. 'I despair for Maneka,' she said and began to weep.

'We must not despair,' Hume told her. 'Tell me what is to be done now, for the best.'

Her answer shocked Hume. 'There is nothing. Everything has been done already. She cannot give birth. Such a thing can happen. I have known it before. They will both die.'

Hume did not leave Maneka's bedside that afternoon, and talked with her when she woke and felt strong enough. He saw she did not realise what was happening, the apparent hopelessness of her position. 'Our baby will be a boy,' she said to him. 'He will be like you my husband and my cousin Atal Thapa. Like both of you. He will be strong and clever.'

She thought of the fall of Kirtipur and of the cruel disfigurement of the men and boys there. 'We must take our baby to your country. That is my hope,' she told Hume. 'Away from the danger to him here. Away from the Gurkha King.' Hume was greatly saddened, believing her hope would never be realised.

That night when Maneka slept, Hume left her bedside and paced up and down the streets, dejected. Then he sat for a long time in his own quarters in the dim lamp light with his unhappy thoughts. Later, Puskar Maske called on him; he had heard from his wife of the looming tragedy. He spoke quietly, kindly trying to console Hume. Hume noticed he wore his talawar at his side.

'It's wise to go out well armed at night, Puskar Maske,' Hume said pointing to the sword.

Puskar Maske drew the sword from its scabbard and laid it on the table in front of Hume, the steel of its long blade gleaming in the light from the lamp. 'No, it is not that, Hume. Tonight, I do not wear it for my own protection.'

Hume looked at the fine weapon and then at Puskar Maske, wondering.

'It has protected me in the past. Protected me well. This sword served me well when we defended Kirtipur the time the Gurkhas first attacked. It slew then, several times it slew. Tonight I have brought it to save life. Not to take life. Tonight it will try to compensate for the killing it has done.'

'It's hardly the time, Puskar Maske,' Hume said. 'What are you doing?'

Puskar Maske asked a servant to bring a pot of water and a bowl. He poured the water over the sword's bright steel, letting it drain into the bowl placed for the purpose. He looked at Hume, a little embarrassed. 'It might work, Hume,' he said, 'but perhaps it is only superstition. I have heard it has worked. With your permission I shall sprinkle this water over Maneka. Water from such a sword is said to induce a birth.'

Hume had little faith in it. But he agreed. A last resort.

They climbed the ladder to the bed where Maneka was sleeping and Puskar Maske told the women there of his intention. Hume bared Maneka's body and Puskar Maske sprinkled the water from the bowl. She awoke and Hume saw the fear in her eyes. She had heard of the custom and realised nothing else could been done—the water from the sword was the last attempt to save her. For a long time she looked at Hume, then asked, 'Will you bring me the little images of Saint Francis and Ganesh from my altar. I want to keep them with me.' He gave them to her; her labour pains stopped and she fell asleep again with him holding her hand.

Very late that night Maneka seemed to grow weaker. Hume had his servant go quickly to ask Father Matteo to come. For a long time the priest knelt beside Maneka's bed and prayed. Then, sadly, with Hume's consent, he performed the last rites for her, gave her the Host for a last Holy Communion and anointed her with the oil of the sacrament of Extreme Unction. It was a sad time for Father Matteo, for Maneka's maids and Hume's servant and for Bachhla and Puskar Maske's second wife and others who came to the house to ask about her. It was the very saddest of nights for Hume.

But then early next morning, at dawn when there was just light enough to count the tiles on the roof-tops, when two crows had come down out of the mist to take the food the maids had put out for them, Maneka awoke and her labour pains began again and she started to sit up.

Hume, at her bedside, held her hand. 'Rest, Maneka,' he told her. 'I shall stay here with you.'

'No,' she said. 'Our baby is coming. It is late but it is coming. It will be here soon. I know that.'

Hume hurried off to send for Bachhla and the midwives. A little later Maneka gave birth to a son. It was to everyone's surprise, delight and thanksgiving. And to Hume's own very great relief. The child was healthy and within hours Maneka lost a little of her weakness. Hume's pleasure was beyond words. Many called to congratulate Maneka and to view the baby with some curiosity, which was understandable enough with the child half-English and half-Newar.

Hume wondered what had helped the child be born in the end and what had saved Maneka. He wondered if it were the pleas to the gods, the sacrifices, or the water from Maske's sword, or simply nature's way of being late sometimes.

Later, when Maneka had recovered, Hume would discuss this with her. She also wondered, was not sure. But Hume saw she always kept the little gilded image of Ganesh in a special place on her altar, and she called her baby son Francis after the saint.

The Gurkha King was marshalling his army for another attack. Not on Kathmandu, as people had expected, it was Lalitpatan he chose. His army, reinforced from Nawakot and the town of Gurkha, assembled close to the walls of Lalitpatan, set up their camps, built crude revetments and put cannon in place. The Gurkha soldiers walked almost to the walls and reminded the people of the fate of the men and boys of Kirtipur, bringing noseless ones to the gates as walking examples of the fate in store them, adding, 'Those who resist will also have their right hands cut off.' Lalitpatan put up some defence, sending detachments out the gates to engage the Gurkhas, but these forays became less frequent as Lalitpatan lost heart.

Then one morning in August one of Jaya Malla's vakils arrived back from Makwanpur with urgent news: 'A British army is on its way to the Valley of Nepal. It has already left Patna and is approaching the Terai.' That same morning, the Gurkha King also heard the news. The Gurkha army, the whole force, left their positions around Lalitpatan and assembled in formation for departure.

Some in Kathmandu believed that the Gurkhas would retreat to Nawakot and their ancient capital of Gurkha to escape the British threat. But it was not to be. The Gurkha King was to hurry out of the valley, down the steep and rugged slopes of the Mahabharats, down into Makwanpur to seek out and confront the British.

The monsoon that year had brought more than usual rain, but the day the Gurkhas left was clear, the sky a deep blue, and the great Himalayan mountains overlooking the valley were free of cloud, their peaks a sparkling white. Hume watched the Gurkha force departing. How different, he thought, from the colourful armies of Mir Kasim and the Nawab of Oudh at the Battle of Buxar, and also, though to a less extent, from the Company's army. The Gurkhas had no elephants with elaborately ornamented howdahs and no cavalry officers with their fine uniforms and bejewelled harnesses and brocaded saddle cloths; they had no regiments of horse at all. Few flags flew and no bands played. They had no large cannon, no supply wagons with their oxen and no camp followers and merchants making up the rear.

The Gurkhas were mountain fighters. They travelled light, with their muskets and talawars, bows, their sharp kukhries and a few small cannon. They carried few provisions and would live off the land, and the villages they passed. They marched out of the valley quickly, in high spirits, led by the Gurkha King himself, as well as Surpratap and other senior generals. Hume could hear the roar of their war-cry as they went, "Ayo gurkha ayo gurkha !", loud at first then growing fainter until it was lost in the distance.

News of the coming of the British army and the Gurkha's departure brought much relief and rejoicing in Kathmandu. Jaya Malla called

Hume to the palace. 'Please accept my warmest thanks for the part you have played in negotiations with the Company, Sir Hume Clarke. My letter to your governor has brought great success.'

'What are your own plans, Sire?' Hume asked. 'Will an army from the Valley of Nepal fight alongside the Company's?'

'It is possible,' he said. 'I have messages from my cousins in Bhaktapur and Lalitpatan. They say they will send soldiers. They praise my initiative in getting British help. Even the treacherous Pradhans have sent me a message of support, and the Satbahalyas.'

'Will you raise an army, Sire?' Hume asked.

'My vakils in Patna will advise the British.'

'Yes, but an army?' Hume repeated his query.

'Certainly, if need be. But tell me Sir Hume Clarke, will it be necessary?'

Jaya Malla answered his own question. 'I do not believe the Gurkha King can stand against your British army. It will annihilate him. That is certain. And they will fight on the Terai or in the lower hills. That is good. Better there than here in the valley.' He looked closely at Hume. 'The Court Astrologer is confident. He has no doubt about a British victory. A great victory.'

About that time Dasain was held in Kathmandu, the great ten-day festival celebrating Durga's slaughtering of the brutish Mahisasura, who came in the form of a black water buffalo, huge and red-eyed, and roamed the land bellowing. He gored with his great horns and breathed fire from his great black nostrils, killing and maiming.

'It was truly a victory of good over evil,' Puskar Maske said when he called at Hume's house. 'And it is the Black Night, Hume. You could come with me to the Temple of Taleju. Many buffalo will be sacrificed there tonight. It will please the goddess.' He smiled. 'She will be pleased and be on the side of your British army.'

They found the courtyard of Taleju's Temple bathed brightly in the light of the near-full-moon. Ministers and generals, the priests, Jaya Malla himself, and many others were there to worship Durga. In front of the Temple, a buffalo was secured to a stout post, a great beast representing the demon Mahisasura, its sharp horns tossed, its white and red eyes rolled, and the moonlight emphasised the blackness of its body.

Priests officiated. Several Newar soldiers stood nearby with long swords, the sharp blades flashing in the moonlight as they swung them through the air to test their arms. Out in the Durbar Square there was a rustling, a soft lowing and occasional bellows, as a hundred or so buffalo waited their turn to be taken to the temple.

When the time came to sacrifice the first buffalo, a priest walked up to the beast and whispered into the its ear. 'He is whispering secret mantras. No doubt he asked for help against the Gurkha King,' Puskar Maske told Hume. Then the priest sprinkled holy water over its great black body. That done, one of the soldiers raised his sword high, held it there for a few moments, then it came slashing down, a mighty stroke taking all his skill and strength. With a grunt the buffalo's head, completely severed, fell to the ground, and the blood spurted high towards Taleju's Temple and into a large kalash a priest placed there for the purpose. For some moments the headless body stood there quivering, then its knees gave way, it sagged, fell heavily and went down rolling on its side. A priest came forward and cut off the end of the buffalo's tail and stuffed it in the mouth, then taking the head by its great horns he placed it before the Taleju Temple. Attendants quickly dragged away the carcass.

Another buffalo was brought in, secured to the post and sacrificed to Durga, then another, and many others. Some were beheaded like the first, some had their throats cut and their blood let drain, others were pierced in the heart or hacked to pieces.

'It is done according to the Tantric rites,' Puskar Maske said. 'Secret rites. I do not follow them, Hume. I have told you that before.'

'You agree with such sacrifices, Puskar Maske?' Hume asked.

He shrugged. 'Many gods demand sacrifices. And I am told that in other countries many animals are slaughtered for their meat, for food. In your country too, I am sure. And I have heard they fight and kill bulls for the sport near Father Michaelangelo's country.'

'You say it is the same, Puskar Maske?'

He thought for a while. 'No, it is better for them here. The gods love those sacrificed. They favour them. They will be raised higher in their next life, an animal reincarnated as a human perhaps. I told you that before, at the stone-throwing at Kumar's festival.'

By the time they left the courtyard many buffalo heads, the ends of their tails in their mouths and horns interlocked, were lying in the moonlight before the Temple of Taleju. And still more beasts were being led in to be sacrificed to Durga.

Walking home through the streets, they passed people sacrificing goats and cocks before temples, particularly the temples of the mother goddesses. Near one temple, a group of people were cutting large pumpkins to pieces with knives. 'They are against blood sacrifices,'

Puskar Maske said. 'Nor will they eat meat. They are of a special cult and are followers of Vishnu.' He looked up at Hume and laughed. 'They are sacrificing pumpkins to Durga. and hope she will accept them.'

'You believe she will?' Hume asked.

Puskar Maske shrugged. 'Some gods would, Hume. But not Durga.'

During the days just after Dasain, a few Gurkha soldiers appeared in the valley again and rumour spread quickly. Most people thought they were the remnants of the Gurkha force, and that the British had annihilated the main body. People waited for the British to enter the valley, said happily that the threat from the Gurkha King had gone forever. But then another of Jaya Malla's vakils returned, and the news he brought shocked Kathmandu, it spread like lightning to Lalitpatan and Bhaktapur and throughout the valley. A battle had been fought in the lower hills to the east of Makwanpur near the fort of Pauwa. It had been a complete victory for the Gurkha King. He had routed the British army.

Soon the Gurkha soldiers returned in greater numbers, more confident than ever, and boasted of their victory. They set up encampments in the valley again and roamed freely just beyond the walls of Kathmandu and Lalitpatan. They hurled insults at the guards on the gates, and fired arrows with threatening messages over the walls to remind people of the fate of the men and boys of Kirtipur. Again a gloom fell over Kathmandu and again people prayed to the gods for protection.

One evening after dark, Maneka's cousin, Sardar Atal Thapa, called at Hume's house, in mufti and amused at how easily he had got through the town gate. 'I will leave immediately if I am not welcome,' he told them.

But Maneka greeted him warmly and Hume had a servant bring a pot of raksi and two bowls.

'I have come to congratulate my cousin on the son she has given you,' Atal Thapa said. 'I heard of her difficulty. I am thankful to see her recovered so well. I have known my cousin for many years. Once I would visit her at Jaya Malla's palace.'

Maneka took the baby from the cradle and held him in her arms so as to display him to full advantage. The baby gurgled as he looked at Atal Thapa. His appearance would have pleased anyone, his fine features, his olive skin, big appealing brown eyes, and already his head of black hair.

Atal Thapa took a long look at the child.

'Can you see my father in him?' Maneka asked. 'Some likeness perhaps.'

'Yes, some likeness,' Atal Thapa told her. 'But he will also carry the likeness of many people from here and in far-off England. I am sure he will have good qualities as a man—a strong body, a good mind—and will become a minister or warrior, perhaps.'

'It is kind of you to say that,' Maneka replied, smiling happily. Then suddenly her mood changed and Hume noticed the pleasure drain from her face. 'It is well he was not a boy in Kirtipur, cousin,' she said quietly.

Atal Thapa turned from her gaze, looked down to the floor for some moments, then took the bowl of raksi Hume had given him and drank it. He raised his face to Maneka and then to Hume. 'Because of Kirtipur I delayed coming here. When I entered your house tonight, I was fearful of your rejection. I had no part in the atrocity, nor had my own soldiers.'

'You accept no responsibility for it? Hume asked .

'I did not agree with it.' Atal Thapa thought for a while. 'At least not fully.' For some time they sat in silence. 'I was thankful I had no part in it,' Atal Thapa repeated. 'But Prithvi Shah has his reasons. He will come to take all the Valley cf Nepal. He will build a greater Nepal strong enough to defend itself. That is essential. It is not an easy task for the Gurkha army. Each of the valley kingdoms—each separately, Kathmandu, Lalitpatan and Bhaktapur—could muster a force larger than we Gurkhas. If we have to fight each kingdom, there will be a great loss of life and much suffering, more by far than we imposed on Kirtipur. Prithvi Shah had the faces there disfigured as an example for the rest of the valley, to strike terror into the people of the three kingdoms, to quench their fighting spirit. His hope is to reduce the loss of life and suffering.'

When Atal Thapa had finished talking, Maneka rose and took her baby son from the cradle again. She held him tightly in her arms as she looked at her cousin. 'It was a terrible atrocity. What great suffering and loss of life,' she exclaimed. 'It cannot be excused. But it is not you I blame, cousin. I know you would not want it. It is the Gurkha King. He had no mercy for my father when he murdered him. Now he has no mercy for the men and little boys of Kirtipur. He will have no mercy for my son.' At that, she asked a servant to bring her cousin food and another bowl of raksi.

Atal Thapa had fought near Pauwa with the Gurkha King, and Hume was anxious for news of the battle with the Company's force. At first the Gurkha sardar was reluctant to speak of it, but with Hume's persistence and encouragement he gave him the account he wanted.

Hume learnt the Company had assembled at Patna a force placed under the command of Major Kinloch. Atal Thapa was not sure of the size of the force, or how many were sepoys and how many were Hume's countrymen, but thought it totalled perhaps five thousand men, well armed, much better armed than the Gurkha army, and well supplied.

'I heard that they left Patna with banners flying and bands playing,' Atal Thapa said, with a hint of a smile. 'True they had many foot soldiers, but also horse regiments, large cannon, and elephants I was told, as well as many heavy supply wagons. We all were surprised and laughed about it amongst ourselves, and wondered if their Major Kinloch had ever climbed a mountain. It was not a force suitable for fighting in my country.'

Hume remembered the Gurkha army leaving the valley.

'And they chose the monsoon time,' Atal Thapa continued, 'with its heavy rains and heat. Why, I do not know. We had our scouts watching them all the way from Patna. Even before they crossed the Chauria Hills they had trouble hauling their supply wagons and heavy cannon over the water-logged ground. They had to abandon some. And Prithvi Shah made sure they got no supplies from the villages. Always a step ahead, he warned the village headmen of Major Kinloch's coming and had them hide their grain.'

'Your Major Kinloch had trouble on the duns,' Atal Thapa commented, trying to hide his distain. 'He seemed to know nothing of the paths to take, and Jaya Malla's vakils who were guiding him knew little more. They spent days cutting through the jungle. They lost wagons and their horses were useless. The white vapours rose up from the swamps with the deadly aul and some went down with the fever.'

'Doesn't the aul take your soldiers also?' Hume asked.

'Certainly it would. We avoid the duns in the monsoon. Tharu people in the villages help us. The gods protect the Tharu from the aul.'

Gaining confidence now, Atal Thapa continued. 'Over the duns, Major Kinloch came on through Makwanpur, heading towards the Mahabharat foothills and up towards our fort at Hariharpur. It was country we knew well. Five years ago Prithvi Shah routed King Digbandan Sen there to take Makwanpur. A year later he routed the Nawab of Bengal; Mir Kasim it was then, who sent a force to take Makwanpur back for Digbandan Sen. We met them one night at Hariharpur, slaughtered the

Nawab's army, killed his general, Gurgin Khan, and captured many muskets and some cannon. We beat them so thoroughly Mir Kasim never dared return.'

'We harassed Major Kinloch as he approached,' Atal Thapa said, warming to his story. 'Never let him rest. Sent detachments down from our forts at night to attack their rear and the stragglers. We saw our mountains had exhausted them, because of the high hills they had to climb, the steep descents, the rough and rocky ground, swollen streams they had crossed, and the flooded rivers. They had to haul their heavy weapons and carry supplies on their backs.'

Now Atal Thapa hesitated and looked at Hume.

'He is still a little diffident, wondering if he is offending me,' Hume said to himself. 'Well he might be. I am British and hearing how a British army was defeated. But I want to know.' Hume assured the Gurkha Sardar, 'I'm not taking offence. I would like to hear more.'

So Atal Thapa said, 'Major Kinloch's force did not reach Hariharpur. Prithvi Shah drew him eastwards towards our fort at Pauwa, and we prepared for him there with great care. We positioned a detachment about two miles away, high on the hills near Sindhuli. Bir Bhadra Thapa commanded it.' Atal Thapa glanced at Maneka. 'He is a relative of ours, cousin. Another detachment was put at Dhungrebas, hidden near Kinloch's line of approach. Then Prithvi Shah reinforced Pauwa with his second army under Bamsharaj Pandey. The trap was set.'

Atal Thapa hesitated again, but this time Hume saw he was trying to hide his pride.

'Major Kinloch was new to our mountains,' Atal Thapa explained, half-apologetically. 'He sent his army, much of it, up the mountain-side towards the Pauwa fort. We waited till they were well up the steep rise, close. Then we let loose our rocks, many hundreds of them, great boulders, an avalanche of rocks that gathered great speed as they rolled, hurtled down the slope, and crashed into the midst of them. The rocks crushed many and broke up their lines. After that our men rushed at Kinloch's army, down from Pauwa we came, down from Sindhuli, out from Dhungrebas. Our war-cry, "Ayo gurkha ayo gurkha !", if I may mention it, roared from our thousands of throats. It filled the valleys, echoed and re-echoed, reverberating around the mountains, striking terror as we intended. We struck at their van, their rear, and soon we were amongst them from all sides. After our muskets had done their work, our talawars and our kukhries cut deeply into them. Their blood flowed over the rocky ground, the mountain side was strewn with the bodies of their dead.'

'You have fought in battle, Sir Hume.' Atal Thapa continued. 'I know how well the British fight, and the Indian sepoys they train. I have often been told that. I have great respect for you British. But on the hills near Pauwa, Major Kinloch had no chance. When night came and he retreated to leave our country and return to India, he had only eight hundred men left, no more. And we had captured most of his weapons, his light cannon and many muskets.'

Hume thought of Kinloch, his campaign a tragedy of errors. His return to Patna would not be a happy one, far from it. The Agent there would take it badly; Calcutta would take it badly.

Soon after completing his account Atal Thapa rose to go. 'I am greatly pleased to see you well again cousin,' he said to Maneka. 'I have very fond memories of you. And I congratulate you both on the beautiful child you have.' Then his face darkened as he said, ' I must tell you the Gurkha King will surely take Kathmandu and the rest of the Valley of Nepal. There will be danger for you both. But I assure you I will give what help I can.'

Then Atal Thapa took his leave to return to the Gurkha encampment in the fields just outside Kathmandu's walls.

Fifteen

One day Maneka said to Hume, 'I have been thinking, my husband, that your gold will not be safe here when the Gurkhas attack. Perhaps you should hide it elsewhere. Why not take it to the farm. Hide it there. Bury it in the fields or perhaps under Dongol's hut. The Gurkha soldiers would not look for gold there. They would not expect it in a poor peasant's home.'

Hume saw the wisdom of it. 'Yes Maneka, but Dongol would need to know. Could he be trusted?'

'Such an amount of gold would frighten him. He would not dare disturb it. He would think that the Snake Gods guard it. He would not even mention it to anyone, knowing some might kill him for it. You would need pay him something. Yes, I am sure you could trust him.'

Hume had a lot of the gold delivered to the farm, keeping some to meet his needs. The peasant Dongol looked at it, disbelieving. 'Is it truly gold, master?' he asked. 'I have seen some gold coins at the markets. But this is so much gold. Is it from the Karkot Raja ?'

Hume did not answer to that. He took a tola's worth, gave it to Dongol and said, 'That is for you. I will leave the rest of the gold here, hidden.'

'You do not want the gold, master?'

'I shall come back for it. Speak of it to no one.'

'Others come. They will see it.'

'We shall bury it. It won't be seen.'

Hume told Dongol to lead the cow and the two young goats from the end of his house, move the fodder from the corner and dig a hole deep in the earthen floor. Hume buried the gold, and they put the earth back and replaced the fodder.

'It is well hidden, master,' Dongol said. 'I shall guard it well.'

'The Karkot Raja will also guard it, Dongol. Be careful of him,' Hume said, not able to resist that extra precaution.

It was past the middle of the year when the Gurkhas returned in force to the Valley of Nepal. This time their immediate prey was not Lalitpatan. It was Kathmandu. They surrounded the town walls, set up their encampments and occupied nearby villages—even Balaju which was very close, and Thamel which was only just outside the walls. During the day, Gurkha soldiers fired their muskets at houses abutting the walls and shot their arrows with threatening messages into the town. They would disfigure, cut the hands off, execute or flay alive all those who resisted. No harm would come to those who did not resist. At night the people of Kathmandu watched the Gurkha camp fires glowing in the surrounding fields.

They were under siege. The Gurkhas let nothing enter the town, no grain or other food. They let no one leave except the dead or the occasional deserter. Families rationed their food and their stocks ran low. Hume was glad he had Dongol increase the plantings on the farm near Deo Patan village and had stored extra supplies of rice and soybeans in his house.

Weeks went by and conditions worsened. The monsoon rains came again, flooding the streets, washing the refuse from the higher parts of the town, the garbage from the houses, and the vermin, excreta and unwanted dung; but then it only accumulated in the lower streets. Filth piled up there, right to the walls and gates. Water stagnated and became foul as the rains washed refuse into the earth and down into the springs and wells.

'I come in the most difficult times. I have come to ask a favour of you. One you might find hard to grant,' the old priest Vajracrya said to Hume.

Hume guessed his need. 'Is it for grain?' he enquired.

'It is for grain. Our people are very hungry now. Their stocks are low. And some are starving. Many come to me asking for help.' He looked at the baby Francis in Maneka's arms. 'Some children are starving too.'

Hume saw the concern on Maneka's face, but said, 'Jaya Malla will have stocks. Have you sought grain from the palace?'

'His stocks were small. He has little left.'

In this way, too, Jaya Malla has failed, Hume thought and was about to remark on it when Maneka spoke.

'Are a lot of our people very hungry?' she asked the priest.

'Very many. And even more will be so soon.'

'And children?'

'It is worse for them. They do not understand the reason.'

Maneka looked at Hume, sadly. 'Can we give some?'

'I will Maneka,' he said and asked his servant to bring a basket of rice and give it to the old priest.

That night in bed Maneka pressed close to Hume. 'I am glad you are my husband,' she said. 'Thank you for giving the rice for me. They are dangerous times for everyone. I often wonder if we will be here to see the end of them.'

'I believe we will Maneka. You are brave and we must have hope.'

Maneka lent and took their baby from a basket. 'And I hope for our son,' she said.

More appeals were made to Hume, and he felt he had an obligation, especially to Puskar Maske and his family, the Capuchin priests and of course Maneka's friends. As the weeks went by, others whose needs had become desperate, came to Hume with their pleas, most apologetic and humble. And some came who were aggressive, wanting to seize his stock. Hume kept his pistol ready, determined that Maneka and their little baby son would not starve.

Disease spread quickly in Kathmandu. Hume saw it first in his own servant who was hit suddenly with vomiting and diarrhoea, then with agonising cramps in his arms and legs. Maneka attended to him. 'Build up the fire and put his bed near the hearth even though the day is warm,' she told her maids. 'Wash his body. Keep giving him water to ease his thirst.' But his condition worsened and Hume could see death in his face. Maneka prayed for him at her altar and her maids prayed to their gods. Then, unexpectedly, after a few days his condition started to improve; a week and he was almost well again.

Hume's servant was more fortunate than many in Kathmandu. Many died each day. Hume looked out on the funeral processions of corpses shrouded in red or yellow carried through the narrow streets on bamboo biers, their relatives and friends grieving, wailing loudly. They would pass through the town gates into the fields and head for the river banks; the Gurkha King had agreed that Kathmandu could burn its dead and caste their ashes to the holy waters.

The time for the Gai Jatra came. When Puskar Maske called on Hume to go with him to the festival, he told him many would attend that year, that the procession of the sacred cows would be long, very long. 'Each family that has suffered a death during the year must send a cow to the Gai Jatra,' he explained. 'Or, if they have no cow, a young boy to represent one. It is important. Only on the day of Gai Jatra does Yama open the gates to the Underworld and let souls enter for their judgement. And the way to the Underworld is difficult. There are fires to be avoided, rivers to be crossed. It is a way beset with dangers of all sorts. People believe the departed souls need a sacred cow to guide them, that they hold their tails and are led safely to the gates and arrive there in good time.'

It was indeed a long procession. When Hume reached the Durbar Square he saw that the cows and boys from many families had already joined in a long line. Musicians played their flutes and drums, the family priests were in their white robes and gilded hats, and monks in their coloured robes. The cows, washed and groomed, were decorated with coloured pigments and coloured cloth. The boys wore cow-head masks with two long wooden horns protruding and large black circles painted round the eyes, and necklaces and gaily coloured cloth draped around their bodies. A length of white cloth trailed behind each boy, symbolising the tails the departed souls would hold.

'And at the Underworld, in the gloom before Yama's Gates, the sacred cow has a further task,' Puskar Maske explained. 'The souls of the dead from everywhere, a great multitude, will be waiting there. The cows will thrust their horns between the gates, holding them open to allow the souls to enter.'

Hume and Puskar Maske watched until the procession finished. 'Yes, the Gai Jatra is truly timely, Hume,' Puskar Maske said as they left the Durbar Square. 'Many souls need help. But there will be no carnival this afternoon, not this year, or any crowds to watch the clowning, the lampooning. No frivolities. Kathmandu is not in the mood for that.'

A month later the Indra Jatra came, the great eight-day festival for Indra the King of Heaven. It is said that once in the earliest of times, Indra's mother, Dagini, wanted parijat flowers as an ornament for her Tij festival. Although not growing in Heaven, these flowers bloomed in abundance in the Valley of Nepal; so Indra, disguised as a human and hidden in a blanket of mist, came to the valley to get them for her. The people of the valley caught him in the act of picking the flowers and, thinking him a common thief—not realising his divinity—bound his hands and feet and imprisoned him in Kathmandu.

Before long Dagini came looking for her son and told people who their prisoner was. They were crest-fallen at their mistake, but at the same time proud to have captured the King of Heaven. Promising that mist and dew would always come to the valley each year to nourish the crops, Dagini had Indra released from prison. People made much of the god, worshipped him and offered sacrifices to him; and they commemorate this every year with the Indra Jatra.

That year Hume went with Puskar Maske to the festival. Even though the Gurkhas were just outside the walls, the people of Kathmandu had thrown off their gloom and were celebrating. People had gathered at the Durbar Square waiting for the hoisting of Indra's pole. There were the men of Kathmandu, women in their bright reds, golds and blues, and their children in their best clothes. The Raj Guru and many Brahman priests were there and Buddhist monks in their robes. Detachments of soldiers stood armed with muskets and kukhries.

As the pole was slowly raised, there was a loud cheering and Indra's name was heard against the roar of muskets, the clashing of cymbals and throbbing of drums. At the exact moment determined by astrologers, Puskar Maske assured Hume, the pole was secured upright. Priests offered sacrifices to Indra. Indra's flag, its sun representing the power of the mind and its moon representing valour, was unfurled at the top of the pole. At the foot of the pole, there was a little cage holding an image of Indra bound as a prisoner—in remembrance of his capture—and beside it stood a little elephant, Indra's vehicle cast in gold.

As the festivities began, people brought out their images of the gods so they, too, could watch; images of the Black Bhairab and of Akash the Blue Bhairab with his viscous fangs and his angry eyes turned upwards towards Heaven. In the Durbar Square near the Monkey God Gate to the Palace, the great face of the White Bhairab, his fangs protruding from his snarling mouth, looked out from his place in the wall. The lattice-work that covered the face at other times had been removed.

The Bhaku demon dancers slashed their swords in an anger that could only be appeased by draughts of blood from the cocks and goats being sacrificed. They dashed through the streets to the palace where a horned buffalo, drunk from raksi and enraged, was waiting for them. Near the palace they fought the maddened beast with swords and daggers, killed it and drank its blood in honour of the Bhairab. Hume watched the elephant dancers in their enormous trunked masks, their great swishing tails knocking people to the ground as they meandered through the streets in a symbolic search for Indra in his cage. Dagini's representative, the Lakhe dancer, pranced along, darting here and there in search of her imprisoned son.

In the late afternoon of the last day of the Indra Jatra, Hume and Puskar Maske walked to the house of the Kumari, the little living goddess of Kathmandu. A royal stand was set up nearby, with Jaya Malla seated on a throne and attended by several of his courtiers and generals including General Josi, and a detachment of the royal guard was there. In front of the Kumari's House were three wooden chariots, one very large and the others smaller, each carrying brightly coloured temples which were shaded by gilded umbrellas and festooned with flowers. The men standing beside the wheels of the chariots were ready to haul them in procession through the town. Bands were playing, masked demons were jumping about, and Buddhist monks were ringing their hand-bells. Brahman priests sacrificed a goat beside the wheels of the Kumari's chariot.

'They sacrifice to pacify the Bhairab, Hume,' Puskar Maske said. 'It is to ensure no one is killed under the chariot's great wheels as it makes its way through the streets. It is necessary. Crowds will press close during the procession.'

The crowd cheered as the little Kumari, bejewelled and dressed as a princess in scarlet and gold, a golden ornament and flowers in her hair and black circles painted around her large almond-shaped eyes, left her house and was helped into her chariot. Her two little boy attendants, one representing Ganesh and the other the Bhairab, were also helped into their chariots.

The chariots moved off, creaking as they were pulled by straining men to the sound of firing muskets by the royal guard, the clanging of the Buddhist monk's bells and the cheering of the now excited crowd. Jaya Malla bowed low to the little Kumari as she passed. Then he tossed coins into the crowd. The three chariots edged their way through the mass of people, then lumbered along the streets of Kathmandu during the rest of the evening, while the little Kumari sat there accepting the adoration of the crowds.

'Later the Kumari will anoint the King,' Puskar Maske said to Hume. 'She will put a red tika mark on his forehead and bless him. It gives him the right to rule in Kathmandu for another year. It is symbolic, Hume. But it is important.'

That evening in the Durbar Square, Hume noticed that long tubes were placed to come from the snarling mouth of the Seto Bhairab, the White Bhairab, in his place on the wall near the Monkey God gate to the palace.

'The White Bhairab has an important place in the revelry,' Puskar Maske told Hume. 'Soon, chan will spill out through the tubes from pots placed behind his face. People will have much liquor to drink.'

'Even this year?' Hume asked.

'Yes, and many will bring their own supply of chan and strong raksi. People have been saving it for the Indra Jatra. It will be the last of their stocks. Many will celebrate tonight. It happens every year. It is permitted.'

By evening a lot of liquor had passed the lips of many of the men of Kathmandu. At first Hume thought the merrymaking was natural enough—a relief from the great tensions of recent months—but by the time night had set in he saw how far the drinking had gone. Men dazed from raksi staggered around the Durbar Square, wandered about the streets then slept on the steps of the pagodas and in doorways of houses. Drunken demon dancers cavorted and drunken musicians roamed about the town, banging their drums, clashing their cymbals, singing. Soldiers, too, were drunk, both Newars and some of the Nagar mercenaries whom Jaya Malla had engaged. Some called loudly to each other, laughing and joking, and tormenting any who were still sober. People became lost and searched for their way home. Some approached the town gates, demanding that they be opened so they could pass through out into the fields. But outside, they would have been easy prey for the Gurkhas and the guards turned them back.

Later that night the moon hung large and yellow over Kathmandu, whitening the open spaces and blackening the shadows. The moonlight streamed down onto the Durbar Square, touching the gilded eaves of the pagodas, the images of the gods, the great bell and the royal palace, the house of the Kumari and Jaya Malla's stand now empty nearby. As he turned a corner near the Jagannath Temple, Puskar Maske placed a hand on Hume's shoulder and quickly drew him back into the shadow of its walls. 'Quiet, Hume,' he whispered. 'Look,' he pointed. 'What do you see?' Hume heard the urgency in his voice.

They peered across the moonlit square. Beside Lord Shiva's Temple, they saw a group of men, a score or more, huddled together in the dark shadows.

'It is strange they are there,' Puskar Maske said. 'So many. They are in uniform, soldiers, armed I think.'

They were certainly armed. Hume could make out the muskets of some of them. As they watched, one stepped out from the shadow of the temple into the moonlight.

Puskar Maske pressed Hume's arm. 'A Gurkha, Hume.'

Silently they watched.

'All Gurkhas,' Puskar Maske said. 'So the Gurkha King has come. They are his soldiers. Many Gurkhas will be inside the walls—in our town. Gurkhas are amongst us.' Hume heard the fear in his voice.

Quickly, and keeping to the shadows, they crept away, past the image of the Black Bhairab towards the palace. Then along past the Kumari's House, beyond the flaming torches, they could see more Gurkhas, a large detachment, entering the Durbar Square. It was then that the alarm was given. A Newar soldier came running. 'Gurkhas!' he yelled. 'Gurkhas! Gurkhas!' he repeated over and over again. 'Gurkhas are here. The gates are open. Gurkhas are in our town!'

Others took up the cry. Soon everyone in Kathmandu knew the Gurkhas had come, people in the Durbar Square, in the streets and, before long, those still in their houses. All knew except those still too dazed with chan and raksi, or sleeping with their drunken dreams.

Great panic reigned in Kathmandu. People remembered the fate of the noseless and lipless men and boys of Kirtipur, their grinning skull-like faces. All had heard the Gurkhas' threats to them. As the torches in the streets were extinguished, people scurried for safety, knocking into each other and hindering each other's way. Fathers marshalled their wives and children. And the priests, lamas, ministers, some sardars and generals, and soldiers still dazed from their strong raksi sought safety. Most fled to their homes. Some found safe places in dark recesses well out of the moonlight, the little courts, in the temples, high up on the eaves of the pagodas and in the military headquarters of the Kot. The streets, the open spaces of the Durbar Square, still bright under the light of the large ascending moon, became clear of people, all but empty.

Hume had been amongst the first to leave the Durbar Square. He ran quickly to his home, to Maneka and his baby son, determined to be there before Gurkha soldiers could molest them. He had prepared as best he could for this, for their protection. He had his stock of food and water on the top floor of his house. And his sword and pistol. Drawing up the ladders, he could hold out there, beat off an attack for a long time if necessary.

Maneka welcomed Hume tearfully, holding her baby son tightly to her bosom. Fear dominated the usual serene beauty of her face, and he took them in his arms, mother and son. 'Don't be frightened Maneka,' he said. 'We are not in danger yet. It might be that the Gurkhas will not seek us.' He pointed to the ladder. 'And if they do we will be safe up there.' Beckoning to Maneka's maids, he made ready for them all to go up the ladders to the top floor of the house.

But before he could move he heard a loud rapping at the door and a call from the night outside. He opened the door to see Father Michaelangelo there, the pointed hood of his white habit high over his head. He ran inside and Hume locked the door tightly again.

Father Michaelangelo pulled the hood clear of his worried face and breathed heavily as he spoke. 'The Devil has come, my son. Up from his Hell. His hoards run rife in Kathmandu. They will slaughter, dismember the people, and rape and pillage. They are going to commit the most obscene of sins, the most heinous evils. May the merciful Christ protect us.' He blessed himself and sat fingering his beads.

'Father Matteo? Is he safe?' Hume asked.

'He is at the church. Some of our flock have gathered there and he is with them. They await the Gurkhas there, wait for mutilation or death and martyrdom in the house of the Lord.'

'Can they defend themselves?' Hume asked.

The Capuchin shrugged. 'How can they against the Gurkha King? Except by prayer.'

'How can I help, Father? You have come to my house. What do you want of me?'

'Go to Jaya Malla, or to the generals. General Josi, perhaps. You have influence with them. Ask them to send soldiers to our church, to make a guard around it. There are women and their children helpless inside.'

Perhaps it could help, Hume thought. But before he answered there was another knocking at the door. He opened it to admit his servant, who seized his hand and knelt to beg protection, then sat trembling beside the Capuchin. Recovering his composure a little, but still stammering, the servant told Hume what he had seen that night.

'I was in the Durbar Square, master. When the Gurkhas came, I hid. I climbed high on the Taleju's Temple and hid there. I should not have hidden there. It was to that temple Jaya Malla came with some of his generals and his soldiers. His Nagars from India and others surrounded the temple. Looking down below I could see them. In the moonlight I could see them clearly. But I also saw the Gurkhas come. There were so many of them. I saw the Gurkhas attack. I was frightened of being seen, so I crept back further under the eaves and hid my face. But I could still hear. I heard the Gurkhas calling their "Ayo gurkha, ayo gurkha !", and their muskets firing, the swords clashing, their cursing and yelling. But also the screams of the wounded people.'

He stopped talking and looked around at Maneka and her maids and the Capuchin as though he had only just noticed them. 'No one is safe here, master. Not now.'

'Please go on,' Hume said.

'I hid up in the temple for a long time whilst there was fighting. Then I thought it was the end. The end of me, master. I heard a terrible explosion, a noise as loud as I had never thought to hear. There was a great flash of flame. The whole temple was lit up, high, even to where

I hid. And the great temple shook with the anger of its goddess. I could smell the gunpowder as the thick smoke rose up. When it started to clear I looked down again and saw all the bodies lying on the temple steps. I saw the rest of the Gurkha soldiers had drawn back. Then, as I watched, I saw Jaya Malla and his generals, surrounded by their own soldiers, leave the temple. They hurried off towards the palace.'

Hume turned to Father Michaelangelo. 'So Jaya Malla is defending Kathmandu. Perhaps he would send a detachment to guard your church.'

This cheered the Capuchin a little. But not for long, because Hume's servant was saying, 'No, master, he is not. He is leaving Kathmandu. Because of all the confusion below, I saw my chance to get away. I climbed down from the temple. I joined in with Jaya Malla's soldiers and hurried off with them. I heard them talking. They had exploded the gunpowder to break a way through the Gurkhas. They said Jaya Malla was leaving Kathmandu, going to Lalitpatan, with his relatives from the palace. He was taking his Nagars from India and his light cannon and any other soldiers who wanted to go with him.'

'Are you sure of that?' Hume asked.

'I am sure, master. He leaves even now.'

With Jaya Malla gone, Hume realised that Kathmandu would not resist the Gurkhas—at least no more than his servant had told them of. And if Kathmandu did not resist, Hume saw no reason why the Gurkha King should harm its people. It was not like Kirtipur, which had resisted for many years. Prithvi Shah had already made a warning of Kirtipur for all the valley. He had no need for another in Kathmandu.

'Your worst fears might be unfounded,' Hume said to Father Michaelangelo. 'Perhaps, now that Jaya Malla has gone, the Gurkhas' occupation will be peaceful.'

But the Capuchin did not agree. 'It's the Devil who has come,' he said and quickly blessed himself again.

'He promised an amnesty if there is no resistance,' Hume pointed out to him.

The Capuchin shook his head vigorously. 'Don't let the Devil deceive you, my son. He is the Prince of Lies. He deceived the poor people of Kirtipur. He promised them an amnesty and then he mutilated them. Remember the men and boys.' The priest looked towards the cradle where Maneka had just placed the baby. 'Even the children's faces he cut.'

'What would you do now that Jaya Malla has gone?' Hume asked.

'We will flee from Kathmandu. Go to Lalitpatan. Follow Jaya Malla there,' the priest replied.

Then Maneka spoke. She had been listening anxiously. 'I think Father Michaelangelo is right,' she said. 'Let us leave now. Let us go to Lalitpatan.'

Father Michaelangelo stood up as though already starting on his way. 'We must do that,' he said. 'To save the child, you must leave Kathmandu.'

Maneka lifted Francis from his cradle, stood beside Hume and took his hand. 'We have to leave immediately,' she said. 'We cannot stay.'

'But the Gurkhas might not harm the people here, Maneka,' Hume said. 'They seem to have no need to.'

'They had no need to harm the children of Kirtipur,' Maneka said, holding their baby closely. 'Yes, we will leave Kathmandu,' Hume agreed.

He gathered together the few things they would need and could carry, some clothing, food for the baby, his pistol and sword, and of course he did not forget the rest of the gold from the cavity behind the bricks on the top floor of the house. 'Please take the Holy Virgin and Ganesh from my altar and bring them with you,' Maneka told her maids. 'And the painting of Christ of the Sacred Heart.' They left the house with Father Michaelangelo and walked along the now deserted streets to the Capuchins' house where fifty or so people were crowded inside.

'We are going to Lalitpatan,' Hume told Father Matteo.

'You might be safer staying here,' the priest replied.

'No. The Devil is here amongst us in Kathmandu. He is here,' Father Michaelangelo said. 'True, he might come to Lalitpatan. But he might not. We shall see. Surely the forces of the Lord will stop him, throw him back into his Hell.'

Father Matteo obviously doubted this, but he did not question his superior. Instead he went into the church to talk to the congregation waiting there, to tell them of the proposal to go to Lalitpatan, and to find out who wanted to go.

'Only a few will go with you,' he told Father Michaelangelo. 'Most of them will take their chances here. I will stay with them and continue my ministry here.'

Twenty of them started walking to Lalitpatan that night with Maneka's maids and Hume's own servant and those from the Capuchins' church. They wanted to catch up with Jaya Malla and his soldiers so they could have protection on the way. Passing near the Durbar Square, Hume saw Gurkhas and a few Newars who had come back out of their houses. And a crowd had gathered around Jaya Malla's royal stand, where torches were alight again and oil lamps were burning in their clay bowls.

Some people stood on Jaya Malla's stand, clearly visible in the light from the torches. One was the Gurkha King. Hume had no doubt of it. 'That is certainly Prithvi Shah.' he said to himself. He recalled that morning on Mount Chandragiri, the morning when he first looked down on the Valley of Nepal. Prithvi Shah had stood there, taller than most, Aryan-looking, black bearded, and Hume imagined the sternness of his face and his hard, dark eyes. Hume was close enough to see his turban with its gold badges and jewels and topped with a plume, his blue tunic brocaded and with a fur collar. In his hand he held his talawar, the torch light glistening on its bejewelled hilt, and his kukhri was held in the red cummerbund around his waist.

Hume moved closer. Most seated on the royal stand with Prithvi Shah were his own generals. Now he could make out Maneka's cousin, Atal Thapa, and Surpratap with the scar on his face and the missing eye. But he also saw Newars there, ministers and generals from Jaya Malla's Court, even General Josi and the Dewar and the Raj Guru.

The three chariots were in front of the House of the Kumari, and the Brahmans were again sacrificing a goat and letting its blood spill over the great wooden wheels. The devil dancers again wore their masks, the Buddhist priests were ringing their hand-bells. Men stood by the great yokes ready to haul the chariots again. And the little Kumari came out of her house with her two boy attendants, and they mounted their chariots which were drawn off to stop before Prithvi Shah on the royal stand.

As Hume watched, Prithvi Shah left the stand, climbed into the Kumari's chariot and stood beside the little living goddess. He joined his hands in a namaste and bowed low, at which she took her coloured powder and, reaching up with her little arms, anointed his forehead, and marked it with the red tika, the blessing through which she gave him the right to rule in Kathmandu.

'He is king here now,' Father Michaelangelo said unhappily. 'Not only the King of Gurkha, but also King of Kathmandu. I pray that Christ protects us.'

They hurried away from the Durbar Square, on through the deserted streets, out through the town gate and into the fields. They followed after Jaya Malla on the way to Lalitpatan.

Sixteen

Outside the walls of Kathmandu in the fields Hume and Maneka, Father Michaelangelo and the others eventually caught up with Jaya Malla and his soldiers, and General Vamsi whom Hume had seen after the fall of Naldum and who had remained loyal to the Malla King. Jaya Malla had sent a vakil ahead to Lalitpatan to advise of his coming, and Tej Narsinha Malla was waiting at the town gate to meet them.

An officer of Tej Narsinha's guard brought Hume and Maneka to quarters in the palace. Maneka lost her fear a little and her tension eased. She fed her baby and put him to bed for the rest of the night. 'I am most thankful to be here. I thank you for bringing me,' she said to Hume. 'Who knows? The Gurkha King might never come to Lalitpatan. The British might send a larger force to help us. Might that be so, my husband?'

'We could hope for that,' he told her, moving close and taking her in his arms.

'Then our baby would be safe.'

'Of course.'

'Not like the boys of Kirtipur?'

'Not like those, Maneka.'

Next morning at the palace, Hume joined with the two Malla kings, both dressed as Newar generals, as well as General Vamsi and Kalidas and Bhinkhuar and the other Pradhans, to discuss what could be done. Jaya Malla sat scowling at the Pradhans, showing no love for them, or trust in them after their years of intrigue, no doubt remembering how they once drove him out of Lalitpatan, and blinded and killed his brother.

Nor did the Pradhans show any love for Jaya Malla. Their black eyes were turned away from him as they sat there, small men in brown tunics, their faces thin and dour. They would remember that, a few years ago when he came to Lalitpatan, Jaya Malla made them walk the streets dressed as women and beg for food, and imprisoned them.

Kalidas was first to speak. 'We all welcome you to Lalitpatan, Sire,' he said, only half-turning towards Jaya Malla. 'You have our loyal support. We will join forces and add the fighting men of Lalitpatan to those you have brought with you. Lalitpatan will be defended, and the

Gurkha King driven from the valley. Then we will restore Kathmandu to you.' The other Pradhans indicated their agreement.

Hume watched Jaya Malla looking back at them, the scowl still on his face. He has no option but to accept their offer, Hume thought. He depends on what support Lalitpatan can give.

Jaya Malla relaxed a little. 'And drive the Gurkhas from the valley, you say?'

'We say that, Sire.'

'The Gurkha force is strong, Kalidas.' Jaya Malla said, doubtfully.

But the following morning General Vamsi called on Hume with disturbing news. He had inspected the Lalitpatan defences and found that few preparations had been made to repel the Gurkhas. The guard on the gates had been strengthened and soldiers had been placed at vantage points on the walls. But that was all. Only a hundred or so Lalitpatan soldiers had been mobilised and those Jaya Malla had brought from Kathmandu were still in their quarters—there was no plan for defence. When General Vamsi complained to the Pradhans, they told him they were in the course of attending to those matters.

That evening Hume had the most disturbing news. General Vamsi heard from a Lalitpatan sardar that the Pradhans were bargaining with the Gurkha King. They were offering to admit the Gurkhas to Lalitpatan, let them take the town with no resistance and hand over Jaya Malla and Tej Narsinha. In return they wanted to keep their birta grants and fortunes and to continue in power in Lalitpatan. The Gurkha King had invited them to meet with him the next day at Tekhudobhan.

The news enraged Jaya Malla, who wanted his Nagar mercenaries to execute the Pradhans immediately, lamenting that he had not done this years previously. But General Vamsi stopped him, arguing that the Pradhans would have the support of the Lalitpatan force, which his own soldiers could not cope with. Jaya Malla eventually agreed. So it was decided that Jaya Malla and Tej Narsinha would go to Bhaktapur with General Vamsi and their soldiers. Hume and Maneka and the others were invited to go with them.

'We will be safe in Bhaktapur, Maneka,' Hume explained when she heard the news. 'It is a stronger town. Its walls are stout. Ranjit Malla can muster a strong army and I'm told he has Tamang mercenaries.

'Will it be safe for our baby to go? It is a long walk across the fields.'

'Yes. We will be with Jaya Malla's soldiers, and the Gurkha King is still busy in Kathmandu.'

To Hume's surprise Father Michaelangelo decided not to go with them to Bhaktapur. 'Those of my flock wish to stay here and to return to their homes in Kathmandu when it is safe,' he said. 'News has come from Father Matteo that Surpratap, the one whose face I healed, says that Christians won't be harmed. I shall stay here with my flock.'

Next morning as they left for Bhaktapur, Hume saw the Pradhans on their way to meet the Gurkha King at Tekhudobhan. 'They seemed apprehensive about the meeting,' General Vamsi told Hume. 'Untrustworthy themselves, they do not trust others. Perhaps they have reason for concern.'

'That is likely,' Hume said. 'They will find it hard to bargain with the Gurkha King.

'It is strange,' General Vamsi remarked. 'I hear that last night one of them, Bhinkhuar I think, gave his fortune to the poor. Why should he do that?'

'Yes, it is strange,' Hume agreed.

At Bhaktapur, Ranjit Malla had accommodation at the palace for the two Malla kings and their retinues, and also for Hume and Maneka and their baby. General Vamsi left to meet Bhaktapur's General Amatya and take his soldiers off to barracks to join some of the men of Bhaktapur. The next day and those following, Bhaktapur was on the alert waiting a Gurkha attack; but the days passed and turned to weeks with no sign of the Gurkha army.

Hume occupied himself with Bhaktapur's defences. He had brought his pistol and sword, and he got a musket from General Vamsi for himself and one for his servant. With General Vamsi he would inspect Bhaktapur's readiness at the gates and on the town walls. Hume improved the security of his own quarters with stout planks to reinforce the door and windows, in case Gurkha soldiers should, in the frenzy of battle, attack Maneka and his son.

It worried Maneka.

'It is only a precaution,' he assured her. 'No more than that. I told you that Bhaktapur is strong. And what is more, Ranjit Malla has engaged Tamang mercenaries to support his own men.'

'The baby is our first concern,' Maneka said.

'Of course.'

Maneka was kept busy with their son, Francis, a good deal of the time. And she set up an altar on a table and put there her painting of the Christ of the Sacred Heart and the little statues she had brought from Kathmandu.

Then one day, much to Hume and Maneka's surprise, Father Michaelangelo arrived. He was alone. The Capuchin's flock had returned to Kathmandu. He had started out with them, but getting to Tekhudobhan he turned and made for Bhaktapur. Hume saw he was greatly upset.

'The Devil is at work again,' he said, feeling for his beads. 'He was at work at Tekhudobhan. I saw it by the river bank. It was the Pradhans of Lalitpatan he sent to Hell, unshriven, without the mercy of even the gods they have.'

'A crowd was gathered on the bank of the Bagmati,' Father Michaelangelo's voice was shrill. 'I saw the Gurkha soldiers lead the Pradhans in, the six of them, naked except for loincloths, their hair tied up on top in a knot away from their necks. The Gurkha executioners took them and started to bind their arms closely to their bodies with strong ropes. Then I heard a loud roaring—one of the Pradhans started roaring like a lion. He broke away. Roaring he ran, waving his arms madly, eyes glaring and his mouth frothing. Past Prithvi Shah he ran, past the Gurkha soldiers, through the crowd, into the fields and away towards the surrounding mountains. It was the last I saw of him.'

The priest stopped talking, blessed himself and grasped his beads. 'And the other five Pradhans. I saw it. They were bound. One, Kalidas I think, was made kneel, head bowed, and a thick string was tied to the rope at his back. A Devil's henchman held it to stop him toppling forward. The executioner stood above him, his talawar raised high. I saw the Devil himself raise a hand, a signal. The sword flashed down swishing and cut off Kalidas's head, severed in one blow. His eyes turned upwards, his head fell to the ground. His body tumbled after it as the henchman let go the string. Then, one by one, the other four Pradhans were beheaded.'

'But that was not all,' Father Michaelangelo continued. 'Funeral pyres had been built beside the river bank. The Pradhans' remains were placed amongst the wood. To my horror, I saw the Pradhans' wives come, dressed in bright saris, bejewelled and with flowers in their hair. They had to be supported as they walked to the funeral pyres. Their eyes were fixed ahead, their faces frozen, frozen in fear I thought, or from the effect of drugs. Satis, they were placed on the wood beside their husbands' bodies, and the pyres were lit. I had to leave that place of horror. But I looked back to see the Devil standing there. I saw the rising flames and heard the satis' screams.'

The Capuchin bowed his head in prayer. Hume sat in silence and Maneka, tears in her eyes, knelt and prayed before the altar she had improvised.

When Father Michaelangelo took his leave, Maneka left the altar and stood close to Hume and took his hand. 'Great evil has come to the valley,' she said. 'And much sadness. We must leave. We must go with you to your home in Hollybrook, Francis and I.'

Hume stood beside Maneka and put his arm around her. 'You are suffering and it saddens me. But you are brave. Please keep being so. I will do my best to care for you and our little son both here and back in Hollybrook.'

When Hume met the three Malla kings, he found them with the Satbahalyas, General Vamsi and Bhaktapur's General Amatya. Ranjit Malla welcomed him. 'I offer you my apologies, Sir Hume Clarke, for not inviting you to my presence earlier,' he said slowly, and Hume saw how he had aged further even since their previous meeting. 'But matters have pressed heavily on me, and on my cousins here. Our valley is under attack, as you of course know. Bhaktapur, my own kingdom, is under threat. It is an unfortunate time for us. I should have liked to be more generous with my hospitality. I hope you will forgive me.'

'You are generous, Sire. I am most grateful for the refuge you have given me and my wife and baby son.' Hume replied.

'Prithvi Shah will come and attack us,' Ranjit Malla continued. 'Once I did not think he would. When Prithvi Shah was a young man he visited Bhaktapur and lived with me—for three years I think it was. We treated him well. He was a friend of my son Bir Narshina and he mourned for him when he was murdered.'

Hume had heard this before. At the mention of the murder, he noticed the Satbahalyas avoided their father's gaze.

'That was a long time ago,' Ranjit Malla said. 'But I remember Prithvi Shah well. Why should he want the Valley of Nepal? There are other places in the mountains he could take. He has already taken some of them. I ask everyone that.' He looked around the table but there was no answer except Jaya Malla's irritated grimace.

'And I remember the Capuchin priests who come from a country near your own,' he said looking at Hume. 'They were agents of the Black Bhairab in their black robes and trunks hanging down at the back, until I gave them white to wear. They are still here with me. I wrote to their Pope once. But of course we have our own gods, who mean much to me. Now, in my old age, I spend much time in worship. I have little time left.' He paused in thought. 'I told you that Prithvi Shah was my guest here once. Do you think he will attack my kingdom, Sir Hume

Clarke?'

'Of course he will attack. You have said that yourself.' Jaya Malla answered for Hume, his voice a growl, his face in an angry frown. 'Of course Prithvi Shah will attack. Without a doubt. Bhaktapur has to be defended. We must be ready, cousin. Prithvi Shah will show us no mercy.'

Jaya Malla looked towards the Satbahalyas. Still frowning, he said bluntly, 'I tell you all, the seven of you, it is I who command here now. Not your father you have long betrayed. I have never trusted you. I do not trust you now. Even now you would sell your father's kingdom to the Gurkha King.'

The Satbahalyas, alarmed, started to object.

'I will forestall your evil acts,' Jaya Malla continued. 'I will put you under guard and confine you to the palace.'

Ranjit Malla did not object. Jaya Malla beckoned to General Amatya, who went away to bring back a detachment of the Tamang mercenaries. They took the Satbahalyas and marched them off.

Some time later, a little before dark with the Himalayan massifs touched with pastel colours of dusk, Hume stood with General Vamsi on the walls of Bhaktapur near the western gate. They looked back over the fields towards Lalitpatan and saw in the distance a few horsemen and behind them a group of foot soldiers, and then more soldiers coming on the higher ground to the right. Alerted, General Vamsi hurried from the wall to find Jaya Malla and call the alarm. Hume stayed on watch and soon saw the Gurkha army advancing in force—thousands of men marching out of the dusk towards Bhaktapur. Quickly he, too, left to join Jaya Malla and his generals in the Durbar Square.

Jaya Malla had already strengthened the guard on each of the town gates and about the Durbar Square, and was dèploying his Nagar mercenaries and his cannon on the walls. 'I have called all the men of Bhaktapur to come with their arms ready to repel the Gurkhas,' he told Hume. 'And I am keeping Ranjit Malla's Tamang mercenaries in reserve. Those not guarding the Satbahalyas are still in their quarters in Kauche Tole. It is near the Nyatapola Temple. We can get them quickly if necessary.'

Night set in and Gurkhas reached the foot of Bhaktapur's hill—a dark night, moonless, lit weakly by pale stars. They came around from the west and gathered down below the eastern gate, out of range of fire. They waited there in silence except for murmurings, only the occasional clash of weapons or a shouted order. Two hours or more went by and

Jaya Malla and his generals used this time well in securing Bhaktapur's defences. Jaya Malla himself inspected the walls and gates, ensured that any gaps were filled, and strengthened positions where he thought it necessary. He mingled with his Nagar mercenaries and the men of Bhaktapur.

'My brave fighting men,' he called, 'You will crush the Gurkhas with me. I routed them at Kirtipur once and I will rout them here. You will defend Bhaktapur stoutly. I will reward you well when we repel the Gurkha horde.'

Towards midnight, a report came that the Gurkhas were mounting Bhaktapur's hill and moving up towards the eastern gate. Jaya Malla hurried there with his generals and Hume. The way was dark and the tall houses blocked even the starlight from the streets. But amongst a group of soldiers also on their way to the eastern gate, Hume thought he glimpsed one of the Satbahalyas.

At the gate, Jaya Malla mounted the wall and looked down on the approaching Gurkhas. 'Attack them! Attack!' he roared as he called to his generals. 'Open your fire. Attack!' Cannon and musket fire shattered the night. The Gurkhas drew back a little and again they waited. Then disturbing news came. A jemidar from Ranjit Malla's Guard reported that the Satbahalyas were out of the palace. The Tamang detachment guarding them had disobeyed orders and freed them.

Soon a flare lit up the eastern gate. Again Jaya Malla opened his fire down on the Gurkha army below the walls. But this time the Gurkhas did not retreat. Their van rushed the gate, now open wide for them to enter. The first Gurkhas ran through, ignoring the fire from the guards. It had no effect, even at close range. That gate taken, the Gurkhas surged into Bhaktapur, their war-cry, "Ayo gurkha, ayo gurkha !", echoing through the night. Then news came that a second Gurkha force was entering Bhaktapur through the northern gate and was advancing towards the Durbar Square. That gate, also, had been opened to admit them, and again the guards' fire had been ineffective, fire from their muskets harmless.

Back in his palace the old Ranjit Malla heard that the Satbahalyas had ordered the gates of Bhaktapur to be opened to admit the Gurkhas and had arranged for blank ammunition to be issued to the guards. The Satbahalyas had gone over to the Gurkha King and taken the Tamang mercenaries with them.

'I curse my sons. I curse the seven of them. Again they have betrayed me in my old age,' Ranjit Malla said angrily but with sadness in his face. 'I ask the just gods to punish them. And may the gods deal with my Tamang soldiers who betrayed me.' He thought for some moments, then called for General Amatya. 'Close up the Tamangs' doors in Kauche Tole,' he ordered. 'See they are strongly battened-up. Set the building on fire. Burn the rest of the Tamang soldiers there. I will not let those join the Gurkha King.'

The men defending Bhaktapur fought ferociously that night. They built barricades in the streets and set houses on fire, their flames rising high in the darkness for light to see the Gurkhas as they came. Jaya Malla and the generals and Hume joined the men of Bhaktapur and the Nagar mercenaries to fight street by street, hand to hand, over the bodies of the dead and wounded. Sweating faces were aglow from the flames, swords flashed in the firelight as they slashed; and small cannon, both Jaya Malla's and the Gurkha's, roared and echoed between the houses in the streets. All through the night the defenders of Bhaktapur fought bravely. But gradually, tired and outnumbered, they retreated, and when the dawn broke they were half-way back towards the Durbar Square.

A heavy pall of smoke hung over Bhaktapur from the burning of the night, which blocked out the early sunlight and cast a grey gloom over the town; buildings smouldered, many houses and the Tamangs' pyre in Kauche Tole. That morning the fighting continued in the streets. Hundreds of Gurkha soldiers climbed onto the roof tops to avoid Jaya Malla's cannon. From vantage points high up on the tiles of the houses, they followed the course of the fighting in the streets below, directing their musket fire and their arrows down at the men of Bhaktapur.

All that day the battle raged and sporadically throughout the night, and Bhaktapur's defenders still fought well and bravely. But by the next day the Gurkhas, advancing from all directions, had won their way through the streets up to the Durbar Square. Still the defenders fought, and still Jaya Malla led them. Many times Gurkha detachments charged into the Square, attacking amongst the temples, fighting under the eaves of the pagodas. Each time they were repulsed. Many men on each side died that day and many were wounded, their bodies lying beneath the images of the gods like litter in the spaces between the temples.

The afternoon brought disaster to Bhaktapur's defenders. While leading a detachment to repel a Gurkha thrust, Jaya Malla was shot in the leg. It was a severe wound, one that not only disabled him then but before long was to cause his death. Nagar mercenaries rushed to his aid and fought off his attackers. They lifted him and carried him across the

Durbar Square, and took him, bleeding and weakened, through the Mula Chok, the Golden Gate with its images of Kali and the Tantric gods, and into the palace. It was the end of the defence of Bhaktapur. As Jaya Malla was out of the battle, the Gurkhas surged into the Durbar Square, their war-cry reverberating loudly amongst the temples.

Leaderless now and confused, the men of Bhaktapur tried to withdraw further but, surrounded, they had no place to go. At bay, they fought for a time. Then a sardar appeared at a palace window and, looking down at the Gurkha King in the Durbar Square below, he waved to signal Ranjit Malla's surrender.

Seventeen

After Ranjit Malla surrendered, the Gurkha King stood at the Golden Gate demanding entry to the palace, and no one dared refuse him or stand in his way. Before he entered he called his brother Surpratap and ordered, 'Care must be taken in occupying Bhaktapur. Tell my generals so. Looting is forbidden. The people of Bhaktapur are not to be harmed and their lives should return to normal. Have the priests attend to the dead. Have the wounded helped, be they my men or those of Bhaktapur. Disarm Jaya Malla's Nagar mercenaries and pay them what is due and send them back to India. Send Ranjit Malla's soldiers back to their homes.'

After Prithvi Shah entered the palace with his retinue, Maneka's cousin, Atal Thapa, left and came over to Hume. 'I am pleased to see you are unharmed, Sir Hume Clarke. I hope my cousin Maneka is well. I worried for her safety in the heat of battle.'

'She is well and safe,' Hume told him, 'although anxious, I am sure. She cares for the baby in our quarters in the palace. Do you wish to visit her?'

Maneka made no attempt to hide her relief at Hume's return. Both smiling and weeping when she saw him, she clung close to him for a long time, and Hume saw her lips moving in a prayer of thanks.

Atal Thapa waited until Maneka regained her composure, then said to her, 'I thank my own gods for your safety, cousin, and for your son's. Many have died these days, and many have suffered wounds. Let us hope it is the end to conflict in the Valley of Nepal.'

Maneka left Hume's arms and looked at her cousin. 'Everyone should hope that,' she said. 'But is it the hope of the Gurkha King? Does he really want the valley to be peaceful again?'

'He does, I assure you,' Atal Thapa told her. 'His lifelong aim has been peace. For our people to be able to live in peace.'

Maneka looked at him doubtfully.

'It is true, cousin. He will be more than King of Gurkha now. He will be King of Nepal. It will be a strong Nepal. He has united much of our mountains, not just Gurkha and Nawakot. He has Makwanpur to the south, Palpa is friendly and he has much control over many of the

Chaubisi princedoms to the west, and further west the Baisi princedoms. Before long Kumaon will come with him, and to the east other Sen Rajas. There will be a nation of Nepal that is able to defend itself.' He glanced at Hume, as he continued, 'Against the British or anyone else. The people of the valley will be secure and so will be able to live in peace again.'

Hume made no comment. He thought that what Atal Thapa said was true enough. It was Maneka who spoke. 'It is strange,' she said, her eyes still glistening from her tears, 'that so many have died in battle, so many wounded—even the boys of Kirtipur disfigured for this peace you speak of. It is a cruel path to peace.'

'Strange perhaps, Maneka, and cruel. I do not disagree. But believe me, cousin, it has been necessary,' Atal Thapa replied.

'Will you go back to Kathmandu, to your house?' Atal Thapa asked, turning to Hume. 'I shall do all I can to see both you and Maneka are well received there.'

Before Hume could reply, the door opened. It was Puskar Maske, a broad smile across his face, amused at Hume's surprise. He joined his hands in a namaste and bowed low to the three of them in turn. 'Perhaps you did not expect me, Hume,' he said.

Hume did not. 'Thank God you are safe, Puskar Maske. I've been concerned for you. But how is it you are here, free apparently?'

'I am safe, Hume, and whole as you can see. But last night I was by no means sure I would be. The fighting here was fierce.'

'You fought last night?' Hume wondered. He had seen nothing of him with Jaya Malla and General Vamsi and the rest, heard nothing of him.

'I was with Prithvi Shah,' he replied, looking serious now, the smile leaving his face.

'You've gone over to them, to the Gurkhas?'

'I fought for the King of Nepal, not the Gurkha King, Puskar Maske replied. 'Not only me. There are many who support Prithvi Shah now—General Josi, Ari Lawat, the Raj Guru and many others, even the old priest Vajracrya, Lady Bachhla. Yes many, Hume.'

Late that day the Malla kings came together to meet with the Gurkha King. Atal Thapa and Puskar Maske had been summoned to attend and they took Hume with them. They found the three kings seated together at one end of a table with their generals, Vamsi and Amatya, in the room where Hume had first met Ranjit Malla on his earlier visit to Bhaktapur. The room was as Hume remembered, richly furnished and with gilded images of the gods, Lord Shiva and Vishnu, Ganesh, Parbati and others. But this time the room was darkening. The sun was gone from the Durbar Square outside and the windows were closed to the dusk light, and the oil lamps struggled in the dimness.

Several of the Gurkha King's retinue were standing at one side of the room. Hume noticed Surpratap with his one eye and the scar on his face, and Puskar Maske pointed out General Ram Krishna Kunwar who had led the Gurkhas into Bhaktapur, and Generals Bih Bhadra Thapa and Bamsharaj Pandey who were the victors against the British army at Pauwa. General Josi and the Raj Guru were also there.

The three Malla kings sat in silence, downcast, depressed. Jaya Malla was with fever and obviously suffering from his wound. Light from the oil lamps glimmered on the gilded image of Vishnu; but the images of the other gods were almost lost in the darkness at the edges of the room.

'The Malla kings have come to their end,' Puskar Maske whispered to Hume. 'They would do well to prepare for their passage to the Underworld. To beseech Yama to be kind to them.'

A door opened and all eyes turned towards it. It was the Gurkha King. He strode into the room with his head held high, proudly, a figure of great authority. He stood at one end of the table and looked along at the Malla kings seated at the other end, almost huddled together.

Hume had seen the Gurkha King only twice: once on Mount Chandragiri, and on the night of the Indra Jatra when leaving Kathmandu and he had watched the little Kumari Goddess place the tika mark on his forehead. Up close now, Hume saw he was indeed a truly commanding figure, with a strong face and dark, penetrating eyes, his bearing erect and confident. He was dressed in his general's uniform of blue and gold, the turban with tall plumes, the red cummerbund holding his kukhri, his sword at his side. When he turned towards the lamplight the jewels in his turban and those decorating the hilt of his sword flashed. He stood there in complete command, the absolute master.

For some time he looked across at the three Malla kings, his face severe, frowning. Then he seated himself and beckoned to those in his retinue to come and stand behind him, not close, a little away from his person.

The silence continued. Light from the lamps flickered on Vishnu's gilded image. All waited for the Gurkha King to speak. Then Hume saw the frown leave his stern face; he broke into a laugh, throwing his head back and laughing loudly. Surpratap joined in his brother's laughter and then the others in his retinue, their laughter resounding around the room.

There was no laughter from the Malla kings. They looked back, their faces tense, the strain of defeat weighing heavily on them. For each of them it was the end. And more than that, it was the end of an ancient dynasty, the end of the Malla Dynasty which their distant ancestor, Ari Malla, had founded some six centuries before.

Hume heard Jaya Malla speak. 'Do not laugh, Gurkhas. There is no cause for laughter at our defeat. True, you have defeated me. That I fully recognise. But I myself have been a worthy foe for you. You must not laugh. Not at our tragedy.'

With that the Gurkha King stopped laughing, as did his retinue behind him, and Hume saw a touch of sympathy in his face.

'There were times when it was I who was the victor,' Jaya Malla continued. 'I was the victor when you first came and attacked Kirtipur. I did not laugh then. Once I defeated you at Nawakot. Once I defeated you at Naldum. For many years, for much of my reign, it was I who kept you from the valley. Victory then was no cause for laughter.'

The Gurkha King, thoughtful now, moved his head slowly in agreement.

'In defeat I will offer you my praise,' Jaya Malla said. 'The Gurkha Kingdom which you came from is small and barbarous. That you cannot deny. Yet you have conquered. I have watched you closely—your victories in the Chaubisi, in Makwanpur, against Mir Kasim the Nawab of Bengal, in the Baisi. You defeated the British when they came. You did all that. I praise you for your triumph here today.'

'But you must know,' Jaya Malla continued, 'that my end and the end of my cousin kings have not come by my own hand or theirs. We have reigned amidst treachery. We have long been betrayed. There were the Pradhans, there are the Satbahalyas and there are others.' He glanced towards those standing behind the Gurkha King. 'Some with you now are traitors. You trust such traitors at your peril.'

The Gurkha King looked along the table to Tej Narsinha Malla. 'I deal with traitors justly,' he said. 'There were your Pradhans of Lalitpatan who were treacherous and evil. It is well known how they disposed of their kings, that they blinded Rajya Malla and murdered Viswajit Malla. And they drove Dalmardan Shah, my brother, from the throne. You accepted his throne then. You let the Pradhans put you in my brother's place. But they had no loyalty to you. They opened the gates of Lalitpatan for me and came to me at Tekhudobhan seeking their reward. I dealt with the traitors justly there. I had their heads cut off. You are as treacherous as they were.'

Hume saw Tej Narsinha Malla wince. But he said nothing and turned his gaze down to the table in front of him.

'Have you no reply?' the Gurkha King asked. 'No reply to my charge of treachery?'

'None,' Tej Narsinha Malla said. 'I am at your mercy.'

'You showed no mercy when you took my brother's throne.'

'True, I showed none then.'

'And I shall show none now. You will leave here under guard, be put in irons and confined at Lakshmipur. You will stay there at my pleasure or till your death.'

Tej Narsinha Malla was silent.

Then the Gurkha King turned and beckoned to Atal Thapa, who left the room to return with Ranjit Malla's seven illegitimate sons, the Satbahalyas, who were now under guard, their arms bound. His frown was dark as he watched them standing there. 'You also are traitors,' he said to them. 'For a long time you have betrayed your father. You, too, sought to let me have a kingdom in return for your own security and so you could keep your own power and wealth. You invited me into Bhaktapur, opened its town gates for me and issued blank ammunition to the guards. In both your father's eyes and mine you stand disgraced.'

There were no smiles on the Satbahalyas' faces, who now were by no means the merrymakers Hume met when he first visited Bhaktapur. They stood there tense with fear.

'And you murdered your own half-brother, Bir Narsinha,' the Gurkha King accused them angrily. 'Your father's legitimate son and his rightful heir. It was your worst crime, the most evil. Bir Narsinha was my friend. I mourned for him. Can you answer to that?'

The Satbahalyas stood, their heads bowed in silence.

The Gurkha King beckoned again to Atal Thapa. 'Take them off,' he ordered. 'Have their faces disfigured, their lips and noses cut away. Confiscate their land and other wealth. Turn them out from Bhaktapur, out into the fields.'

Ranjit Malla looked at his sons. 'They have not been worthy sons,' he murmured. 'They murdered Bir Narsinha and have caused me much misery in my old age. It is the last time I will look on them.'

The Satbahalyas were taken away and the Gurkha King turned to Jaya Malla. 'You claim to be a worthy foe,' he said. 'That is true. For many years you thwarted me, holding my army at bay. But I hold no grudge against you. Tell me what you intend to do? What do you desire?'

Jaya Malla spoke slowly now; as Hume saw his fever bore badly on him. 'There is little I desire,' he said. 'I have little time left. For long I ruled my kingdom with the favour of the gods, who have been kind to me and I enjoyed my reign. I built many temples and paid much to repair the Swayambhunath. Long have I worshipped Lord Shiva and Vishnu, Ganesh and Kali, Taleju, and all the gods and goddesses, and I made countless sacrifices to them. It is time, now, for me to go. All I ask is to be taken to the Ayra Ghat where I will await my journey to the Underworld and meet Yama.'

'That is granted,' Prithvi Shah agreed. 'Anything else you want I will give you. Which of your possessions would you wish go to the poor?'

'There is nothing,' Jaya Malla replied. Then, hesitating, he said, 'But there is one small thing you might do for me. I would like from you an umbrella and a pair of shoes.'

There were murmurs of surprise and the Gurkha King was puzzled and hesitated, thinking. Hume wondered what problem he saw in granting such simple things, they were mere trifles. But the request worried him, and he called the Raj Guru who came and spoke with him at length.

The Gurkha King asked for an umbrella and shoes to be brought, and he offered them to Jaya Malla, saying, 'I will meet your request as I promised. You can have the umbrella and the shoes, knowing that one means my crown and the other means my territory. But you will not come back to enjoy them in my own lifetime, not until after the lifetime of my grandson.'

It was a condition that the dying Malla King accepted.

The Gurkha King then turned to Ranjit Malla and his face softened a little. 'I am in debt to you, old friend,' he said. 'I remember well the years I stayed as your guest in Bhaktapur. Your kingdom was a civilised one and I learnt much then. Your hospitality is a debt I have not repaid.'

'And my memory of you is still ripe,' the old King replied. 'I am rich with memories. You were a youth then, my son's friend, between you both there was a sworn friendship. Bir Narsinha's death was a tragedy for both of us. He was only in his thirty-second year when they murdered him. Yes, I remember you well. Three years, I think, you stayed in Bhaktapur. You learnt much from us—to speak our Newari tongue, to write with pen and paper.'

'I read poetry to you and taught you to compose verses. You learnt our arts of government. I remember well the time when we stood together to watch my own Kumari pass, and it was to you the little goddess gave the blue lotus flower. It was your forehead she anointed with the tika mark, giving you her blessing to rule in Bhaktapur that year. She mistook you for me, thought you were the King of Bhaktapur. I did not take offence. You took no advantage of me then.'

The Gurkha King listened. 'And I shall take no advantage of you now in your defeat.'

Hume wondered if he would let Ranjit Malla stay on the throne of Bhaktapur and rule on his behalf. It would not be for long. Ranjit Malla was old, his death could not be far away; and he had weakened in his old age, lost his interest in affairs, his thoughts now mainly of his gods. Now the Satbahalyas were gone, there could be no threat.

The Gurkha King started to speak, but Ranjit Malla interrupted him. 'I have nothing left to take advantage of,' he said. 'The gods have favoured you, giving you the Valley of Nepal. I have no dispute with them. Who am I to do that? It is their will, their design perhaps. Take Bhaktapur and rule it well.'

'What do you wish to do?' the Gurkha King asked.

'My remaining days will not be many and I must spend them fruitfully, in worship of the gods. I will make sacrifices and live what life remains to me in the favour of the gods, and in their favour I will die. I will leave the Valley of Nepal and journey down to India and the holy Ganges, and in the holy city of Benares I will end my days in worship.'

'It is a wise choice you make,' the Gurkha King told him. 'I grant you leave to go. And more, I will provide a guard and porters for you and meet expenses you incur.'

Eighteen

Next morning, Hume and Maneka and their son with Maneka's maids and Hume's own servant left Bhaktapur. Before they set out for Kathmandu, Hume called on Jaya Malla to pay his respects and take leave of him. He found Jaya Malla in a high fever, only half-conscious, with bearers waiting to carry him to the Ayra Ghat to die and for his body to be burnt. Jaya Malla recognised Hume and said, 'They must not carry me away without my thanking you, Sir Hume Clarke. I remember you did much for me. You wrote to your Company asking them to send their army. You sought support for me from my two cousin kings. And you fought bravely here in Bhaktapur. I am much in your debt.'

Hume accepted this, although he knew his help was of little value in the end. 'And I have much to thank you for,' he replied. 'You welcomed me in your beautiful valley and you gave me a house and farm.' He hesitated before he continued, 'And I have Maneka for my wife and the son she has given me.'

Hume noticed a faint smile on Jaya Malla's face as the bearers carried him away.

In the Durbar Square Hume found Ranjit Malla setting off for India and Benares with the entourage the Gurkha King had provided. The old man was again cursing his illegitimate sons, blaming them for the disaster that had befallen him. He condemned them to low-caste menial work and a life of beggary, and condemned their children to an untimely end. They took their leave of each other. Then looking back, the last Hume saw of Ranjit Malla was his walking slowly around the temples in the Durbar Square and bidding farewell to Taleju and the other gods and goddesses.

As Hume and Maneka, who carried their baby son, crossed the fields on their way to Kathmandu, they saw the autumn harvest was now finished in the villages, the paddy cut and threshed and winnowed and most of the rice stored. Hume thought that Dongol, also, would have finished his harvest, and before long he would need to go to the farm to get his share and, of course, the gold he had buried under Dongol's hut.

In the villages the peasants were preparing for a festival. Musicians had gathered with their instruments, goats and cocks had been herded ready for sacrificing and great pots of chan had been brewed; and the people had the image of a goddess on display.

'It is Mahalaxmi,' Maneka told Hume. 'She is the Goddess of Wealth and the Harvest and is a wife of Lord Vishnu. She will protect the stored grain. Many peasants hope she will make it multiply in the bins.'

'Does she?' Hume asked, laughing

'No, I do not think so. And it is the men who cook for the feast at Mahalaxmi's festival. Do men cook food in your country, in Hollybrook?'

'Sometimes,' Hume told her. 'Not often.'

Maneka walked on in silence, then asked, 'Will we leave the valley soon? Go down to Calcutta and over the sea to your home?'

'Are you still sure you want that, Maneka?'

'I do. You know that is what I want. But your customs are so different. You know it frightens me sometimes. Are you sure that I would be able to learn the ways of your country? Be like an English wife to you there?

Hume took her hand. 'You will learn, Maneka. It will take a little time. You will be all I want in a wife.'

As Hume found, there were already changes in Kathmandu. Mostly Gurkha soldiers were seen on streets, as few Newars were in uniform and Jaya Malla's Nagar mercenaries had already gone back to India. Gurkhas had replaced many of the Newar ministers and generals, although some Newars had found favour with Prithvi Shah, including General Josi and Puskar Maske.

Gurkhas had moved into some houses, their Newar occupants had been moved outside the town walls to Thamel or Balaju and other villages further off. But for many people life had not changed under Prithvi Shah's rule. Newars continued with their crafts and their trade, Newars and Gurkhas alike worshipped the gods, conducted the festivals and sacrificed. And the markets were as busy as ever with peasants bringing ample produce from their farms.

But the lives of a few people of Kathmandu were to undergo a great change. They would be recast completely, not in the Valley of Nepal but in India. Soon after Hume returned to Kathmandu and occupied the house in Makhan Tole again, the Capuchin priests Father Michaelangelo and Father Matteo called on him. They were very worried.

'The Devil even yet continues with his work,' Father Michaelangelo told Hume, crossing himself. 'He has prevailed against us and the holy Church, and against God himself. His great evil continues. So our mission in the Valley of Nepal is ended.'

'The Gurkha King has banished us.' Father Matteo explained. 'He has forbidden us the sacrifice of the Mass. He is taking back the house where we live and have our church. We must leave the valley. He will brook no delay.'

'Didn't Surpratap help?' Hume asked.

Surpratap pleaded for us, but failed,' Father Matteo replied. 'The Gurkha King, he is the King of Nepal now, forbids our bible. The bayonet follows the bible he claims. He has heard it said.'

Hume did not disagree, but Maneka was unhappy with what she heard. 'It is not true,' she said. 'How could it be? You are men of peace. It is the Gurkha King who has brought war and death to the valley and so much suffering. Who will minister to the Christians when you have gone?'

'There will be none here,' Father Michaelangelo told her. 'None.'

'It's not only we Capuchins who are banished, not only the priests,' Father Matteo said. 'It is all Christians, all of our flock in Kathmandu and Bhaktapur, the few in Kirtipur and any others in the valley. We are all banished.'

Maneka, too, was concerned. 'Where will you go?' she asked. 'Where will all the Christians go? Most are poor. It will be difficult for them.'

'We will go down into India, to Bettiah, near Sagauli. We will all go there. The Prefect of our mission at Bettiah will accept us. I have no doubt of that.'

The Capuchins left to prepare for their departure. Maneka took her son in her arms and sat in silence looking at Hume. 'Yes, it is time to leave the valley,' he told her. 'I know that pleases you.'

She came and stood close to him and took his hand. Hume looked down to see her smiling happily. Then she went and knelt before her little altar and prayed.

The next days were busy ones for them. The furniture Hume had bought, the household goods and the personal belongings they could not carry, as well as a little gold, he gave to Maneka's maids and his own servant, who returned to their families. His Italian pistol from Pistoia, Hume gave to Puskar Maske as a keepsake, and Maneka gave him her painting of the Christ of the Sacred Heart. The grain and other stores, Hume asked the Raj Guru to distribute to the poor.

There was also the gold Hume had buried under the floor of Dongol's hut. He went to get that. But arriving at the farm he found the harvest long finished and the paddy fields in stubble—no sign of a winter vegetable planting or any animals in the fields. He knocked at the door of Dongol's hut, but drew no response. Inside, he saw the hut deserted, no stock of grain, the pots and other utensils gone, and the hearth had been cold for a long time. The farm implements were missing and there was no sign whatever of Dongol or his family. Where the fodder had been at the end of the hut, Hume saw a hole in the earthen floor. It was where he had buried the gold. The gold had gone.

Hume enquired about Dongol at Deo Patan village and of the peasants he had engaged the previous year. But with no result. Some thought Dongol had joined with the Gurkha army. One peasant thought Dongol might have been killed during the attack on Bhaktapur, that his wife and children had returned to their home village although he did not know which. Another peasant thought the demon Ghanta Karna might have risen from the dead and devoured the Dongol family or spirited them away to one of his bestial lairs. Dongol had left apparently without making any farewells to neighbouring peasants. He had disappeared and Hume's gold had gone with no explanation.

It was a cold December morning in 1769 when Hume and Maneka finally left the Valley of Nepal. The white mist hung low and thick over Kathmandu, filling the streets and market places and bathing the houses and the temples in its opaque whiteness. Hume and Maneka and their son left their house in Makhan Tole and walked through the mist to the Capuchins' house.

The street there was crowded and the two priests were waiting outside their house with fifty or so of their flock, those who were to follow their religion in Bettiah. Some were in tears, some were hesitating, not sure whether to go or stay. Their relatives and friends were saying goodbye to them. Lady Bachhla was there to farewell Maneka. Puskar Maske came out of the crowd to Hume.

'How is it you aren't leaving for Bettiah, Puskar Maske?' Hume asked. 'You are a Christian. You told me that not long after I first met you. You have attended the Capuchins' church.'

'Yes, Hume. But I am also Hindu, a Shestra. I also told you that,' he said, smiling. 'I have had the best of both worlds here on earth. In prospect, both heavens, too, I hope.'

'You are leaving the Christian Church, Puskar Maske?'

'No, Hume. It is the Christian Church that is leaving me,' he replied. 'My life is here, the valley is my home. My family is here and most of my gods. And my work. We will have much to do in our mountains now. Prithvi Shah will need the support of all of us.'

Hume could not disagree.

'I am sad to be losing you, Hume,' Puskar Maske said, feeling for Hume's hand. 'Truly sad. I will miss your friendship.'

Hume returned the affection. 'And I yours, Puskar Maske,' he assured him.

'It is the way of the gods, perhaps. But we might meet again,' Puskar Maske said.

They talked on for some time and at last exchanged namastes and made their farewells. Hume looked across at Atal Thapa with Maneka and their son Francis, making his farewells. He walked over to them and took his leave of him. By now the Capuchins and their flock were moving off and Hume and Maneka joined them.

They walked out of the town gate into the fields. They crossed the Vishnumati River and set off towards Thankot village through the mist, the thick white mist that the King of Heaven's mother, Dagini, promised would always come to the valley to nourish the crops. The Capuchin priests from Bhaktapur and their flock who had decided to go to Bettiah were waiting for them, and also a few from Lalitpatan. And there were several young noseless men, their faces horribly disfigured, from Kirtipur. They all walked in a long file across the valley through the mist, following the Capuchins in their white habits with their pointed hoods pulled up over their heads.

They passed to the west of Kirtipur and through Thankot, and climbed up the sloping ground, high up towards the Chandragiri Pass. The mist had cleared when they were on the side of the Chandragiri Mountain, and Hume looked back over the Valley of Nepal. He knew it all so well now, the towns of Kathmandu and Lalitpatan and Bhaktapur, the red brick and the tiled roofs of the houses within the town walls, the gilded roofs of the many temples. The eaves of the pagodas were now sparkling in the sunlight. He could make out the Swayambhunath and the Bodhnath and the holy Pashupatinath for Shiva as Lord of the Animals. Hume looked over the fields stretching away, some green with the growing vegetable crops, some black in fallow and some brown still with the paddy stubble. He looked at the villages dotting the valley and up to the terraced farms on the sides of the surrounding mountains.

And beyond all this, not far to the north, rearing high in the air, were the mighty Himalayas, white, glittering in the bright winter sunlight against a deep blue sky. Maneka stood beside Hume as they watched the great mountains, and she, too, was dazzled by their massive beauty. Hume's eyes travelled slowly along the great white peaks of Langtang Lirung, Dorje Lakpa, Ganesh's Himal and others.

Hume looked back to the Swayambhunath with its painted all-seeing eyes of the Adi Buddha. Those eyes had seen so much since he had come to the Valley of Nepal, he thought. They had witnessed the defeat of the three kingdoms, the end of the Malla kings, and the establishment of Gurkha rule. They had seen many woundings and deaths in battle. There was the tragedy of Kirtipur, the cutting away of lips and noses of the men and boys. The great eyes had watched the incineration of the Tamang soldiers at Bhaktapur, the beheading of the Pradhans and the burning of their wives as satis, and the punishment of Ranjit Malla's seven illegitimate sons. Hume wondered what the future was, what the great painted eyes were yet to see. Then Maneka took his hand to draw him on, and his gaze and thoughts were broken.

They left the valley and the great mountains to their future. Hume carried his baby son and kept Maneka close to him as they followed the Capuchins over the Chandragiri Pass and started on their descent, down the steep slopes and along the rocky tracks on their way down to Makwanpur and then into India.

At Bettiah they found that the Christians from the Valley of Nepal were well accepted and were given a place to live and settle. And Hume found Alexander's grave. It was a sad hour for him, as his thoughts went back to his boyhood days with his brother, and to his father. Hume commissioned a tombstone for Alexander, which was worded to tell briefly of his exploits in battle, to keep the memory of him alive.

By the time they reached Calcutta, Hume found that Governor General Clive had already left and returned to England. He was debriefed by members of the British East India Company Council and learnt that the Company had, at that time, lost interest in the Valley of Nepal. Being defeated once they were loath to engage in war again with as formidable a mountain general as the Gurkha King. In any case, the Company was too busy consolidating its gains in India.

The Indiaman "Pelham" was due to sail soon, in the January of 1770, and had empty cabins. There was nothing to keep Hume in Calcutta. Maneka, Hume and their son Francis embarked and sailed for England and his estate in Hollybrook.

THE GREAT MOUNTAINS WEEP

One

It was July 1839 when Adam Clarke, a young man of twenty-five years, arrived in Nepal. He was the second son of Sir Francis Clarke, and the grandson of Sir Hume Clarke, who had been in the Valley of Nepal some seventy years earlier, and Maneka the Nepalese lady he married there.

Finishing his studies at Oxford and graduating with a Bachelor of Arts Degree, Adam took employment with the British East India Company. They sent him to India; and when he reached Calcutta he was told of a vacancy in the British Residency in Kathmandu and that he was the right man for the post. They knew of his family connection with Nepal and that he spoke Newari, the old language of the valley, and could get by in Nepali, the language of the Gurkhas. Maneka had taught him these.

He went off from Calcutta with a detachment of sepoys for the Residency garrison. They travelled during the worst of the monsoon rains, across India, across the Nepalese Terai and the aul-infested duns with their jungles and swamps, and up into the cool air of the Mahabharats. They climbed up the steep and rugged slopes of Mount Chandragiri; and from there, through banks of dark monsoon cloud, Adam caught glimpses of the great Himalayan massifs rearing high in the sky not far to the north. Then they walked down into the valley and to Kathmandu, and on to the British Residency in nearby Lainchaur.

At the Residency a Captain O'Keefe showed Adam to the bungalow that was to be his, and invited him to drinks that evening after he had settled in. His long journey finished and, for the first time in weeks, out of the weather, washed and shaven and dressed in dry clothing, Adam enjoyed the luxury of the bungalow—comparative luxury that is.

It was one of several bungalows in the Residency grounds, austere but pleasant enough, built of brick with floors of hard pressed earth, its walls limed white, its roof of burnt clay tiles. It had a living room with a stone fireplace for winter warmth, a bedroom, a kitchen and quarters for servants. It was furnished sparsely but sufficiently, with the necessary tables and chairs, cupboards, a great four-poster bed, a bookcase, and easy chairs near the hearth. There was a small iron safe where Adam put the ruby pendant which his grandmother had given him; the very same pendant his ancestor, Sir Alexander Clarke, had taken from the Nawab Shuja-ud-daula's treasury at Murshidabad years before, after the battle of Plassey. The walls were bare of ornaments, except for an old cutlass and a mask of the elephant-headed God Ganesh, left there by a previous occupant. Out through the front window, Adam could see the other bungalows and the main Residency building, all set amongst lawns and flower beds. To the back of the bungalow, beyond the trees and shrubs, their leaves dripping in the rain and hanging low, the ground sloped down towards the Vishnumati River; and in the distance through the wet haze were the valley's surrounding mountains.

When Adam called on Captain O'Keefe he found him changed into the evening dress of his regiment, the red and gold jacket and the blue trousers with red stripes. The captain was a sparsely built man with reddish hair and the rather rigid bearing of a military officer. His bungalow was similar to Adam's but he had improved its comfort. Carpets from India and Tibet lay on the floor and his regimental pennant and his sabre and pistols were hanging on the wall. A fine tiger pelt with its gold and black stripes, fierce glass eyes, and long white fangs, was spread on the floor before the hearth. In a corner the captain had a large brass casting of a many-armed, three-faced god, which Adam took to be Lord Shiva.

Captain O'Keefe poured whiskies. 'Irish. Not scotch,' he said, handing one to Adam. 'Welcome to the Residency, Mr Clarke. Welcome to our prison. Let us drink to your pleasant stay.'

Adam thanked him. 'Prison, you say?'

The Captain shrugged. 'Yes, I don't want to complain, but we're confined to the Residency here. Can walk out around the nearby fields in the mornings and evenings. But not much more. We don't at all have the run of the country. The Gurkhas don't want us here and keep us very much to ourselves.'

'They're not friendly?'

'Not at all. Might be different for you, though.'

So Adam mentioned his connection with Nepal, his grandmother and his Nepalese quartering.

'Yes, I've heard. Good for you, Mr Clarke,' Captain O'Keefe smiled. 'I might tell you I married a lady from the Nawab Jafar's family in Calcutta. Dead now, to my great sorrow. We have grown-up children in India.'

Adam went on to talk about events in England, although they were seven months back then—of the young Queen Victoria, the London theatres and about the Parliament at Westminster where his father represented the Hollybrook Borough.

But Captain O'Keefe was little interested. 'I've long lost touch, Mr Clarke,' he said. 'Lost interest almost, in either England or Ireland. I'm Irish of course. Fought here with the Irish Dragoons. Born in Belfast, but never went back these thirty years. Never took home leave.'

Captain O'Keefe refilled their glasses. 'Have you contacts here in Kathmandu, Mr Clarke?'

'Yes, Dor Maske.' Adam replied. 'The son of a friend my grandfather once had. Have you had dealings with him?'

'Not myself. But I know of him. He has a trading business. He's an influential man here.'

The servant brought in a visitor, whom Captain O'Keefe introduced to Adam as Dr Jones the Residency medical officer. The doctor welcomed Adam then turned to the captain to say the Resident wished to see him immediately, with no delay. The captain went off.

Dr Jones looked at Adam and said, 'You seem in good health, Mr Clarke, after your journey from Calcutta. He looked closely into Adam's face and eyes and felt his forehead. 'No fever?' he asked.

'None, thank you,' Adam told him.

'And the sepoys who came with you. No fever there?'

'None. Not as far as I could see.'

'I must examine them too. You've done well. The duns are full of the aul, as they call it, at this time of year. Malaria. Bad air in the miasmas that rise from the swamps.'

'We crossed the duns quickly. Avoided the white mists as best we could. Covered our faces and hands.' Adam remembered hearing how his grandfather had done that. 'In Patna a priest from Bettiah gave all of us an infusion. He said it was from the bark of the Cinchona tree, a new remedy they had from the Americas.'

'Yes, quinine,' the doctor said. 'It seems to help.'

They talked on. Doctor Jones would be glad when the monsoon finished. He thought the valley beautiful, from what he had seen of it. At the window, he pointed out the bungalow of the Assistant Resident, Mr St Clair, and his family.

A peon came with a letter for Adam. He was surprised to find it was from Dor Maske inviting him to call the next morning, saying he would send a carriage. 'Strange how Dor Maske knows I'm here,' Adam said, 'after only a few hours.'

The doctor shook his head. 'I'm not surprised. Dor Maske is well informed. Very well informed. You will see.' But the doctor changed the subject, looking worried as he spoke. 'I can tell you, Mr Clarke, today hasn't been a good one for us at the Residency. A tragic one perhaps. Bhim Sen Thapa has been accused again of poisoning the baby prince. It will be the end of him. Yes, a tragedy for him and us. A great man, Bhim Sen Thapa. You must have heard of him.'

'Their prime minister, once?'

'Prime minister here for thirty years. A very great man. Not that I condone everything he's done. Not at all. By no means all. The king here, Rajendra Shah, imprisoned Bhim Sen Thapa today, and the court physicians. The Resident has just heard. It's the end of the Thapas, Mr Clarke. Ranjang Pandey and the rest are in power now, and the Pandeys are no friends of ours.'

'You expect trouble?' Adam asked.

'No need for alarm yet. But the Resident wants Captain O'Keefe to double the guard on the Residency.'

When the Resident called Adam later that evening, he went with some trepidation. Mr Brian Hodgson was a senior official with the company; and Adam, much his junior, was about to start his first posting. Mr Hodgson had long experience of Nepal, having been in Kathmandu for nearly twenty years, first as assistant to Resident Gardner and then as Resident himself. And he was a scholar of a high order, having already contributed much to a knowledge of the flora and fauna of the hills and of aboriginal peoples, and he was a student of Buddhism.

Mr Hodgson stood up slowly from his desk to welcome Adam. 'Glad you're here, Mr Clarke. I've been waiting for you to join us.' He pointed to chairs near an open window. 'A little cooler there. Beastly weather just now. The monsoon of course. But pleasant the rest of the year.'

Adam thought the Resident was not a robust man, and more the scholar than the soldier.

The Resident sat looking at Adam, intently. So Adam said, 'Of course my grandmother was Nepalese.'

'I know. That's why I agreed you come here. I've important work for you and I believe you're the man for it. I understand your family has a connection with a Dor Maske.'

Adam told him of Dor Maske's message asking him to call next morning; he asked if he should accept.

'Yes indeed. It's important you do,' the Resident told him.

'Perhaps he has memories of my grandparents.'

'He should. Golden memories, Mr Clarke.'

'Golden, sir?'

'It is said that your grandfather started the Maskes on their way to wealth. Sir Hume Clarke brought gold with him to Kathmandu which he multiplied several times by minting coins for Tibet. Dor Maske's father was with him in the venture, and had a share. The Maskes built on that. Dor Maske can be very useful to me in these worrying times. More worrying than in all my years here. They talk of war. Dangerous for us.'

'Dangerous, sir?'

'Yes, dangerous. You know that although we beat Nepal in 1815, it was only after the hardest of struggles. The Gurkhas had taken a great deal of territory on the Terai and in the hills far to the west of here; and they'd got into the lands of the Sikhs, lands under our protection. So we had to call a halt. Yes, it was certainly a hard struggle for us, Mr Clarke. For a time the Gurkhas thrashed us—our best forces—at Kalanga, at Jaithak and Parsa, and in Palpa and other places. After that they fought furiously at Almora and in the Deonthal Hills; it was there that the tide of war turned in our favour and we beat them. A great many soldiers on each side died, Mr Clarke, and many were wounded. There was much suffering. I don't want it to happen again. I don't intend it to.'

Adam indicated his agreement.

'In the end we were fortunate to have them sign the Treaty of Sagauli,' the Resident continued. 'The Treaty made them give up most of the territory they'd taken, agree to return criminals who sought refuge in their country to escape our justice, and stop plotting with the Indian States against us. It made them accept a British Resident in Kathmandu. That's how I'm here.'

The Resident did not disguise his worry. 'Now they want war with us again, Mr Clarke. They want to undo the Treaty. To get revenge. Many in the Durbar do. Certainly the Pandeys and Samraja Devi who is the Senior Queen.'

'To make matters worse,' the Resident continued, 'the Durbar is a hotbed of intrigue. Their King, Rajendra Shah, is weak and capricious, and his relatives the Chautariyas are not much better. There's the Heir Apparent, who is little more than a boy, but already unstable and cruel. Laxmi Devi, the Junior Queen, is not against us; but she thinks of little else than having her own son succeed to the throne instead of the Heir Apparent, she's obsessive about it.'

'You've doubled the guard on the Residency,' Adam said.

'Yes, a precaution. I used to get on well with Bhim Sen and the other

Thapas. But the Pandeys have the power now,' the Resident said unhappily. 'They have the Senior Queen's support. They've put Bhim Sen in prison again, brought up the old charge of poisoning the king's baby son. It's the end of him this time. That's the situation you've come to. It is what you have to help me deal with.'

'I shall do my best, sir.'

'It's crucial that you do, Mr Clarke. I must avoid another war with them.'

'But surely, sir, their chance of victory is slight.'

'Maybe. I have an army ready in India on their southern border, twenty thousand men there under Colonel Oglander.'

'They know that, sir?'

'Of course.'

'They're not deterred, sir ?'

The Resident shrugged. 'Not the Pandeys or the Senior Queen or the army itself.'

'They don't count the costs.'

'They do not. It is I who count the costs. The Gurkhas are mountain fighters, skilful, brave and ferocious. We must manage the Durbar, and we need the Thapas back. The Pandey war-mongers must go.'

Adam could clearly see his determination.

The Resident looked at Adam closely, 'No doubt you're wondering what part you'll play, Mr Clarke. Well I'm assigning you to the Thapas. Most of the Thapa leaders are dead or banished, but there's your Dor Maske. True he's a Newar, not a Thapa, but he always supports the Thapas. He's rich, a financier as well as a merchant. He has much influence in Kathmandu. You'll be my contact with Dor Maske. Does it please you?'

'It's for you to say, sir. Yes it does.'

Next morning Dor Maske sent a syce driving a small carriage to the Residency for Adam, with a Nepalese who introduced himself as Tanka Rana. As they drove away, the rain eased and the blue sky came through breaks in the clouds. Adam could see the Swayambhunath, the ancient Buddhist Chaitya, across the Vishnumati rising from its wooded hill. Its gilded spire sparkled where the sun's rays touched it, and its great painted eyes of the Adi Buddha looked sternly out over the valley.

'I am a jemidar,' Tanka Rana told Adam. 'I am a soldier but I am no longer with my regiment.' He pointed to the west. 'I fought against your country once. Far away. I fought at Kalanga where your Major

General Gillespie was killed. But I am not with my regiment now because I am with Sri Dor Maske.'

He must have been little more than a boy at Kalanga more than twenty years ago, Adam thought. He looked no more than forty, with his smooth brown skin, his dark, almond-shaped eyes alert, and his jaunty topi cap.

The syce drove the carriage at a quick pace, bumping over the rutted tracks, its wheels spraying the mud, and swerving to miss peasants coming in from the fields carrying their produce for the market in baskets at the ends of long poles over their shoulders. The syce skirted the walls of Kathmandu and came to the Rani Pokhari, the Queen's Lake, where Adam asked Tanka Rana to stop so he could view the pleasant scene: the little temple in the centre of the lake, the dainty arched bridge, and overgrown foliage covered by rain-drops, ivy running wild. Past the little lake, over the valley's surrounding mountains, Adam saw a great white peak appear from behind the clouds. the top of a giant of a mountain that reached high in the air and overhung the valley, its snow and ice glittering silver in the sunlight.

'It is the Gosain Than,' Tanka said. 'It is looking down at the valley. It wants the monsoon to finish.'

The carriage passed the ancient Temple of Mahenkal, which was used by Hindus to worship Mahadeo and by Buddhists to worship the Bodhisattva Padma Pani. It skirted the parade ground of the Tundikhel, a mile long nearly, which was busy with Gurkha regiments at drill and with much activity around several buildings, which Adam learnt were magazines, a foundry for the casting of cannon, and cantonments.

The syce turned the pony through an open gateway and along a drive bordered with lawns and flower gardens to a grand house. A servant in a frock-coat led Adam up the wide steps, past the tall colonnades, over the tiled verandah and in through the front doors. At the end of the room, an old man dressed in a silk tunic and white jodphurs was lying on a couch. Adam looked down at Dor Maske, a small thin man, his complexion darker than Adam's own and with a hooked nose, a bald pate. His skin was stretched tightly over his face, his black almond-shaped eyes darted as he looked back at Adam.

'So you are Adam Clarke, a grandson of my father's friend,' he said, moving stiffly as he joined his hands in a welcoming namaste. His knuckles were gnarled and arthritic. Dor Maske was some years older than Adam's father.

'My father sends his greetings. He asked me to extend his regards to you, his best wishes,' Adam said, handing him his father's letter of introduction.

Dor Maske bowed his head slightly, opened the letter and read quickly, then looking at Adam he said, 'I see you have much of my country in you, Mr Clarke; but you are large like your grandfather was. My own father, Puskar Maske, used to speak of him. He saved his life once. It was near Buxar, before the battle there. My father always remembered it with much gratitude.'

Adam looked around at Dor Maske's room, which was larger than any in his father's house in Hollybrook, and richly furnished. A chandelier was hanging from the ceiling over oriental carpets, and a grand piano stood in one corner near large gilded castings of several gods. There were paintings of the late King George and of a Gurkha noble whom Adam took to be the great Gurkha King, and one of an English landscape. Dor Maske had great success as a trader.

'It is like an English room, is it not, Mr Clarke?' Dor Maske pointed to the painting of the English landscape. 'It is from Calcutta. My father bought it years ago. He said it reminded him of your grandfather. He was told it is a scene in Kent, near your home in Hollybrook perhaps. What would you say?'

It was a pleasant enough landscape. The wheat had ripened in the fields and the last of the harvest was being brought in. The cattle grazed in lush meadows and the hedgerows were already bright with berries; and the oaks and elms had started to take on their autumn colours. It was a sunny scene with the day still warm, Adam imagined, and just enough breeze to move the few white whiffs of clouds slowly across the sky. Dor Maske waited for Adam to say the painting was of Hollybrook.

'Yes, it could be Hollybrook, near our estate perhaps,' Adam said.

Dor Maske seemed pleased with that. 'I think Maneka settled happily in Hollybrook.'

'I understand she had difficulties at first,' Adam said. 'But after a time she adjusted well. She ran the Clarke household, mothered her children and took her place in the neighbourhood as Lady Clarke. She spent a good deal of time working for the local church and helped raise money for the parish poor.'

'I am pleased to hear that,' Dor Maske said. 'I was only a young boy, but I remember her.'

'They were troubled times, those days in the Valley of Nepal,' Adam said. He well remembered his grandfather talking about them and of Prithvi Shah, the Gurkha King who took the Valley of Nepal from the old Malla kings.

'True, and for decades more,' Dor Maske agreed. 'Then the war with the British came. But my father prospered. He found good openings for trade in wool and gold from Tibet and weapons for the Gurkha army. And also items for the nobles and generals here—English furniture, clocks, mirrors, carpets and drapes, ornaments, wines and spirits. They were getting a taste for good living and they had gold to pay.'

A young Nepalese woman came in carrying a tray with tea and rice cakes. Dor Maske took her hand, 'This is Lalit, the youngest of my womenfolk. She is my favourite, Mr Clarke.'

Adam looked at Lalit, the red sari she was wearing, the golden ornament in her black hair, and her golden bangles, jewelled earrings, silver anklets. Momentarily he had an image of his grandmother, Maneka, when sometimes she had changed her English dress for a sari and jewellery, and had worn the pendant with its great red ruby, which later she left to him. But that was when he was a young boy. Lalit standing there was an entirely different experience for him. She was certainly attractive, he thought, beautiful, perhaps, beneath the red sari drawn up to her black eyes. Immediately he felt an affinity with her, the Nepalese quarter of him claiming her. Lalit poured the tea. Then Adam watched her as she walked away, her cholo blouse brief at the back to expose the olive skin of her slender midriff .

'Troubled times are back in Nepal,' Dor Maske said. 'Bhim Sen Thapa is in prison again. I am a Newar, not a Gurkha. I am not a Thapa by blood, but I am a Thapa in spirit. I know Bhim Sen well. He ruled wisely for many years after the war with the British ended in 1815. We owe much to Bhim Sen, and so do the British.' Dor Maske's old face frowned. 'Times will be difficult with Bhim Sen Thapa gone. The Pandeys have power and will make trouble—war perhaps. They talk openly of war.'

Dor Maske shrugged. 'It is the old charge against Bhim Sen, poisoning the baby Prince two years ago. They try again to wring a written confession from him. I hear the torturers' irons are red-hot. My people tell me that.'

'Will he confess?' Adam asked.

Dor Maske shook his head. 'He will not confess. He did not before and he will not now. Bhim Sen is not the poisoner.' Dor Maske lent towards Adam and said softly, 'It was the King, Rajendra Shah himself, who had the poison dealt. He poisoned his own son. I have no doubt of it. Poisoned his own son so he could frame Bhim Sen. You should tell Resident Hodgson that.'

Adam looked doubtful and Dor Maske explained. 'Rajendra Shah is an imbecile, a weakling. The Pandeys put him up to it.'

Then Dor Maske said, 'The Resident will have spoken to you of me.'

'I am to be his contact with you.'

'Yes, he would want that. Tell him I agree.'

'Why not deal with you directly?' Adam asked.

'He does not want it. Nor do I. I do not deal with the British Residency. Let us say the British are not popular here. Not at all popular in the Durbar. I deal with the British in Patna and I buy much from them. But I do not deal directly with the Residency.'

Adam waited but Dor Maske did not explain. Instead, he told Adam that his house would always be open to him. He said he was placing a carriage and syce at Adam's disposal, and had already arranged with King Rajendra Shah for him to be free to move around the valley and not to be confined to the Residency. Tanka Rana would escort him.

With that Dor Maske lent back on the couch, for a while the lids hung heavy over his eyes and then they closed. For a few moments Adam sat looking at Dor Maske's face as he slept, the hooked nose and bald pate. Lalit, the golden ornament shining in her black hair, came up quietly and told Adam that Dor Maske would sleep for some time, it was his habit at mid-day now. She had alerted the syce and Tanka Rana, and they were waiting for him. She walked with Adam out onto the verandah and stood there between the colonnades. And Adam imagined her smiling behind the sari still pulled up to her eyes.

Passing Kathmandu as they rode back to the Residency, Adam stopped the carriage and asked Tanka Rana to go with him into the town. They walked along the cobbled streets between the tall terraced houses of burnt brick and tile, their overhanging verandahs and facades decorated with fine old wood-carvings. They made their way through the crowd, of small wiry men for the most part, brown-skinned and almond-eyed, some wearing jaunty Nepalese caps. The women wore their saris and jewellery and children played in loincloths. Adam sought out Makhan Tole and wondered which had been his grandfather's house.

Following Tanka Rana, Adam found himself in the Durbar Square. He took his time walking around the temples, the many pagodas with their eaves curving gracefully and their gilded roofs glittering in the sunlight. There were Rajendra Shah's palace with its Monkey God Gate, and the house of the Kumari who was the little living Goddess of Kathmandu. He stood for a long time looking at the Black Bhairab.

'The Durbar Square is truly the heart of Kathmandu as my grandfather called it,' Adam told himself.

For a while they sheltered beside the Jagannath Temple against a monsoon shower, out of the rain which dripped from the eaves of the pagodas and washed the pavements. Then as the rain eased Adam heard yelling coming from near the palace, and a young man came running quickly out of the Monkey God Gate, looking back over his shoulder at a group of soldiers chasing him.

Tanka quickly pulled Adam back near the Temple. 'It is best we are not seen, Mr Clarke.'

Adam saw that a boy was leading the soldiers, urging them on, his sword in hand. He was dressed in the uniform of a Gurkha general, his blue tunic heavily embroidered in gold, a kukhri in the red cummerbund around his waist, and his turban braided and bejewelled.

'Please take care, Mr Clarke,' Tanka Rana cautioned. 'It is the Heir Apparent, the King's elder son Surendra Shah. He is dangerous and best avoided.'

Looking again at the soldiers, Adam was amazed to see they wore the uniform of the Irish Dragoons. It puzzled him—they could not be the Company's soldiers yelling, running amok in the Durbar, he was sure of that. Then as they came closer, he saw their faces were whitened with chalk and their uniforms were ill-fitting and soiled, torn in places.

The soldiers ran past and Adam left Tanka Rana and hurried to the other side of the temple to watch. He saw them chasing the young man around the Durbar Square, the Heir Apparent flashing his sword, the soldiers yelling, brandishing their kukhries. Then they passed out of sight to the north of the Square.

Tanka Rana, greatly perturbed, urged Adam to leave and return to the Residency immediately. They drove off in silence, with Tanka Rana downcast, embarrassed. At length he said, 'Please forgive me, Mr Clarke. I am sorry you should have seen. But it is the Pandeys. They dress peasants in your uniform. I am sorry they make fun of your soldiers. You must forgive me.'

It certainly angered Adam. 'And what of the Heir Apparent?' he asked. 'How does he come into it?'

'The Pandeys encourage him. You must beware of him. He is dangerous and cruel.'

'And who is the young man?'

Tanka Rana shrugged. 'He is Jung Bahadur, an aide at the palace. I think he will escape them.'

Two

That evening Adam was invited to dine with the St Clair family—Mr Alfred St Clair, his wife Agnes and their daughter Sarah. Dr Jones and Captain O'Keefe were also guests. Mr St Clair welcomed Adam heartily, taking his hand in a firm grip and saying they needed him in the Residency. Mr St Clair was past middle-age, strongly built, red-faced. He spoke loudly and seemed rather too sure of himself. Mrs St Clair welcomed Adam politely but hardly warmly. She was a matronly woman, still comely, her brown hair touched with grey, dressed in dark blue and white. Her eyes had fixed on Adam's face as he entered the room, and she looked at him keenly as he was introduced to her.

Mr St Clair introduced his daughter, and Adam was long to remember his first meeting with Sarah St Clair. She had just turned twenty then. Dressed in a white blouse and a long green skirt of Indian silk, her light brown hair was plaited and tied with a bow. Speaking softly, a little shyly, she welcomed him, then her mother took her away, saying she would let Adam join the men for drinks.

Going into dinner, Adam was surprised to find a table almost the equal of his mother's back in Hollybrook, with its white cloth, candles burning in a candelabrum in the centre, the silverware, fine china, glasses and decanters all sparkling under the candlelight. The rest of the room was only dimly lit by the glow from oil lamps in the corners and any light the night outside sent through the windows, which were open to catch the cool breeze.

Mr St Clair gave a satisfied smile from his end of the table. 'You see Mrs St Clair keeps up standards, Mr Clarke. Even here. Even in this remotest of all valleys, away from everywhere.'

'Of course I do,' Mrs St Clair agreed. 'I do try. I like to do as we'd do at home. It is difficult for me, very difficult. But it's important. We've always been used to such things.'

Adam complimented her, told her he had not known such comfort for months, not since he had left his home in Kent.

'You're from Kent then, Mr Clarke,' she said. 'Such a lovely place. Our house is in London, Kensington you know. A very nice house. But I'm afraid we seldom use it.' She glanced at her husband with a touch of irritation. 'We go to our house only on home leave. That is not often. Very seldom indeed. I was down in Kent once or twice, Mr Clarke. It's very nice. Did you live there long?'

'All my life,' Adam said, 'I was born there.'

'Oh, so you are English then.'

'Yes. My father is Sir Francis Clarke, the sixth baronet. The family estate is in Hollybrook.'

Mrs St Clair thought for a few moments. It seemed Adam had impressed her. Then she asked, 'You are the eldest son, Mr Clarke?'

'The younger. My brother helps manage the estate.'

Adam thought she might ask about his Nepalese ancestry, but Dr Jones was saying, 'Mr Clarke will have news from England, Agnes. I'm sure we'd all like to hear. Very little news comes here. Calcutta neglects us. The last letter from home they sent on to me was a year old, almost a year.'

Adam wondered what would interest them. 'Our new queen was settling in well when I left England,' he said. 'Becoming better known and well accepted by most.'

'Still only young though, little more than a lass.' said Captain O'Keefe. 'It's not fair on her, or on Britain, or Ireland for that matter. They wouldn't have the young Victoria in Hanover. I heard Hanover went to the old king's brother, the Duke of Cumberland, a mature man. Better to have had him.'

'Not a popular man,' Adam pointed out.

'A young lady, the Queen, but she'll get every support,' the doctor said. 'Has Lord Melbourne to help her, I think.'

'And she'll have someone else soon who is closer to her than Melbourne, if what's being said is right,' Adam told them. 'There's a royal marriage coming up. Much talk of it. It's her cousin Albert, a prince from Saxe-Coburg.'

Captain O'Keefe showed his displeasure. 'Another German. Probably can't even speak English. And a cousin. I don't believe cousins should marry.'

Mrs St Clair disagreed. 'Come now, captain. I think it's lovely, our young Queen having a prince. And she certainly should be married. Every woman needs a man beside her. A queen certainly does.' She turned to her daughter. 'It's very romantic, Sarah. Don't you think so?'

Sarah agreed. Then speaking softly to Adam, she asked, 'Will you like it here, Mr Clarke? I know you have seen something of Kathmandu.'

'Too early for me to say yet, Miss St Clair. But, yes, I think I will.'

'Will you be here long? A long posting?' she asked.

'I expect so,' he told her, and saw it pleased her.

'There's so little to do here for some of us, Mr Clarke. It's really a shame.'

Adam was agreeing when the main course came. Mr St Clair proposed a toast to the Queen and her prince. Adam found the St Clairs' meal excellent, a roast of venison—the nearby hills being well supplied with deer—and vegetables grown in the Residency garden, and Cape wine which had travelled well enough up from Calcutta.

Across the table, Captain O'Keefe was telling the doctor and Mr St Clair how he would like to go into the hills to hunt. He had shot a few tigers in his time in Bengal.

Adam started to talk to Sarah, but her mother interrupted. 'We are great readers here, Mr Clarke. Very interested in good literature. We have quite a library with us. We have *Emma* and *Pride and Prejudice*, lovely books, by Jane Austen, you know. We've read them, Sarah and I. And of course there's dear old Sir Walter Scott. We have several of his.'

Mr St Clair had been listening. 'Don't read much, myself, Mr Clarke, but there's one book here I like, a long poem. Not that I read much poetry. What is it Agnes?' he asked his wife.

'*The Ancient Mariner*, I suppose you mean. By Mr Coleridge, I think.' She looked to Adam for confirmation.

'That's it,' Mr St Clair agreed. 'I think of the poor devil of a sailor when I'm aboard ship myself, the tropical sea becalmed, the burning sun a copper colour I recall, the old man mad with thirst. Was becaimed myself once while going on home leave. Off Madagascar, the sea was like glass and an albatross kept flying round. Hot as hell. Remember, Agnes?'

'I remember it only too well,' she replied. 'Are you sure it was an albatross, Alfred?'

Mrs St Clair felt a need to explain the Resident's absence. 'Mr Hodgson is always most welcome here, Mr Clarke. Always. But I'm afraid he seldom honours us with his presence. He has little time to spare. He's a very busy man.'

'That's so,' Mr St Clair confirmed. 'Mr Hodgson has a heavy load on his shoulders. Official work. And he's a famous scholar. Studies the native animals and flora here. Examines specimens they bring in and makes notes. It takes up the rest of his time.'

When they had finished the meal, the two ladies left the table and Mr St Clair passed the port. The conversation lagged and the three of them sipped their drinks, looking towards Adam expectantly. Then Mr St Clair said, 'You called on Dor Maske this morning, Mr Clarke.'

Adam told them of Dor Maske's warm welcome; and of his wish to have the Pandeys out and the Thapas back in power, his willingness to help the Resident in this. He told them that Dor Maske had accepted him as Mr Hodgson's emissary, and had made a carriage available and arranged for him to be free to move around the valley.

Dr Jones seemed satisfied, thinking it would be a great help to the Resident. But Mr St Clair had his reservations. 'I've nothing against Dor Maske personally,' he said. 'I've never met the man. But I can tell you that for decades he's supplied the Gurkhas with a good deal of their weaponry, muskets, light cannon, mortars and ammunition, even heavier cannon nowadays. Gets them up from Delhi and Lucknow, some from China across the Himalayas, and also, God forbid, from the Company's own arsenal down in Patna.'

'So you think the Resident should reject his help?' Captain O'Keefe asked.

'Not only that. I'd put an end to Dor Maske's business altogether. Stop him getting weapons for them.'

'You'd reject his help to get the Thapas back in power in the Durbar?' Dr Jones asked.

'Yes. We don't need friends there. Neither Thapas nor Pandeys.' Mr St Clair rapped the table to emphasise his point. 'Control the Gurkhas, I say. Bring in our army if there's trouble. Make short work of them. What's the Company's army for?'

Captain O'Keefe objected. 'Come, Alfred. You're going too far. You know well enough I'm against another war with the Gurkhas. It would be a bloody affair. I fought against them in 1814, and in 1815 too. I was at Kalanga with our Irish Dragoons. They killed most of us there.'

He looked at Adam. 'You must know of our war with the Gurkhas, Mr Clarke. We had fifty thousand against them on the Terai and the lower hills. We beat them in the end but they slaughtered us at first. Gurkha cannon, muskets, kukhries. They killed our Major General Gillespie at Kalanga. I was there. As fine a soldier as you could wish for. A man I respected greatly. And I fought on the Terai, Mr Clarke. At Parsa we lost hundreds of our men. I was at Parsa. If Dor Maske can help, then so much the better.'

'Certainly,' Dr Jones agreed.

Of course Adam knew how fiercely the Gurkhas fought. He thought of Major General Marley who, defeated on the Terai, demoralised and unable to face the Gurkhas again, deserted his post. One morning before dawn, the major general packed his belongings and quietly left his tent, alone, left his twenty thousand men without a leader, mounted his horse and returned to India.

Mr St Clair refilled his glass and lent towards Adam. 'Let me tell you my view, Adam, if I may call you Adam. General Ochterlony should have taken Kathmandu back in 1815. He had them beaten then. Don't let us make the mistake again. Take them now. Why not? There's Colonel Oglander and his regiments down near the Makwanpur border. Bring them up here. Why not take Nepal? We've taken much of India. Why is Nepal different?'

'It is different,' Captain O'Keefe told him, 'It's because the Gurkhas are here in their mountains.'

'Good time to send an army up and take the place now,' Mr St Clair persisted. 'There's turmoil in the Durbar, from what I hear. A weak king with two troublesome queens up to their necks in intrigue, and ministers and other nobles murdering each other.' He laughed, 'And a mad boy, the Heir Apparent.'

Adam told them he had watched the Heir Apparent and his mock Irish Dragoons chasing Jung Bahadur that afternoon.

'Uniform of the Irish Dragoons!' Captain O'Keefe said, annoyed. 'I hear they do it. Insulting. That certainly has to be stopped.'

'So you see my point,' Mr St Clair said loudly. 'That's the people we try to deal with. Must have the Company in control here. Good for both us and them. And just think, Adam, what use we'd make of valley here. Delightful climate, except for the few weeks of the monsoon, and not so bad even then. Beautiful place, those great white mountains, green fields and clear rivers. Picturesque old towns, I understand, with their gods and pagodas and all that. We could police the place, build accommodation and sports grounds—polo, cricket and the rest—make it safe and comfortable. What a place for our people, wives and children and all of us, away from Calcutta's heat now and then. Surely we deserve that.'

Mrs St Clair had sent Adam a note saying she expected him for cards. He found her in her sitting-room, with its floral curtains, chintz coverings on the chairs, a Persian carpet and several paintings on the walls. The mantelpiece interested Adam, cluttered with bric-a-brac. There were ivory elephants and brass vases from India, and miniatures of the family in silver frames. A small clock ticked away under its glass dome amongst hand-painted porcelain pieces. Mrs St Clair had set up a small table near the window, with a pack of cards and a cribbage board.

'I'm so glad you could come,' she greeted Adam. 'These dreary wet afternoons. I hope you play cribbage, Mr Clarke. I like to play.'

He told her he had played.

'Just the two of us. Sarah doesn't like to play.'

'No, I would like to play today, mamma,' Sarah said as she came into the room. She gave Adam a welcoming smile. This time she had taken her plaits out and her hair hung softly around her face and onto her shoulders. The white blouse she wore was frilled and lacy, and a gold locket hung on a chain over her breast.

'I'm afraid Sarah doesn't play cribbage very well,' Mrs St Clair said.

'Perhaps, mamma. But I hope Mr Clarke will be patient with me. Will you, Mr Clarke?'

'It is I who will need your patience, Miss St Clair,' Adam said. 'I've played very little and I'm sure I don't play well.'

Mrs St Clair sat Adam at the table and put the little ivory pegs, counters for the three of them, in the holes at the end of the cribbage board. She shuffled the cards and put the pack on the table to cut for the deal. Sarah won, and her fingers—bare of rings Adam noticed—nimbly dealt out the cards. The counting came back to Adam: two for the fifteens, two for the pairs, the runs and flushes, and one for the knave noddy. Mrs St Clair took charge of the board and moved the pegs along as they scored. Occasionally Adam's attention waned and, looking out the window, through the rain and across the Vishnumati, he thought of the great Buddhist Chaitya, the Swayambhunath, and promised himself a visit to it soon. He thought of Bhim Sen Thapa in prison, of the torturers' hot irons as Dor Maske had said. Here in the almost English sitting room, it seemed unreal.

'So you've won again, Sarah,' Mrs St Clair said, a little annoyed.

Sarah had won more than her share. 'You asked me to be patient, Miss St Clair, but you've won most,' Adam said. 'You were too modest. You're too good for us.'

She smiled back. 'You're too kind, Mr Clarke.'

'The servants will make tea,' her mother said. 'Will you go and see to it, Sarah?'

With Sarah gone, Mrs St Clair turned to Adam. 'Sarah has been with us for more than two years now, Mr Clarke. It's nice. She came to us in Calcutta and then up here. I used to miss her very much. She was at school in England, of course, at Saint Ann's College in Devon. A very good school. Do you know it?'

'I've heard it mentioned,' Adam answered.

Mrs St Clair sat looking at Adam intently, staring again. 'And your grandmother, Mr Clarke. I hear she came from here, was Nepalese.'

'Yes, many years ago now. Her name was Maneka, a noble lady.'

'Noble?'

'Yes, a lady in the court of Jaya Malla, a King of old Kathmandu.'

Sarah returned followed by a servant with the tea. Mrs St Clair cleared away the cards and the cribbage board, and they set the tea things on the table—the usual English china and silver spoons, and a cake on a stand. Sarah poured.

'Sarah does our baking,' Mrs St Clair said as she cut the cake.

'I do,' Sarah agreed. 'I like making cakes.'

'It's not China tea,' Mrs St Clair said. 'It's Indian.'

'Of course we ladies are cooped up in the Residency here,' Mrs St Clair said with a frown. 'Different from Calcutta. It wasn't so bad there. Mr St Clair was appointed to Kathmandu unexpectedly. To my own disappointment I must say. It is difficult for me but I accept it because it's my lot. It's the lot of a wife. But I do worry about Sarah and I have plans for her to return to England. Of course I'll miss her, but it's for her own sake. It's been terribly difficult for her here. Ghastly really. Hasn't it Sarah?'

'Not quite that bad, mamma.' Sarah turned to Adam. 'But mamma is right, Mr Clarke, saying we are cooped up here in the Residency. I have hardly ever been out of it, except for walks in the fields, and I've seen nothing of Kathmandu. It disappoints me.'

'I can understand that, Miss St Clair. Unfortunate for you,' Adam said sympathetically.

'Yes, very.'

'You have to accept it, Sarah,' Mrs St Clair said.

'Do I mamma?' Then Sarah said to Adam, 'You're very lucky, Mr Clarke. I hear you have the run of the country almost. You can go where you like.' She sat looking at Adam uncertainly, pleading with her blue eyes. 'Would I be too bold to suggest you should escort me, Mr Clarke? Just once or twice. Just to show me around Kathmandu.'

Adam could hardly refuse her. 'Of course, Miss St Clair. I'd be delighted to.'

'It would be nice. Thank you, Mr Clarke. You are kind.' Sarah was pleased and showed her gratitude by smiling warmly now.

But Adam saw it did not please Mrs St Clair, who was frowning at her daughter. 'That was forward of you, Sarah. I do not approve. You must know that. You must not impose on Mr Clarke.'

Adam looked at Sarah and saw the suggestion of a blush. 'Really, mamma. I'm not imposing. Am I, Mr Clarke?'

Adam had to tell her she was not.

'You are, Sarah.' Mrs St Clair turned to Adam. 'I realise we are here in a strange world, Mr Clarke. Very strange indeed. It's very different from England, very different from Calcutta even. But I do not make allowances and still follow the proper conventions. I try to be the very essence of propriety. And I am. Anyone would tell you so. Is it any wonder I do not approve of what Sarah has asked you? I won't have her imposing on you.'

Sarah blushed. 'Really, mamma,' she said again.

The strength of Mrs St Clair's reaction surprised Adam. To his mind Sarah's suggestion could be readily excused in the circumstances. So he said, 'No, I assure you, Mrs St Clair, Sarah is not imposing on me. By no means. I should like to be able to show her something of Kathmandu. But it's for you to decide.'

Sarah, embarrassed, sat looking down at the table, her hair falling around her face, then she got up quickly and hurried out of the room.

Mrs St Clair, unbending, watched after her. 'Please forgive us. I think Sarah will be better back in England.'

When the time came for Bhim Sen Thapa's trial, Dor Maske arranged for Adam to attend with Tanka Rana, so that the interest of the British would be clear to all. News of the trial had spread quickly, and people had come from all parts of the valley to hear of Bhim Sen's fate—the fate of one of their most famous men, the great minister who had led Nepal for more than a generation. An officer of the guard admitted them through the Monkey God Gate to the palace. They walked with the Gurkha nobles, officials and military officers, and others entitled to be present at the trial, along the narrow passages to the inner court where the trial was to be held.

At one end of the court a long wooden platform covered by a red carpet and backed with purple drapes was set up as a dais. Flames from two large oil lamps struggled against the overhanging gloom of the overcast sky and the shadows of the ancient walls. A gilded image of Vishnu the great protector was at one side of the dais and soldiers of the royal guard stood nearby with their swords drawn.

King Rajendra Shah was seated on a white cushion on a large arm chair of a throne placed at the centre of the dais. He wore the dress of a Gurkha general, a long tunic embroidered in gold, and a kukhri was in his red cummerbund and his sword at his side; his face was thin under his black turban with its crown heavy with jewels and a plume flowing to the back. He sat quite still, his black beady eyes fixed ahead. The Senior Queen, Samraja Devi, sat to one side of him and Adam thought her a severe-looking woman, ungainly, in her voluminous and many-pleated skirts, dark-coloured blouse and sari. The young Heir Apparent sat to the other side of Rajendra Shah, also dressed as a Gurkha general, like his father but without a crown. Tanka Rana pointed out others on the dais: Ranjang Pandey the prime minister with his face expressionless, his brothers Karbar Pandey and Kulraj Pandey, the Raj Guru, Dal Pandey and the Lama Bhatta from the Swayambhunath. A little away from the rest to the front of the dais sat an old Brahman. 'He is Kanak Singh Mahat, the Ditha, the Chief Justice,' Tanka said.

Rajendra Shah signalled and two officers of the royal guard escorted Bhim Sen Thapa onto the dais, the iron shackles still heavy on his ankles but the chains removed. He, too, wore the uniform of a Gurkha general, but it was ill-fitting now, his tunic devoid of honours and his turban without jewels. Adam watched as this broken man shuffled forward, moving with difficulty, now stooped, his head bowed. Adam looked at Bhim Sen's face; how tired it was and aged beyond even his advanced years, his jowls twisting occasionally with a nervous tic. Then soldiers brought in two dishevelled figures who were still in irons and dragging their heavy chains, and stood over them as they sat crouched at one end of the dais. They were the court physician and his deputy.

An official stepped forward and read the charge against Bhim Sen Thapa, the poisoning of the baby prince, using the court physicians for the purpose. Bhim Sen raised his head and started to deny it, but the officer of the guard silenced him. Then the Ditha rose with a document in his hand, and turning his head so as not to see Bhim Sen, said, 'I have in my hand, Sire, Bhim Sen Thapa's confession to the murder of your royal son, the baby prince. He admits without reservation of any kind that he ordered the physicians to carry out the poisoning, that he went to the room of the prince that day just two years ago to ensure the physicians did their evil work. It is a written confession that I have.' The Ditha held up the document. 'It is for all to see. It is in order, I assure you, Sire. It is properly signed by Bhim Sen Thapa.'

There was a low murmur from those watching in the court, expressions of approval on some faces. 'Many Pandeys are here,' Tanka Rana whispered to Adam. 'And two Thapas who would approve are here—they are Indra Bar and Rambam Thapa—treacherous men who have long sided with the Pandeys.'

But on other faces in the court Adam saw disbelief and silent anger.

Bhim Sen turned towards those gathered in the court; his demeanour suddenly changed, he was erect now and his head was held high. No one stirred or murmured. All was still except for the flickering of the oil lamps on the dais, their light playing through the gloom on Vishnu's gilded image. 'I deny the charge,' Bhim Sen called loudly, and his voice, strong and deep, filled the court and reverberated back from the dark walls. Even with those few words, Adam saw that he was no longer the broken man, an object of pity. Again he was the supreme commander, the man of power who had led Nepal as its undisputed leader for more than three decades.

'I did not make this confession,' he went on. 'I call on the great Lord Shiva to hear me. I call on the merciful Vishnu.' He glanced at the god's image on the dais. 'These are times of evil. The evil of the Pandeys. You must ask who wrote the confession. Who forged my name?' He looked briefly at Rajendra Shah and then at the Ditha. 'Was it you Ditha, for my enemies, the Thapa's enemies?'

The Ditha, eyes downcast, did not reply.

Bhim Sen turned towards the Pandeys on the dais. 'You are the vultures,' he said. 'May the gods destroy you. You plot my death. Stand and admit it. Do it now. Do it for all to hear.'

Ranjang and his fellow Pandeys sat in silence. The King sat staring fixedly ahead, and the Senior Queen, her lips compressed, looked sourly at Bhim Sen. The Heir Apparent pointed to the physicians crouching at one end of the dais, then laughed and made some remark to his father. A heavy, expectant silence hung over those gathered in the court.

'You accuse me of this crime,' Bhim Sen continued, anger ringing in his voice. 'You accuse one who has served the gods so well. I gave gold and silver doors for the Pashupatinath, Lord Shiva's great temple, the most holy temple of Shiva Lord of the Animals.' He looked at Rajendra Shah. 'I was your steward, Sire, when we built the Tripureswara Temple, the ghats on the Bagmati nearby and Hanuman's image. It was I who had the great wooden beams of the Swayambhunath replaced, those there having rotted with great age. Yes, I have served the gods well. Is that the sign of a poisoner?'

'Am I a poisoner?' Bhim Sen looked down into the court. 'One who has served so long and loyally? For thirty years and more I served, as your leader, prime minister, commander-in-chief. It was I who pursued the great tradition set by Prithvi Shah, your illustrious forebear, Sire, and the father of our nation. It was I who pushed the boundaries of our nation westwards—far to the west. My able General Amar Singh Thapa took Kumaon and Garhwal, then moved on into the territory of the Sikhs. He fought the Sikhs at Ganesh Ghat and put Kangra, the very gate to Kashmir, under siege.'

'When the British called a halt we fought them, the conquerors of India, the aggressors from beyond the seas. We terrified them and, even yet, they tremble in fear of us. I will remind you of Kalanga where the British learnt to fear us and where their gallant General Gillespie paid with his life; and of Jaithak where we crushed the British and where their General Martindale froze with fear; and Jitpur where we routed their General Wood and he too froze in his terror of us. At Parsa and Sumanpur, close by in Makwanpur, our fury slew the British, and their General Marley fled in the grip of panic. He rose one morning before dawn and fled to India, alone, leaving his men and cannon, and deserted his army. I ask again, were those the actions of the poisoner of a royal prince?'

Adam noticed Ranjang Pandey beckon to an officer of the guard, who went up to Bhim Sen as if to silence him. But Bhim Sen brushed him aside. 'I remind you of our brave defence of Almora. It was I who supported our great General Amar Singh Thapa in his struggle against the British in the west, up to his last gallant action in the Deonthal hills. It was I who dealt with the aggressor Ochterlony and kept the British out of our sacred valley.' He stepped forward as if to get closer to those assembled in the court. 'I call on all here present to rise and speak for me.'

But no one did. A murmur ran through the gathering, nothing more.

This time it was the Rajendra Shah himself who beckoned to the officer of the guard. The officer called his soldiers, who seized Bhim Sen and escorted him forcibly from the dais to take him through the Basantpur Chowk back to the prison. Other soldiers took the court physicians off.

Adam looked up at those on the dais. He still saw little emotion on their faces, a touch of satisfaction perhaps, but certainly no triumph. The King rose and departed and after him the Senior Queen and the Heir Apparent. The Pandeys and the others followed. The oil lamp at one end of the dais burnt low and then flickered out and the gilded image of the God Vishnu receded into the gloom. Adam left the court with Tanka Rana and in the gathering dusk walked past the darkening temples and the tall pagodas of the Durbar Square, and returned to the Residency.

Three

When next Adam called on Dor Maske, an elderly lady took him up a staircase to a room where he was in bed. Looking up, Dor Maske introduced her to Adam. 'She is Maya,' he said. 'My wife, Mr Clarke. We are married now. Once she was the wife of my friend who died.'

Maya's hands came together in a namaste and she smiled at Adam. 'Yes, he is my husband, my old husband. He is not well today and must stay in bed. It is I who care for nim.' She was a small but portly woman and wore a brown sari draped over her shoulder. 'I also make you welcome to this house, Mr Clarke. Now, he wants to talk with you.'

She went from the room.

'Bhim Sen Thapa is dead,' Dor Maske said, pulling himself up with some pain against the pillows. 'It is said he killed himself, that he cut his throat with a kukhri. Yesterday he died.'

'Bhim Sen did that?' Adam queried this, thinking it was not in keeping with his spirited defence at his trial.

'Great pressure was brought on him. The Senior Queen and the Pandeys were behind it. They were about to bring a terrible disgrace on Bhim Sen's womenfolk, his wives, daughters and concubines. They were to be stripped naked, marched through the streets of Kathmandu and have indecent acts committed against them. They were to be totally degraded and become objects of derision. Bhim Sen would not have that.'

'So he did kill himself.'

'He did. But with the help of officers of Rajendra Shah's guard. They threatened even worse for his womenfolk. Then they gave him the kukhri.'

'He confessed to the poisoning?'

Dor Maske shifted irritably. 'I told you Bhim Sen was not the poisoner. It was the King. The confession the Ditha read was not Bhim Sen's. His name was forged. You will come to see one day.'

'Bhim Sen's tragedy did not end there,' Dor Maske continued. 'Even his corpse is disgraced. Last night his body was cut into pieces, and these have been strewn around Kathmandu, thrown amongst the filth of the gutters. Later they will be taken to the river bank and left there for the vultures. There is no funeral pyre for Bhim Sen. No priests. His ashes will not be cast on the holy waters. Yet he has done so much for the gods.'

'And the physicians,' Adam asked. 'What of them?'

'They were dealt with immediately after the trial. The court physician, being a Brahman and twice born, could not be executed. So with hot irons they burnt much of his skull away to expose his brain and burnt away his cheeks to expose his jaw bones. He cannot live for long. The deputy physician they executed. He was impaled and, whilst skewered on his pole and still alive, they cut his heart out. That was their fate, Mr Clarke. It is how the Pandeys dealt with them.'

True Bhim Sen had committed his own cruelties, Adam thought, many cruelties no doubt. To secure his power thirty years ago, he had crushed the Pandeys, executed and exiled many; and he had burnt Rana Bahadur's queen, Rajeswari Devi, as a sati on the river bank near Sanku village along with the ex-King's fourteen concubines. It was a vile crime, inexcusable. But Adam realised that Bhim Sen had been a great leader. His punishment and that of the court physicians turned Adam even more against the Pandeys.

'Who will lead the Thapas now, Dor Maske?' Adam asked.

Dor Maske shrugged, 'It is difficult, Mr Clarke. There might be Jung Bahadur one day; he has seven brothers to support him. But not yet, he is still young. I hear you saw the Heir Apparent and his soldiers chasing him in the Durbar Square. He escaped, of course, by hiding in a well. The most likely leader is Mathabar Singh Thapa, but the British hold him in India, in Simla. I do not like him. He is arrogant, overbearing, rude, but he is a nephew of Bhim Sen and well-placed to lead the Thapas. He could control the army.'

'But he is our prisoner.'

'Yes, the British hold him. Your East India Company treats him well; it pays him a pension of a thousand rupees a month.'

'Still, they hold him,' Adam said.

'Yes, but Mathabar Singh is no enemy of the British. True he went into India without the Resident's permission. The British captured him one night when he was crossing the Sutlej on his way to visit the Sikh leader Ranjit Singh. They believed he sought an alliance with the Sikhs for Nepal against the British. But it was not that. Mathabar Singh was seeking Ranjit Singh's support for the Thapas against the Pandeys here in Kathmandu.'

'Still, they hold him in Simla,' Adam repeated.

'It suits Mathabar Singh Thapa. It is not yet safe for him to return here. Not now. The Pandeys and the Senior Queen would quickly murder him. He will return when the time is right. The British should help in that because it is very much in their own interest. Tell the Resident so, and that I shall advise him when the time is right.'

Dor Maske sank back into the pillows, tired from his talking. After a while he smiled and surprised Adam by saying, 'You are young and healthy, Mr Clarke. I know of the St Clair's daughter. I can see she would be discontented with her life in the Residency. She is also young and needs company. And attractive I believe, in your English way.' Dor Maske thought for some moments, 'And there are women in my own household who would interest you. They know of you and I am sure they will find your company agreeable. There is Lalit whom you have seen. We are Newars, Mr Clarke, and the gods give us some latitude.'

Maya returned and took Adam from the room, down the staircase to the ground floor and to the back of the house. Here there was nothing of the luxury of the reception room, or the flower gardens as at the front of the house. Maya led Adam along a terrace of burnt brick, past a kitchen darkened by years of smoke where several maids were working. Nearby a score of fowls pecked for food and several well-fed cows ground lazily at their cud. Two peasants were at work in the field, one pulling a wooden plough and the other guiding it, preparing the soil for a new crop; a few pigs followed them to forage in the furrows.

Maya stopped at an open doorway that had an image of a serpent painted on its lintel, in black with a red tika mark and white cotton trimmings; people had left offerings of pots of milk, and rice and honey and flowers. A small oil lamp was burning and an aroma of incense filled the air.

'It is Naga Panchami,' Maya told Adam. 'Everyone worships the Snake Gods today.'

She led him from the terrace into a large, well-cared-for room, its floor tiled with bricks, the wooden furniture scrubbed clean; and the large hearth was stacked with wood ready for burning. An image of the elephant-headed, pot-bellied God Ganesh was to one side of the hearth.

Maya asked Adam to sit at a table. 'We have food prepared for you, Mr Clarke,' she said.

A servant carried in a platter and placed it before Adam. Lalit stood at the door and Maya had her enter. The two women sat opposite Adam as he ate the meal of curried chicken, rice, cauliflower, potato and hot chilli. Maya watched quite openly, pleased he accepted the food. Lalit was more circumspect, glancing in Adam's direction occasionally, but most of the time looking towards the hearth or sitting with her eyes lowered.

This time Lalit had not drawn her sari up to her eyes and Adam knew now he had not been mistaken. He thought her face was a delight. Her olive skin was a little darker than his own, her features shapely and her black eyes almond-shaped. She had a red tika mark on her forehead. This time she wore a light blue sari with borders embroidered in red, and again her jewellery, the bangles, anklets and earrings, and the golden ornament in her hair.

The servant brought a clay pot and bowl and poured a drink for Adam. He sipped the liquor, to find it potent, almost breathtaking.

'It is raksi,' Maya said. 'Do you find it pleasant?'

'Strong. Yes, pleasant,' he told her as its warmth penetrated his chest. He had heard of raksi, the strong rice spirit.

'Do you like our food too?' Maya asked. 'Do you have such food in your own country?'

Adam told her he enjoyed it, that English food was not so spicy.

'Dor Maske has told us about you,' she said. 'You are not a soldier.'

Adam explained he was an official of the British East India Company.

'Dor Maske told us you are from England, a country far away,' Maya said. 'You came from over the sea. We have never seen the sea. Would you tell us about it?'

Adam told her about the sea, its calms and storms and changing colours, the saltiness. He tried to give her some idea of the great expanse of the blue oceans, and told her of the ships with their white sails. Maya listened attentively, intervening now and then for further explanations. Then she asked about England, and Adam told her something of it.

Maya turned to Lalit who had been listening attentively. 'You, too, have a question for Mr Clarke, Lalit. I am sure he will answer it for you.'

'Indeed I will, Lalit,' Adam said, smiling to encourage her.

'Yes I will ask,' Lalit said to Maya. She looked at Adam, 'I have heard you are not only of England. You are also of Nepal. Your father was born in Kathmandu.'

'Yes,' Adam replied, 'I am of both England and your country. My grandmother was Maneka, a lady of Jaya Malla's court, the old King of Kathmandu.'

Lalit looked at him. 'I can see it in your face.'

'Does that please you?' Adam ventured.

She smiled. 'Yes, it does please me.'

Adam wondered about Lalit, who she was, what her place was in Dor Maske's household. She was young to be another wife, he thought, and Dor Maske had not introduced her as his daughter. Perhaps she was his concubine in spite of his advancing age and his poor health.

Now the meal was finished, Adam left the table and followed Maya and Lalit out to the terrace. A peasant was waiting there, and he told Maya he had finished cleaning the wells. Maya thanked him and explained to Adam, 'Everyone cleans the wells on Naga Panchami, Mr Clarke. It is a good time. The Snake Gods are away visiting their ancestors, so we can clean the wells without disturbing them.' She took her leave of Adam. 'I must see that the work is properly done. Lalit will take you to your carriage.'

They found Tanka Rana waiting with the carriage. As Adam was leaving, Lalit looked up at him and asked shyly, 'Will you visit Dor Maske another time, Mr Clarke?'

'I will,' Adam told her. 'And I will look forward to seeing you again.'

Four

'I am pleased you came quickly, Mr Clarke,' Dor Maske said, holding up a paper. 'My people have brought this to me. It will alarm you. It is what Rajendra Shah will say when he addresses the army today. There can be no doubt that the hands of the Pandeys and the Senior Queen are in it. He will seek the army's favour by promising them war with the British.' Dor Maske handed the paper to Adam. 'Read for yourself, Mr Clarke.'

Alarmed, Adam read Rajendra Shah's address to the army:

> "The English Government is powerful, abounding in wealth and in all other resources for war. I have kept well with the English so long, because I am unable to cope with them. Besides, I am bound by a treaty of amity, and have no excuse to break it. Nor have I money to support a war. Troops I have, and arms and ammunition in plenty, but no money. This is the reason I have reduced your pay. I want treasure to fight the English. Take lower pay for a year or two, and when I have some money in hand, then I will throw off the mask and indulge you with war."

Adam showed his anger.

'And there's more to it,' Dor Maske said. 'A Gurkha detachment has entered the Ramnagar Territory near our southern border. It has reclaimed ninety villages for Nepal—territory the British got under the Treaty of Sagauli twenty years ago.'

'An outrage, Dor Maske. A declaration of war almost,' Adam said.

'Will the British take it so?'

'There are many who would.'

'Your Governor General in Calcutta?'

'I'm not sure. Perhaps not. He is likely to take the Resident's advice.'

'The Resident's advice?'

'He's a man of peace.'

'And you, Mr Clarke?'

'I do not want war.'

Dor Maske sat looking at Adam for some moments, a smile touching his face. 'Yes, your blood itself would be in conflict.'

Adam thought it over. In war he would certainly side with Britain, he decided. There could be no doubt of that. After all he was English, and an official of the British East India Company.

One of Dor Maske's womenfolk came into the room, not to serve them tea but with another paper which she handed to him. He studied it then went to some trouble thanking her, complimenting her on getting it for him so quickly.

Dor Maske's lips turned down disparagingly as he pointed to the paper she had brought him. 'It is not unexpected,' he said. 'The army will reply to the King. She brought me a copy of their text. Again Pandey hands are in it. There is no doubt.'

Adam now read the army's reply to the King:

> "True the English Government is great, but care the wild dogs of Nepal how large a herd they attack? They are sure to get their bellies filled. You want no money for making war, for the war shall support itself. We will plunder Lucknow and Patna. We must first get rid of the Resident who sees and forestalls all. We must be able, unseen, to watch the moment of attack. It will soon come. It is come. Give the word and we will destroy the Resident, and then war will follow of course. You want an excuse for war. There is one ready made. Let us act without being watched by the Resident, and we will soon make the Ganges our boundary. Or if the English, as they say are your friends and want peace, why do they keep possession of half your dominions? Let them restore Kamaon and Sikkim. These are yours, demand them back. And if they refuse, drive out the Resident and let us have war."

'They are very threatening words,' Adam said.

'True, but only words as yet.'

'The safety of the Residency?' Adam asked.

'Safe at present, perhaps. There are some moderates around the King,' Dor Maske replied.

In Lainchaur on his way back to the Residency, Adam saw placards attached to trees by the roadside and he had the syce stop the carriage. As he read them, again his anger rose. They predicted the end of the British, claiming their forces were over-extended in Afghanistan and China, that the fighting there would cripple them. They said the Burmese had spurned the British Resident at the Court of Ava and had expelled him from their country. They urged Nepal to do the same, to throw the

British Resident out. Then Nepal would invade India and drive the British back into the sea.

Back at the Residency, Adam told the Resident of the King's address to the army and the army's reply, and also of the placards on the trees in Lainchaur. The Resident showed little emotion, just gave an occasional frown, a shrug. He sat in silence for some minutes, considering, then excused himself and left, saying, 'There is much to be done, there must not be war.'

After the Resident had gone, Mr St Clair restrained himself no longer. 'What indignity,' he said loudly. 'What insults. They scorn us, hold us all in contempt, the British Crown, Lord Auckland, the Company and the Resident. What an insult from these pests, these wild dogs as they call themselves. They want war with us. Then let them have it!'

Captain O'Keefe objected. He again reminded Mr St Clair that he had fought the Gurkhas at Kalanga where the Irish Dragoons were routed and the gallant Major General Gillespie was killed, and then at Parsa where the Gurkhas slaughtered many of the Company's soldiers.

Mr St Clair ignored him. 'Why is it Adam? And I ask all of you this. I cannot understand it. Why is Nepal different? We run other Indian States; we control their Durbars and their appointments most of the time. We tax them, ensure their justice is reasonable and regulate their armies. Conduct their foreign relations too. Residents there have real power. I know it, I had much to do with them. Why not Nepal?'

'They say our army is extended,' he went on, ' Over-extended. That the fighting in Afghanistan and China will cripple us. That they'll drive us back into the sea. What audacity. And what a pack of lies.'

'No, Alfred. There is something in what they say,' Captain O'Keefe objected again. 'You know well enough there's trouble in Afghanistan. Our Afghan friend Shah Suja's has let us down. He's not popular. Can't raise an army from his own people to fight on our side. We've got twenty thousand of our own troops in Kabul. But it's not enough, not by any means.'

But Mr St Clair was not to be subdued. 'We'll thrash them in China, Captain.'

It was Dr Jones who objected. 'Can't agree with opium. We shouldn't be there. To send an army to make the Chinese take our opium isn't good.'

Mr St Clair came back again. 'The Indians murdered our Resident in Jaipur. Will that happen here? Will it be like Burma? We all know the Burmese forced our Resident from the Court of Ava. So now the Nepalese jeer at us about it. I knew the Resident in Burma. It was Major Burney, a fine fellow. Major Burney wanted another war against Burma and advised the Company to attack again. I know that. I was in Calcutta then.'

Mr St Clair shook his head sadly, disapprovingly. 'But the Company refused, rejected Burney's advice. I was amazed. Could hardly believe it. Burma's kings humiliated Burney. Tharrawaddy especially. It was sound advice Burney gave. Our Residents must not be humiliated. I would have sent our army into Burma again. There is a lesson for us here in Nepal. I say that.'

No one spoke for a while. Then Dr Jones said hopefully, 'Of course, it might come to nothing. The Resident will find a way out. We must have faith in him.'

When Mrs St Clair next invited Adam to play cribbage, Sarah joined them. After the game, whilst they were taking tea, she said, 'I see you leaving the Residency some mornings in your carriage, Mr Clarke. How I envy you. Have you forgotten me? Of course you did promise.'

Adam looked at her mother expecting her disapproval. But Mrs St Clair was resigned. 'Sarah will have her own way,' she sighed. 'I must say she has pestered me. Not at all in a daughterly fashion, in my opinion. I have told you I've always acted with great propriety, and always will, even in this strange place. Certainly I do not agree, but I shall not object. If you are sure Sarah is not imposing on you, you may take her to see something of Kathmandu. Not that I myself have any desire to.'

Sarah sat smiling. 'Thank you mamma. And please do not worry. No harm will come to me. Will it, Mr Clarke?'

Adam hesitated. 'There are signs of trouble, Sarah.'

'Maybe, but I will be safe. Won't I, Mr Clarke?

Mrs St Clair answered for him. 'Of course Sarah will be safe. She is a British young lady.'

Adam mentioned possible trouble to Mrs St Clair; but she insisted that the Gurkhas would nor dare molest her daughter.

So one morning soon after, Adam helped Sarah up into the carriage, introduced her to Tanka Rana, and had the syce drive them into Kathmandu. The truth was that Adam, with the threats from the Gurkhas in mind, was not at all sure that he should be taking Sarah.

But he heard her saying, 'Now, Mr Clarke, I want to see everything. Otherwise I shall be really very annoyed with you.' Her blue eyes looked up at him. 'I hope you don't mind me saying that.'

'Not at all, Miss St Clair,' he told her. Even in the long brown dress she wore, and a straw hat, her appearance was appealing. Adam could not imagine her annoying him.

'Mamma is so old-fashioned,' she said. 'I had to persuade her to let me come with you. It took some doing.'

'I hope you didn't annoy your mother.'

'Perhaps I did. It doesn't matter.'

They spent the next hour exploring Kathmandu. Sarah was certainly interested and very excited. They walked through the narrow streets between the tall terraced houses, with Sarah pulling up the hems of her dress a little and stepping carefully to avoid the garbage there. She brushed past the wandering cows, sometimes patted their rumps with almost the aplomb of a milkmaid on the estate in Hollybrook, Adam thought; and she took no offence at the goats and pigs that shared the streets.

Many people were out that morning, and they would stop and look at Sarah then stand aside to clear the way in front of her. They pointed at her and talked amongst themselves, but from what Adam could hear there was only curiosity and no hostility.

Best of all, Sarah liked the Durbar Square, the temples, the great pagodas, Annapurna's Temple and Ganesh's Temple with its golden roof. She was fascinated with the house of the Kumari, the little-girl living Goddess of Kathmandu. She wanted to know about the Kumari, so Adam told her of her part in the festivals—how one of her predecessors placed the red tika mark on the Gurkha King's forehead the night of the Indra Jatra when he took Kathmandu from the old Malla king. He told her how—to test their courage—little girl candidates for the Kumari are put alone in a dark room amongst the still bleeding heads of sacrificed buffaloes. That did not seem to worry Sarah, but Adam noticed she did not stay long before the image of the Black Bhairab, the Bhairab of Death, garlanded with human skulls, his fangs menacing and great anger in his face.

Tanka pointed to a house near the Singh Satal Temple at one end of the Durbar Square, 'It is the house of Gagan Singh,' he told Adam, speaking quietly. 'He is the Junior Queen Laxmi Devi's lover. So it is said. He was once a chodbar in her service.' Tanka explained that a chodbar was a servant in the palace who was allowed to enter the women's quarters. 'Now he is Laxmi Devi's favourite. She gave him this house.'

Adam had the syce drive outside the town's walls, to show Sarah a little of the countryside before going back to the Residency. Their return took them along the edge of the Tundikhel, where Adam expected to see the usual activity of soldiers about the cantonments and regiments at drill. But this time it was different. They saw angry soldiers gathered in groups, some talking to each other loudly, some yelling and some listening to their leaders haranguing them from gun carriages and other vantage points. Some of the soldiers had laid down their arms, but many still carried their muskets, their swords and kukhries.

'It is best not to delay here, Mr Clarke,' Tanka Rana said.

Adam agreed and the syce whipped the pony along. But a group of soldiers—fifty or more who had left the Tundikhel and were gathered at the roadside—stopped them, some of them running out in front and a couple of them grasping the pony's bridle. Soldiers milled around the carriage, pressing in on it. A motley lot, Adam thought. A few were obviously from an elite regiment; but many had uniforms unkempt and hanging off them, or wore a peasant's waist-cloth below their military jackets. But for all that Adam thought they looked fierce enough, more dangerous than the Company's sepoys.

Suddenly a soldier hoisted himself up into the carriage and seized Sarah's arm to pull her down to the road. But Adam and Tanka Rana were onto him immediately. They wrenched him away from Sarah, manhandled him out of the carriage and threw him back to the road. Tanka Rana went after the soldier, but he ran off quickly and was soon lost amongst the crowd.

Returning to the carriage, Tanka Rana explained, 'It is very serious, Mr Clarke. They are very angry. Some are peasants who want to be paid what is owing to them and then be discharged back to their farms. But most are even more angry. They rave against Rajendra Shah, and they are demanding that the Resident be driven out of Nepal. They threaten to attack the Residency. Many in the army will mutiny tonight, I think.'

Sarah assured Adam she was unharmed, not to worry about her, but he saw her face was white and the sleeve of her blouse torn. Adam had the syce whip the pony on again, and this time the soldiers stood back and let them pass. He made all haste back to the Residency.

At the Residency, Adam alerted the Resident, who acted immediately. He told Captain O'Keefe to assemble everyone in the St Clairs' bungalow, so they could make a stand together should it come to that. They armed themselves from the Residency's arsenal. Captain O'Keefe had the sepoys fortify the bungalow with bags of earth and rocks, and branches cut from nearby trees. He placed the garrison's four cannon at the front of the Residency buildings and put a detachment there. The rest of the garrison he positioned along the perimeter of the Residency grounds, the greater strength where they bordered a Gurkha parade ground.

And so they waited through the afternoon. Captain O'Keefe made frequent inspections of his soldiers; Adam wondered if his thoughts went back to the battles he had fought, to the bloody defeats by the Gurkhas at Kalanga and Parsa. The captain was business-like, obviously the experienced soldier, and calm. Dr Jones brought his box of medicines and his tools of trade, putting them away out of sight. Mr St Clair locked his liquor cupboard.

As the afternoon wore on, Mrs St Clair came up to Adam. 'I'm sure they wouldn't dare attack us.' She pointed through the window to the cannon. 'If they did come, I know our cannon would frighten them off. Terrify them. I've seen our guns firing at practice. They are terrible. No one could stand up to them. I believe the Gurkhas could not. Barbarians really. Captain O'Keefe agrees with me they could not. And even if the Gurkhas got to our bungalow, you men would be here with your swords and muskets.'

'Of course we would, Mrs St Clair,' Adam assured her.

'We are British,' Mrs St Clair said. 'You are too, Adam. You are mainly British.'

But Adam wondered if Mrs St Clair could imagine a detachment of a hundred or more yelling Gurkha soldiers, madly excited men scenting the kill, their swords drawn, sharp kukhries in hand, screaming into the bungalow to slaughter those left alive by the Gurkhas' guns. At the same time, however, Adam was British enough to know the value of such an attitude, such confidence. And Mrs St Clair was also British enough to go and arrange for the two servants remaining to prepare afternoon tea.

Adam spent a good deal of time in Sarah's company that afternoon. 'Your mother is taking things well,' he told her. 'A brave lady.'

'She is. But I expect it of mamma. The big things will not upset her. Just the little things.' Sarah laughed, 'Things like me. Of course mamma is right. We can defend ourselves.'

'Of course, Sarah.'

Sarah had taken one of the hand guns, a new rifle, a Baker Adam saw; she wanted him to explain it to her and show her how to use it. The thought of her firing it worried Adam. He looked at her hands and arms, the slender shoulders under her blouse, her slight body. 'It's not for you, Sarah,' he said. 'They're not easy to fire. They'll kick badly.'

Sarah frowned. 'No show me, please. I might need to know how.'

Adam explained the rifle to her, a breech-loader, how to put in the ball and powder, replace the flints from spares if needed, and how to take aim and fire. He took care to tell her how to hold it, warning her again about the recoil. She asked him to repeat the instructions several times, till she was satisfied.

Once she said to him, 'I know your Christian name is Adam, Mr Clarke. It's a nice name. Would you tell me about your home in Hollybrook, about your grandfather and Maneka? I should like to hear.'

So Adam talked about his grandparents, until Mrs Clarke called them for afternoon tea. She had set things out on the table, as though they were safe in an English cottage, with her best china, her silver, and cakes on a tray. 'I have standards to keep to,' she said, laughing. 'I've always done so. That is true, Alfred. Isn't it?'

'It is true, Agnes. I've always admired you for it. Particularly now,' her husband confirmed. 'I'm sure we all admire you for it.'

A little after dusk a scout reported to Captain O'Keefe that Gurkhas were in Lazimpath and headed for Lainchaur, where the Residency was. Captain O'Keefe had the garrison on the ready and asked those in the St Clair's bungalow to stay at their posts. Then in the distance Adam could hear shouting and the discharge of fire-arms. There was no doubt, the Gurkhas were coming in the direction of the Residency. Sarah, at her post near Adam's, asked him to be sure she could use her rifle properly.

'It is exciting, Mr Clarke,' she said as she practised her aim through the bungalow window.

Adam could make out the tension of her face, and reached over and took her hand to reassure her. 'It is, Sarah. You will remember it always,' he said.

With no moon and early monsoon clouds blocking out the stars, the night darkened. Adam could make out little beyond the nearby cannon, only the outlines of the trees and shrubbery, and one of the sepoys on guard on the periphery. As he watched, it seemed the noise of the Gurkha soldiers was growing louder. The tension in the bungalow increased. Again they waited.

Mr St Clair was first to see the burning. He pointed and they crowded around him following his direction to see. Not far away, a red glow broke the darkness. As they watched, the glow increased. A flame licked upwards, then another, and soon the flames lit that part of the night.

'It's Pashkar Shah's house,' the Resident said.

The Chautariya Pashkar Shah was a relative of the King, and, under the prime minister, had nominal responsibility for the army. The Gurkhas have chosen well, Adam thought: symbolic, attacking the King through his cousin.

They peered through the darkness at the raging fire, until gradually the flames burnt low and subsided and the darkness of the night took over again. And they themselves stayed at their posts, alerted, ready for their own turn. But by dawn the Gurkhas had still not come. They found they had moved from Lainchaur, left the neighbourhood. The Residency had not been their goal.

That morning on his way to Dor Maske's house to get information for the Resident, Adam could see no sign of the mutineers. The roads were quiet, but a pall of smoke hung over the town and soldiers were gathered again on the Tundikhel.

Dor Maske was waiting. 'You were not molested in the Residency last night, Mr Clarke. They burnt the house of Pashkar Shah, the King's cousin. You would have seen the flames.'

'Yes, we watched it burning.'

'They did not stop there. They returned to Kathmandu for more burning. They burnt five more houses, homes of members of Ranjang Pandey's Ministry.'

'Smoke was still creating a haze about the town when I passed.'

'I hear it terrified the King,' Dor Maske said. 'He had not foreseen the trouble. It seems the mutiny is over. The King took advice from his relatives, the Chautariyas, when Fath Jang and Guru Prasad called on him this morning. Rajendra Shah agreed to appear before the army again, reluctantly because he fears them. He has now addressed the army on the Tundikhel for a second time, and has promised to increase their pay and redress their grievances. The soldiers have accepted and are returning to their cantonments.'

'It is welcome news, Dor Maske. We'll be thankful at the Residency.'

News of the end of the mutiny that day was indeed welcome at the Residency. The Resident told Captain O'Keefe to return the garrison to their quarters, except for a patrol around the boundary and the sepoy gun crews. The tension eased in the St Clairs' bungalow. Mr St Clair opened up his supply of liquor and served drinks, and Mrs St Clair provided an evening meal.

The meal was a quiet affair, with the stress of the past twenty-four hours bearing heavily on them. At the table they joined in a short prayer of thanks. The Resident praised Captain O'Keefe's management of the garrison and he thanked all concerned for their readiness and calmness. Sarah, sitting next to Adam, turned and whispered a special thanks to him.

Mrs St Clair, pleased but not entirely happy, looked glumly along the table. 'I have to apologise. It's not my usual standard. By no means. Is it Alfred?' she asked.

'Come now, Agnes,' her husband said. 'You've done well. What could you expect? Who would expect even this? There's been a mutiny, Agnes. Lucky to have a meal. Lucky to still be here, perhaps.'

Mrs St Clair brightened a little. 'Of course we would still be here. I know the Gurkha army was on the rampage. But I said they wouldn't dare attack us. They did not. We are British.'

No one remarked on that and the meal went on with little talk.

A few days later when Adam called on Mrs St Clair to apologise for taking Sarah into trouble with the Gurkha soldiers near the Tundikhel, he found her in her sitting room with an apron covering her dress and wearing long gloves. She was at the table where they played cribbage and had the bric-a-brac down from the mantelpiece, dusting it, polishing the metal pieces.

'You've caught me at work, Mr Clarke. I do work, you know,' she said by way of welcome. 'I keep up standards in my house. Just as I always do in other things. Even here in Kathmandu.'

'Will I call again later?' Adam asked.

'No, stay. I've been wanting to see you. I have something to say to you.' She frowned as she took off her gloves. 'Yes, I will say what I think. You have disappointed me badly. I trusted you. I might have known Sarah would not be safe with you.'

Adam was surprised, remembering he had warned her of possible trouble. 'I have come here to apologise, Mrs St Clair,' he protested.

But Mrs St Clair went on. 'You were escorting a young lady, a British young lady. Leading her into that pack of ruffians! Such a thing. It's never happened to me. Mr St Clair has never done that. Sarah doesn't deserve it. Not at all.'

Adam tried again to apologise.

'I want no apologies,' she told him. 'Not for Sarah or myself. Not even from their King. I know about them. What they did to the old Bhim Sen.'

Mrs St Clair got up and started replacing her bric-a-brac, moving from the table to the mantelpiece. 'No, Mr Clarke, you must realise Sarah is a lady. She is English.' She stopped and looked at Adam. 'You do not understand. You are not English, Mr Clarke.'

Of course there was his Nepalese grandmother, but her taunt irritated Adam. He was about to object when he heard Mrs St Clair sobbing, and when she turned he saw tears in her eyes.

It was Sarah who saved Adam. She came into the room and before going to her mother went up to Adam, took his arm and walked to the door with him, saying quietly, 'I'm so sorry, Mr Clarke. Mamma gets like this sometimes. She will get over it. Mamma always does.' Adam saw the concern on Sarah's face. 'But please, do not take offence. For my sake, please do not.'

Five

One evening, just as the rice harvest was finishing, Dor Maske invited Adam to his house. Adam drove there through fields brown with the stubble where peasants were harvesting the last of the paddy, threshing it on roadways and other hard surfaces, and winnowing the grain; others carried the rice to the storage bins. The afternoon was cool and crisp, the air crystal clear under the blue sky, and always there were the great icy mountains to the north. The people were pleased that the hard work of the harvest was finishing, and happy they had a good harvest to ensure supplies for the coming year. Some smiled up at him as he drove past and some joined their hands in friendly namastes.

Dor Maske was waiting for Adam. 'The harvest has finished,' he said. 'And my household will celebrate the harvest moon. Would you like to join us? My womenfolk will make Yomarhi cakes for a feast.'

Adam went with Dor Maske to the back part of his house, along the terrace where the fowls were busy pecking at the grains of rice that had been spilt, and past the smoke-blackened kitchen and the servants' quarters, to the large room where some time ago Dor Maske's wife, Maya, had served him a meal. The God Ganesh was still there beside the hearth, his image shimmering in the glow from the fire, which was lit both for warmth and to heat a steaming cooking-stove. Dor Maske's womenfolk were waiting for him, Maya and Lalit and another three, whom Dor Maske introduced to Adam as Uma, Bhu and Ratna. Each was dressed in her best for the occasion in bright saris and wearing jewellery and ornaments in their hair. They welcomed Adam and Dor Maske with their namastes and stood there waiting for Dor Maske to speak.

Dor Maske went to the table, which held a great bowl of dough made from rice flour, a pot of dark sugar and a heap of sesame seed. 'I see you are prepared,' he said to his wife. 'I am waiting for the Yomarhi cakes to be made.'

The women set to work. They blended dough, sugar and sesame seed and drew off pieces which could be conveniently held in a hand. Adam watched as their fingers moulded the cakes into the shape of figs.

'They are skilful, are they not?' Dor Maske said to Adam. 'Newar women have done this through the ages to mark the end of the harvest. For how long no one knows. It is said that in very early times a beggar came to the house of a merchant on the evening of the harvest moon. The merchant took him in and gave him Yomarhi cakes to eat. But he proved to be no beggar. He was the God Kuber in disguise, Kuber a God of Wealth. Grateful, Kuber revealed his true identity and made a present of figs to the merchant. From then on the merchant's business prospered.'

Dor Maske called to Lalit, 'Please bring a Yomarhi cake to Mr Clarke.'

Lalit held it out in her open hand for Adam's inspection.

'Yes, it's like a fig,' he said. 'You've shaped it well.'

She smiled up at him, pleased. 'It is yet to be cooked,' she said, pointing to the steaming stove.

The women worked busily at the table and they shaped many cakes as figs and steamed them over the stove. Then they made other shapes from the dough: images of a peasant farmer and his wife, of the elephant-headed Ganesh, a fish, and various types of fruit. Lalit would bring them over to Adam, holding them out for his approval, and apparently pleased with his praise. She was giving him much attention and this pleased Dor Maske.

Soon many of the Yomarhi cakes were cooked and laid out on the table. Dor Maske signalled to his wife, who left the room and returned with the others of the household, Tanka Rana, the syce, the farm hands and the servants. Dor Maske took some of the cakes, put them in a clay pot which a servant had brought in, and placed the filled pot near the image of Ganesh. Then Tanka Rana prayed over the pot whilst the rest in the room watched in silence.

'He is thanking the harvest gods,' Dor Maske explained to Adam. 'Now we will hide the pot of Yomarhi cakes in a bin of rice. It will stay there for four days. If we do this, the God Kuber might make our stock of rice increase many times.'

'Could that be?' Adam asked.

Dor Maske shrugged. 'It has never happened to my knowledge. But some believe it possible. Some families in the valley hope for it.'

The servant took the pot away to hide it in a rice bin.

The ceremony now finished, Maya gave generous helpings from the remaining cakes to Tanka Rana, the farm hands, the syce and the servants. They thanked her and went away, taking their cakes back to their own quarters. Dor Maske, his womenfolk and Adam sat around the long table to enjoy the sweet cakes that were left.

Night had set in by the time they had eaten. Dor Maske spoke to Lalit, then took his leave of Adam. The womenfolk climbed the ladder at the end of the room to their quarters. Except for Lalit, who came up to Adam.

'Dor Maske has asked me to show you an image of a god,' she said, not sure of herself and avoiding Adam's gaze. 'He said it is a god which your grandmother, Maneka, gave to his father once. Will you please come with me?'

Adam followed Lalit, her bangles and anklets tinkling, out along the terrace and through a dark corridor to the front part of the house which was now lit by an occasional oil lamp, then up a ladder to the floor above, and still another ladder to a room at the top.

'This is my own room,' Lalit said. 'It has been mine since I was a child. Dor Maske has always been kind to me.' She opened the wooden shutter on the window. 'Now there will be light for you to see,' she said.

Outside the window in the cold night, the light from the full moon lit the countryside, the fields below, the village beyond and the surrounding mountains. And to the north the great Himalayas were massive shapes of silver overhanging the valley. Adam watched with Lalit, who stood beside him quietly, not breaking the spell.

After a time Adam felt Lalit's hand on his arm. 'Dor Maske told me to show it to you,' she said, looking back. Adam turned, and there hanging on the wall was a painting of the Christ of the Sacred Heart. He could see it clearly enough in the moonlit room, and recalled his grandmother speaking of it.

'A Christian god, I think.' Lalit said.

'He is, Lalit,' Adam told her.

'He is a god with a sad face,' she said.

Adam turned back to the window with Lalit still beside him, near enough for him to sense the warmth of her body through the cold air. He moved closer to her, then took her hand and she let it lie there, trembling a little, in his.

Adam felt his desire for her surge within him. Putting his arms around her he drew her to him tightly with the passion that he felt; and she yielded and he held her there, the softness of her body against his. The moonlight played on her face as she looked up at him. For a little while he held her, her warmth against the cold night, and thrilled at the possibility she offered.

Then Adam let her go. Holding her at arm's length and looking down into her face, he said, 'You are beautiful, Lalit. As beautiful as Maneka must have been.'

Adam went to leave, but Lalit sought his hand and held it. 'Will you visit Dor Maske again?' she asked. 'Will you come to see me?'

'Yes, Lalit. I want to and will look forward to it,' he said, smiling down at her.

Adam found his own way down the ladders and out of Dor Maske's house. The patient syce was waiting. He boarded the carriage and, still with the thought of Lalit delighting him, made his way back to the Residency.

About that time Sarah St Clair called on Adam in his bungalow. 'I've come to make amends for mamma,' she said, when Adam's servant showed her in and seated her near the warmth of the fire, the December days being cold. 'Mamma behaved really terribly to you. I'm ashamed of her.'

Sarah's hand twisted the necklace hanging down over her blouse, self-consciously.

'I'm glad you've come,' Adam told her.

'I've come to apologise for mamma.'

'You don't have to.'

'No I want to. You must be annoyed with her.'

'Not at all. But perhaps your mother is making too much of it. I hope you'll excuse me saying so, Miss St Clair. No harm came to you. And you're a brave young lady.'

'Thank you. No, I enjoyed it really. It was an excitement for me with the soldiers. How different from my life in the Residency. And I loved the old town and all its temples. I'm grateful to you for it. I want to go with you again, if you'll take me.'

'Your mother?'

'She'll get over it. She'll agree in another week or so. But I'd like to make an excuse for her, if I may.'

'Of course.'

Sarah hesitated before she went on. 'Forgive me, but I think this is the first time you have been with the Company in such a place. You could not know. Some ladies, wives of the officials and the soldiers, hate such a life. Mamma dislikes it also. She misses England and home terribly, and sometimes it gets just too much for her.'

'Then she gets upset?'

'Yes. Of course she complains to daddy. But that is not always enough for her. When something happens, like the mutiny and with those soldiers near the Tundikhel, she gets very upset, out of all proportion. Do not think too badly of her, Mr Clarke. She'll get over it.'

'Yes, I understand. Thank you for telling me.'

Her excuses made Sarah shifted in her chair, undecided Adam thought, whether she should leave. Then the servant brought in tea.

'Let me pour it,' she said. 'I'm in no hurry. I told mamma I was calling on you.'

Sarah poured the tea, her blue eyes glancing around the room. 'I have been wondering what your bungalow would be like, Mr Clarke. It's not fair. Daddy can get all sorts of things from the Company and, of course, there are all mamma's things. But we're a family. The Company doesn't provide much for their single men. I am afraid you're not well done by.' She looked sad.

Adam smiled at her concern. True, the room had little, was Spartan you could say. But be replied, 'No, you mustn't feel sorry for me, Miss St Clair. I need little. I have all I need here.'

She looked around the room again, doubtfully, saying half to herself, 'Perhaps it will be different one day. You will come to need more.'

'Yes, perhaps.' Then to tease her a little, Adam asked, 'And when will that be, Miss St Clair?'

She did not answer and sat there a little confused, embarrassed, a blush coming up on her cheeks.

'You mean when I am married and have a family?' Adam asked, smiling.

'Yes, I did mean that.' She avoided his eyes.

'I hope you don't think me too forward,' Sarah said as she was leaving.

Adam did not and he told her so. 'I thought you behaved very properly, Sarah.' He used her Christian name. 'And I'm looking forward to your calling on me again.'

Before long Sarah did call again. It was with a formal little note from Mrs St Clair inviting him to their bungalow on Christmas Day.

Christmas day in the St Clair's bungalow in that remote valley had more than a touch of England. On a cold morning with snow on the hills the St Clairs welcomed their guests at the door, Mr St Clair with a firm handshake, Mrs St Clair and Sarah with quick kisses. The room was warm with Persian carpets and the curtains drawn, and the fire burning brightly in the hearth under the mantelpiece holding Mrs St Clair's bric-a-brac. The Resident conducted a short service, reading from the Church of England's Book of Common Prayer. Then a servant entered with a tray of drinks.

Mrs St Clair made her way towards Adam. 'I am so glad you've come, Adam,' she said, smiling and taking his hand. 'It's too long since we've had you here. It must not happen again. We're really one big family in the Residency. It's nice like that. And we must play cribbage together soon. I know Sarah wants to play.'

'I'd be delighted, Mrs St Clair,' Adam replied, he hoped convincingly enough.

'Yes. I enjoy playing cards with you,' Mrs St Clair said. 'I shall arrange something soon. I should like to talk to you longer. I shall. But now you must excuse me. I have things to attend to.'

She went off and Sarah joined Adam. 'I see mamma is paying you attention. It's nice. I told you she'd get over it.'

'You were right then, Sarah.'

'I am sometimes. Nearly always with mamma. Will you play cards with us again?'

'Yes, I told your mother so.'

'Come,' she said, pulling at Adam's sleeve. 'I have something .'

She led him out to the hall and took a parcel from a table. 'You can open it now. It's a Christmas present for you.'

Adam understood that the custom in the Residency was not to exchange Christmas presents. They did not have the run of Kathmandu to buy things there, and a few years ago it had become little more than exchanging bottles of spirits brought up from the Company's stores in India.

Adam opened the parcel to find a scarf.

'I knitted it myself. It's fine wool from the mountains,' Sarah explained. 'I hope you like it. It will be warm.'

Adam put the scarf around his neck. 'I do Sarah. It's nice and warm. I can tell already. You're a clever young lady. Thank you.'

'Well we must wrap it up again.' She reached up taking it from around his neck. As she did Adam bent and kissed her. She blushed, then hurried back to join the other guests.

Christmas day went off well. Dr Jones and Captain O'Keefe were in good spirits and Mr St Clair was relaxed and talking more quietly. Even the Resident threw off his cares of office and his work on the flora and fauna for a while. Mrs St Clair had gone to a good deal of trouble with the Christmas dinner, and Adam thought they would not have done much better on his father's estate in Hollybrook. There were roasts of wild bore and venison and an excellent Christmas pudding with flaming brandy sauce. And Mr St Clair served the best wines he had from Calcutta including an excellent port.

Six

The months went by and social life for those in the Residency continued in much the same vein. They visited each other's bungalows for drinks, the St Clairs gave their dinner parties, Adam played cribbage with Mrs St Clair and Sarah, and the Resident was busy with his work.

Adam found himself waiting for Dor Maske to call him to his house again, but he did not and it disappointed him, disconcerted him when he realised he was waiting not only for further news of happenings in the Durbar but also, and more importantly, to see Lalit again.

Adam thought a good deal about Lalit. Dor Maske seemed to encourage a relationship, but Adam was not sure what to do about it. Newar customs in such matters were still strange to him. He still knew nothing of Lalit herself and her place in Dor Maske's household, or the family she came from. He assumed most of Dor Maske's women were concubines whom he had acquired over the years. Again he wondered if Lalit was Dor Maske's latest acquisition in spite of his age and ill-health, or perhaps a slave like the maids in the kitchen, a much favoured slave, or perhaps she was a relative.

When at last one day Dor Maske did speak of Lalit, Adam learnt that she was not his concubine or his slave. 'Lalit is from the west of Nepal, from Doti,' he explained. 'She is the daughter of a high caste Chhetri. Her parents died when she was a small girl and I took her into my house. I am her guardian, she has no one else.'

When Adam asked if he could see Lalit, Dor Maske said, 'Lalit is not here today. She is a helper to Laxmi Devi, the Junior Queen, a lady-in-waiting you might say. Lalit is often at the palace away from my house for a week or so at a time.'

Although the mutiny in the army had finished, trouble with the Gurkhas came again. One day Adam, with Tanka Rana, chanced upon a mock battle at the Military Headquarters of the Kot. It angered him greatly. On the parade ground there, he again saw peasants dressed to mock the Irish Dragoons, their faces whitened with chalk, their uniforms soiled, ill-fitting and torn in places. Twenty or more of them were armed with muskets and kukhries. They stood in an irregular formation and before them was a yokel—Adam had to call him that—dressed as a British general, his uniform as dishevelled as the rest. Opposite these, fifty paces away, a Gurkha detachment from an elite regiment was lined up, also armed. And before them stood a Gurkha commander.

'The commander is the son of Prime Minister Ranjang Pandey,' Tanka Rana told Adam, agitated. 'We should leave here, Mr Clarke. It is not for us to see.'

'That may be, Tanka Rana,' Adam replied. 'But I wish to see.'

Across on the far side of the parade ground, Adam saw a group of spectators. And from the distance he recognised the Heir Apparent amongst them, remembering him from the trial of Bhim Sen Thapa.

'Most of the others are Pandeys,' Tanka Rana said. 'And there is Kulraj Pandey who is the Prime Minister's brother. Adam had seen him also at Bhim Sen Thapa's trial.

Kulraj Pandey spoke to the Heir Apparent then signalled for the battle to begin. The two commanders gave their orders and the two sides raised their muskets. One volley rang out, then another and another. Soon the parade ground was filled with a haze of smoke and the stench of burnt powder. Two of the mock Dragoons fell.

'A mock battle, of course,' Adam said. But Tanka Rana had moved away behind a wall and did not answer.

More volleys were fired. The smoke was thick now and Adam had to strain to see. The elite Gurkha detachment charged, swords drawn and raised high and ready, yelling their war cry "Ayo gurkha ayo gurkha!" till it echoed around the Kot. In seconds they were onto the mock Dragoons. The attack raged for some minutes before the order to withdraw came. Yes, surely a mock battle, Adam assured himself.

When the smoke cleared and the Gurkha detachment formed up again, Adam looked across the parade ground to see the Heir Apparent cheering excitedly, with the Pandeys encouraging him, urging him on. He also saw several mock Dragoons lying wounded on the parade ground. In places the stone was dark from their bleeding.

Tanka Rana called to Adam to leave, but he waited, watching the Heir Apparent come out onto the parade ground and walk amongst the fallen. Standing over one of them and scowling down, he called to a Gurkha soldier. The Heir Apparent spoke and the Gurkha drew his sword and slashed down at the mock Dragoon to take his life away. Adam could hear the Heir Apparent's laughter.

Adam left quickly, taking the carriage back to the Residency. 'It happens,' Tanka Rana said. 'Kulraj Pandey arranges it. It is to make the

Heir Apparent believe British soldiers cannot fight. You must excuse us, Mr Clarke.'

'The Pandeys, Tanka Rana, I cannot excuse them.'

On the way back to the Residency Adam noticed that more placards had been put up on the trees; some were even in front of the Residency itself. They claimed it was time for Nepal to strike at the British, and the Resident must be driven out. In the days that followed, unruly groups of soldiers appeared near the Residency, hurling insults, firing their muskets into the air and yelling their war-cry. On top of it all, the Gurkhas still occupied the ninety villages in Ramnagar they had taken earlier in the year.

The Resident called a meeting of Mr St Clair, Dr Jones, Captain O'Keefe and Adam. He seated them before the fire burning in the hearth, took a letter from his desk and joined them. Adam felt concern for him—he was obviously worried and not looking in good health.

The Resident held up the letter. 'From the Governor General in Calcutta,' he told them. 'I've kept Lord Auckland informed of the unfortunate events here, and they have worried him. Lord Auckland cannot decide on what course to take. He seems inclined towards war with Nepal, to send an army in and take these beautiful hills once and for all. '

Mr St Clair indicated his approval.

'Calcutta has advanced a brigade to Nepal's southern frontier,' the Resident told them. 'Under Colonel Oliver there are three native infantry regiments, the 6th Light Cavalry, artillery and irregular infantry. It's available to me in place of Oglander's force. For my use. Lord Auckland believes that Nepal's taking the Ramnagar villages could justify an all-out war.'

'One brigade only, sir?' Captain O'Keefe queried.

'Not a small force, Captain.'

'Mainly native infantry though.' The captain looked doubtful.

'Yes, but Lord Auckland has an alternative to war,' the Resident said. 'He thinks I might still be able to change the power in the Durbar. Get the Pandeys and the Senior Queen out, and those friendly with us in. Lord Auckland asks for my advice.'

Adam noticed Mr St Clair's disappointment, knowing what the Resident's advice would be.

'Yes, I advised against war,' the Resident said. 'Except for the Ramnagar villages. We'll retake them by force if necessary. I'll get the

Pandeys out of the Durbar if I can. Lord Auckland will leave it to me. He authorises me,' the Resident said, reading from Lord Auckland's letter, 'to promote to the utmost degree, consistent with prudence, the object of procuring the removal of the present Ministers of Nepal and the appointment of a friendly and honest administration in their place. I will do it.' He passed the letter around for each of them to read.

Not long after the meeting Adam accompanied the Resident on the audience he demanded with King Rajendra Shah. They left the Residency in fine style, the Resident sat in his carriage, stiffly, in uniform and beplumed, and Adam followed in a carriage behind him. They had a mounted escort from the Residency garrison, four sowars ahead and as many to the rear, who were armed with swords and muskets at their saddles. The horses were beautifully groomed and their harnesses sparkled in the winter sunshine.

They left the Residency at a fast trot, Captain O'Keefe leading, and kept a quick pace through Lazimpath into Kathmandu and the Durbar Square itself. The Resident alighted, accepted the escort's salute, their swords drawn, and walked quickly towards the palace with Adam following. A detachment of the royal guard was there and the commander welcomed them politely, led them into the palace through the labyrinth of courts and passages to the King.

Rajendra Shah was waiting, seated near a gilded image of Vishnu, with two soldiers of the royal guard standing by. He wore the dress of a Gurkha general, the same as Adam had seen him in at Bhim Sen's trial, the bejewelled turban and blue tunic, which this time was lined with fur for the winter. The room was cold and dark, lit only by an oil lamp, its flame flickering and the odour from the burning oil pervading the whole room. Rajendra Shah's beady eyes were unsteady with apprehension as his hands joined in a namaste to welcome the Resident and Adam.

'Please be seated', he said. 'Your visit honours me. I trust all goes well with you and with the great Lord Auckland in Calcutta. I sincerely wish our friendship to continue.'

'It is my wish too, Sire,' the Resident replied. 'That is why I have sought an audience with you. It is also Lord Auckland's wish. He has always made that clear to me.'

Rajendra Shah bowed his head in acceptance. 'I have found a way to cement our friendship with the British. I know these are troubled times for the Governor General in Afghanistan and China, as I understand and so I am told. To help, I propose to offer Lord Auckland the services of my army to use as he might wish. In Afghanistan. Against the war-like Sikhs. And in China. As he might decide.'

'A generous offer, Sire,' the Resident replied, his lips turned down, no sign of acceptance in his tone. 'But I suggest there are better ways to cement our friendship.'

Rajendra Shah's eyes turned away.

'Much has saddened me in Kathmandu,' the Resident continued. 'Saddened me greatly, Sire. For two years or more now I have watched events in the Durbar with great displeasure.'

'Great displeasure? In spite of our friendship? It surprises me.'

'It should not, Sire,' the Resident barely hid his irritation. 'I see there is much I must remind you of. I remember Bhim Sen's trial, his death and the treatment of his corpse—the persecution of the Thapas. I was not pleased with that. Nor was I pleased when your soldiers entered Ramnagar and took ninety of our villages.'

Rajendra Shah still avoided their eyes.

'Nor do your courts of law please me, Sire. I see no justice for Indian merchants who are wronged. I know you harbour fugitives, those escaping from the Company's justice. And I know you seek allies to war with us, the Sikhs, at the Court of Ava, at Peking, and elsewhere. All that displeases me.'

The Resident's plain speaking surprised Adam.

'I object to harassment from your soldiers,' the Resident continued. I object to the exaggerations in the placards I see posted near the Residency, placards threatening to drive me out, and urging war with us. And I object, Sire, to the scurrilous mocking of our brave Irish Dragoons. I have more.'

Rajendra Shah's hands moved defensively. 'No. I shall explain.'

'I would remind you, Sire, I have a strong force waiting on your southern border.'

'That I know. I shall explain.' Rajendra Shah lent forward, speaking softly as if not to be overheard. 'True, things have been done to endanger our friendship. That I admit. It is no fault of mine. Nor my wish. I am not well served. My queens are troublesome. My son, the Heir Apparent, also troubles me. They are strong-willed, difficult to control. There are ministers who advise me badly. There are changes I need make.'

'That is so. Lord Auckland considers that you must make changes, Sire. It is necessary and proper for you to dismiss from office those who have disturbed the friendly feelings between our governments. I, too, wish you to make changes. The Pandeys are not my friends. You must replace them. I should like you to inform me of the changes.'

Rajendra Shah winced. 'It is my intention.'

'That pleases me. Let me add, Sire, my army waits for you to leave the Ramnagar villages. It is impatient and will brook no delay.'

Rajendra Shah indicated his agreement. He sat for several minutes, eyes downcast, his shoulders sagging.

Abruptly, the Resident stood to take his leave. Rajendra Shah rose and in silence they exchanged namastes. The commander of the guard came forward and led the Resident and Adam from the palace. They boarded the carriages, the escort fell into place and at a fast trot they left the Durbar Square to return to the Residency.

Within weeks Nepal had withdrawn from the Ramnagar villages, and Rajendra Shah advised the Resident of changes he made in the Durbar. He dismissed Prime Minister Ranjang Pandey and other Pandey ministers, and appointed a coalition ministry of moderates comprising Chautariyas and Brahmans, with Chautariya Fath Jang as prime minister.

Seven

In October of the year 1841 there was unexpected news. The Senior Queen was dead—Samraja Devi, the queen who had dominated Rajendra Shah and who was behind much of the intrigue and plotting in the Durbar. The supporter of the Pandeys, she had responsibility for the decline of the Thapas and for Bhim Sen Thapa's fall from power, and his torture, death, and the horrible desecration of his corpse. Samraja Devi, no friend of the British, had long been eager for war with them. Adam recalled seeing her at Bhim Sen Thapa's trial, a severe looking woman dressed in voluminous dark skirts and sari.

Samraja Devi had left Kathmandu and descended the steep mountain tracks down to the Terai on a hunting expedition. The monsoon had just finished and the days on the plains were becoming pleasant. It was a time to hunt elephants, tigers, leopards and other game that abounded there. She had with her a hunting party from the Durbar, the Pandeys and Chautariya relatives of the King, and a large retinue of beaters and servants and many scores of porters. But she took ill in Makwanpur, in the town of Hetaura, developed a high fever and in a few days was dead.

Rumour had it that the Senior Queen had been poisoned. Then fingers were pointed at the King himself. News of the Senior Queen's death spread into India, to Calcutta, and copies of a newspaper came to Nepal with an article accusing Rajendra Shah of poisoning his wife.

The article worried the Resident. He had no evidence against Rajendra Shah, in fact no evidence of any poisoner. Even in Kathmandu where it was by no means unknown, poisoning was a serious charge. And this was worse because it was a charge against the King.

The reaction was quick. Adam was with the Resident when a carriage, escorted by a detachment of the royal guard, horses coming at a fast canter, hooves kicking up the dust, turned into the Residency driveway and came to a noisy halt. Through the window they saw the King and the Heir Apparent alight, hurry to the door and knock loudly.

'We're in for it, Mr Clarke. I've been afraid of this,' the Resident said grimacing. He threw up his hands. 'How do I explain?'

The peon admitted the angry King and his son. The Resident greeted them and asked them to be seated. 'You both are welcome here, Sire.

Perhaps an appointment might have been made. But no matter, you are welcome.'

'An appointment is not necessary, Mr Resident,' the young Heir Apparent snapped, glaring at him. 'It is you who are not welcome here.'

'I am here by right,' the Resident said abruptly and turned to the King. 'To what do I deserve this honour?'

Rajendra Shah's thin face scowled. 'It is no honour, Resident. Not for you.' He waved a copy of a newspaper. 'I am accused of poisoning the Queen. It is an evil lie. A lie of the scurrilous British. I will have a retraction. I demand one.'

'I regret the article, Sire,' the Resident told him. 'But you must understand that it was not my doing. Nor the Company's doing. We do not accuse you. You see it is an Indian newspaper.'

'It is. But you British control India and you teach them lies,' the Heir Apparent smirked.

The Resident ignored him.

'You will get me a retraction.' Rajendra Shah grasped the kukhri at his side.

'It's beyond my power.'

'I demand it.'

'You might do that. It is your privilege.'

The King sat, his hand on his kukhri, rage in his thin face, his breath coming in quick gulps. 'That is no reply for me. I demand a retraction!' His voice rose almost to a scream. 'I tell you, Mr Resident, I will fight you British. I have wanted it for a long time. I will crush your East India Company and drive it out of India. Drive it back into the evil sea. I know you British are now weak. I know you are beaten.'

'In Afghanistan you are beaten. In China the Emperor has your measure. I restrain myself no longer, Mr Resident. I demand a retraction.' Rajendra Shah snarled. 'It is a retraction. Or it is war.'

Adam wondered at the fury of it. The Resident said nothing, but sat looking at the King, a distasteful look.

After some moments, Rajendra Shah brought himself under better control and his tone was almost pleading as he said, 'It was not I who poisoned Samraja Devi. You must believe me. No agent of mine put poison in her food. Not I. She was my wife. All should know that if I find the poisoner his punishment will be terrible. I will have the skin torn from his body, not the smallest piece left. I will have his raw flesh rubbed with salt and the juice of the lime. Rubbed slowly, day by day, till he is dead.'

Adam noticed the Heir Apparent's smile.

'How could I poison her? I took the greatest care of Samraja Devi,' Rajendra Shah continued. 'She was my wife. I gave her everything she wanted and refused her nothing. I bent to her slightest wish.'

The Heir Apparent turned towards his father, a smirk again on his face. 'That is true, father. True, you bent to my mother's wishes. And her wish was for your power. You gave it to her? No, she took it from you. She left you nothing, left you naked. You are no ruler, no real King.'

This startled Rajendra Shah.

The Heir Apparent continued, 'And now Laxmi Devi is your Queen. Will you bend to her, father? Will she have your power? You puppet King,' he sneered.

Rajendra Shah was lost for words, his face tight with anger.

'Will you give Laxmi Devi's son the throne? Yes, she will take it from you. The puppet King will agree,' the Heir Apparent taunted.

Rajendra Shah rose from his chair waving a clenched fist at his son as the Resident and Adam watched, amazed.

'Laxmi Devi will come to take all from you, father. Already she even takes her own body from you, this Laxmi Devi,' the Heir Apparent goaded. 'She has Gagan Singh for a lover. Not you, father. This Gagan Singh cuckolds you.' He laughed loudly. 'A humble servant cuckolds the puppet King.'

Rajendra Shah grasped his son, cursing, calling on the gods and raining blows on him. For some moments the Heir Apparent fought back, then, disengaging himself, he rushed from the Residency, took a horse from one of the royal guard and rode off.

As Rajendra Shah returned to his chair. The Resident rose and went to the window. He beckoned to Adam to join him. They stood there looking out over the Residency grounds until the King was ready to talk to them again.

After some minutes Rajendra Shah, downcast, his eyes avoiding them, apologised to the Resident for his outburst, and for the altercation with his son. It was the Resident who returned to the poisoning. They discussed the matter, and he suggested that a letter be sent from the King to Lord Auckland in Calcutta. Rajendra Shah agreed, saying the letter would assert his innocence and outline the terrible punishment he would deal to any poisoner of Samraja Devi.

One evening a little later, Lalit had Tanka Rana take a message to Adam asking him to come to Dor Maske's house. He found her waiting for him at the door. His pulse quickened as he looked at her.

'I have been waiting for you,' she said. 'I am pleased you could come.' He went up to her and took her hand.

'I have to talk to you, but not here,' she said, looking around as though she might be overheard. 'Please come with me.' Lalit took Adam up the ladders to her room.

The dusk was quickening, but there was still light to see. The painting of Christ of the Sacred Heart was there, Adam noticed, and he saw a mask of the God Ganesh and an image of Lord Shiva's wife, Parbati. Apart from these, the room was simply furnished with cupboards, a table and chairs, a bed of quilts and a coverlet, and a small mirror on the wall.

Lalit pointed to her mirror. 'Do your English ladies have mirrors?'

'Yes, they do,' he said.

'Dor Maske gave it to me. It is nice to have.'

'That was kind of him.' Adam knew there were few mirrors in Nepal. He pictured Lalit using it, setting her hair, applying salve to darken around her eyes a little, choosing necklaces to wear, fixing flowers in her hair.

Lalit lit an oil lamp, which flickered at first then burned steadily. She went over to the window to draw the shutters closed.

'We must not be overheard,' she said. 'It would be dangerous. What I have to say is secret.' She sat with Adam at the table. 'Has Dor Maske told you what is arranged?'

'He has not. I'm mystified, Lalit.'

'I will tell you. It is Laxmi Devi, who was the Junior Queen. She commands that you come to her.'

'Commands?'

'Please do not take offence. She is now the Senior Queen. She demands your presence tonight. It is late tonight. She expects you to come.'

'She told you so, Lalit?'

'She did. I am one of her helpers, a lady-in-waiting, as your grandmother was once. That is where I have been. I am with her when not here in Dor Maske's house. I hope you will agree.' Lalit's dark eyes were troubled as she waited Adam's reply.

'What does Laxmi Devi want from me?' Adam asked.

'She will tell you. It is your help she wants. She has enemies, the

Pandeys and others. Prime Minister Fath Jang perhaps.'

Lalit shuddered, 'I know she fears she will be poisoned, and her sons. She has her maids taste their food.'

Of course Adam was going to agree, he wanted to please Lalit. And the meeting could prove valuable for the Resident. 'You want me to go to Laxmi Devi, Lalit. You, yourself?'

'I do. She has commanded me to bring you, and will be angry if I fail her.'

'Then I do agree.'

The worry lifted from Lalit's face. 'That pleases me,' she said, smiling warmly and feeling for Adam's sleeve.

Lalit's touch delighted Adam. He took her hand and she let it rest there. He sat watching her as her eyes softened and a touch of colour rose on her olive skin. Adam lent forward and she smiled as he kissed her. Giving way to his feelings for her, he rose and took her in his arms, and finding the bare skin of her back below her blouse, he held her tightly. It startled her, but Adam felt her relax and she stayed close to him, until, slowly pulling away, she put her hand up to his face and shook her head saying, 'Not now. It is not the time.' Lalit sat in silence for some minutes, composing herself before she spoke of the arrangements for the audience with Laxmi Devi.

'She wants you to come in secret at midnight,' Lalit said. 'I will wait for you at the house of Gagan Singh near the Singh Satal Temple in the Durbar Square.'

Towards midnight Adam accompanied Lalit and Gagan Singh to the audience with Laxmi Devi. Gagan Singh thanked him for coming, making a self-depreciating remark about his being Laxmi Devi's servant. They walked across the deserted Durbar Square, keeping to the shadows of the temples, towards the Monkey God Gate. Gagan Singh led them through the dark courts and corridors of the palace to Laxmi Devi's quarters.

The room, with its dark wood panelling and heavy, low beams overhead, was lit by several oil lamps, the air was hazy with their smoke and had the odour of the burning oil. Thick carpets covered the floor and several images of goddesses stood in the shadows near the walls—Durga, Parbati, Saraswati, the Queen's namesake Laxmi and others.

Laxmi Devi was seated with her two little sons close beside her. She was younger than Adam had expected, only little more than his own age. She wore a sari of gold-coloured silk, a profusion of gold jewellery, and had a silver nose stud, and vermilion powder in her hair. Her large black eyes watched as Gagan Singh seated Adam at one side of the room. She was not unattractive Adam thought, but he saw her lips were tightly drawn and there was a hardness in her face. Even then, on that first meeting, Adam judged her to be a woman of strength and determination, but also of ruthlessness.

Laxmi Devi asked Lalit to gather up the two little princes and take them to another room. She beckoned Gagan Singh to come and stand beside her, then she welcomed Adam.

'Lalit has spoken of you, Mr Clarke. I have been told that a little of our blood runs in you.' She looked to Gagan Singh for conformation and Adam heard him mention Maneka.

'Yes, I have heard of Maneka. It was the old Malla king she served. That was long ago. But Nepal is just as troubled now.'

Her eyes studied Adam, waiting for a response. 'So I understand, Madam,' he agreed.

She spoke softly to Gagan Singh then said to Adam, 'I wish to tell you that I am no enemy of the British. I have no designs on your Company's lands in India. Not even on Kumaon and Garhwal, which you took from us in 1815. I have no desire at all for conquests. I wish to live in peace with the British.'

'Peace is also our desire, Madam,' Adam told her.

Her face hardened. 'But I will bring changes in the Durbar. You must know of the troubles we have here. Of the Heir Apparent. You, too, must hold him in contempt. He is a vile creature, cruel. And he is insane and an enemy of the British. He must never rule.' Again she waited for Adam's reaction: he could hardly disagree.

'My elder son must succeed Rajendra Shah, not the Heir Apparent,' she said. 'I shall see to that. My own son would be your friend. My sons are reared to admire the British, not to hate them.'

Adam indicated his approval.

Laxmi Devi again consulted with Gagan Singh. 'I need your help, Mr Clarke. It is why I asked you here.'

'I'll give what help I can, Madam; if it is appropriate for me.'

'Your Company holds one of my countrymen in India, in Simla I believe. He is Mathabar Singh Thapa, a man of strength. I want him back. We need him in Nepal to help govern. He will ensure that my son will succeed Rajendra Shah. The British must let him return. Can the Resident Hodgson arrange it?'

Adam remembered Dor Maske speaking of Mathabar Singh. 'Is the time right?' he asked. 'I have heard he has many enemies here. Would his life be safe?'

'It is now we want him. I want your Resident to arrange it.'

'I will speak to him, Madam.'

She thanked Adam. For the first time he saw Laxmi Devi show a hint of a smile. Then she beckoned to Gagan Singh to escort him from the palace. The audience was closed.

Eight

During the months that followed, Fath Jang's ministry brought no stability to the Durbar, and intrigue and turmoil continued. The Heir Apparent, young as he was, schemed openly against his father. The Pandeys invented more troubles in Afghanistan and the Opium War in China, arguing that it was time to strike at the British. Yet again placards appeared in the streets, urging war and threatening the Resident.

Laxmi Devi watched all this and stood away from it, acting with intelligence and foresight. Before long, governors of the districts, village chiefs and merchants came to the Durbar wanting power vested in Laxmi Devi. They drew up a Petition of Rights, which provided for the King to act on her advice, to which he had no option but to agree.

The Resident had followed events in the Durbar with the greatest of interest and, where possible, had brought his influence on Rajendra Shah for the support of Laxmi Devi. The change pleased him. He took some credit for it himself, but he thought there was still more to be done. 'We've progressed, Mr Clarke,' he said to Adam. 'It is different from the days of the Pandeys and the Senior Queen. Laxmi Devi certainly doesn't want war, and doesn't look outside Nepal. She told you that. She looks no further than the Durbar itself, to consolidate her power there. To get her own son on the throne one day.'

'It's a credit to you, sir,' Adam complimented him.

'Thank you. Yes, a little perhaps,' the Resident acknowledged modestly. 'But we must make sure Laxmi Devi stays in power. The Pandeys are still here, and I wouldn't trust Rajendra Shah not to twist yet again. And the Heir Apparent, God forbid. No, Laxmi Devi's position isn't secure enough. Fath Jang is weak and goes where the wind blows him, and the Chautariyas don't like her much. Yes, she needs a strong prime minister. One who is a friend of ours. A Thapa no doubt. You told me Laxmi Devi wants this Mathabar Singh Thapa. I'm inclined to agree.'

'Laxmi Devi is sure of him, sir. Says the time is right.'

The Resident frowned. Adam saw the tiredness in his face, and he realised again that Mr Hodgson was not a robust man, and not well perhaps.

'I don't like the man, Mr Clarke,' the Resident continued. 'He's too confident by half, overbearing and blunt, and rude at times. I had dealings with him a few years ago. Bhim Sen sent him to Calcutta to get the Company to give back the Terai lands we'd taken in 1815. Sent him against my wishes, I must say.' The Resident smiled. 'And what did he take with him, Mr Clarke? No less than three thousand Gurkhas from elite regiments, loads of valuable presents for everyone from King George down, tremendous elephant tusks, kukhries, rich furs from the Himalayas, embroidered work, tigers, a leopard said to have been suckled by a Nepalese woman, and a rhinoceros. They received Mathabar Singh with courtesy and when he was leaving they gave him presents, the latest rifles, mirrors, jewellery, a sun dial, thermometers, an accordion and model ships for the children. But that's all he took back to Kathmandu,' the Resident said, satisfied. 'He got no territory from the Company.'

'Laxmi Devi wants him, sir.'

'Yes, I think she's right. No doubt he would finish off the Pandeys if he got the chance. Frighten the King out of any wits he might have, and get the Heir Apparent under control, or have him murdered, perhaps, for Laxmi Devi. Couldn't countenance that though. Yes, I'll write to Lord Auckland asking that he be returned to Nepal.'

'It seems satisfactory, sir.'

'I hope so, Mr Clarke. And there's something else. But I'll let Mr St Clair tell you himself.'

Back in his bungalow that afternoon, Adam rewarded himself with an Irish whisky and relaxed. He felt that a little self-congratulatory indulgence was not unwarranted. Had not he himself played a part in bringing about the changes in the Kathmandu Durbar? Not the main part certainly, but a part. He had faith that Mr Hodgson would acknowledge it and mention his name in the letter to Lord Auckland. Adam imagined a reply coming with at least a phrase in it for him, a 'Well done, Mr Clarke' or something like that. Then his reverie was broken by a servant with a message from Captain O'Keefe inviting him to drinks that evening, drinks for a special occasion.

Arriving at the Captain's bungalow, Adam found Mr and Mrs St Clair and Dr Jones already there. Dr Jones winked and waved his glass towards Mr St Clair. 'Getting rid of him at last. We'll see the last of him in a week or so. Put up with him for too long.'

'Yes,' Captain O'Keefe told Adam. 'We're losing the St Clairs. Alfred has home leave, the Resident heard today.'

Mr St Clair was in a happy mood. 'Let me congratulate you on your good fortune,' Adam said.

He replied, his face beaming, 'Thank you. It's high time. Seven years, four in Calcutta, three here in these mountains. The Company's come good at last. Great to get back in England for a long spell. Badly need it.'

'Mrs St Clair will be delighted.'

'Indeed she is. In her seventh heaven. And she deserves it. Been a champion. Marvellous help to me.'

'And Sarah, of course. She's not here though?' Adam said.

'Not yet.' Mr St Clair lent towards Adam and lowered his voice, 'Funny young lady, Sarah. Not so bucked up about it. It surprised me. But then it's not all that long since she was home.'

Mrs St Clair came over to them. 'Does Adam know our good news, Alfred?'

'I do. I must congratulate you too,' Adam told her.

She laughed, almost giggled. 'Thank you. I'm really, really looking forward to it. I simply cannot wait to be back in London again. Back in our nice house.' She looked at her husband, 'It's been such a long time, Alfred. All those years.'

He took her hand and patted it. 'You deserve it, my dear.'

'Yes Alfred, I think I do. I'll simply love the shops again, real shops. And the plays you spoke of once, Mr Clarke. I do love the theatre. Sarah does too.'

It was not until they had nearly finished drinks that Sarah came, looking pretty in her green skirt of Indian silk, a white blouse and a necklace, with her hair drawn back and tied in a bun. Captain O'Keefe welcomed her with more than a touch of gallantry and congratulated her, as did Dr Jones. She smiled and thanked them, then came up to Adam.

'Back home again, Sarah. You must be looking forward to it.' Adam said.

She hesitated a little. 'Yes, I suppose I am. Yes, of course. It will be nice, Mr Clarke.'

'And the voyage, Sarah. You like the sea?'

'Sometimes, when the weather is nice. Not the rough weather.'

'But you're an old sailor, Sarah.'

'Perhaps, I am,' she said with a hint of irritation. 'I should rather not talk about it.'

Sarah stood looking at Adam, and he was wondering what else to talk about when Mrs St Clair joined them. 'Sarah will need to help me with her packing, won't you Sarah. There's a lot to do. Although we'll be able to leave things here till we return, we won't have to take everything with us.' She looked at her daughter. 'Sarah will need to take all hers things, though.'

'Will I mamma?'

'Of course, dear. You won't want to be coming back with us when home leave finishes.' She turned to Adam. 'I hate to think of home leave finishing. But it is a long time away yet. Thank goodness for that.'

Sarah frowned. 'I'd like to decide myself, mamma.'

'Would you, Sarah. But you'll settle in England. I just know you will. You must, a young lady of your age.'

'Why is that, mamma?' Sarah asked, pouting.

'You will see, dear. I shall miss you terribly. But that's the way it is for us women. You will see.'

The evening was drawing to a close. Dr Jones left and Mr and Mrs St Clair were taking their leave of Captain O'Keefe.

'Would you walk back with me, Mr Clarke?' Sarah asked. 'Please. I should like that.'

Out in the night Sarah led Adam not to the St Clairs' bungalow, which was no distance away, but to a bench in the Residency grounds near the part of the garden which Adam had occasionally helped her tend. She sat beside him.

'Is it too cold for you?' she asked.

'It isn't, Sarah', he told her, although in truth with the winter not long over Kathmandu's nights were still cold.

'I just want to talk with you, Adam. Just a little while. Do you mind me calling you Adam again?'

'Not at all. I like it. But home leave doesn't seem to please you very much, Sarah. '

'No. I want to stay here.'

It surprised him. 'Why on earth do you want to stay here? A young lady like you. Are you sure?'

'I am. I do want to stay here,' she said.

'But England has so much more to offer you. There's more to do. Here you are cooped up in the Residency, left to yourself too much.'

'That doesn't matter, not to me.'

'You must like it here then?'

'Yes, I do.'

'Why do you, I wonder?'

'No, I cannot tell you that.'

He looked down at her. There was just enough light to make out her pretty face looking back up him—a worried face. Adam felt sorry for her. 'Sarah,' he said gently, 'you will find many things you like in England. You will find young men you will like. Many will like you, I can promise you that.' She said nothing and Adam felt her shivering. 'It's too cold for you, Sarah.'

She moved closer to him. He put his arms around her, bent and kissed her on the forehead, and she clung to him, sought his lips with hers. For some moments he held her, until she drew away and got up from the bench. 'I shall always remember you, Adam. I shall, always,' she whispered. Then she hurried away, back to the St Clairs' bungalow.

Although pleased for the St Clairs sake, it was with some regret that the others in the Residency saw the St Clairs leave. They would miss their company, miss it for at least a protracted period, forever perhaps if Mr St Clair went to a different post at the end of his home leave. The St Clairs had brought family life to the Residency and more than a touch of England. There had been the drinks with Mr St Clair and his views, rather extreme though they might be. Mrs St Clair's dinners, her afternoon teas and the cribbage had been pleasant. And there was Sarah. Adam had come to look on Sarah almost as a sister.

The St Clairs left the Residency one April morning, after the mists had risen, with an escort of sepoys from the garrison and a score of porters carrying their baggage and provisions for the difficult journey to Calcutta. They all stood out in front of the Residency seeing them off. Adam went with them through the valley, past the town of Kathmandu and Thankot village, then up to the Chandragiri Pass. There the St Clairs made their farewells to him.

Mr St Clair gave him a hearty handshake and laughingly charged him with the care of the Heir Apparent. Mrs St Clair was both happy and fearful, pleased to be starting on her way back to London but not daring to look down from the pass to the rugged descent she would have to make.

Sarah stood by quietly and Adam saw the tears brimming in her eyes. Then as the party was leaving and her mother called her, she came up to Adam and whispered, 'I want to write to you from London, Adam. I hope you will remember me.'

'I will remember you, and I will look forward to a letter from you,' he told her.

Nine

Some time after the St Clairs went on home leave, the Resident received instructions that Adam was to report to Calcutta. There had been a change in governor-generals; Lord Auckland had returned to England and Lord Ellenborough had replaced him. Nothing was said about Adam's duties in Calcutta, how long he was to stay there or, in fact, whether he would return to Kathmandu at all. But Mr Hodgson was sure that Adam would return, assuming—although not at all happy with the idea—that the new Governor-General simply wanted a first-hand account of what was happening in Nepal.

Mr Hodgson went to a good deal of trouble in briefing Adam for his visit to Calcutta. He made sure he fully appreciated the recent improvements in the Durbar, particularly with the Petition of Rights and the transfer of power to Laxmi Devi. Adam was to stress that Laxmi Devi was not interested in war with the British and presented no threat. But he was also to point out to Lord Ellenborough that Mr Hodgson's work in Nepal was by no means finished, that he, as Resident, must still do what he could to influence events in the Durbar. The Pandeys were still about, the imbecile king could not be relied on, and the Heir Apparent still ran loose and uncontrolled; and Fath Jang was a weak and indolent prime minister. Adam was to make sure Calcutta agreed to the release of Mathabar Singh Thapa, to let him return to Kathmandu where he would become a strong prime minister. Adam himself had no problem with all this. They were his views too, so he agreed fully. Had not he played a part himself?

When he went to make his farewell to Lalit, Adam found her in her room. He stood beside her near the window that looked out over the green fields and farm houses to the Himalayan massifs glittering in the afternoon sunlight. The breeze fanning the valley wafted in through the window, to play on Lalit's hair and rustle the silk of her sari.

Lalit looked sadly at Adam. 'You are leaving Kathmandu,' she said. 'You will go to Calcutta.'

'A new governor-general is there, Lord Ellenborough has sent for me, Lalit.'

'So you will leave. I hoped perhaps you would not.'

'But it will not be long, Lalit. Weeks only before I return.'

'Have they told you so?'

'They have not. But I will come back to you.'

'How do you know?' she asked anxiously. 'There must be other places you could go to. In India or back to your own country perhaps. So far away.'

Adam took her hand. He saw the worry in her face and felt the full force of his affection for her. He drew her close to him. 'I love you Lalit,' he said. 'I must tell you that now. I will not let anything take you from me. You are very dear to me. I promise I will come back to you.'

Lalit's eyes were soft as she looked up at him. 'You will really come back to me?'

'I love you,' Adam said again. 'I promise to come back to you.'

'Thank you. I am very grateful,' she said.

'And you will be waiting for me when I return, Lalit?' Adam asked.

She moved closer into his arms. 'I promise that. You are very dear to me.'

Adam was to remember the deep pleasure of that April afternoon for a long time: the declaration of his love for Lalit, her nearness, her charms, and her tenderness towards him. They talked on till the sun was setting on the afternoon and it was time for Adam to take his leave. They lingered over it, enraptured with each other, unwilling to break the spell. Then dusk came and the room darkened. Adam descended the ladders and left Dor Maske's house to find the waiting syce, and he returned to the Residency to pack for his departure the next morning.

Adam left Kathmandu with a small escort from the Residency garrison, to make his way down the steep and rugged descent into Makwanpur and on through India. In Bettiah the Capuchins' mission made him welcome. Adam took the opportunity to visit the grave of Alexander Hume, his grandfather's brother who had fought in the Battle of Buxar two generations ago and was killed in action against the Nawab of Oudh's men. He found the tombstone, that his grandfather had put there to keep his brother's memory alive, hidden in the undergrowth.

The prefect at Bettiah was interested in Nepal, regretting it was many years since they had a mission there. He sought Adam's opinion about sending a priest again to Kathmandu, and wondered if permission could be obtained from the Durbar, what Mr Hodgson's reaction would be, and whether many people would come to church and to be converted to Christianity. Adam answered cautiously, not knowing Mr Hodgson's view and not wanting to build up the prefect's hopes.

He had heard no expression of interest for a Christian mission in Kathmandu. The days of the good Capuchin fathers during the time of the later Malla kings were long forgotten. Only once since then, back at the turn of the century, had a Christian priest come to Kathmandu. But his mission was a disaster. True, the Durbar did not meet the commitments it made when it invited him, giving him no church, no decent housing and hardly enough food; and few Nepalese came to be converted. But the priest's conduct fell far short, very short indeed, of what was undoubtedly expected of him. He turned out to have an inordinate appetite for sin, mortal sin, serious sins of several types, living for fornication, strong liquor and other people's money. Much of his time in Kathmandu he spent drinking, stealing and impregnating young women. He was recalled, of course. Back in India, charged with living in concubinage, embezzlement, and murder by conducting abortion, he was imprisoned for breaking the laws of the land and excommunicated for breaking the laws of the Church. It was a sad tale. Adam made no mention of it to the prefect, nor he to Adam.

Adam had a long wait in Calcutta before the Governor-General and the Company Secretary received him. Their welcome was pleasant enough, and Lord Ellenborough mentioned Captain Sir Alexander Clarke and Adam's grandfather, Sir Hume Clarke. Then he said, 'Now take your time, Mr Clarke, and tell me all about the Kathmandu Durbar.' Adam spoke at length and Lord Ellenborough listened intently.

Adam told him about the turmoil in the Durbar, starting with Bhim Sen Thapa's trial and death, the end of Thapa power and the rise of the Pandeys who had support from the Senior Queen and King Rajendra Shah. He talked about the insults to the Resident and the Company, the Heir Apparent's mock battles denigrating the Irish Dragoons, the posters harassing the Resident, and the mutiny of the army.

'They threatened war with us, sir,' he said. 'The army demanded war. Many in the Durbar believed the British forces were weakened, being over-occupied in Afghanistan and in the war in China. Many believed it was a time to attack the Company and drive the British back into the sea from whence they came, as they would say.'

'Things improved after Laxmi Devi's rise to power,' Adam told them. 'She does not want war with us. But others in the Durbar still do; and the Pandeys might well regain the favour of Rajendra Shah, who is capricious to the extreme, and the untrustworthy Heir Apparent. Laxmi Devi needs support. Her Prime Minister Fath Jang is weak.'

Adam went on to give the fullest possible account of the part Mr Hodgson was playing and emphasised the great importance of continuing his influence in the Durbar. Finally he raised the need for Mathabar Singh Thapa to return to Kathmandu and support Laxmi Devi.

Finished what he had to say, Adam sat back satisfied. Having played a part in the events himself, he expected a measure of praise from the Governor General, at least a congratulatory remark. But Lord Ellenborough sat in silence for a long time looking at Adam. Then he turned to the Company Secretary, frowning and tapping his desk with his fingers. His response dumbfounded Adam.

'I'm afraid, Mr Clarke, that you have confirmed my worst fears. I already know something of Mr Hodgson's interference in Nepal's affairs. I do not agree that his influence in their Durbar is important. On the contrary, I am against it. Irrevocably against it. It must stop. We must not interfere in such matters. Not at all. I have already written to Mr Hodgson to that effect. In future he must desist from any part whatsoever in the intrigues going on in the Kathmandu Durbar. That is their affair, not ours. We must not meddle. That is my policy not only for Nepal but for all our frontier States.' Lord Ellenborough looked at Adam keenly. 'Do you agree, Mr Clarke?'

What could Adam say? Lord Ellenborough was the Governor-General and Adam was only a junior official. He hesitated for some time wondering what to say for the best. Then taking his courage in hands, realising he might be putting his whole future with the Company at risk, he said, 'With respect, sir, I do not agree. At least I do not fully agree. Surely Mr Hodgson's intervention has done much to stop Nepal being at war with us.'

'Is that so, Mr Clarke? Then I suggest your judgement is not good,' Lord Ellenborough said coldly. 'It is my army that stops Nepal attacking us. It is not Mr Hodgson. My army is why we are at peace with Nepal. It is not because the Resident enters into their intrigues. But of course you do not have the facts. Believe me, the force I have in India is strong. It is enough, far more than enough, to make short shrift of anything Nepal could muster, what any State in India could muster. You must realise that. And Mr Hodgson must understand I could deal quickly with any threat Nepal might come to pose.'

Lord Ellenborough did not wait for Adam to reply. He had stated his policy and that was it. Adam saw he was about to end the session, so he said, 'There's the matter of Mathabar Singh, sir. May I ask if he will be returned to Nepal?'

Lord Ellenborough turned to the Company Secretary, speaking quietly, but Adam gathered he wanted to be informed about Mathabar Singh. He thought for some moments then said to Adam, 'I certainly don't see why we should be still holding him and paying him a handsome stipend. I'll consider the matter.'

Adam was hardly a happy man when he returned to his bungalow that day. He had been told the Resident's approach was wrong and had been wrong apparently for many years. He himself had been wrong. Lord Auckland who had fully supported Mr Hodgson must have been wrong. Adam was amazed how suddenly policy could change.

He thought of the fierce mountain battles a generation back, at Kalanga and Jaithak and Parsa where the Gurkhas slaughtered many of the Company's soldiers, and Almora and Malaon where many Gurkhas died. No doubt Lord Ellenborough would have the victory in the end, he thought, but at what a price. Adam favoured Mr Hodgson's policy.

But his spirits were raised by a letter from Lalit written in her own unaccustomed hand. He smiled as he pictured her laboriously putting the words on paper, the few lines in Newari saying she hoped he was in good health and was looking forward to his return. But it was enough, what he wanted to hear, and a letter he treasured for a long time.

A letter from Sarah St Clair, posted from the Cape, reached Adam in Calcutta, a long letter describing the ship and the voyage in some detail. He read that Mrs St Clair was complaining a good deal about the ship's facilities and could hardly wait to be in England, and Mr St Clair seemed bored with the voyage. Sarah herself loved the sea and was enjoying it all, but she missed Kathmandu and everyone in the Residency. She would return with her parents at the end of home leave; she would have her mother agree to that, one way or another. Sarah sent her kindest regards and pleasant memories.

When Lord Ellenborough called for Adam again, both he and the Company Secretary welcomed him in a friendly enough way. Lord Ellenborough came straight to the point, saying, 'About this Mathabar Singh Thapa, Mr Clarke. I can tell you I've decided to let him return to Nepal. I'm told he proclaims friendship with us. Not that I trust him. He let us down once before. You might not know.' He turned to the Secretary. 'Would you like to tell Mr Clarke about Mathabar Singh?

'Certainly, sir. We caught him back in '38, Mr Clarke, trying to cross the Sutlej one night. On his way to talk with the Sikh, Ranjit Singh, and perhaps on to the Shah of Persia. To get them to join in war against us. No doubt at all about it.'

Dor Maske had assured Adam that Mathabar Singh went to seek Ranjit Singh's support against the Pandeys, not against the British. But he saw no point in interrupting.

'We clapped him in prison for a year. Thought he'd come to his senses. But what does he do? We release him, and off he goes to Ranjit Singh.' The Secretary smiled. 'We put a little pressure on Ranjit Singh, just a little, mind you. Ranjit Singh was hurt—pretended to be, I'd say. He denied any collusion with Nepal. Was annoyed we'd suggested it. He handed Mathabar Singh over to us and we've held him ever since. He's in Simla. We've treated him well though. Pay him a thousand rupees a month upkeep.'

'Did you know that, Mr Clarke?' Lord Ellenborough asked.

'I've been told something of Mathabar Singh, sir.'

'Just as well, because I'm sending you back to Kathmandu with him. See he gets there.'

'It's a wise move, sir. Returning Mathabar Singh,' Adam ventured.

'And why is that, Mr Clarke?' Lord Ellenborough asked, doubtfully.

'He's needed there, sir. He'll bring stability to the Durbar. Get the army under control.'

Lord Ellenborough frowned and started tapping his desk again. 'No, Mr Clarke. What Mathabar Singh does in Nepal, what happens to him dead or alive is not my concern. I have no reason for holding him, no reason for some time; but until recently Mathabar Singh himself wanted to stay in India. He's a suspicious man, I understand, and feared his life would be endangered in Kathmandu. But now he says his King has asked him back, and he's decided to go. His King can have him.'

Lord Ellenborough lent over his desk towards Adam. 'I tell you again, Mr Clarke. We must not meddle in Nepal's affairs. Previously I mentioned that I told Mr Hodgson so. I have written to Mr Hodgson in that vein yet again, and in no uncertain terms. He knows that in future it is I who shall decide what we do in Nepal. He will not. I'm sure you agree, Mr Clarke.'

With that the Governor-General and the Secretary rose for Adam to take his leave. They wished him a safe journey to Simla and then on to Kathmandu. And they wished him good progress with his work in Nepal.

Ten

Adam found that Mathabar Singh Thapa had already left Simla and was at Gorakpur near the border of Nepal, with a deputation from Rajendra Shah inviting him back and a guard of honour sent by Queen Laxmi Devi. Mathabar Singh was approaching middle-age, an impressive man, large, towering over most men, well-built and strong. It was said he could crack a walnut between his thumb and forefinger and overcome half-a-dozen men at a time in unarmed combat. He wore the blue uniform of a Gurkha general, his kukhri in his red cummerbund, and he bore himself erect, proudly, his head held high.

'So Ellenborough has sent you to accompany me, Mr Clarke,' Mathabar Singh said loudly when Adam met him, his hands joined in a namaste and with only the suggestion of a bow. 'Ellenborough might have sought my permission first. But you are not unwelcome. I do not object. Tell me, Mr Clarke, what news have you from Calcutta?'

There was little Adam had to say or was prepared to say. Just a few general remarks.

Mathabar Singh frowned. 'Trivialities. Come now, Ellenborough is not Auckland. I know of his order to Hodgson to keep out of our concerns. I do not agree with Ellenborough. I will not reject Hodgson's help, but he must understand it is I who will govern Nepal. Tell him so, Mr Clarke.'

Mathabar Singh continued, clenching his fist to emphasise each point. 'Yes, I will govern. The army is mine. I will control the weakling Fath Jang and his Chautariyas. Rajendra Shah is the King whom the gods have given me, so I shall serve him. I shall also serve Queen Laxmi Devi.' Mathabar Singh's anger rose and his voice deepened to a growl. 'And the Pandeys, Mr Clarke. I will revenge Bhim Sen Thapa. I curse the Pandey torturers and murderers and will have their heads.'

That said, Mathabar Singh relaxed a little. He bade Adam sit at a table with him and asked servants to bring rice and a dish of venison, and a bowl of raksi for Adam only as he did not take strong liquor himself. During the meal, Mathabar Singh talked about his hunting tigers, elephants and other big game on the Terai, and the grand visit he once made to Calcutta. The Company's army impressed him greatly. As

Adam noted, Mathabar Singh had a very active mind, and by the end of the meal he had no doubt Mathabar Singh would take control in the Kathmandu Durbar.

It was a large party that crossed the border into Nepal, over the duns, which were safe at that time of the year from the miasmas which brought the deadly aul, and on to Bhimphedi, then climbed high up the steep rugged Mahabharat Ranges, up the rocky tracks and ladders.

Mathabar Singh decided to wait on the side of the Chandragiri Mountain overlooking the valley for news from Kathmandu confirming the safety of his return. But as the days went by, Adam began to wonder if his return was really safe. He knew the Pandeys must be dreading it and that Rajendra Shah was capricious to the extreme. And he saw that Mathabar Singh was uneasy, losing his temper quickly with those about him, brooding and keeping to himself most of the time.

When two crows perched on a tree near where he was sitting, Mathabar Singh lost his temper. He jumped up and tried to shoo them off but they stayed put, craning their necks to peer down at him. He threw a rock at them, but with a flutter of wings the crows perched on a lower branch even closer to him. He shouted up at them, cursing, and threw more rocks but failed to dislodge them, and the crows set up a loud and raucous squawking. With that Mathabar Singh seized a musket from a nearby soldier and, still cursing, fired at the birds. His shot missed, but it dislodged the crows and they flew off down towards the valley, with Mathabar Singh waving his arms angrily after them until their squawking was lost in the distance below. 'I do not like the crows,' he told Adam. 'They are Yama's messengers from the Underworld. They can be messengers of death.'

At last a small detachment climbed up from the valley with a captain in command. Adam remembered him, Jung Bahadur, whom he had once seen in the Durbar Square being chased by the Heir Apparent and his mock Dragoons, and whom Dor Maske had mentioned as a possible leader of the Thapas one day. Mathabar Singh welcomed him and the two men embraced. 'Let me introduce Jung Bahadur, my nephew, he is my sister's son,' he said to Adam.

Mathabar Singh's return to Nepal turned out to be already widely known, and people gathered along the roadside to welcome him as he passed on his way to Kathmandu. Many had also gathered in the Durbar Square. Rajendra Shah, Laxmi Devi and the Heir Apparent were seated on a dais near the house of the little Kumari, and they invited Mathabar Singh to join them. The King and queen were lavish with their welcome—a welcome for all to see—and even the Heir Apparent joined in with long and courteous namastes. That day Mathabar Singh basked in the royal favour and the plaudits of the crowd. His homecoming must have satisfied him fully.

Back at the British Residency Mr Hodgson lost no time in calling for Adam to report on his stay in Calcutta. Adam found him at his desk, looking tired and paler than usual. He welcomed Adam back, then, with a touch of suspicion in his voice and his mouth turned down a little, said, 'So you briefed our new Governor-General, Mr Clarke? Lord Ellenborough must have learnt a great deal from you.'

Adam had known that Lord Ellenborough's change of policy towards Nepal would annoy Mr Hodgson, but the remark surprised him with its strong hint of blame. 'No, on the contrary, sir.' Adam defended his loyalty to the Resident. 'I assure you I gave Lord Ellenborough a very good account of the work you've done. I spoke of it in glowing terms. Emphasised the need for it to continue. But I'm afraid it didn't please him.'

'He said so?'

'As much and more. He said he's changed Lord Auckland's policy. And your's, sir. He laid it all down to me.'

Mr Hodgson grimaced. 'How unfortunate. What does he know about Nepal? He's so far away.'

'Lord Ellenborough wants no interference in Nepal's affairs, sir. Wants to let Nepal be. Says his army would crush the Gurkhas if that became necessary. Says he'd make short shrift of them.'

Mr Hodgson sighed and pointed to a letter on his desk. 'Yes, I have another letter from him. He keeps telling me such things. But crush the Gurkhas at what cost? At what cost! No, I do not agree. I'll never agree. I've made that clear to the Governor-General.'

'A difficult situation, sir.'

The Resident shrugged. 'Yes, but I know what is necessary in Kathmandu. We will continue as before. We'll ensure that those who get power in the Durbar are our friends. Or do our best to.' He studied Adam for some moments. 'I should like you to agree, Mr Clarke.'

Adam agreed. He preferred Mr Hodgson's way and he wanted to continue to play a part. If some of Lord Ellenborough's ire should fall on him, well so be it, he thought.

'Mathabar Singh has returned, sir,' Adam said.

The Resident brightened a little. 'Yes. That is something. At least my advice is followed there. Mathabar Singh must take power quickly. I must see to it.'

There was a letter waiting at the Residency for Adam, from Sarah St Clair. He read that she was hardly pleased to be back in London and was missing Nepal. She asked Adam for an early reply to tell her about what was happening in Kathmandu, and enquired about his own work and health. She often thought of him, she said, and hoped he was taking care of himself. Sarah concluded by saying that she fully intended to return to Kathmandu when her father's home leave finished. Adam wondered about Sarah. When he replied he again suggested that life in England must be more congenial for so attractive a young lady.

That evening, Adam joined Dr Jones and Captain O'Keefe for drinks. They were certainly pleased to see him back, to have someone else to talk to. Now that the St Clairs were gone and with the Resident usually busy with his official duties and his work on the flora and fauna of the mountains, they had lacked company except their own. They asked Adam to give an account of his visit to Calcutta, enquiring about the friends and officials they knew and whom he might have met. And they wanted to know about Mathabar Singh and Lord Ellenborough. They already knew how he had changed Lord Auckland's approach to Nepal.

'You know that Ellenborough has called Mr Hodgson to Calcutta,' Dr Jones said.

Adam was surprised,

'Mr Hodgson has refused to go,' Dr Jones said with a hint of a smile. 'Perhaps his health wouldn't stand it.'

'He's ill, then?'

'Not a robust man. But that's not the reason. He thinks if he went to Calcutta, Ellenborough wouldn't let him come back here. He's right of course. He won't have a bar of Ellenborough. Ellenborough wrote to Rajendra Shah recently to tell of his policy of non-interference. Mr Hodgson refuses to pass the letter on. He's still determined to influence events in the Durbar.'

'So he should,' Captain O'Keefe said. 'Someone has to. I don't agree with Ellenborough's idea of crushing the Gurkhas. Our army might do it in the end. But what a price? I know these mountain fighters. I say yet again I was at Kalanga and there were Parsa and Sumanpur, Almora and other battles. I know how they fight, these Gurkhas. Lord Ellenborough doesn't.'

The discussion went on and each of them agreed that Mr Hodgson's approach was the better one. There was a need to foster an effective and friendly government in the Durbar.

The welcome Adam had looked forward to so much during his stay in Calcutta did not come till the following morning, when Tanka Rana brought a message from Lalit asking him to come and saying she would be waiting in the house of Gagan Singh near the Durbar Square.

Lalit opened the door to him, and he drew her close in the embrace he had waited so long for. Then he released her and stood back, watching her smile, shyly at first then with pleasure as she welcomed him. As she stood there all Adam's memories were met fully, and again he delighted in her charm. She was exactly as he had pictured her, the soft beauty of her face. She was wearing a brightly coloured sari of silk and bangles and anklets, and had a tika mark on her brow and a golden ornament in her hair.

Adam stepped closer, again to take her in an embrace. But she raised her hand to stop him, held it gently against his chest.

'No, I cannot now. Not now,' she said. 'Yet again, you must forgive me. There is something else. But I promise that soon we shall be together. Very soon.'

'What else is there, Lalit ?' Adam asked.

He saw her concern. 'I have waited for you. But so has Laxmi Devi who wants you to come to her. She is waiting for you now. Do you mind? I hope you will agree.'

Adam found Laxmi Devi as before, her two little sons beside her and with Gagan Singh in attendance. It was the same room, the oil lamps alight and the odour of the burning oil, the images of the goddesses. Laxmi Devi asked Lalit to take the children, who had—so far at least—survived the threat of poison, from the room. Gagan Singh seated Adam, as before, some distance from the Queen, then returned to her side.

Adam noticed the approval in Laxmi Devi's face. 'You have done well to bring Mathabar Singh back to Nepal, Mr Clarke. I am grateful.'

In truth Adam had little to do with Mathabar Singh's return, but he accepted her gratitude.

'I have high hopes of Mathabar Singh, Mr Clarke. An able man, a man of power to support my rule. He will silence those who intrigue against me.'

'Yes, a powerful man it seems,' Adam said.

'I have a message for the British Resident,' Laxmi Devi told him. 'You will tell him I want Mathabar Singh as my prime minister. He must call on Rajendra Shah to insist he appoint Mathabar Singh quickly.'

'There is another thing, Mr Clarke,' Laxmi Devi said. 'Tell the British Resident I want you as my contact with him, to pass information between us. You will be admitted to the palace and be free to come and go. I have already arranged it.'

She asked Gagan Singh to give Adam a paper, which was her authority for the palace guards to let him pass. 'You might come to me, Mr Clarke. Or to my loyal supporter, Gagan Singh.' Then with a hint of a smile she added an inducement, 'And you might come here to the palace to visit Lalit, Mr Clarke. Feel free to do so. I would not object.'

Eleven

When he was appointed prime minister and commander-in-chief of the army, Mathabar Singh Thapa lost no time in exercising power. He disposed of the Chautariya Fath Jang by making him Governor of Palpa. He appointed Thapas to influential positions, in place of the Pandeys and also some Chautariyas and Brahmans. His nephew, Jung Bahadur, he promoted to colonel and gave him an important army command. The army gave Mathabar Singh unquestioning loyalty, and he raised three new regiments to add further to its support. Laxmi Devi supported Mathabar Singh strongly, being sure he would help her put her own son on the throne one day instead of the Heir Apparent. Thus Mathabar Singh became the virtual dictator of Nepal.

Mathabar Singh struck quickly against the Pandey leaders, and the vengeance he wreaked on them broke them as a power in the Kathmandu Durbar. Almost immediately he had the King appoint a court to investigate the old charge against Bhim Sen Thapa of poisoning the baby prince back in '37.

'The court has found Bhim Sen innocent of the crime,' Dor Maske told Adam. 'His name, Mathabar Singh Thapa's name and those of other Thapas have been cleared of any guilt. It is as I told you, Mr Clarke. Bhim Sen was not the murderer.'

'Was it Rajendra Shah?' Adam queried, remembering Dor Maske had claimed that the King himself was the poisoner.

'That matter was not raised. The court placed the guilt fully on the Pandeys.'

'And Bhim Sen's confession?' Adam remembered the Ditha, the Chief Justice, had read out a confession at Bhim Sen's trial.

'The Ditha admitted to the court that it was false.' Dor Maske's old face saddened. 'I have pity for him. True he wrote the confession. But it was not his responsibility. I believe he wrote it at Rajendra Shah's command, used the very words the King directed. He had no option but to obey.'

'The punishment?' Adam asked.

'Death. The court sentenced many to death.'

The following Saturday afternoon—Saturdays being regarded as ill-omened and therefore appropriate—the Pandeys were executed on the river bank to the south of Kathmandu, down below a road leading to the holy Swayambhunath with its great painted all-seeing eyes of the Adi Buddha. It was a place littered—from earlier executions—with bones bared of their flesh by the vultures and jackals and bleached white in the sun.

A detachment from an elite Gurkha regiment stood to attention near the river and many people gathered to watch from the road above. Men of the Payra caste, the executioners, waited down on the river bank, passing the time chatting with each other and taking turns to sharpen their swords on a stone.

A murmur ran through the crowd as the condemned men approached along the roadway, escorted by a group of soldiers and followed by their relatives and Pandey supporters. Each condemned man was naked save for a loin cloth, his arms bound at his back and his hair tied in a knob at the top of his head. That is each except the once prime minister, Ranjang Pandey. Ill and on the very verge of death, he was far beyond walking, so was carried in a basket on a peasant's back. He was set down on the roadside to watch, and the others were led down to the river bank.

Karbar Pandey was the first to be taken and made kneel, then have a cord tied to the rope binding his arms behind him. One of the Payra men edged Karbar Pandey's body forward for a clear view of the back of his neck whilst another held the cord to stop him falling forward on his face. An executioner stood over Karbar Pandey, his sword held high ready to strike, his eyes turned towards the detachment's commander, waiting his order.

But before the order came a man from amongst the Pandeys' followers who was carrying a sword—Karbar Pandey's own sword—hurried down from the roadside and spoke to the commander. With the commander's agreement the executioner discarded his own sword and took Karbar Pandey's; he tested its sharpness, nodded his approval and then again stood ready over the doomed man. But the order to strike was delayed a second time. Another Pandey follower came down from the road and, with the commander's agreement, went and knelt beside Karbar Pandey. He took Karbar Pandey's head between his hands and held it. This time the order came. The sword shimmered in the afternoon sunlight as the executioner struck. The Pandey follower held Kabar Pandey's severed head as the blood gushed. Then he placed it on the ground, carefully, as gently as he could. He returned to the roadside in his belief that this act—holding the head of a man he thought innocent at the instant of execution—would ensure a propitious future life for him.

Kulraj Pandey, who had organised battles against the mock Irish Dragoons for the Heir Apparent, was the second man beheaded. Then the others were executed, amongst them Indar Bir and Rambam, both renegade Thapas who had sided with the Pandeys. The last was the Ditha, the Chief Justice, an official caught in the web of intrigue—no doubt an innocent man.

The people on the roadside had watched intently, some murmuring their approval each time the executioner's sword cut, some silent and angry. The dying Ranjang Pandey, set up in pride of place to the front of the crowd, had looked down to see his colleagues die, his own eyes glazed as life ebbed from them. Towards dusk, with the killings finished the bodies of the condemned men were left as carrion for the jackals' feast, and the people dispersed to return to their homes. Ranjang Pandey was carried to his house, where he died soon after.

Back in Kathmandu, other punishments were carried out. Bodman Karki had his lips and nose cut off and Bansraj Bashniat's nose was cut away. All Pandeys who had played a part in the affairs of the State or the army had their property confiscated, and fifty or more were banished from Nepal with their families. The power of the Pandeys was truly broken.

'The King has honoured the memory of Bhim Sen Thapa,' Dor Maske told Adam. 'He has proclaimed him one of Nepal's greatest sons, and is restoring all Thapa property which was confiscated after Bhim Sen's trial. Thapas banished then are free to return to Nepal.'

'You approve of the killings, Dor Maske?' Adam asked.

'It is the custom, Mr Clarke. No novelty for us.' He shrugged. 'No novelty for the British either, I would say. Not in India.'

Adam did not dispute the point.

'But Mathabar Singh will need to take care,' Dor Maske continued. 'True, now the Pandeys are gone no one has the mettle to stand up to him. Not openly. Not the Chautariyas, nor the Brahmans. But he must not overreach himself. Already people fear him.'

In the British Residency there was little talk of the execution of the Pandeys. Captain O'Keefe accepted it as the way things were, a fact of life. Dr Jones shrugged it away saying it was not his affair. The Resident, too, seemed reluctant to talk about the killings, perhaps because he had played a part in Mathabar Singh's return and must have foreseen their likelihood. After a while the execution of the Pandeys passed to the back of people's minds as they busied themselves with their affairs.

Twelve

The next time Adam went to the palace, one night, it was at Lalit's invitation. As Laxmi Devi, and her two sons and Gagan Singh were occupied elsewhere, he found her alone in the queen's quarters. Lalit was as beautiful as ever, her brown eyes soft, her face aglow with the warmth of her smile as she welcomed him.

'How beautiful you look tonight, Lalit,' Adam said, taking her in his arms and holding her close to him. She responded until, pulling herself away, she said, 'Not here. I shall show you.'

Adam followed her out along a corridor, and up a stairway to a narrow passage on the floor above. It was unlit and too dark to see clearly. But at one place a ray of light came up from a cleft in the floor, and Lalit cautioned Adam to take care as he stepped by. There was a trapdoor, not fitting well. 'The light is coming from an audience room below. It is used by the King at times,' Lalit explained. Looking down through the cleft, Adam caught a narrow glimpse of the King's room.

At a nearby door Lalit took Adam's hand. 'Come,' she said.

The small room was lit by the glow from an oil lamp burning in a corner and a window high up near the ceiling which let in a little of the night outside. As Adam grew accustomed he looked around to see a room furnished much as Lalit's in Dor Maske's house. The image of Lord Shiva's wife, Parbati, was touched by the light from the lamp and was reflected in the mirror over a dressing table.

'A gift from Laxmi Devi,' Lalit said pointing to the mirror. 'And also from the Queen,' she pointed to a carpet on the floor. 'She, too, is kind to me.'

The flickering oil lamp's glow played on Lalit, on the golden ornament in her hair and shimmered on her silk sari. It gave a sparkle to the stones in her necklace and her bangles. Adam stepped close to her. She looked up at him, gave a little smile, then shyly lowered her eyes and turned her face away. But when Adam put his arms around her and drew her close and held her, she pressed her softness against him, returning the desire he felt for her.

'I have waited Lalit, a long time,' Adam whispered.

She pressed even closer to him.

'You are very dear to me, my beautiful Lalit,' he said.

'It pleases me to hear you say that. And you are very dear to me.'

Adam took the ornament from Lalit's hair, put his arms around her and unfastened her necklace. He tried to take off her sari, fumbling, it was strange to him. So she took the silk in her hand and, twisting, dropped the sari to her waist, exposing her cholo blouse.

Again Adam fumbled trying to undo the blouse, until her hands again came to help him, her fingers finding the cords and untying them. Adam looked down to Lalit's face and to her bare breasts. Embarrassed now, she lowered her eyes. For some time he held her close, then feeling quickly for her waist he loosened her sari and let it fall from her, and after it her skirt and petticoat. Lalit clung to him in her nakedness, the warmth of her body, her head buried in his shoulder, her arms reaching around him. As he held her there, her heart pounded against his chest. Then, gently, he took her to the bed of quilts.

She lay there closely in Adam's arms and he felt the softness of her body trembling a little. 'I frighten you, Lalit?' he asked.

'Yes. But it is not you,' she whispered. 'It is strange for me. I need a little time.'

He caressed her until her trembling stopped and she relaxed. But Adam could wait no longer. He took Lalit to him. There was a sharp little cry from her at first, and then they completed the love they had for each other.

The oil lamp burnt low and spluttered and went out as Lalit lay quietly beside Adam under the quilts. He looked up through the darkness to the beam of the night light coming through the high window and settling on the opposite wall. His thoughts went to their future. Right then Adam decided he would marry Lalit, and take her with him back to England one day.

Lalit's hand felt for Adam's under the quilts and held it, and she asked, 'Would you tell me about England, about your home in Hollybrook?'

'I will,' he replied. 'But you must have a name for me. It is Adam. You can call me that.'

'I know it is. But I cannot. Not yet. One day I would like to.'

It is their custom, Adam thought. He went on to tell Lalit about life in England and Hollybrook, and spoke a lot about Maneka, saying how life there had pleased her, how she ran his grandfather's house, cared for her children and followed her adopted religion, helping often at the parish church.

'Was it difficult for her in a strange country?' Lalit asked.

'For some time, I was told, but then she managed and was happy. I was only a boy when she died, but I remember her well.'

And Lalit asked Adam to tell her about his younger days. He told her about his parents, life on the family estate, his school, university, then how he came to her country. 'But Lalit,' he said. 'You have me talk but you tell me nothing about yourself.'

She hesitated. 'There is so little to tell. You know Dor Maske cares for me. He always has. Before that, I remember little. I was a small girl when I went to his house.'

'What happened to your parents, Lalit?' Adam asked.

'They died long ago. It is best for Dor Maske to tell you of them. I should like you to ask him.'

'Your service with Laxmi Devi. There is that.'

'Dor Maske arranged it for me. He is very kind. I help the Queen with her wardrobe, keep her papers tidy, and take messages for her to Gagan Singh. And I care for the two little princes sometimes.'

Lalit asked more questions about England, until they came more slowly and then stopped altogether, and Adam heard her breathing deeply, asleep. He stayed with her, holding her whilst she slept, then lent and gently kissed her forehead, rose from the bed and dressed quietly. He found his way along the dark passage taking care to avoid the faulty trapdoor there, then down the stairway and out of the palace into the night, where the morning mists were already coming down in wisps around the pagodas and the images of the gods in the Durbar Square. He found the syce where he had left him near Gagan Singh's house, apologised for the long wait he had caused him and tipped him generously with an English shilling. Adam took the carriage back to the Residency.

It was only a day or so later that Dor Maske amazed Adam by saying with no warning at all, 'You might consider yourself married to Lalit, Mr Clarke'

Adam had him repeat it, to make sure.

'Yes, you are married to each other. It happened two nights back.' He watched Adam's reaction, his dark eyes twinkling, a broad smile coming over his old face.

'I don't understand, Dor Maske. Has Lalit spoken to you?'

'She has not. I assure you she has not. But much information reaches me. I have many sources. I can tell you that I am not at all displeased.'

'Will you explain, Dor Maske?'

'You have both eloped, Mr Clarke. Lalit has eloped from my house. I have a right to decide on that. I am her guardian. As for you, Mr Clarke, it seems you have eloped with her.'

'You still do not explain.'

'I am a Newar, Mr Clarke. Elopement is one way to marry. We accept it. Our gods accept it and it is often practised in the villages.'

The idea was entirely new to Adam and totally unexpected. But with just a little hesitation, he decided he liked it. 'Does Lalit regard herself as married?' he asked.

'No, not yet. But when I claim she has eloped with you, and make it plain to her, she will. She will have no option. Do you agree you are married, Mr Clarke?'

Adam waited only momentarily before he replied. 'I should like to, Dor Maske. Yes, I do.'

'I had expected that reply and it gratifies me. Lalit is very fond of you, devoted. I shall tell her you are married to each other, and that I approve of it.'

'And her family, Dor Maske. What of their approval?'

'I am her family. Her parents are dead. I shall tell you about them now, Mr Clarke. You have a right to know.'

Dor Maske told Adam how years ago his business had taken him into India, to Lucknow. As he was returning to Nepal, he stopped at the town of Nepalganj in the west to trade with a merchant, a Chhetri from Silgarhi, who had come down from the hills with his wife and a little daughter to meet him. To his dismay, Dor Maske found both the merchant and his wife were stricken with the aul, that deadly fever from the miasmas on the duns. The Chhetri had given his little daughter to a Tantric to be a devdasi, a gift to the God Krishna, on the condition that the god deliver them from their illness.

'But both the merchant and his wife died. So I thought Krishna had no right to the child,' Dor Maske said, a sly smile on his old face. 'He had not carried out his part of the bargain with the Chhetri. So I bought her from the priest. She was a pretty little girl.'

'It was Lalit?'

'Yes, of course.'

'You say a devdasi?'

Adam learnt that devdasies attend the God Krishna in the temple, his slaves you could say. They play an important part in the Tantric rituals. At puberty they are married to the god and the priests deflower them, ceremoniously, using a stone lingam usually. Devdasies assist in the worship of the god, and are trained to dance before Krishna's image, to cooperate in rituals portraying his amorous affairs, his carnality, to practise the erotic arts. Privileged people may use them in copulation.'

'You saved Lalit from that, Dor Maske.'

'You can look at it so. But devdasies have advantages. The priests care for them. When they leave the temples, many become well-sought-after courtesans. It is said Krishna treats them well in their future life.'

Dor Maske saw Adam's doubts.

'The gods have never blessed me with children, Mr Clarke. That is why I bought Lalit from the priest.'

Adam talked on with Dor Maske, but that was the crux of it. As he took his leave, Dor Maske told him Laxmi Devi wanted Lalit to stay in her service for some time yet, and that he was in no position to object. But it would not keep them apart altogether. He reminded Adam that his house was always available to him, and said that he had heard Adam was welcome at the palace.

The months that followed were a delight for Adam and, he was sure, for Lalit also. Many a time Adam felt thankful it was he, and not the God Krishna, who had won her. Lalit had heard of the custom of marriage by elopement, and she willingly accepted Dor Maske's verdict that they were man and wife. It was Adam who would sometimes talk of confirming it with a ceremony in a church or temple. Wanting a tangible symbol of the marriage, he found a goldsmith and asked him to make a gold ring to fit Lalit's finger. There was also the ruby pendant his grandmother had left him, the keepsake he had brought with him to Nepal. And he decided Lalit should have it.

Adam called on Lalit one October afternoon. The monsoon had finished, and it was a sunny day, the air still warm enough with just a touch of the coming winter. Lalit had picked flowers from Dor Maske's garden, and had put a few in her hair and the rest in a vase in her room beside the window opening to the green fields and village and to the mighty Himalayas, white and shining away to the north.

He took Lalit's hand and slipped the ring onto her finger. 'It's a wedding ring, my dear wife,' he said. 'It's a custom in my country.'

'To show I am a married woman,' she replied. 'It is like the vermilion powder in my hair. I shall cherish it always. It will never leave my hand.'

She held it out for Adam to see and it pleased him greatly, feeling it secured her more closely to him. 'There is something else,' he said, taking the ruby pendant and holding it out to her. 'It was my grandmother's once. A present my grandfather gave her. It came from India long ago. Now I give it to you Lalit. It is just right that I do .'

She took the pendant to the window, to the afternoon sunlight, and watched the great ruby glow rich red and the diamonds around it sparkle. 'It is so beautiful,' she said. 'Fit for the gods. I can see the flames. I can almost feel them burning me. Thank you Adam.'

'Take care of the flames, Lalit. Do not let them burn you,' Adam told her, laughing.

'It is so beautiful,' she said again. 'Perhaps it is too good for me. Even Laxmi Devi has none like it.'

'No it is not, Lalit. And Laxmi Devi is not as beautiful as you. I assure you of that,' Adam said as he took the pendant and put its chain around her neck, the great ruby settling over her breast, a gleaming red against the whiteness of her blouse.

After Adam left, Lalit put the pendant for safe keeping with her other jewellery in the cupboard in her room. She would wear it at times in Dor Maske's house but not at the palace, fearing perhaps Laxmi Devi or other ladies of the court would want it.

No one in the Residency objected to Adam's marriage to Lalit and they all wanted to meet her. Captain O'Keefe congratulated Adam and spoke at some length of his own happy marriage with the lady from the family of Mir Jafar, once Nawab of Bengal. Adam also had Dr Jones' congratulations; but the doctor suggested, politely enough, that he should take Lalit to Bettiah as soon as possible and have the Catholic fathers marry them.

The Resident was more circumspect, congratulating Adam but suggesting it best for him not to bring Lalit to live in the Residency at that stage. 'I might as well tell you now,' he said. 'It will be widely known soon. You had better consider what a new Resident's attitude to your Nepalese wife might be. My time here as Resident could be coming to an end.'

'Have you asked for a posting elsewhere, sir?' Adam asked.

'Not at all. I'm needed here. They need my help, as I've made it clear to Lord Ellenborough several times. Now Rajendra Shah has also made it clear to him and has written to the Governor-General asking that I stay here.'

'Surely Lord Ellenborough will agree,' Adam said, although not at all sure.

The Resident was silent for some minutes, looking through the window to the Residency gardens before turning slowly to Adam before saying, 'We will have to wait on Ellenborough's reply. Let us hope it's favourable.' Then as Adam was leaving he said, 'Of course you might bring your Lalit to the Residency on a visit, Mr Clarke. I'm sure we'd all like to meet her one afternoon.'

It was Christmas Day when Lalit came with Adam to the Residency. The Resident had arranged a small function in his office for Dr Jones and Captain O'Keefe and Adam and Lalit if she came, just with tea and cakes, and spirits for those wanting them.

Lalit looked as beautiful as ever in her richly embroidered sari and she wore the ruby pendant. Adam called for her and took her to the Residency early, in good time for her to look over his bungalow. Not that there was much to show. The living room, the kitchen, his bed room, the servants' quarters, all were sparsely furnished, and there was really nothing by way of ornaments, and little on the walls. Lalit was shy but interested. She gave a little smile at the large four-poster bed.

'Is it your sword?' Lalit asked, seeing the cutlass on the wall of the living room. 'Are you also a soldier, then?'

Adam told her the cutlass was there when he had come to the bungalow.

'You worship Ganesh, too?' she asked, looking at his image on the wall.

'In a way, Lalit,' Adam told her. 'I know he's a kind and helpful god.'

'Yes, I like him too.'

'Is my bungalow like you expected, Lalit? he asked.

She thought for some moments. 'No, it is not. I thought it would be more like Dor Maske's room or Laxmi Devi's perhaps. I thought your Company was rich and you would have more.'

Adam remembered Sarah St Clair also had thought his bungalow too Spartan and that the Company did not do well for him.

'The Company is rich, Lalit. Believe me. But I have all the things I need here. All I lack here is you.'

She smiled. 'I want to come to you, to live with you. I hope I will one day. But please forgive me for a while more. I must serve Laxmi Devi.'

Captain O'Keefe came and Lalit started to draw the silk of her sari up to her face, but Adam stopped her, not wanting her to have to hide the beauty. He introduced her to the captain, who greeted her gallantly, took her hand and kissed it. 'You are very welcome at the Residency. And may I compliment you on your beautiful sari,' the captain said. Seeing the pendant, its great glowing ruby and great diamonds, Captain O'Keefe was taken aback. He would surely know its worth, Adam thought. Then the captain praised it and told Lalit how it suited her.

In the main Residency building, Mr Hodgson had his servant go to some trouble to prepare for Lalit's visit. His room was warm with the log fire burning. And he had arranged for an afternoon tea to be set out with fine china, silver spoons and forks and a Christmas cake which was iced white on top and decorated with green holly leaves and red berries. But he was rather tense, Adam thought, and formal, although his welcome was certainly friendly. Dr Jones, too, made Lalit welcome, even though he doubted the validity of their marriage.

During afternoon tea each did his best to put Lalit at ease. Adam interpreted for Dr Jones as he talked about Christmas and the Christ Child. The Resident took the opportunity to talk about his great interest, the flowers and trees in the valley and the surrounding hills, using his Nepali. Lalit listened but was hardly at ease, the situation was so strange for her. She responded more to Captain O'Keefe's talk of the Indian lady he had married, and their children.

'Your wife, Captain?' she asked shyly, 'Did she go to the Christian religion?'

'No, she kept her Hindu faith,' the Captain told her.

'Did she ever go with you to England?'

'No. Nor to Ireland. I never returned. If I had she might have gone with me. Would you like to see England, Lalit?'

'Oh yes,' she said.

The afternoon tea that day finished on a pleasant note. The Resident seemed more relaxed. Dr Jones cut a large slab of the cake and had it wrapped for Lalit to take back with her. And Captain O'Keefe continued a little with his gallantry, telling Lalit how she was needed in the Residency. As he took her back to the palace, Lalit told Adam how she enjoyed the afternoon.

Thirteen

After months of Mr Hodgson's refusals to stop involving himself in the affairs of the Durbar, Lord Ellenborough dismissed him. The Company's Secretary wrote conveying, too bluntly Adam thought, the Governor General's order that Mr Hodgson, "... would be relieved of his situation of Resident at the Court of Nepal at the earliest period at which the season and the exigencies of the public service might have permitted such relief to take place". And to rub salt into the wound, as it were, Lord Ellenborough offered Mr Hodgson an appointment as the Company's assistant sub-commissioner at Simla. Mr Hodgson tendered his resignation and Ellenborough accepted it.

Captain O'Keefe, Dr Jones and Adam were disappointed and annoyed at the treatment meted out to Mr Hodgson. They thought it totally unfair and unworthy of Lord Ellenborough, to say the least. Mr Hodgson had served in Kathmandu for two decades and had served the Company well, and Nepal well in their opinion. He had worked through many troubled times in the Durbar, times which could easily have erupted into war again, and heavy loss of life on each side as Captain O'Keefe often emphasised. They thought that the offer of the junior position in Simla was an insult, no more than a paltry act of revenge on Ellenborough's part and a petty reaction to the Resident's strong will.

When Mr Hodgson came to leave Nepal, he did not go without a recognition of his worth, expressions of esteem in fact, from some in the Durbar, from Dor Maske and many others. And his departure was hardly a happy occasion for those left in the Residency. The evening before his departure, Dr Jones, Captain O'Keefe and Adam met with him for farewell drinks. They wished him well for the future, without knowing what that might be, and good luck with his studies of flora and fauna as well as his study of Buddhism. Mr Hodgson told them that, although they were losing him, they would be regaining the St Clairs. He had heard from Calcutta that Mr and Mrs St Clair would return to Kathmandu after their home leave. And also Sarah, Adam thought, judging from further letters he had from her saying she still intended to come back. Before he left, Mr Hodgson said that a Major Henry Lawrence would come to take his place as Resident.

The day Major Lawrence came to Kathmandu he made it clear, crystal clear, to all in the Residency that Lord Ellenborough's policy of non-intervention in Nepal's affairs would be followed to the letter. Even during the first meeting Major Lawrence called in his office, Adam realised how different he was from Mr Hodgson; he was very much in command, formal and much the soldier. Major Lawrence pointed out very bluntly that his own duty, and theirs in helping him, was to keep an eye on the Gurkha army, to check any contacts the Durbar might attempt with Indian States, to ensure Nepal was fair with British trade, and to see that Nepal returned people seeking asylum from the Company's law. That was all. Nothing else interested him, or them.

In future the Nepalese were to be left to conduct their intrigues alone, to fight each other for power or to murder each other if they wanted to. He assured them that If the Gurkhas should want to wage war, the Governor General would not delay in sending an army to crush them. Then dismissing Captain O'Keefe and Dr Jones, Major Lawrence asked Adam to stay on.

He stared at Adam for some moments before he said, 'You're a special problem for me, Mr Clarke. Lord Ellenborough told me of you. He sent you back to Kathmandu only because you spoke their languages well. But he thought you too much a Hodgson man, and told me to do something about it.'

Alarmed, Adam wondered what that would be.

But Major Lawrence was not wondering. 'I know of your Dor Maske. I won't stop that. You will continue to sound him out for the intelligence I need about their army and any contacts they try with the Indian States, our trade and our criminals. Let me be clear. That's all. Nothing else.'

'Certainly, sir,' Adam replied, relieved at not being confined to work in the Residency.

'I warn you, Mr Clarke. You will take no other action, and you will take no part in their intrigues. No part whatsoever. Keep away from the palace. You will not visit their queen. You might have been Mr Hodgson's go-between with her, but you're not mine. You understand?'

It was clear enough.

'One false step, Mr Clarke, and you leave Nepal immediately. You go back to Calcutta.'

Of course Adam's problem was Lalit, who was now at the palace in Laxmi Devi's service much of the time and not so often at Dor Maske's house. He hardly wanted to be denied the palace, for Lalit's sake as well as his own. 'You might not be aware that I am married, sir,' he said.

'Married? No, I was not aware. You surprise me. To whom, Mr Clarke?'

Adam told the Resident about Lalit, that she was Dor Maske's ward, in Laxmi Devi's service and that she lived in the palace much of the time.

Major Lawrence shook his head doubtfully. 'Even more of a problem than I thought,' he murmured to himself. Then he said, 'Bring her to your bungalow. Surely it's large enough for you both. Why haven't you?'

Adam started to explain, but the Resident interrupted. 'You say married. There's no priest here. Who married you?'

Adam told him of his marriage by elopement.

For a long time Major Lawrence stared at Adam in disbelief, then asked him to repeat what he had said, to make sure he had heard correctly. 'I find it incredible, Mr Clarke. I can hardly believe it.'

Adam explained that marriage by elopement was an accepted custom, but the new Resident cut him short.

'It is not my custom, Mr Clarke,' Major Lawrence said coldly. 'Nor is it the Company's. Not to my knowledge. I can't imagine it.'

Adam started to explain further, but the Resident said, 'No, you shall not bring her to the Residency. Not until you're properly married. You must understand that.'

'You still deny me visits to the palace, sir?' Adam asked.

'I do. I have given you your orders. It's your problem. Go and find your own way out of it.'

At that Major Lawrence dismissed Adam, saying as he left, 'I have heard, Mr Clarke, that cows and women cause much of the trouble in Nepal. I hadn't expected it so soon.'

Not long after that the Heir Apparent, enraged at his father not letting him have the throne, gathered together a large army detachment of three thousand strong and went down into Makwanpur towards the Indian border. Rajendra Shah and Mathabar Singh hastened after him.

'They caught up with the Heir Apparent at Hetaura,' Dor Maske told Adam. 'But he refused to return to Kathmandu unless his father abdicated. He threatened to move his troops into India to join with the British, saying they would support him for the throne. Father and son quarrelled furiously, degraded each other, and came to blows as Mathabar Singh and the generals were watching.'

'Then Mathabar Singh showed his hand,' Dor Maske continued.

'Without doubt he committed himself to side with the Heir Apparent. He had the army detachment go against the King. Except for a few—sixteen of them—senior men amongst them who were angered by Mathabar Singh's disloyalty, as they saw it. Next day the sixteen were beheaded for their trouble, beheaded at Dhupoabasa summarily and without a trial.'

'An evil act, Dor Maske,' Adam said. 'Who ordered it?'

'Mathabar Singh I think, or perhaps the Heir Apparent. I am told he watched the killings gleefully. Eventually the King gave way and gave full power to the Heir Apparent—full power to rule Nepal. He agreed to stay on the throne only as a figurehead.'

'And the Queen? What of Laxmi Devi?' Adam asked, remembering her powers under the Petition of Rights and knowing her high expectations of Mathabar Singh, her belief that he would help her have her own son on the throne instead of the Heir Apparent.

Dor Maske's laugh was cynical. 'She is out-manoeuvred, and beside herself with rage. Her regard for Mathabar Singh has turned to loathing because he has espoused the Heir Apparent. He is no longer of use to her, and is now a hated enemy.'

'And the King's revenge on Mathabar Singh?' Adam asked.

Dor Maske shrugged. 'It is strange. Rajendra Shah has bestowed honours on Mathabar Singh. He has made him minister for life, conferred on him the title of Kala Bahadur and presented him with four large gold medals. And he has given him a sword, a symbol that he will protect Mathabar Singh's life.

'So he has regained the King's favour it seems.'

'What do the King's honours mean, Mr Clarke? Rajendra Shah is an capricious. His words can to lead to the opposite—exactly so.'

Late one night not long after, Adam went to the palace to be with Lalit. Inside he made his way as usual along the corridor near Laxmi Devi's quarters, up the stairway to the floor above, which was dark now with the lateness of the night and the oil lamps out, and along the narrow passage towards Lalit's room. That night he could hardly miss noticing the faulty trapdoor in the floor, because light came up strongly through the cleft from the King's audience room below, piercing the blackness of the passage. Entering Lalit's room, he was disappointed. She was absent, had gone to Dor Maske's house.

As Adam went to leave, he heard voices coming up from under the trapdoor, and, curious to see, he knelt and peered through the cleft down to the room below. Rajendra Shah and Laxmi Devi were there seated at one end of the room. Standing near them were Gagan Singh, the queen's favourite, and Jung Bahadur, Mathabar Singh Thapa's nephew. Both were armed with muskets. Adam could see clearly. Large oil lamps gave ample light and their burning oil filled the room with only a slight haze. Vishnu's gilded image was near Rajendra Shah, and at the other end of the room the floor was raised to a gallery behind a lattice-work screen.

An attendant came into the room, spoke to Rajendra Shah, was dismissed and left. Adam saw Gagan Singh and Jung Bahadur mount the raised gallery and go behind the lattice screen.

Moments later a door opened and Mathabar Singh strode into the room, as impressive as ever, in the full dress of a Gurkha general, his large build and his demeanour showing his strength and confidence. The golden medals the King had recently bestowed on him shone in the light from the oil lamps. At his side he carried the sword, the King's gift to him, the symbol guaranteeing his life. As he faced Rajendra Shah and the Laxmi Devi, he joined his hands in a namaste and bowed low.

But at that moment a shot rang out from behind the lattice, and Adam saw Mathabar Singh's head jerk and his hands part from the last namaste he would ever make. He raised his arms towards the King, calling to him and beseeching him not to harm his family, to care for them. More shots came from behind the lattice and Mathabar Singh's strong body swayed as he continued to plead with Rajendra Shah. Then he fell to the floor. In an instant Jung Bahadur and Gagan Singh were onto him with their swords. Again Mathabar Singh raised his hands in a last supplication. Then Adam saw the swords slashing to cut his outstretched arms away.

Adam had seen enough, perhaps too much. He rose from the cleft in the trapdoor and, quickly, silently—doing all he could not to be noticed—crept along the dark passage and the corridors and out of the palace into the night. In the Durbar Square he saw soldiers of the King's guard standing in the shadow of a pagoda and heard others elsewhere, their murmuring, the shuffling of their feet. Adam stayed close to the Jagannath Temple, hidden in the shadows there. Soon soldiers came carrying the remains of Mathabar Singh, which had been lowered from a palace window on ropes, and took them off. Adam hurried back to the Residency, to get there under cover of what remained of the night.

The morning after the death of Mathabar Singh, Major Lawrence called a meeting at the Residency. Adam went there with some anxiety, fearing he had been seen at the palace the night before. But it was not that. Major Lawrence told them he had agreed to receive a deputation from the Durbar and wanted him present.

'Captain O'Keefe has news that Mathabar Singh is dead,' the Resident said.

'Yes,' Captain O'Keefe confirmed. 'My havildar tells me word is around Kathmandu that Mathabar Singh was killed last night in the palace.'

'Unexpected, unfortunate to say the least,' Adam said, feigning surprise.

'Unfortunate maybe, Mr Clarke. But hardly unexpected. Not in Kathmandu,' the Resident said sourly. 'Now they bother me with this deputation. Want to report it to me, I believe. A murder, no doubt.'

They did not have long to wait for the deputation. Adam heard hurried hoof beats pounding towards the Residency, the riders reined in their horses and dismounted. This time Adam's surprise was genuine, entirely so. It was Jung Bahadur followed by two attendants, his brothers Adam guessed from their appearance.

Jung Bahadur thanked the Resident for receiving him and hoped he was meeting him in good health. 'My King has sent me to you,' he said. 'I am to tell you the prime minister, Mathabar Singh Thapa, has been executed.'

'Executed!' the Resident repeated. 'How am I concerned with that?'

'I come on the King's order.'

'Executed. On what charges, might I ask?'

'The King found his offences most serious. There were several crimes,' Jung Bahadur said. 'He was guilty of the killings at Dhupoasbasa, murdering sixteen of our brave soldiers there. He was about to take the Brahmans' lands. He increased taxes. Most serious was his treason. Mathabar Singh took to himself the royal powers, powers only the King might wield. He deserved a traitor's death.'

'His trial?' the Resident asked.

'Rajendra Shah's verdict. The King is the supreme magistrate.'

'The executioners?'

'The King appointed them. They were properly appointed I assure you, Major Lawrence.'

There was not a flicker of guilt on Jung Bahadur's face, it gave nothing away.

'He was executed inside the palace, I've heard,' the Resident said, this time showing his doubt. 'Executed at night. Hardly British justice, I might point out.'

'British justice, Major Lawrence?' Jung Bahadur repeated, his face darkening. 'I am not here to talk with you of that. I can tell you that Mathabar Singh had to be executed privately. Much of our army supported him. Rajendra Shah had no wish to disturb the army, and rightly so. No doubt the Resident would agree.'

'It is not my place to agree or to disagree. It is no concern of mine. Not at all,' said Major Lawrence.

'Of course it is not, Resident. But I have been charged to tell you.' Jung Bahadur said. 'And I shall say that I myself also condemn Mathabar Singh. Powerful as he was, he did not govern wisely. He was a murderer at Dhupoasbasa and he did not stop the intrigues in the Durbar; nor did he bring stability there.'

Major Lawrence sat staring at Jung Bahadur, saying acidly, 'They are your own affairs, Jung Bahadur. Absurd to my mind. But, I warn you. Keep the peace between our nations. Keep your army under good control. I assure you our strength is great. We would crush you.'

This might well have intimidated a lesser man, but not Jung Bahadur. Calmly returning the Resident's stare, he said, 'Yes, that might be true. I have long known your strength. But you would pay a price.'

'Not too great a price.'

'You might think that. But there will be no cause for war. Our two nations will gain much from friendship. I will tell you, Major Lawrence, that our two nations will come to live happily together. I have no doubt of it.'

'Well let us hope so,' the Resident said bluntly. He stood up to end the session and Jung Bahadur and his attendants made their adieus and left.

Major Lawrence waited till they heard the deputation's horses cantering away, then he said, 'Murder! No doubt at all. It doesn't surprise me.'

No one disagreed. 'The King himself is behind it,' Captain O'Keefe suggested.

'At his orders, perhaps,' the Resident replied.

'The Queen?' Captain O'Keefe ventured.

'Possibly. Her man could do it for her. What's his name, Mr Clarke?'

'Gagan Singh, sir.'

'What do you think, Mr Clarke?' the Resident asked.

'Yes, Gagan Singh could be involved,' Adam agreed, saying no more than necessary—careful not to give himself away.

Mathabar Singh's murder brought an end to Thapa power in the Durbar, and the Heir Apparent lost his support. Queen Laxmi Devi resumed the powers which the Petition of Rights had given her and regained a measure of control over the King. The Chautariya Fath Jang was again made prime minister, but his duties were confined to matters in western Nepal and relations with China and the British. In his cabinet were the aged Dalbanjan Pandey who had no significant duties, General Abhiman Rana with some responsibility for eastern Nepal, and Gagan Singh who had the real power. Laxmi Devi saw to that. He was made a general and commander-in-chief of the army, and was given command of seven regiments all stationed in Kathmandu; and he had control of ordnance and all military supplies. He also controlled matters relating to the Durbar.

Jung Bahadur was the only Thapa—a Thapa on his mother's side—who had survived, and was made a minister and a general with the command of his three regiments. Without delay, he made good use of his new rank to favour his seven brothers. Each of them, Bhakta Bir, Bom Bahadur, Badri Nar Singh, Krishna Bahadur, Rana Udip, Jagats and Dhir Shamsher, he appointed to positions of command, thus ensuring their support and their unquestioning loyalty.

Fourteen

News came that the St Clairs were approaching the valley and Adam drove out to Thankot to meet them. The first he saw of their party was Mr St Clair walking along the road with some of the sepoy reliefs for the Residency garrison.

'Welcome back,' Adam called, genuinely pleased to have the St Clairs in Nepal again. Mr St Clair acknowledged it, but only coldly.

Adam wondered at this, but pointed to the carriage. 'You've had a hard climb up here. Ride with me for the last few miles.'

Mr St Clair thanked Adam but said, 'No, I'll walk on, Mr Clarke. Perhaps Mrs St Clair might want to ride.'

Mrs St Clair came into view with more of the sepoys. Bedraggled, Adam thought, with her long skirts creased and muddy, her hair dishevelled. Not at all as she would be seen in London, Adam mused smiling to himself, or in the Residency, or anywhere for that matter. He felt some concern for her, a woman past middle-age having to make such a long walk and a steep and difficult climb up into the valley. She was tired no doubt, but she was walking strongly as she came up to him.

Adam welcomed her also. 'I must say, all in the Residency are pleased to have you back, Mrs St Clair. It's been a long time. Everyone has missed you.'

She stood looking at Adam, staring into his face. He recalled she had done this more than once, not long after he had first met her.

'Is there something wrong?' he asked.

'No there is not, Mr Clarke. I was thinking of your Nepalese grandmother.'

'Would you like to drive to the Residency?' Adam offered. 'You must be tired after the long climb. Sarah must be too.'

Adam helped her into the carriage. The rest of the sepoys and the train of porters had come into view, and he stood looking along the road for Sarah.

'It's no use you looking for Sarah. If that's what you're doing,' Mrs St Clair called from the carriage. 'She won't be coming to Kathmandu.'

Adam was surprised, remembering Sarah's letters.

'Sarah's staying in Calcutta,' Mrs St Clair said. 'I am glad. She's a wise young lady.'

Mrs St Clair said no more. They drove back to the Residency in silence, passing on the way Mr St Clair, who again refused Adam's offer.

Adam wondered about the St Clairs. He saw little of them for some time after they returned to the Residency. Mr St Clair would pass the time of day with him politely enough, but that was all. He saw nothing of Mrs St Clair. She was busy settling into their bungalow again, unpacking what she had brought back from England, taking out again what she had packed and left in Kathmandu. She was busy getting servants again, instructing them and setting them to her way of work, the cleaning, dusting and the rest. Adam imagined her lining her mantelpiece again with her bric-a-brac and adding more pieces she had acquired.

The next time Major Lawrence called Dr Jones, Captain O'Keefe, Mr St Clair and Adam to his office, it was to tell them that, short as his stay in Kathmandu was, the Governor General was recalling him to Calcutta for a more senior posting elsewhere and that his replacement would come to Kathmandu in due course. They congratulated him and wished him well. It was expected of them, the thing to do.

Adam heard himself saying, 'You must be satisfied with your time here, sir.' It was sarcasm, of course. Immediately he could have bitten his tongue out. It was rude. No doubt he was still annoyed with Major Lawrence for forbidding him access to the palace to be with Lalit and for not accepting their marriage. But it was more than that.

During Major Lawrence's residency, turmoil and intrigue had worsened in the Durbar. Soldiers had been killed at Dhupoasbasa. Mathabar Singh had been murdered, and his murderers had done well out of it. Gagan Singh had effective control in Nepal. The Thapas, friends of the British, had been ousted. And the Durbar was as unstable as ever with Rajendra Shah, Laxmi Devi and the Heir Apparent still playing for power.

But to Adam's surprise, and some relief, the Resident replied, 'Thank you, Mr Clarke. Yes, I am satisfied. And I'm sure the Governor General is. My stay here has had at least some measure of success.'

Dr Jones and Captain O'Keefe were non-committal, but Mr St Clair agreed, saying, 'More than some measure, sir, I'd say. I'm back only recently. But from what I hear, there's been much improvement. No more meddling with the Durbar.'

It pleased the Resident.

Then Captain O'Keefe said, 'There's their army, sir. Building it up further worries me.'

'No need to worry, Captain,' the Resident replied. 'No need at all. Prime Minister Fath Jang came to me some time ago full of friendship. He said the Sikhs had asked Nepal for help in their war with us. But Fath Jang would have none of it. He told the Sikhs that when they'd taken Delhi it would be time enough to think of it. Can you imagine the Sikhs ever taking Delhi, Captain?'

Before the meeting finished, the Resident warned them against interfering in the affairs of the Durbar after he had left, saying yet again they must not get involved in the squabbles there. He spoke of Rajendra Shah: 'I can see why people call him an imbecile. He gave me a letter to send on to the Governor General about Mathabar Singh's murder. It amazed me. He claimed he put the traitor Thapa to death with his own hands—killed him with his own gun and sword.' The Resident smiled. 'I have no idea why he said it. I certainly don't believe him. He hardly had the courage even to face Mathabar Singh, let alone fire a gun at him. Might have mangled the corpse though. Others killed Mathabar Singh.'

Adam knew it well enough.

'Major Lawrence continued. 'After I go you must remember the Governor General won't take trouble from Nepal, believe me. He'd send in our army and make short shrift of them. I wouldn't mind if he did. Candidly, I'd like to annex Nepal. Many of us would. Good climate, a nice valley around Kathmandu. It would make a good retreat for us from Calcutta.'

Captain O'Keefe looked doubtful, but Mr St Clair agreed with enthusiasm.

When she settled into her bungalow again, Mrs St Clair invited Adam to a game of cribbage. He found things much the same as before her home leave. The table was set up near the window with a pack of cards and a cribbage board. Her sitting-room was still as English as ever with floral curtains, the chintz coverings and the paintings. The mantelpiece above the hearth was again full of bric-a-brac: the little ivory elephants, Indian brass vases and the clock under its glass dome, the porcelain pieces and miniatures in their silver frames.

'I'm so glad you could come, Adam,' Mrs St Clair welcomed him. 'We've seen little of you. But I have been really busy. It was such a job settling in again. Everything was so dusty. And the new servants, I won't say more.'

Adam thought she seemed friendly enough.

'We had a lovely time in England, just lovely. We went back to our house in Kensington. It's a very nice house and near to everything. Mr St Clair bought a sulky and a dear little pony so we could get around.'

'Into Kent?' Adam asked, thinking of Hollybrook.

'No. But Sarah did. Several times, I think.'

Of course Adam was wondering about Sarah. And he noticed Mrs St Clair had not mentioned Lalit and his marriage.

'I shopped a lot,' she said with a smile, and a little guiltily. 'The London shops are really wonderful. What I miss out here for Mr St Clair's sake. We visited our relatives and our friends, nice friends. And nice dinner parties. We went on picnics in the countryside.'

'You were busy, Mrs St Clair! You enjoyed yourself.'

'Immensely. And we attended the theatre a lot. We saw *The Lady of Lyons* by that clever Lord Lytton, and Browning's *Strafford*.'

Mrs St Clair went on and on about her stay in England until she said, 'But I'm talking too much, and I invited you for cards.'

As they played, Mrs St Clair kept the score on the cribbage board with the little ivory pegs. The counting came back to Adam: two for a pair, one for the jack noddy and the rest. Between hands, Mrs St Clair told Adam more about her home leave. Then she asked a servant to bring in the afternoon tea, the fine china, silver spoons and cakes.

'Sarah isn't here to pour tea today, Adam,' she said, looking at him keenly.

'I was wondering about Sarah,' Adam said.

'She's staying in Calcutta and will return to England.'

'Has she changed her mind? She wrote to me, you know.'

'Yes, I do. Sarah should not have come back from England with us. I wanted Mr St Clair to refuse her, but he wouldn't. Men are so blind sometimes. Sarah has every opportunity in London. She met several young gentlemen. There is one, Lord Sinter's eldest son, who I'm sure is very fond of her. I was really devastated when she took the ship back with us.'

For some moments Mrs St Clair sat looking at Adam again, then said, 'I believe you are married.'

'Yes.'

'You told Sarah in your letter. But it was held up. She got it only in Calcutta. I'm glad for you. I must congratulate you.'

'Well thank you, Mrs St Clair,' Adam said.

'Of course it's best for you, marrying a Nepalese lady. And being partly Nepalese yourself. You must extend my best wishes to her,' Mrs

St Clair added.

'I'll arrange for her to meet you.'

'Yes. Perhaps. I shall see. Sarah will return to England from Calcutta. It is very wise of her. I shall miss her, of course. Dreadfully. But it is for her own sake. I certainly didn't want her to come out to India with us. Certainly not back to Kathmandu. If I may say, Adam, she's grown into a charming young lady. And George Sinter is a man from a very good family.'

Just then Mr St Clair came back to the bungalow. 'I'm sure Adam would like a drink, Alfred. So would I,' Mrs St Clair told him. 'We have seen very little of him since we returned. We played cribbage this afternoon.'

Mr St Clair poured drinks and sat opposite Adam, not speaking.

Mrs St Clair shook her head, showing her irritation. 'Come Alfred,' she said. 'Please don't keep it up any longer. I shall explain. I will.' She turned to Adam. 'Perhaps you do not know, Adam. But your marriage hurt Sarah terribly. She was shocked when she read your letter in Calcutta. That is why she has not come to Kathmandu with us. It is why she will return to England soon. I shall miss her. But it is best for her.'

Adam had, of course, half expected it. 'What can I say?' he asked.

'Nothing to me,' Mrs St Clair told him. 'Nothing at all. I'm so glad things have worked out for the best.' A little worried, she looked towards her husband. 'Won't you agree now, Alfred?'

'I will not, Agnes. I'll tell Mr Clarke, now, to his face, that he's been unfair with Sarah. Unfair at the very least. I won't go further than that. Perhaps I could, but I won't.'

Adam started to defend himself but Mrs St Clair cut in. 'Alfred, I've told you Adam is blameless, entirely so. I told you I made Sarah show me his letters in Calcutta, all of them. And I read them. I hope you'll excuse me for that,' she said, turning to Adam. 'There was nothing. On the contrary, Adam told Sarah several times that she should stay in London or words to that effect. Mr Clarke did not encourage Sarah in any way. Isn't that so, Adam?'

Adam assured them that was. He told them how much he regretted Sarah's unhappiness and wondered what he could possibly do to help rectify matters.

'There is nothing, Mr Clarke,' Mr St Clair told him bluntly. He poured Adam another drink and, when Adam left to return to his bungalow, had lost some of his coldness.

Looking back on it, Adam always thought that Lalit was at her happiest one day late in August towards the end of the monsoon. It was the Krishna Jayanti, the festival for the birth on earth of the God Krishna. He called for her at Dor Maske's house with the carriage to take her to the Krishnamandir Temple at Lalitpatan for the birthday celebration. Adam found Lalit waiting for him, dressed especially for the occasion in her red silk sari trimmed with gold and carrying a woollen shawl. Her hair was fixed with a golden ornament and its shining blackness touched with vermilion powder. The ruby pendant he had given her glowed a blood-red on her breast. She welcomed him warmly, although a little anxiously he thought. He helped her up into the carriage and had the syce drive off towards Lalitpatan.

In the carriage Lalit sat quietly, glancing shyly at Adam a few times till he asked what troubled her.

She hesitated before she replied, 'It is perhaps nothing. But I believe it is.'

'What do you believe, Lalit?'

Again she hesitated. Adam turned towards her to see a little smile playing on her lips. 'How do English ladies tell their husbands of such news?' she asked.

'What news, Lalit?' Adam looked to ensure the syce was on the right road to Lalitpatan.

'It is important news. It is news I hope you will like to hear.'

'I'm sure I shall, Lalit. But tell me.'

She lent closer to him, saying softly, 'I am carrying a child for you. It seems so.'

Adam took Lalit's hand, bent and kissed her cheek. 'It's a wonderful surprise, Lalit. Wonderful news,' he said after only a few seconds' hesitation.

He was indeed surprised, not that he ought to have been. Adam should have guessed. The possibility had often crossed his mind, and now it had happened for him. 'Of course it's important news, Lalit. Most important. I am delighted. I'm very happy indeed.'

Adam watched the pleasure in her face, the warm smile, her dark eyes moist and glistening. 'I was anxious,' she said. 'Now, I am not.'

'Our son or daughter?' Adam asked, kissing her again.

'A son for you, perhaps.'

'It doesn't matter, Lalit. I shall have you and our child.'

She lent back happily as they made their way on to Lalitpatan to celebrate Lord Krishna's birthday.

Adam learnt that Krishna, who was the eighth reincarnation of the great God Vishnu, was one of the most adored of all the gods, the personification of good over evil, of gallantry and of virtuous manhood. He was born on Earth in the very distant past, on the stroke of twelve, it is said, at midnight of the seventh day of the dark fortnight of the month of Shrawan. He was born of Devaki, the daughter of the demon King Kansa, and her husband Vasudev.

Krishna was the most beautiful of babies, his eyes were lotus-shaped, his skin shone like the blue of a dark sapphire, his body giving forth a celestial radiance. He came to Earth already crowned with jewels and dressed in yellow silk, and his four arms held his conch shell, mace, disc and a glowing lotus blossom. He stood before his earthly parents and all the gods celebrated. A storm raged, lightning lit the sky and the thunder rumbled against loud music from the heavens. Later, when the storm was over, fruit suddenly appeared on trees, and flowers rained down from the clear blue sky.

On their way to Lalitpatan Adam and Lalit saw many images of Krishna displayed at the front of houses, along the roadside and outside temples, images often clothed in colourful garments, bedecked with flowers, and sometimes decorated with precious stones or other jewellery. And they passed many people on their way to the festival carrying their own images of Krishna.

They found the Durbar Square at Lalitpatan, with its ancient palace and pagodas and images of the gods, already crowded with people. Most, Adam noticed, were women and girls, who were also dressed for the occasion in bright saris and wearing their jewellery. In the processions people carried images of Krishna and held their banners high to declare his divinity. Priests and lamas mingled in the crowd and bands played drums, cymbals and flutes. Adam and Lalit walked up to the great Krishnamandir Temple, which was built of grey stone two centuries earlier, and looked up at its three tiers of balconies which were decorated with fine stone carvings of scenes from the holy Ramayana.

Lalit led Adam into the temple, dark inside now with the coming dusk, and up a stairway to the second floor, to a large gilded image of Krishna, which, lit by the light of the burning oil lamps, glowed through the darkness. It was an image exuding great authority, a truly god-like power, Adam thought. The god was surrounded by offerings of milk and butter, rice, cotton, flowers and coins. Lalit made her offering of coins to the god and bowed low in prayer; and the priest in attendance gave her his blessing, dabbing red sindar powder on her forehead and giving her a flower to put in her hair. She looked at Adam smiling, expectantly Adam thought, so he, too, offered coins to the god and received a blessing and the red powder from the priest.

'I prayed for our child,' Lalit whispered to Adam as they walked down out of the temple.

The tiers of balconies around the Krishnamandir Temple were already filled with women and girls, who sat holding little oil lamps on their knees and sticks of incense, waiting for midnight the hour of Krishna's birth. Lalit and Adam found a place to sit in front of the temple near a pillar which held the image of the bird-god Garuda, Lord Vishnu's carrier. A pundit offered to tell stories of Krishna's childhood.

He told them that, although Krishna's entry to this world had been illustrious, truly brilliant, he immediately met with difficulties. The demon King Kansa had heard a voice from Heaven saying that he would die by the hand of the eighth son born of his daughter Devaki and her husband Vasudev. So for safety, King Kansa had put to death the first six boys born to them. The seventh escaped him because Lord Vishnu transferred the foetus from Devaki's womb to that of Rohini, who lived in Gokhul with a family of cowherds, and who gave birth to Balarama, a pleasant boy and really a reincarnation of the Snake God Ananta.

When Devaki was pregnant for the eighth time, her father, King Kansa, put her and her husband, Vasudev, in iron chains and imprisoned them under guard in a dungeon in his castle, intending to surely be able to kill their child when it came. But again Lord Vishnu was watching. At midnight when the baby boy was born, he caused the parents' chains to be broken, the guards to be drugged, and the dungeon doors to be opened. Vasudev took his child and carried it through the still raging storm, the lightning and thunder to Gokhul, where it joined its brother, Balarama, and was reared by a family of cowherds. The child was of course Krishna.

The pundit spoke of Krishna's boyhood. Krishna loved his life with the cowherds and their children and his brother, Balarama. He helped tend the cows in the fields, played with them, drank their milk and ate the butter they gave. He was an impish young boy, sometimes tormenting the milkmaids, taking their curds and hiding them and thieving butter from them. As Krishna grew older his strength grew mightily. Once, to protect Gokhul from rains that would have flooded the land, he held up a nearby mountain with one finger.

And the Pundit told them that as a young man Krishna travelled widely with Balarama into many parts of India and Nepal, performing brave deeds for the good of mankind with no thought of reward for himself. Krishna became a prodigious lover adored by women, by his many hundreds of wives and thousands of milkmaids who would leave their homes and husbands to follow him, enraptured, fascinated by his beauty and godly charm and captivated by the music of his flute.

The pundit went on to say that the demon King Kansa did not give up his pursuit of Krishna. Enraged by his own failures, he sent out murderers who killed many who might be the god, young men, Brahmans who worshipped Lord Vishnu, and, in revengeful desperation, the sacred cows. These murders were in vain. But finally King Kansa managed to entice Krishna to a great wrestling tournament, with a plan to kill the god by unfair means. Krishna accepted. With his supernatural strength he won each bout in spite of trickery. Then tiring of King Kansa's evil, he mounted the royal platform, grasped the demon king by the hair and slew him.

Adam thanked the pundit, and he left.

'Krishna is a manly god. And he is kind,' Lalit said, 'He was a beautiful child.'

'He had the demon king to trouble him,' Adam remarked.

Lalit thought for a while, frowning. Then she smiled as she said, 'Yes, but there is no King Kansa now.'

By midnight the Krishnamandir Temple was packed with women who crowded together along the temple's tiers of balconies, spilling over to the court below; and some, the more adventurous young, sat on the temple's many roofs. Most were wrapped in shawls against the cold of the night air and all had lit their little oil lamps and rested them on their knees. Some burnt incense. As midnight approached their worship of Lord Krishna intensified. They prayed, their heads bent low over the oil lamps on their knees. Their bodies swayed as they repeated Krishna's name over and over again and some of Lord Vishnu's other thousand names, Narayan, Rama, Surya, Gopal, Hari and many more, until the night air throbbed with their chanting.

Adam and Lalit left a little after midnight. Looking back as they walked across the Durbar Square, they saw the Krishnamandir Temple still alight with the glow of hundreds of little oil lamps. And behind them in the shadows women with their shawls drawn up around their heads were still praying and chanting, still celebrating Krishna's birth. They strolled back to the carriage and the waiting syce and rode back to Dor Maske's house. Adam stayed with his wife that night and returned to the Residency next morning.

Fifteen

September was half way through with the moon going into the dark half of the month of Ashwin, and it was time for the Sorah Sraddha in Kathmandu. It is said that during this dark fortnight the spirits of ancestors come back from the Underworld to the homes of their families. It is a special time for caring for the needs of the departed souls, for venerating and worshiping them, and offering presents to them.

In many homes people say prayers for the dead. First they pray to the great Gods of the Hindu Trinity, Brahma, Vishnu and Shiva, then to the ancient sages and respected kings and other leaders of the past, and after that to each of those departed from the family by name back through the generations. They make offerings to the dead of pure water and pindas cakes made with rice or barley flour and rolled into little balls, which are later fed to the sacred cows. To pay homage to their ancestors, many people attend the Pashupatinath and other temples or go to the sacred rivers, to the burning ghats and the other holy places.

It was 14th September 1846 when Adam next called on Dor Maske. He always remembered the date. He had to wait till dusk for Dor Maske to return from the Pashupatinath, where he had gone early to worship his own dead. Seeing her husband tired from the journey, Maya went to take him to his bed, but he objected and wanted to go to his couch in the reception room, saying he had important news for Adam.

'I have many dead to remember, Mr Clarke,' he said. 'To pay homage to. Many more than I have living. And there are those recently departed, Bhim Sen Thapa and now Mathabar Singh. It is a sad time for me.'

Adam sympathised with him, but wondered what was the important news he had.

Dor Maske did not delay. Once he had settled his old body on the couch, his black eyes became alert, darting over Adam, and he said, 'Gagan Singh's turn is coming, Mr Clarke. Very soon he, too, will be a departed soul to remember.'

Dor Maske talked about Gagan Singh's rise to power, his being commander-in-chief of the army and wielding the ministerial authority

Laxmi Devi had given him: authority surpassing that of Prime Minister Fath Jang. Gagan Singh had become more and more resented by the Gurkha nobles, the Chautariyas in particular, many of whom were jealous of him and embittered because he, once only a chodbar, a palace menial allowed to enter the quarters of the ladies of the court, had been preferred to them.

'You of course know that Gagan Singh is Queen Laxmi Devi's lover, Mr Clarke,' Dor Maske said. 'The King wants revenge, and talks of it to his two sons, the Heir Apparent and the younger Mihla Sahib. He talks of the disgrace it brings to him—to them also—and to his throne. And he urges his sons to protect the family honour, to avenge him.'

'Why now, Dor Maske?' Adam asked, surprised. 'For a long time Rajendra Shah has known Gagan Singh is Laxmi Devi's lover. It's common knowledge in Kathmandu.'

Dor Maske shrugged. 'The King is capricious and an imbecile. Also, he resents Gagan Singh's new-found power.'

'So the Heir Apparent would support his father in this?' Adam queried, remembering how he had once insulted his father at the Residency, calling him a puppet King and saying Gagan Singh was cuckolding him.

'It is not his father's honour, Mr Clarke. The Heir Apparent cares little about that. He thinks that without Gagan Singh's support, Laxmi Devi's power will go. So will the threat of her own son succeeding to the throne. But it is not the Heir Apparent who is plotting. The King has chosen the younger prince to help arrange Gagan Singh's murder.'

'Mihla Sahib is a mere boy.'

Dor Maske shrugged. 'Yes, but he is suitable. He is too young to raise suspicion. The King has sent him to Prime Minister Fath Jang with the proposal, and to two ministers, Dalbanjan Pandey and General Abhiman Rana, and also to Kishore Pandey.'

'Have they agreed?' Adam asked.

'They have. I hear they hired their assassin. A Brahman named Lal Jha, I believe. A rascal.'

'Does Gagan Singh suspect?'

'Not at all. The King shows him much favour to keep him off his guard. Fawns on him, almost.'

'Of course you will alert Gagan Singh,' Adam said, alarmed at the prospect of yet another murder in the Durbar, and Laxmi Devi's loss of support.

Dor Maske shook his head slowly for a moment or two before he replied. 'No, Mr Clarke, I will not intervene. I am old and, as you see, in failing health. I no longer have the Thapas to support. True, I have no love for Fath Jang and the Pandeys who are left, and less for the imbecile King and his cruel heir. But I will let their plot unfold.'

'You will acquiesce in murder, Dor Maske?'

'It is not my doing, Mr Clarke. Whatever I would do, Gagan Singh's fate is sealed. This plot or the next, he is finished.'

'There is Laxmi Devi. She loses his support.'

'That matters little, Mr Clarke. Laxmi Devi's fate also is sealed. It was sealed the night of Mathabar Singh's murder.'

'Who would you want to rule Nepal, Dor Maske?'

Again he shrugged. 'I cannot answer that, Mr Clarke. It is unfortunate, perhaps a tragedy that I cannot. But there is one who will come to rule my country whether I want it or not.'

'Is it Jung Bahadur?' Adam ventured.

'We shall see, Mr Clarke,' Dor Maske said with no pleasure in his smile.

Dor Maske's decision not to alert Gagan Singh to the plot against his life worried Adam. Dor Maske had said Gagan Singh's fate was sealed, but that was a matter for the future Adam thought. As he left Dor Maske, he decided that he himself would alert Gagan Singh of the King's plot against his life. 'Drive to Gagan Singh's house near the Durbar Square,' he directed the syce as he climbed into the carriage.

But Adam was not to alert Gagan Singh. Leaving his carriage with the syce, he approached Gagan Singh's house through the darkness and saw its door and window open and lit by the oil lamps inside. A crowd was gathering in front where several torches were burning, their glow flickering out towards the Durbar Square and touching the nearby temples. Adam found people staring through the open window at an inert figure inside, others pointing to nearby roof tops. Most were talking excitedly. He had come too late. Gagan Singh was dead.

A man in the crowd called to Adam, 'Gagan Singh was at prayer, worshipping his gods. The shot through the open window killed him.' Another man pointed to a roof top, saying, 'The assassin fled over the tiles. Men are chasing after him.' Adam also learnt that Gagan Singh's son, Captain Wazir Singh, had already gone to the palace to tell Laxmi Devi of his father's murder.

As Adam watched, two women, the wives of Gagan Singh, came slowly out from Gagan Singh's house, fearful and weeping, beside themselves with grief, to meet the sympathetic murmurs from the crowd.

Before long the men, who had gone in search of the assassin, returned. 'We found no sign of him,' they said.

Suddenly there was a hush, and all faces in the crowd turned in the direction of the palace. Coming out from the dark of the night, out past Narayan-Vishnu's Temple, past Garuda's statue and Lord Shiva's Kabindrapur Temple, and into the flickering light from the burning torches, Adam saw Laxmi Devi. She was hurrying, almost at a run, her black hair untied and streaming, and the hem of her white sari, a sari hurriedly donned no doubt, trailing behind her. In one hand she held a heavy sword, the Sword of State. Two of her ladies-in-waiting came running after her, having difficulty in keeping up with her. In front of Gagan Singh's house the crowd made way for Laxmi Devi, and, as the light played on her face Adam saw it was distorted in its fury, her lips tightly drawn, her eyes glowing with rage. Looking at her young ladies, Adam realised one of them was Lalit.

Laxmi Devi hurried into Gagan Singh's house as the crowd watched through the open window. For a time she stood there looking down on Gagan Singh, her lover of many years, his corpse turned on its back, its face upwards with the eyes not yet closed. For minutes she stood there, and Adam saw tears streaming down her cheeks. Laxmi Devi looked back through the open window out into the crowd, and, holding the sword high with her two hands, she gave a scream that rent the night air and echoed amongst the temples of the Durbar Square.

Laxmi Devi came out from the house to stand in the space which the people quickly cleared for her. Then again holding the sword high above her head, she looked up past the tops of the pagodas to the stars in the black sky and, in a voice that must have pierced the heavens with its shrillness, she swore vengeance on Gagan Singh's murderers, and called upon all the gods to help her.

'Death to the murderers! Death to those who plotted this unholy and vile evil!' she called loudly. 'Death for their great villainy. Death quickly for them. Not one of them will survive the night. That I swear. I will revenge my fond and faithful minister. Tonight, Yama already awaits his murderers.'

With that Laxmi Devi made to leave, but seeing Gagan Singh's widows she stopped and spoke to them. 'You will not burn on your husband's pyre,' she told them. 'You will not become satis with him. That I order, and I will be obeyed. I will arrange for the burning of Gagan Singh's body. It will be a great funeral. He will be honoured. Honoured as he rightly deserves.'

On her arrival at Gagan Singh's house Lalit had gone to stand beside Adam, and the two had listened to Laxmi Devi. 'It is a terrible thing to happen. So sad a night for the Queen,' Lalit said. 'She has lost her lover. It is so unfair. Gagan Singh was a kind and gentle person.'

Adam remembered Gagan Singh's part in the murder of Mathabar Singh Thapa, but said nothing.

Lalit felt for Adam's hand and said, 'You must take care. We, also, are lovers. You are my husband. Nothing must take you away from me.'

Adam felt Lalit's hand trembling in his own. He started to reassure her, but Laxmi Devi was calling her. 'The Queen needs me,' Lalit said. 'I must go with her. She is going to the military headquarters, to the Kot. She will seek those who murdered her lover.'

Adam watched after Laxmi Devi as she hurried off into the night, carrying the Sword of State. Followed by Lalit and her maid, she hurried back past Lord Shiva's Temple and the Kasthamandap, until, out of the light of the burning torches, he lost them in the darkness of the Durbar Square.

A little later the blare of trumpets broke the night. It was Laxmi Devi's summons, the signal for all ministers and generals and all senior officials and soldiers to assemble at the Kot. Without delay she was to look amongst them for her lover's slayers. The crowd in front of Gagan Singh's house started to disperse and Adam decided to go to the Kot himself, wondering what was to happen there and wanting most of all to be near Lalit.

As he neared the Kot Adam felt a hand on his arm. He turned quickly and was surprised to see Tanka Rana. 'I think it is best for you not to be here, Mr Clarke. Best to go back to the Residency.' Tanka Rana told him. 'Who knows what will happen here tonight?'

'You yourself are here, Tanka Rana.'

'I have no choice, Mr Clarke. I am a soldier again. I have joined with Jung Bahadur.'

'I too shall stay, Tanka Rana.'

'You are British, and from the British Residency. You should not stay.'

Adam bent towards Tanka Rana. 'Do I look British, Tanka Rana? Would you take me for British in the night?.'

Tanka Rana looked at Adam's face. 'Perhaps not, Mr Clarke. No, I would not.'

'You say you're with Jung Bahadur?' Adam queried. 'Has he come here with his regiments?'

'Jung Bahadur has news of Gagan Singh's murder. He is here with his three regiments and his seven brothers are with him. His regiments are armed, they are ready to protect the Queen.'

'He fears Laxmi Devi is in danger?'

'He has told her that she is in danger. He told her that those who murdered Gagan Singh might come to her next. And they might also come to her sons. He has agreed that she must find the plotters without delay and execute them. He will help her do so.'

'Are the plotters known?' Adam asked, remembering Dor Maske had told him that the King himself had initiated the murder, and involved Fath Jang, Dalbanjan Pandey, Kishore Pandey and General Abhiman in the plot. 'Does Laxmi Devi know? Does Jung Bahadur know?'

'It seems Laxmi Devi does not know, Mr Clarke. She has ordered that a council be set up to identify the plotters. Jung Bahadur advised her to do this.'

That night the darkness of the Kot building, its parade ground and open gateways were lit by the yellow flames of many torches as people crowded there: Chautariyas, Brahmans, Thapas and Pandeys, Jung Bahadur and his seven brothers and others obeying the summons of Laxmi Devi's trumpets. Adam could see the plotters of Gagan Singh's murder there—the King, Dalbanjan Pandey, Kishore Pandey, General Abhiman—but not yet Prime Minister Fath Jang. One plotter, Kishore Pandey, was in irons, sitting on the ground with his legs shackled and arms bound. Adam learnt from Tanka Rana that Laxmi Devi, believing that Kishore Pandey had played a large part in the murder, had ordered General Abhiman to put him in irons.

'Has she evidence of that?' Adam asked, wondering if the plotters had been uncovered.

Tanka Rana shook his head doubtfully. Laxmi Devi has never liked the Pandeys, Kishore Pandey in particular. That is all, I think.'

Tanka Rana and Adam saw Laxmi Devi came out from the Kot building and stand over Kishore Pandey. Looking down at him she charged him with the murder, her voice loud and shrill, fury in her face. 'Your deed is vile, the vilest of deeds!' she cried, repeating it several times, the words seething between her teeth. 'You stole the life of my most faithful minister.'

'It is best I am not here,' Tanka Rana said to Adam and went off to rejoin his regiment.

Kishore Pandey looked up at her, protesting. He denied any part in the crime, saying Gagan Singh's life had been sacred to him, that he was involved in no plot, and the gods would surely bear witness to it.

Laxmi Devi would accept none of it. 'Murderer you are, Kishore Pandey,' she screamed. 'And now a liar. You are truly a murderer. Your life will pay for it.'

Kishore Pandey continued to proclaim his innocence, again denying any plot and swearing his loyalty. But Laxmi Devi called to General Abhiman, 'Come General. With your sword. You will use it in my service. This Kishore Pandey I will execute. A vile murderer. You will behead him. Now. It is my order.'

Adam saw General Abhiman's hand go to the hilt of his sword as if to draw it, then he stopped. He looked away, avoiding Laxmi Devi's eyes and, turning to the King, asked, 'Am I to behead Kishore Pandey, Sire? Is it your command?'

'Has Kishore Pandey confessed to the murder?' Rajendra Shah asked, knowing full well he had not.

'No he has not, Sire. He proclaims his innocence, and proclaims it strongly,' the general replied.

A cunning smile crossed the King's face, 'No, General. You will not behead Kishore Pandey. A council will try him.'

'A council is to identify all the murderers, Sire,' Jung Bahadur said. 'The Queen has ordered it. I shall arrange it immediately.'

This time there was concern in the King's face. 'Not yet, Jung Bahadur,' he said. 'Fath Jang is missing. He is needed on a council. His good judgement is needed.'

Adam smiled wryly.

With that Rajendra Shah left, saying that he himself would go to fetch Fath Jang. Laxmi Devi flounced off into the Kot building, and Adam saw her looking down from a window on the upper floor. Framed in the window Adam could also see a figure moving behind Laxmi Devi, whom he took to be Lalit.

Anxious for Lalit, Adam went into the lower chamber of the Kot seeking to join her, but at the foot of the ladder to the upper floor soldiers barred his way. So he waited there near the ladder and looked around the dimly lit room, through the haze from the oil lamps at others who had also come in from the parade ground. Amongst them were three of Jung Bahadur's brothers, Krishna Bahadur, Bom Bahadur and Dhir Shamsher; also three of the plotters, General Abhiman, Kishore Pandey still in irons, and Dalbanjan Pandey.

Adam was still waiting there when Jung Bahadur came in from the parade ground and, brushing past the soldiers, mounted the ladder to go to Laxmi Devi on the upper floor. Adam tried to follow him to join Lalit, but again the soldiers barred his way. Close on Jung Bahadur's heels, Prime Minister Fath Jang strode into the lower chamber, his face tense and frowning, and with him other Chautariyas including his son Kharak.

Fath Jang waited there to make sure Jung Bahadur had climbed the ladder to the upper floor, then went over to General Abhiman. Speaking softly, although Adam nearby made out the gist of it, he said, 'I have the gravest of news for you, General. Jung Bahadur spoke with me just now.'

'He knows then,' the general replied, alarmed. 'Is the King back? We will need him.'

'The King has not returned, General,' Fath Jang replied, not disguising his disgust. 'I am told he went to the British Residency. Went there to report the murder.'

'To the British?' General Abhiman queried, in disbelief.

'Yes, it might surprise you, General. Gagan Singh's death is no concern of the British. In truth, the King is afraid to return here.'

'Then we are undone. Jung Bahadur must know.'

'No, General, I believe he does not know. He did not speak of that. Jung Bahadur told me you refused Laxmi Devi's order, her order to behead Kishore Pandey. And he told me of Laxmi Devi's rage. To appease her, Jung Bahadur proposed that he execute both you and Kishore Pandey. He will arrange it now, without delay. He said that I would continue as prime minister and he would be the army's commander-in-chief. He said he had Laxmi Devi's sanction to it.'

'You did not agree,' General Abhiman said grimly.

'I did not, General. I told him your refusal to behead Kishore Pandey was proper, in accordance with the King's command. I said that Kishore Pandey should be tried by a council. I knew that with the King's connivance he would be found not guilty—no harm would come to him. No doubt you agree?'

General Abhiman did not reply. Fully alerted, he took his kukhri and kept looking towards the ladder, to be ready for Jung Bahadur should he come down. 'So he wants my life, the murderer,' he snarled. 'We shall see. It will be Jung Bahadur's life, not mine.' The general beckoned to officers from his command. 'Bring my own soldiers to the Kot and have them stand-by ready,' he ordered.

It was not long before General Abhiman's regiment arrived. His soldiers marched through the gates and assembled on the parade ground near the outer walls, trying to keep away from the crowd, and away from Jung Bahadur's soldiers. Looking from the doorway out through the torchlight, Adam was dismayed, alarmed to see the soldiers of General Abhiman's regiments loading their muskets. Fully alerted to what could erupt, and the danger to Lalit, he was determined to take her away from the Kot and back to the safety of Dor Maske's house. He forced himself past the soldiers and tried again to mount the ladder to the upper floor.

But again Adam's way to Lalit was blocked. This time by Laxmi Devi. She came hurrying down the ladder, still clutching the sword, her clothing disordered, her hair still dishevelled and falling loosely about her. And now Adam saw clearly the fury in her face as she looked at those in the lower chamber. Then her voice rose to a scream that reverberated from the walls as she called, 'Who has killed my faithful minister, my brave general? Who has killed Gagan Singh? Name him, I order you! Who is the murderer?'

But no one answered her.

Then Fath Jang spoke, 'A council will seek out the murderer, Madam. I assure you the King will call a council together. In good time he will call a council.'

Laxmi Devi ignored him. With another scream of rage, holding her sword high above her head, she rushed at Kishore Pandey, in irons and his hands bound, to slay him. But the three ministers, Kishore Pandey's fellow plotters, General Abhiman, Fath Jang and Dalbanjan Pandey, moved quickly. Two seized Laxmi Devi and the other grasped her sword, pulling it away before it could fall to cut off Kishore Pandey's life. For some moments they held Laxmi Devi, tears streamed down her face and her breath was broken with her sobbing; and then they led her to the ladder and stood at its foot watching her climb back to the upper floor.

At that moment the blast of musket shots rang out; from whose guns Adam was never to be sure. The walls of the lower chamber echoed their thunder and Fath Jang and Dalbanjan Pandey fell dead. General Abhiman, badly wounded, crawled towards the door trying to join his regiment out on the parade ground, calling out to accuse Jung Bahadur of treachery. But the general also was to die. Jung Bahadur's brother, Krishna, ran up to silence him, and cut his body in two with a great slash of his sword.

In an instant Fath Jang's son, Kharak, came rushing into the lower chamber. Seeing Krishna Bahadur with his sword still drawn and standing over General Abhiman's severed body and seeing his father dead, he assumed Jung Bahadur's brothers were responsible. He drew his kukhri and slashed at Bom Bahadur cutting a deep gash across his head. He turned on Krishna Bahadur with his kukhri to wound him also. Then swinging back on Bom Bahadur, who was blinded by the blood gushing from his wound, Kharek raised his kukhri ready for a fatal blow. But it was Kharek himself who was to die. Hearing the commotion in the lower chamber, Jung Bahadur hurried down the ladder and, seeing his brother's danger, seized a rifle and shot Kharek in the chest. As Kharek fell, Dhir Shamsher, the youngest of the Bahadur brothers, dispatched him with a cut of his sword.

Terror raged in the Kot that night, raged in the crowded lower chamber with its air hazy from the burning oil lamps and pungent from burnt powder, and outside on the parade ground lit by the flaming torches. Passions burnt ferociously. Swords clashed and kukhries cut as officials and soldiers took to one another, killed in order to save themselves. All feared for their own lives. Blood was spilt with many not knowing why, no longer knowing friend from enemy. A detachment from Jung Bahadur's regiments, well armed with double-barrel guns, came charging into the lower chamber to protect Jung Bahadur and his brothers. They rallied behind Jung Bahadur to attack—to shoot down Chautariyas, Pandeys, Brahmans, officials, generals and anyone not known to be of Jung Bahadur's party.

Adam left the carnage in the lower chamber and climbed up the ladder. He found Lalit standing a little away from Laxmi Devi, who was looking from a window down to the parade ground below. Seeing Adam, Lalit ran to him and he took her trembling in his arms.

It took some time before Lalit could speak. 'I hear the guns and the screaming. They are killing each other. Many must be dead.'

'Some are dead, Lalit.'

She pulled away from him. 'They are still killing. I can hear it.'

'They are, Lalit. A tragedy.'

Lalit looked towards Laxmi Devi. 'The Queen is enraged.' she whispered. 'She is so angry. I have never seen such hatred in her. I would not have believed. It is evil.'

'A tragedy,' Adam repeated.

Lalit sought Adam's arms again. 'I am frightened,' she said, and he felt her trembling again, 'I am frightened for your life.'

'You must come with me, Lalit,' Adam said. 'We must leave whilst we still have time. Even more will happen here tonight. There is great danger. I will take you to Dor Maske's house.'

Lalit hesitated, looking towards Laxmi Devi. 'No, Lalit. You must leave the Queen and come with me. Come now,' Adam said, grasping her arm and pulling her towards the top of the ladder.

But they could not leave then. Firing broke out on the parade ground again, and Adam went to a window to see. General Abhiman's regiment had left the Kot, no doubt after hearing of the death of their leader; and Jung Bahadur's soldiers had blocked the gateways and had surrounded the parade ground. Adam watched the massacre. Jung Bahadur's regiments set to work slaughtering, firing volley after volley into the crowd, trying to avoid only those known to be of their party. Many fell, and through the torch light Adam could see bodies roughly taken to be piled on top of each other, the blood flowing freely over the ground towards a gateway out to the street.

Above the clamour he heard Laxmi Devi calling from her window down to the soldiers below. She urged them on with their killing, her voice still loud and shrill. 'Kill my enemies!' she was screaming. 'Destroy them all. Kill for your queen.' Many more fell and the pile of bodies on the parade ground rose, blood flowed in a flood.

The slaughter was continuing when Jung Bahadur climbed back up the ladder to the upper floor followed by one of his brothers and stood beside Laxmi Devi. For some time the two looked down on the parade ground. Then Adam saw the Queen turn to him, her face composed now, a nod of satisfaction, and heard her say, 'You have done well, General. You have earned my gratitude. You are now prime minister and commander-in-chief of the army. You will continue to serve me well.'

There was a lull in the firing now and Adam wondered if it was safe to leave and take Lalit to Dor Maske's house. But Jung Bahadur left Laxmi Devi's side and walked over to him. 'Mr Clarke,' he said, his concern clearly showing on his face. 'I am surprised to see you here. It does not please me. I am not pleased that you have seen this unfortunate event. I fear for your safety. And that I cannot guarantee.' He looked at Lalit. 'Yes, I think I know why you are here, Mr Clarke. But you must leave immediately. The two of you must leave.' With that and without waiting for any response from Adam, he called to his brother to escort them from the Kot. Then he returned to Laxmi Devi's side.

In the lower chamber, its floor strewn with the dead and wounded, Jung Bahadur's brother told Adam and Lalit to wait until the firing outside became less frequent then stopped. Out on the parade ground, lit dimly now by the grey of dawn with the torches burnt-out-butts, they made their way towards the gate, Adam taking Lalit's arm to guide her feet around the flow of blood, around the groaning wounded lying there and around the bodies of the dead not yet tossed onto the pile. Soldiers of Jung Bahadur's regiments were in control, and several, Tanka Rana amongst them, spoke to Jung Bahadur's brother to claim victory and seek his praise.

It was then that Adam heard the shot. Glancing around, he saw a figure on the wall, the marksman, a grey shape shrouded by the morning mist that was now coming to cover the tragedy of the Kot. At that same moment Lalit at his side gave a cry, and he felt her hand clutch at his own. He held her as she fell against him.

Jung Bahadur's brother showed great concern, said the shot was meant for him. Tanka Rana and the others gathered around as Adam held Lalit. Blood now stained her blouse and sari, her face was deathly pale, her breath was coming in gasps. Adam lifted Lalit into his arms and her dark eyes opened and looked into his, her lips moved as though trying to find words. Lalit's eyes closed again, and Adam carried her over the parade ground and out through the gate away from the Kot. There, along the road near Vishnu's Temple, they found a carriage for Adam to take Lalit to Dor Maske's house, where Tanka Rana would ask Dr Jones to come quickly.'

Adam drove off holding Lalit in his arms, urging the syce to make all speed. The carriage rattled along the narrow streets of Kathmandu which were now deserted and grey in the morning mist. Anxiously, he looked down into Lalit's face and prayed to both her gods and his own that her wound would not be fatal and that she would recover.

Outside the old town, Adam saw the vultures already flying down into Kathmandu, their wings beating the air as they came down out of the mist to home in on the corpses heaped on the parade ground of the Kot. Passing the Tundikhel he saw much activity there, soldiers were already preparing for a feu-de-joie, which later that morning would honour Jung Bahadur as the new prime minister of Nepal. There would be ringing of temple bells, the blare of trumpets, a salute of nineteen guns, and a grand parade of many regiments.

Then as the carriage neared Dor Maske's house, Adam felt Lalit's breathing falter. He saw her slowly open her eyes, saw her smile sadly as she looked up at him. He held her hand as, again, her lips moved to seek the words, and this time he thought he heard a faint farewell. Seconds later, Adam felt Lalit's breathing stop.

Sixteen

Adam Clarke stood looking back over the Kathmandu Valley from high on the Chandragiri Mountain. It was winter, the air crisp and cold, and the mighty Himalayan peaks to the north were close and dominating, white giants rearing up into the bluest of skies, the sunlight gleaming on their great faces of snow and ice and rock. Adam had resigned from the British East India Company and was starting on his long journey home; down the steep and rugged descent into Makwanpur, on into India and across to Calcutta, and then a passage to England and to the Clarke estate in Hollybrook.

Looking back down over the valley, he saw the patchwork of the peasants' fields, some still green from the monsoon rains, some brown with the stubble from the harvest and some now black from the ploughing and ready for another planting. He saw the many villages dotting the fields; Kirtipur on its hill, Kathmandu and nearby Lalitpatan and Bhaktapur, the terracotta of their tiled roof tops, their palaces and temples, the golden roofs of their pagodas sparkling where the sunlight touched. There were the ancient chaityas, the Swayambhunath and, further off, the Bodhnath and Lord Shiva's great temple, the Pashupatinath.

Adam's thoughts, the saddest of thoughts, lingered on the Pashupatinath. It was to the burning ghats near that great temple on the banks of the Bagmati that he had gone with Lalit's body to her funeral pyre. He had walked there with the priests, his three colleagues at the British Residency, Captain O'Keefe, Mr St Clair and Dr Jones, as well as one of Jung Bahadur's brothers sent to pay the new prime minister's respects; and with the ailing Dor Maske who was carried in a basket on a servant's back

Adam had followed the bier with Lalit's body lying under a red satin shroud and bedecked with flowers, Adam's flowers. He had watched the burning. Later, when the embers of the pyre were cold and black, he had taken Lalit's ashes from the priests and, with the greatest of care, had cast them on the Bagmati's holy waters.

From Chandragiri, Adam looked towards Lazimpath and on to Lainchaur where the British Residency was. All at the Residency were united in their sympathy for Adam at Lalit's death. Mrs St Clair wept when she offered Adam her condolences, and afterwards would have tears in her eyes whenever she looked at him. She was affected the most by the massacre, trying to put it out of her mind and refusing to talk of it except to urge her husband to retire from the Company's service and take her back to England. Captain O'Keefe was very sympathetic. Dr Jones attempted to console Adam by saying that Lalit died quickly with little pain and was saved the lingering agony that might well have come from the wound he saw. Mr St Clair was profuse with his condolences, there being a marked change in his attitude to Adam. He went out of his way to seek Adam's company and spoke of the friendship he felt towards him. Several times he spoke about his daughter Sarah. 'Sarah will be in Calcutta when you arrive. Still awaiting a passage to England,' he had said to Adam before he left the Residency. He handed him a letter. 'I have written to Sarah. I would be pleased if you would give her my letter.'

As Adam looked down from Chandragiri towards the Tundikhel, towards Dor Maske's house, he thought of his meeting with the old man when he took his final leave of him. Dor Maske had been greatly depressed. There was Lalit's dying. There was the slaughter at the Kot.

'It was Jung Bahadur with his brothers and his regiments who did the killing, Mr Clarke, was it not?' Dor Maske had said. 'Jung Bahadur's rise is swift, far too swift. The blood was still flowing on the Kot, running out to the street, as he was made prime minister and the army commander. Almost all who could oppose him are now dead.' Exhausted by the effort of his talking, Dor Maske had lent back on his couch and murmured, 'What has Jung Bahadur in store for us, Mr Clarke? Very many died that night. Three hundred or more died. Ministers and generals fell, Chautariyas, Brahmans, what was left of the Pandeys, Nepal's leaders and their sons—almost all of them and many soldiers. It was the greatest of tragedies, and it forebodes badly for my country. Badly for many generations to come. Only Jung Bahadur is left, or almost so. Jung Bahadur Rana and his seven brothers. Only the Ranas are left. What is the future for my country?'

'Good-bye old friend,' Adam had said to him. 'I am sure the mists will rise again one day and the blue sky show through.' The two embraced. Dor Maske's eyes closed and soon he slept. For some minutes Adam waited, looking down at the old man, his hooked nose, his bald pate, the skin tight over the bones of his face, and his frailty. Then Adam left, knowing that Dor Maske himself would come to have only very little of his country's future.

After leaving Dor Maske, Adam had mounted the ladders to the room that was once Lalit's. It was much as she had left it. There were the mask of the elephant-headed, pot-bellied god, Ganesh, and the image of Lord Shiva's wife, Parbati. He looked at the cupboard and the table and chairs and the little mirror Dor Maske had given Lalit, and there was the bed with its quilts and coverlet. The painting of the Christ of the Sacred Heart, which once belonged to his grandmother, Maneka, was still hanging on the wall, and Adam decided to take with him.

Standing by the window Adam had looked out over the fields, past the village to the great white Himalayan massifs to the north. He thought of the first time he had done that, the night of the feast for the harvest moon when they had made the Yomarhi cakes. Then, Lalit had stood beside him with the warmth of her body close and the cold moonlight lighting the beauty of her face. He thought of the time he had given Lalit her wedding ring and the ruby pendant which Alexander, his grandfather's brother, had taken long ago from the treasury of the Nawab of Bengal at Murshidabad after the Battle of Plassey.

Wanting a keepsake, something that had once been Lalit's, Adam had gone to the cupboard, and there, amongst her jewellery, her bracelets and anklets and the rest, he saw the ruby pendant glowing. He took it to the window and for some time stood in the sunlight watching the fires burning in the great red ruby and its diamonds sparkling. He took the ruby pendant to remember Lalit by.

From the Chandragiri mountain, Adam looked down over the valley and wondered what was in store for it. He took a last look at the great white Himalayan massifs. 'They should be weeping,' he said to himself, 'the great mountains.' Then he continued on his journey, down into Makwanpur, on into India to Calcutta, then back to England.

THE RISING MIST

One

It was a cold evening in the January of 1990 when Harry Clarke arrived at the Hotel Laxmi and followed the porter through the glass doors and across the foyer's wide marble floor to reception. The receptionist welcomed him with her hands joined in a namaste. 'Sorry sir,' she said, pointing to the oil lamp on the counter. 'A black-out. It happens. The electricity will come on again soon.'

It was bright where the lamp light fell but dark around the edges of the foyer, in the corners. Harry noticed the aroma of the burning oil. He rather liked it; it was incense-like and he thought it somehow fitting for Kathmandu.

The receptionist checked his passport and registered him. 'From Australia,' she said. 'Several journalists have come here lately. From different countries. More than usual.'

A young woman came in through the glass doors and went up to the reception counter for her key. 'Flat four, please,' she said.

The receptionist took the key from the board. 'A cold night, Miss Jackson. Your flat will be cold, but the electricity will come on again soon.'

'I hope it does,' she said.

Harry saw she was in her late twenties, her fair hair falling on her shoulders, a nice face; and she was rugged up against the cold. Harry gave her a smile, but she met his gaze then looked away, turned and went back over the foyer and out through the hotel doors. Attractive, Harry thought.

'Your room's 17,' the receptionist said to Harry. 'If you like it, sir. Ground floor.'

She took a key from the board and beckoned to the porter, and Harry followed both of them over the foyer past several dimly lit shops with Tibetan carpets hanging at the doors and tourist ware inside, and past a door marked "Pad's Bar". The long corridor to the ground floor rooms was lit by candles burning in little peacock-shaped clay bowls placed on the carpet along the bottom of the walls. A nice idea, he thought.

'Do you have peacocks here in the wild?' he asked.

'In the hills,' she said.

The receptionist opened a door and ushered him in, drew the curtains to close out the last of the dusk and lit the candles. When she left, Harry went to the dressing table and peered into the mirror at his face close-up, lit by the candle light. It stared back at him out of the darkness, his fair hair and reddish skin, and his blue and rounded eyes showed no trace at all of the Mongoloid fold. It was not like the Nepalese faces he had seen so far—those of the stewardesses on the Royal Nepal Airline's Boeing 727 up from Delhi, the porters and customs people at the Kathmandu airport, the taxi driver and the receptionist. Of course it was very long ago, he told himself.

Harry poured a scotch and sat back in an armchair thinking the hotel seemed good so far, very good in fact, better than he had expected even though the glossy brochure had said it was four-star and had a picture of a fine brick building with pagoda-like tiled roofs, and extensive gardens and green lawns. Harry was still surprised to be in Kathmandu, in Nepal, up in the very shadow of the Himalayas. That afternoon he had watched the great mountains from the Boeing 727. First they were a long white line on the horizon, then white humps, then they grew as the aircraft approached to become white giants towering high into the blue sky with their winter snows gleaming in the afternoon sunlight; the roof of the world. Harry had been impressed.

The idea of going to Nepal had never entered Harry's head until he called on an old relative, a distant cousin, Mary Clarke. He had telephoned her before leaving England to return to Australia, and one Sunday afternoon had caught the train to Hollybrook in Kent to visit her. He found the Clarke's house in Connor St large and old, and with big grounds as he walked up the path through the overgrown garden to the front door. An old lady in black with a white lace collar opened it.

'I'm so glad you've come,' she welcomed. 'I'm Mary Clarke. So you're Alan's son. Henry, isn't it?'

'Harry or Henry,' he said, smiling at her. 'It doesn't matter.'

She led him through the hall to a reception room and gave him a chair near a bay window overlooking the garden. A table was set for afternoon tea with fine china and a cake on a cut-glass dish. Harry saw it was a room of the past, with old mahogany furniture and Persian carpets and a chandelier now converted to electricity; there was a touch of eau-de-Cologne in the air. There were Chinese vases, a painting of the Christ of the Sacred Heart over the mantelpiece and a large brass casting of a Hindu god in a corner. Several paintings were around the walls, portraits of the Clarke ancestors Harry guessed.

'They're your ancestors, too, Henry.' Mary Clarke said. 'I remember your father came here once. During the war, nearly fifty years ago now. He was an airman in your air force.'

She must be nearly ninety, Harry thought. 'My father died twenty years ago. I was a boy at school. He mentioned his family in England to me. Not that he told me much about it.'

'You aren't like your father. He was darker. Black hair, eyes like mine.'

'I take after my mother.'

'There aren't many Clarkes left now, not our Clarkes,' she said smiling sadly. 'In England it's really only me.'

Harry nodded sympathetically.

'Tony went to America,' she said. 'And settled there. He was the tenth baronet. Now he's dead, too.'

'It's a shame,' Harry said, to be polite.

'Is it? Perhaps it is. Times are different now.'

She pointed out the window. 'It was all Clarke land once; an estate with farms and pastures and many tenant farmers. And the Hollybrook village. The Clarkes were good squires, members of parliament too. Now you see it's all houses.' She laughed. 'Suburbia, you'd call it.'

Valuable real estate, Harry thought.

She read his mind. 'Much of the land was sold long ago, piece by piece. We have only a little of it now, and the garden is far too big. There's no Clarke estate now. Not like it used to be.'

'It must be a loss to you,' Harry said.

'Not to me. I have other things to think of.' She glanced at the picture of the Christ over the mantelpiece. 'Are you a Catholic, Henry?'

'Christened a Catholic. Went to a Catholic school for a while.'

'The Clarkes have always been Catholics. I hope you go to Mass on a Sunday?'

Harry had not been to church for nearly twenty years. 'Not now, I'm afraid,' he told her.

'Not at all?'

'Occasionally,' he said, because she was old.

'You should. My religion means much to me. Very much.'

She went away to make tea and Harry got up to look at the portraits around the wall, all six of them. The first was of a young man in military uniform and the second was of a large, fair-haired man. The next portrait surprised Harry. The face there was different, it was brown-skinned with dark hair and black almond-shaped eyes, almost an Asian face. More than a touch of India or China, Harry could not decide. He turned to the last three portraits. These, too, were of dark-haired, black-eyed men, but progressively each lost some of the Asian look. Harry was wondering about it when Mary Clarke returned with a pot of tea.

'So you've seen him,' she said putting the teapot on the table and fixing the cosy over it. 'He was the seventh baronet. Sir Francis Clarke. Didn't you know he was only half-English?'

'No. Can't say I've ever heard of him.'

'His father was Sir Hume.' She pointed to the portrait of the large fair-haired man. 'Hume Clarke went out to India in 1764, then to a country up in the Himalayas. Nepal it is now. He married a Nepalese young lady there, her name was Maneka, and Sir Francis was their son. You hadn't heard of that? Your father never told you?'

'Never mentioned him to me.'

'Your father knew. He saw the portrait when he came here. I remember, as though it were yesterday.'

'Thought it didn't affect us, I suppose. It happened a long time ago.'

'Oh yes, you Australian people don't bother much about ancestors. I've seen that. But we still do. The earlier Clarke baronets have their portraits in the hallway. You must see them, too, before you go.'

'And there's more,' she went on. 'One of Francis' sons, Adam Clarke, went out to Nepal for the British East India Company and lived there for several years. He, also, married a Nepalese lady. She was Lalit. A lovely name I always think. But she was killed. She was shot in a terrible massacre. Shot dead. It was a terrible mistake.'

'A long time ago now?'

'It was, Henry. Half-way through last century. Adam returned to England, to the estate here. Lalit's death was a terrible thing for him. But he married again. She was also a lady he knew in Nepal, a young lady named Sarah St Clair who was with her parents in the British Residency in Kathmandu. It seems she was very much in love with him. He found her in Calcutta on his way back to England and they travelled on the same ship. They lived here on the estate. Had children. You didn't know all this, Henry?'

'Not at all. It's all news to me.'

'You might like to see this,' Mary Clarke said, taking a padded box from the pocket of her dress. She opened it to show a pendant with a great ruby, sparkling red, surrounded by large diamonds. 'Have you ever seen the like?' she asked as she handed it to Harry.

'How magnificent it is,' he said.

'There would be few like it,' Mary Clarke said. 'The ruby is perfect and very rare. We've had it for more than two hundred years. Alexander got it in India at Murshidabad, from the defeated Nawab's treasury after the Battle of Plassey. A reward for his valour, I suppose. Unfortunately he had little time to enjoy it before he was killed. Then Sir Hume got it and gave it to Maneka who brought it to England with her. Years later Adam Clarke took it to Nepal and gave it to Lalit. He brought it back home when she was killed, and always kept it with him to remember her by.'

'It must be valuable,' Harry said.

'It is, Henry. It's a Burmese ruby, pigeon's blood. What do you think it's worth?'

Harry placed the pendant on his knee to let the light from the window play on the jewels. For some time he watched the diamonds sparkling and the great ruby's red flames before handing it back to his cousin.

'Half a million?' he said. 'But I'm no expert.'

She smiled. 'More, much more. It's worth three million. Our pounds that is. I've had a buyer waiting for a long time, a man from the Middle East.'

'So much.' It surprised Harry. 'Will you sell it?' He wondered what she would do with the money, at her age.

She looked down at the pendant saying, 'It's helped keep our past alive, the Clarkes'. It has helped. But it seems there's no more past to come now. Yes, I shall sell it. In certain circumstances.'

'Certain circumstances?'

'I have no use for the money. You can see that. I'm old, and still well-off. The money ought to go back to Nepal.'

'But you said it came from India,' Harry said. 'From the Nawab's treasury.'

'The money ought to go to Maneka's country, and Lalit's too. I would want that. Perhaps I'm too romantic.'

She looked at Harry. 'What they could do with the money, I don't know. It's a large sum. What could they do best with it? I could not see to that, I could not go there.'

Harry nodded agreement.

Then she asked quietly, 'Why don't you visit Nepal, Henry? Stay there a while on your way back to Australia. It would be only a small detour for you. See what the money could do.'

Harry was surprised. 'No, I'm sorry, I'm afraid not,' he did not hesitate. 'There's my newspaper in Sydney waiting for me.'

'Yes, but you're a journalist, Henry. It would be a good story for you.'

'Not my thing though, I'm afraid, and there's a lot of work waiting for me in Sydney.'

'It's the land of one of some of your forbears. You, too, have a responsibility, Henry.'

Harry could not see how he had much of a responsibility. He had only just heard of this ancestor who had stolen the ruby pendant a long way back. He had already decided it was stolen.

'I'm asking you because you are a Clarke,' Mary Clarke persisted. 'You look like Sir Hume, you know. As he must have been at your age, late-twenties. Fair hair too, and a big man. You're the only one I could ask now. I know I'm romantic, but I think it only proper that a Clarke should return the ruby, the money it brings.'

Harry did not agree, it was not at all his way of thinking.

A little later as he was leaving, Mary Clarke brought out two old journals which had been in the family for generations, one written by Hume Clarke and the other by his grandson, Adam, and gave them to Harry. Again she asked him to go to Nepal for her. When she persisted he agreed to think it over, and to look through the journals.

But back in London Harry changed his mind about going to Nepal. He learnt of trouble looming there, reading in the London newspapers that Nepal's major political parties—which were banned, had been for many years—were now active and united in a struggle for democracy, a struggle which was coming to a head. He read that a conference in Kathmandu on the 18th of January had appealed to the people to demand a democratic government, and had launched a movement for democracy—a non-violent movement. Chandra Shekhar, a leader of India's Janata Dal, had attended and had told the Nepalese people that they must struggle for their democracy. Harry also read that President Mitterrand, Willy Brandt, Rajiv Gandhi and leaders from Britain, Japan and other countries had sent messages of support. And he sensed good copy there. This was much more his thing, he thought. So he phoned his chief-of-staff on the *Sydney Mail* and arranged to go to Kathmandu to cover events for them.

During the following few days Harry studied up on Nepal; he went to the British Museum to read about the people, about their history, their religion and customs. The tourist literature told him Nepal is a must for tourists, and a trekker's paradise. He read up on Nepal's politics to find it an autocracy with a King who had almost absolute power. Harry found that the economy was backward and Nepal was one of the poorest countries in the world. He read the journals Mary Clarke had given him and began to be interested in his ancestors. The airline people arranged his detour to Kathmandu and booked him into the Hotel Laxmi, a good hotel they assured him.

Before he left England Harry called again on Mary Clarke for afternoon tea. 'Yes, I'll make a detour to Kathmandu,' he told her. 'I'll see how the money from your ruby pendant might best be spent. And I think you'll be pleased to know I read the journals and am getting interested in our ancestors.'

'I am delighted,' she said, smiling warmly at him. 'Of course you are a Clarke, Henry; one of our Clarkes even though you are an Australian. I'll sell the ruby and have the money ready. And I remember that years ago a Nepalese young man called on father. Ram Maske his name was, from the family that befriended our ancestors. He might still be alive. You could get in touch with him.'

'There is another thing, Henry,' she said as he was leaving. 'I know nothing of the problems in Nepal, but I do want to approve how the money is going to be spent. That is most important to me.'

Harry thought that was fair enough. After all, it was her money.

Harry had finished a second scotch by the time the electricity came on again in the Hotel Laxmi. The lights were now bright and the air-conditioner hummed, working. The room was good—what would be expected in a quality hotel anywhere. He unpacked his bags, shaved, showered away the long flight from Europe, and dressed in a comfortable lounge suit for dinner.

The head waiter showed Harry to a table, a small one near the window. 'I hope this suits you, sir,' he apologised. 'We're full here tonight. Three tours. Japanese, Americans, Germans. And you are English, sir?'

'No, Australian.'

'Ah yes, I thought you were. We have many Australians come here and they are very welcome. I think it is your first visit to Nepal, Mr Clarke, and I hope you will enjoy being with us.' He called a waiter, who came and took Harry's order.

Harry liked the look of the restaurant, its tables with their red cloths and candles ready for when the electricity failed. Its decorative wood-carvings, and the busy waiters in red jackets and bright Nepalese topi caps gave it a distinctive ambience.

Another hotel guest came and sat opposite. 'Do you mind?' she asked in an English accent. 'My usual table. I eat here sometimes.'

'Not at all,' Harry assured her. He recalled seeing her at the reception counter earlier. She studied the menu. Yes, she was in her late twenties, he thought as he stole a glance or two at her face to see a pretty little nose, blue eyes, soft lips and turquoise earrings.

She put the menu down and looked up at Harry. 'I suppose you're a tourist here, Mr...?'

'Clarke, Harry Clarke from Sydney. No, not a tourist. I'll do some writing for my paper.'

'Oh, an Australian,' she said. 'You're covering the trouble here, I suppose.'

'Yes. Got here only a couple of hours ago. Have you been to Australia?'

'No. I might go there one day to have a look. I've read a lot about it, and seen it on TV of course. Met a few Australians here and there.

They ate in silence with Harry wondering who she was, what she was doing in Nepal. 'You're a tourist Miss... ?' He addressed her as "Miss", noticing that she wore no wedding ring. 'Going on a trek? Climbing one of the mountains perhaps?'

'Oh excuse me, I didn't introduce myself. I'm Anne Jackson, Ms Jackson. I repeat Ms. I'm certainly not here on a holiday. I work in Kathmandu.'

'You're English?'

'Of course. You must have picked my accent.'

'You live in the hotel?' Harry asked.

'The hotel has some flats nearby. 'She pointed to the window out into the night. 'Much cheaper. Not luxurious by any means, and a terrible kitchen. But I manage. I often eat here.'

She excused herself and left. Harry watched as she walked across the restaurant. A shapely figure, he thought, in her skirt and jumper. He noticed that other men in the restaurant watched her too.

With the meal finished Harry went into the hotel foyer and through the door into Pad's Bar. He found it well set-up and spacious with polished woodwork, carpeted and a lounge with a dozen or so arm chairs. A large brass peacock decorated much of the far wall, and glass doors opened to the garden. He took a high stool at the bar counter and looked along the shelves which were well-stocked with bottles whose labels claimed many countries, and had a score or so of miniature flags, a gleaming kukhri and a set of war medals.

The barman came up to him and joined his hands in a namaste. 'I am Pad, Padam Bahadur Rai. You are Mr Clarke I think, and you are a journalist from Australia. Let me welcome you,' he said. 'Welcome to Nepal, to the hotel, and to my bar of course.'

'Thank you,' Harry said. 'You have a nice bar here.' Harry looked back at him to see a shorter than average man, a young sixty perhaps, with almond-shaped eyes, black hair, high cheek bones and the skin on his face smooth with a touch of yellow in the brown. He was dressed in a neat white coat, a striped shirt and a blue bow-tie.

Pad poured a beer for Harry and one for himself. 'Australians often stay at the Laxmi. But I can tell you I saw very many Australians once.' Pad's face broadened in a grin. 'It was at Tobruk in North Africa, in World War Two when I was with the 7th Gurkha Rifles.'

Harry looked at the medals on the shelf behind the bar and saw the Military Medal amongst them. 'Yes, a lot of Australians fought in Tobruk.'

'For more than a year I was there.'

As they talked Harry learnt that Pad came from the Solu Khumbu area, from a family farm high in the hills underneath the great Mount Everest. In his late teens he had been enlisted in the Brigade of Gurkhas, having gone down from the hills to pass examinations and be selected against strong competition. He had spent the prime years of his life, some twenty five years of them, with the Gurkhas, fighting in Malaya as well as North Africa. Pad had also been stationed in Hong Kong for a while and at Church Crookham in England until he was demobilised as a sergeant and given his pension in 1970.

Pad had left Harry to serve other customers when an old man came into the bar wearing the regalia of a Grand Masonic Lodge. Harry knew the regalia from work he had done on Freemasonry. There was the long frock coat, the apron with blue and gold ribbons and a fringe of gold, the blue collar with gold edging and embroidery of golden flowers; he was wearing the gilded jewel of a district grand inspector of workings, which was the square, the level and the plumb rule set inside a circle.

Harry's thoughts went straight to his ancestor's journal as the old man stood there before him. He was small, almost bald-headed, with a hooked nose, brown skin stretching tightly over a bony face and black almond-shaped eyes. He was just as Harry had pictured Dor Maske, the

Dor Maske of one hundred and fifty years ago, a friend of his ancestor, Adam Clarke.

'I have just returned from our temple so you must excuse my regalia,' he said to Harry. 'They told me you had booked into the hotel. I take it you are of the Clarkes of Hollybrook in Kent. Please let me introduce myself. I am Ram Maske. Let me welcome you to my country.'

'Thank you. I am pleased to be here and to meet you. My cousin in England mentioned you, Ram Maske. She is Mary Clarke.'

'I met her once. As a young man I visited England and called on the Clarkes in Hollybrook. In the past our families had much friendship. In the distant past it is true, but some things can pass down the generations. Yes I am very pleased to meet you, Mr Clarke.'

Leaving the bar to go and change from his regalia, he said to Harry, 'This is my own hotel, one of my business ventures. I have a room here and live here part of the time. You might come and join me and we can talk.'

Two

Ram Maske welcomed Harry to his room in the hotel, had him seated, poured a scotch for him and a fruit juice for himself, then said, 'I'm told you are a journalist, Mr Clarke and here to report on our trouble. Journalists are here from many countries.'

'It is one reason,' Adam told him.

Ram Maske's worry showed on his old face. 'Yes, there is trouble and it worries me greatly. There is much unrest. Many people are against the Government and, I'm afraid, the King. Most people want democracy, their own elected parliament and their own political parties to represent them. But others disagree and blood is still being spilt.'

'But the movement for democracy's non-violent.' Harry said, remembering the London newspapers.

Ram Maske sighed. 'No, my country history is a bloody one, Mr Clarke. We have not been brothers. It is very sad for me. I am a Newar, a man of Nepal and of the Hindu faith. But I am also a Freemason. I want all to be brothers. You know we are a brotherhood.'

Harry saw a gleam in the old man's eyes as he went on, 'Our temple is a very holy place, Mr Clarke. Our gods smile their favour on it. Lord Shiva's image is there, and it is Brahma who is our great architect of the universe. We conduct ourselves properly in the temple, try for perfection with our rituals. It is well set up with furniture: King Solomon's chair, our wardens' desks, tracing boards and the other things. Our implements are gold, pure gold—the square and compass, the level and the plumb.' Ram Maske's pride was obvious. 'And it is my doing. My energy set up our lodge, and my money.'

'But the trouble,' Harry reminded him. 'The movement for democracy?'

It turned out that Ram Maske needed no encouragement to talk about that. First he spoke about the century of Rana rule, which he said was the background to his country's trouble. 'It was a hundred years of brutal tyranny, Mr Clarke,' he said angrily. 'A century of poverty and backwardness for the people of Nepal.'

He told Harry that Rana rule started in 1846, when Jung Bahadur Rana came to power; after he and his seven brothers had killed most of

Nepal's ministers and senior soldiers in the great massacre at the Military Headquarters of the Kot. Appointed prime minister and the army's commander-in-chief, Jung Bahadur soon exiled the powerful Queen to India, confined the King to the palace and seized absolute power to himself. To ensure such power stayed in the Rana family, he drew up a Roll of Succession which provided for his own sons, and then his brothers and their sons, to rule Nepal after him.

Ram Maske told Harry how the Rana prime ministers, one after the other, built up huge fortunes for themselves. 'They lived in great luxury, Mr Clarke,' he said. 'They gave lavish parties, ate from golden plates and spent a great deal on gorgeous uniforms and jewellery. They built great palaces, kept harems often with a hundred concubines and maids as well as wives.'

'The people suffered under Rana rule,' he told Harry. 'The Ranas kept Nepal in its dark ages; closed to the outside world, closed to new ideas, to learning, closed especially to any threat to Rana power. Justice was corrupt, Mr Clarke. Secret police were everywhere. Murder was rife.' Ram Maske spoke of Rana Jung Bahadur's murder of Bir Basnet and twenty of his kinsmen in the Bhandarkhal gardens; of Rana Dhir Shamsher's murder of the Thapa and Basnet families; of the four Rana Shamsher brothers who murdered their uncle, Prime Minister Rana Udip Singh. Ram Maske's anger rose further as he spoke of the bully Rana Juddha Shamsher's corrupt trial on the football ground in 1946—of young men of the Praja Parishad, a liberal, non-violent organisation, who had published the *Janata* newspaper calling for democracy. He had them whipped and tortured with hot irons to wring confessions from them, to make them name their ringleaders. Four of their young leaders, found guilty of high treason, were taken late one night from the gaol in Kathmandu and executed. 'That crime was less than fifty years ago, Mr Clarke,' Ram Maske pointed out. 'And slavery and the burning of widows as satis were not unknown. Only one or two schools existed then, no hospitals to speak of or doctors, no industry worth mentioning, no electric power, no proper roads connecting up the country.'

But Ram Maske spoke well of the kind King Tribhuban, saying that he would sometimes climb the stairs of the Taleju Temple at dusk and look out over the roof tops of Kathmandu. If he saw a chimney without smoke, he would think the people in the house had nothing to cook and would send food to them. He praised the Nepali Congress, formed by young Nepalese men committed to end the Ranas' rule, and its Liberation Army which fought and finally broke Rana power in 1951. He told

Harry that King Tribhuban, on 18th February 1951, issued a proclamation annulling Rana power and promising a democratic government for Nepal. 'The people were delighted then,' he said. 'And their hopes ran high.'

Then Ram Maske shook his head sorrowfully, saying, 'But the promised democracy came to nothing, Mr Clarke. King Tribhuban died and his son, King Mahendra tried it for a while, but then dissolved the elected parliament, made political parties illegal and set up the Panchayat parliamentary system which gives power to the King and his ministers. The present King, his son King Birendra, has continued the Panchayat system.'

'No, it is not non-violent, our movement for democracy, far from it,' Ram Maske said. 'People fight the Panchayat system. Bombs tear our towns, brothers shoot brothers and torture each other, execute each other. Our prisons overflow.'

'You must yourself favour a democracy, Ram Maske,' Harry said.

'Of course.'

'You are against the King?'

'I am against his ministers who mislead him, not against the King himself. Our Kings are sacred. They are descendants of our great God Vishnu and are governed by their dharma. They must rule for the good of the people.'

Harry decided that he liked the look of Ram Maske. He saw no guile in his old face and his black eyes were alert, but soft enough. So he told him about Mary Clarke's ruby pendant, which she now intended to sell and give the money it brought to Nepal, that she wanted him to advise her on how the money might best be spent.

'So you have that, as well as report on our trouble for your paper,' Ram Maske said. 'You surprise me. The pendant is very valuable, no doubt.'

'Five million US dollars. About that.'

'A significant amount. Your cousin is very generous.'

'There must be many ways the money could be spent and spent well,' Harry ventured.

Ram Maske agreed. 'Yes, many ways. Very many ways indeed. There is so much to be done in Nepal that it is very hard to choose. I will think of it. There are those in the ministries who will advise you. And there will be others when they hear of the large gift. But I suggest you talk to our Planning Ministry at the Singha Durbar. I shall ask the Director to see you.'

As Harry was leaving, Ram Maske said, 'You need to find out more about us, Mr Clarke. You will have a big story soon about our movement for democracy. Look around, see as much as you can quickly. You don't have much time. Please don't hesitate to come to me for help I can give.'

Three

Next morning after breakfast Harry stood in the bright daylight of the hotel foyer with the aroma of the oil lamps still lingering in the air. The shops were open and he looked through the jewellery crafted in Nepal, at the turquoise from China, diamonds from India, coral from the Red Sea and garnets and aquamarine. There were the richly coloured carpets of wool or silk, Tibetan and Nepalese, carvings in wood and bone and some in ivory, and castings of the Hindu and Buddhist gods and goddesses in polished brass or gilded. In one show-case Harry was amused to see two gilded figures, a male god with three faces and six arms and a goddess—images of Lord Shiva and his wife Parbati—cast together in an eternal act of lovemaking. A score or so of little brass figures, not gods this time but men and women, were also in acts of making love, some in the most imaginative positions.

Outside, the mist had been thick and white, blanketing everything and reducing all to vague shapes. It had cleared with only a few wisps hanging about when Harry went out to walk in the hotel's fine garden. Its well-kept lawns and abundant flower beds stretched away to a little white stupa which stood on top of a grassed hill, and the trees still had a touch of autumn foliage. Along the far border stood high walls of ancient brick in russet colours, and beyond the walls, were buildings with the sun shining on their terracotta roofs. In one corner of the garden a tiny temple was almost covered with red powder and adorned with freshly cut flowers.

Harry left the hotel and walked into the old town. He found it quaint, something like parts of London must have been two hundred years ago. The streets were narrow and cobbled. The old brick and tiled roofed houses were three or four storeys high and abutted each other. Each had windows with wooden shutters, their verandahs supported by wooden buttresses overhanging the street. Their facades were decorated with fine old wood carvings: houses little changed, Harry thought, since Hume and Maneka lived there more than two hundred years ago. He found his way along the crowded streets, amongst Nepalese men in western dress or jackets and jodhpurs and jaunty topi caps, women in saris and many children, and gurus and a Buddhist monk in a red robe.

Tourists were out and about. Occasionally a car or truck with its horn blaring would edge carefully through the crowd. Cows would wander by and a rickshaw edge its way through. Harry came to one of Kathmandu's many squares, which was warm in the sunlight and had a market offering bright yellow oranges, cauliflowers, garden peas, onions, garlic, potatoes, red chillies, bananas, buffalo meat and fish. Harry sat for a while on a low wall near a little temple and watched the people. Later he found Makhan Tole and wondered what house his ancestor Hume Clarke had lived in.

As Harry turned into the Durbar Square, like many before him he was not prepared for it—the expanse of the ancient builders' art—the temples for Lord Shiva, Vishnu, Kali, Taleju and the many gods and goddesses, and he walked in wonder past towering pagodas with their gilded roofs sparkling in the sunlight. There was the house of the Kumari, who was the little living goddess of Kathmandu. He took his time exploring it all, the old administrative buildings, ancient walls of red brick mellowed by the ages, tall columns, the rambling old palace and the great Taleju Bell.

For a long time Harry stood gazing at the great fearsome image of the Black Bhairab, with its six arms, its red eyes glaring from surrounding whites, its fanged mouth snarling, human skulls decorating its head and neck. Many people were in the Durbar Square that day. Nepalese sat on the steps of the pagodas enjoying the warm sunshine, as well as ascetic saddhus and monks and other holy men; and there were many tourists with their cameras

That evening when Harry called at Pad's Bar, the electricity was off again so oil lamps were burning and candles lit the bar counter. Anne Jackson, whom he had met at dinner the previous night, sat at the bar with a half-finished drink in front of her, her head bent as she read from a batch of papers with the help of a flickering candle. Occasionally she looked up from her papers, tossed her hair back and let her gaze wander along the shelves behind the counter. As he sipped his scotch Harry watched her through the oil lamp's haze, wondering if she would look in his direction and hoping to catch her eye. But she did not. After she finished her drink she gathered up her papers and gave Harry just a hint of a smile as she passed him to leave.

Pad walked up to Harry as she left. 'A charming young lady, Mr Clarke. She's Anne Jackson and she lives in one of the flats on the other side of the garden, past the brick wall. She works in one of the ministries. Been here a couple of years.'

The morning Harry was to go to the Planning Ministry in the Singha Durbar, as Ram Maske had arranged, one of their advisers called for him at the Hotel Laxmi and waited in the hotel foyer, a fresh-faced man in his early forties and hair in a crew-cut.

'Harry Clarke, I believe,' he said with an American accent, extending his hand. 'Pleased to meet you, Harry. I'm Bruce Singer. Tej Shamsher asked me to call for you. He's the Director. Australian, aren't you?'

'Yes. Pleased to meet you Mr Singer,' Harry replied.

'Call me Bruce, please, Harry. I've got a car waiting. The mist is cleared and we can be off when you like.'

At the Singha Durbar the sentries admitted them through the tall gates and they drove along the road past the formal gardens up to the great white building of imposing facades, great verandahs and tall colonnades. 'Built nearly a century ago for the Rana Chandra Shamsher,' Bruce Singer told Harry. 'The architect was Jogendra Babu from India. Built it as a palace for the Rana prime ministers. Hundreds of porters, poor devils, carried everything on their backs, thousands of feet up the steep mountains into the valley. They were heavy loads—marble, huge glass lamps, tiles, pipes, furniture, a great piano, you name it.'

Harry followed Bruce through a side entrance and up several flights of a wide marble stairway to a long balcony overlooking a great central courtyard.

'Bombed and burnt out a few years back. Gutted,' Bruce said. 'But it's repaired now, as you see. With aid money.'

'Some building. It's magnificent,' Harry said.

'Great shell really. There are better things to spend money on.'

Bruce laughed as they stood looking out over the courtyard at the rows of balconies. 'Imagine the Ranas here, Harry,' he said. 'A hundred rooms or more. The Ranas and their harems. Hundreds of women. Dozens of wives and concubines, maids, beautiful young girls.'

'A virile lot. Those were the days then, Bruce.'

'Perhaps. Are you a married man yourself, Harry?'

'Not yet.'

'Not even one wife then. A girl friend perhaps?'

'Several over the years.'

'They were a bad lot, the Ranas, Harry.'

'Seems they left the Nepalese with a lot of catching up to do.'

'That's right. People had to start from nothing here only forty years ago. The Ranas bled the place. Left a bad legacy.'

'The Ranas ruled here till 1951,' Bruce continued. 'They had absolute power for a century. Kept the Kings locked in their palace like the Shoguns did in Japan. The Ranas hogged it, Harry. Robbed the country's treasury. Took forests for themselves, and land. Built great mansions like this here. Lived high.' Bruce scowled. 'And they kept the people down, cowered and ignorant. Kept the country closed to foreigners, to ideas, to democracy. I could go on and on, Harry. The Ranas left a hell of a mess when the country got rid of them in '51. It'll still take Nepal a long time to get out of it.'

Bruce led into his office. 'I won't apologise for it,' he said. 'All the same here. No money to fit the rooms out.'

The room surprised Harry. There was an old desk and a couple of chairs, a dilapidated sofa with broken springs and threadbare coverings. The carpet was dusty and worn, the heavy brown curtains had seen better days and there was no heating to warm the cold morning. A peon came in and Bruce sent him off to tell the Director that Mr Clarke had arrived.

'Tej Shamsher's a modern-day Rana,' he told Harry. 'A good fellow, very able. He'll impress you. He's devoted and a hard worker. Wants to make up for his ancestors' wrongs.'

The Director's office was in much the same state as Bruce's, no better. Tej Shamsher greeted Harry with a polite namaste and excellent English. He seated the two on the old sofa, sent a peon off to get tea, then pulled his own chair close. He was a fine looking man, tall and slender with a pleasant smile, light-brown skin and black eyes under heavy brows. Like many senior officials, he wore a tweed jacket, jodhpurs, a cummerbund around his waist and, rather jauntily, a colourful Nepalese topi cap. Very much the Nepalese gentleman, Harry thought.

For a few minutes Tej Shamsher talked about Australia. He had been to Sydney once on a short visit, had not expected it to be so big and spread-out, and so modern. Ram Maske had told him of Mary Clarke's gift of five million dollars, and he was curious.

'My cousin is selling a ruby pendant, which the Clarkes have had in the family for more than two hundred years', Harry explained. 'An ancestor Sir Alexander Clarke got it from the treasury of Shuja-ud-daula, the defeated Nawab after the battle of Plassey. And I can tell you the that the Clarkes used to have connections with your country. Alexander's brother, Hume, came to the Valley of Nepal where he married Maneka a lady of King Jaya Malla's court. And their grandson, Adam, was in the British Residency here.'

'It's interesting, Mr Clarke,' Tej Shamsher said. 'I have not heard of your ancestors, but then I'm no historian. Of course they were was difficult times. And they were not good at keeping records; or perhaps they were lost in the turmoil.'

Harry noticed a faint smile cross Tej Shamsher's face. 'But was not the ruby pendant shall we say borrowed from the then Nawab?' he asked. 'Borrowed from India? Not borrowed from Nepal? Should not the money go back to India? Nepal is not India.'

Harry pointed out that his cousin wanted to give the money to Nepal.

Tej Shamsher smiled openly this time. 'Of course. Seeing that is so, we should certainly accept the gift. I have no doubt about that. We would be most grateful. And I assure you the money would be put to good use. At the proper time we would write to your cousin thanking her. The letter would go from the King.'

'Thank you, she would appreciate that. But I must say Mary Clarke wants to approve the use of the money before she makes the gift. She has asked me to advise her on that.'

'You don't trust us to know what our own country needs, Mr Clarke?' Tej Shamsher asked quietly.

'My cousin wants it that way. It isn't a matter of trust. I should need help in advising her. I know little about your country.'

'Of course,' Tej Shamsher agreed. 'I understand. You will need to learn about us. Of course we'll help you.' He glanced at Bruce Singer. 'If you agree, Mr Singer will help you. I spoke to him after I heard from Ram Maske. Perhaps he'll show you one of our factory estates. Mr Singer knows us well, his advice is good.'

Tej Shamsher took a paper from his desk and handed it to Harry. 'And you might find this helpful. It lists projects I'm asked for money for; good projects, most of them. Countries do help us, Britain, Switzerland and several European countries, Japan, China, the US and of course India, to mention some. But you'll see there's a lot to be done in Nepal. So very much.'

Harry looked quickly through the list. The large projects would cost in the tens of millions of dollars and more, for roads, irrigation, electricity, education and health. But the villages also needed drinking water, health posts, sanitation, minor roads, schools, and cooperatives. There were many other projects like aid for factories, farm development, family planning, hotels and other facilities for tourists. Tej Shamsher watched Harry as he read and when he looked up, said, 'Take the list away with you, Mr Clarke. It's a long one. I think you will find it hard to choose. I know that we do, even with all the expertise of our own people and

Mr Singer here.'

Tej Shamsher thought for a while. 'But I would make a special mention of our family planning, Mr Clarke. It is very important for us. Our population is running away. We have eighteen million now, up three million in ten years. And you'll see we are a country with few resources. I can assure you that more money for our family planning would do a very great deal of good.'

When Tej Shamsher glanced at his watch, Harry and Bruce Singer rose to take their leave.

'Ram Maske also tells me you're a journalist, Mr Clarke,' Tej Shamsher said. 'And here also for news about our troubles for your Sydney paper. That's good. I think other countries ought to know more about us.' He walked to the door with them and joining his hands in a namaste. 'I want to extend our hospitality to you. You bring a fine gift. Before you leave I would like to arrange a dinner for you at one of our best hotels.'

Leaving the Singha Durbar with Harry, Bruce Singer asked the driver to park the car in the Durbar Marg. He pointed towards the great iron gates of the royal palace at the end of the street. 'It's the Narayan Hity Palace, Harry,' he said. 'The King lives there, not in the old palace in the Durbar Square. But what about a meal? Not a bad place near here, the Sun Kosi. It's Tibetan food, wonton soup and momos, things like that. Suit you, Harry?'

They took a table near the log fire and the waiter brought Star beers. Harry looked to the end of the room to the open kitchen which was white-tiled and spotlessly clean.

'Yes, it's one of the nicest little eating places anywhere,' Bruce said. 'Warm in here out of the cold. So you have a Nepalese ancestor, Harry?'

'Yes, I found out only recently.'

Bruce studied Harry for a moment or two. 'You don't look like it.'

'It's a long way back.'

'Interesting though.'

'Perhaps.'

'So you're going to write up the trouble here for your paper?'

'I'll cover it. Do you expect bad trouble?'

'People here are fed up with the Panchayats. They want democracy, Harry. And good for them. They deserve it. But their god-damn government's dead against it. Some bad things are happening here, Harry. Killings, torture. It's bad.'

'Do you think it will come to a head soon?'

'Perhaps. People in the US Embassy here are fed up too. One of our congressmen, a big shot in foreign affairs, flew over from Washington last month. He did some straight talking with the King here and the politicians. Advised them to get a democracy going and lift their ban on political parties.'

'Are they going to?'

Bruce shrugged. 'I'm not sure. It's not my territory, so I can't help you there. But your cousin's five million is a different matter. I must say she's generous. Five million dollars wouldn't touch the big projects; but it's a godsend for a few smaller ones.'

Bruce Singer explained that he was from USAID which was the United State's foreign aid organisation. An economist, he had previously worked in South Korea and the Philippines. He had been with the Nepal Planning Ministry for the last four years, and helped them select different projects coming up and get them funded in their plan.

'Yes, as I said, Nepal will still take a long time to get out of the mess the Ranas left,' Bruce continued. 'But they've made a start. Their tourist business is coming on well, with some good hotels and good trekking. They have a few reasonable roads now and a new one down to India instead of the old Raj Path. Some hydroelectric projects are operating, and there are some important irrigation projects, Sun Kosi, Pokhara and others. And they have some factories. They've got industrial estates in some of their towns, Hetauda, Butwal, Nepalganj and others, two here in the Kathmandu Valley. It's not much for a country with eighteen million people, but it's something, Harry.'

'What do you have in mind for the five million?'

'Nothing specific yet. But I can tell you they've got to industrialise. Get more going in their factory estates.'

'A factory?'

'Yes, a modern one, Harry, efficient, up-to-date machinery and all that. Tell you what, I'll take you to look at what's happening at the Balaju Industrial Estate so you can see what they have in mind there.'

They had finished their meal and Bruce waved towards two young women sitting at one of the other tables, one fair-haired and the other Nepalese, both dressed in multi-coloured woollen jumpers and blue jeans. 'I'll ask them to join us for coffee,' he said. 'You'll like them, Harry. I know them well. They're interesting people.'

So the two young women joined Bruce and Harry at their table near the fire. 'Meet Anne Jackson,' Bruce said.

'Oh, I've already met Mr Clarke,' Anne said. 'He was at my table for dinner the other evening.'

'And I saw you in Pad's Bar,' Harry said. 'You were busy with your papers.'

'I often am.'

'And this is Bhu Vamsi,' Bruce said. 'They're both with the Ministry of Development here. I see something of them at the office.'

The two women settled themselves in the chairs and looked at Harry, appraising him. 'Have you got anything for your paper on the trouble here, Mr Clarke?' Anne Jackson asked.

'Not yet. Give me time,' Harry said. 'I'm looking around. There'll be plenty, I suppose.'

'Yes,' Bhu said. 'And it's most important. But there are also other things happening in Nepal.'

'What things?' Harry asked.

'We could let him have some material. Don't you think, Anne?' Bhu said.

Anne was doubtful but she said, 'Well I suppose it could be of interest in Australia. It depends on how he writes it up. Maybe he could come to our Ministry and talk about it.' She looked at Harry. 'If you want to, Mr Clarke, why not?'

Bruce Singer was encouraging. 'Might be a good idea, Harry. They know Nepal well, and travel about a lot from one end of the country to the other—Ilam to Nepalganj and further on. They oversight their Ministry's dozen or so employment centres throughout Nepal, and are in touch with a lot of what's happening in the country areas. Employment centre staff get people into work and train people in skills needed locally. They're busy places and they do a good job.'

'We'd do more if your Ministry let us, Mr Singer,' Anne said.

'We don't let you?' Bruce queried.

'Money's our problem, Mr Singer. You know that well enough.'

'It's a problem everywhere, Miss Jackson.'

'Of course.'

Harry watched after the young women as they paid their bill and left the restaurant. 'Attractive girls, both of them,' he commented.

Bruce agreed. 'But don't call Anne a girl, Harry, not to her face. She wouldn't like it. She holds down an important job and is a liberated woman.'

'Is she?'

'Sure. Absolutely. A hard worker too, devoted to her job and completely wrapped up in it. It's her life, it seems.' Bruce smiled, 'No time at all to spare for men, Harry. At least not since she's been here.'

'Not gay, is she?' Harry asked as they were leaving the Sun Kosi.

Bruce Singer looked at Harry, eyebrows raised, then laughed. 'Good Lord no. I wouldn't think so. You saw her, Harry. Pretty face, nice figure, wears her jumper beautifully and she looks as feminine as you'd get.'

Four

When Harry called at the Himalayan Travel Agency in Durbar Marg to lease a car for travelling around the valley, they had a small toyota for him, and also Krishna Sarki who was one of their best drivers and spoke English well. From the start Harry liked the look of Krishna Sarki, a young man, confident, dressed neatly in his carefully ironed white shirt and grey trousers. In the car, Krishna Sarki suggested going to the Durbar Square, saying all tourists wanted to see the old temples. But Harry told him he was not a tourist, had already been there and wanted a good look around Kathmandu.

Krishna drove out to Lazimpat and Gyaneswar, and to newer parts of Kathmandu with their modern houses and shops. They visited the Tribhuban University and the National Museum on the road to the great Swayambhunath, then drove past some of the foreign embassies, a modern hospital in Maharajganj and several very impressive hotels. And Krishna drove Harry around the Tundikhel, which was once the home of Gurkha regiments and now a great park surrounded by the Kathmandu suburbs.

Harry also wanted to see the poorer parts, so Krishna drove out past Gana Bahal to a place heavy with the squalor of underdevelopment, a different world with none of the charm of the old town. The streets were too narrow for the sun to ever find them, and unsanitary with foul gutters and garbage strewn about. Cows wandered through the streets sure of their right of way, and stray dogs and the odd pig foraged in the garbage. The houses were old and neglected, the little shops dark and the little cafes black with many years of smoke and fumes from cooking. Krishna drove carefully past people sitting on doorsteps, women washing their pots in the gutters, cripples, and the occasional beggar. The poverty shocked Harry—the unemployment, the people caught there unable to help themselves and apparently with no help available.

'Do you live around here, Krishna?' Harry asked.

'Not here, in Kirtipur, some miles away.'

'Is it like this?'

'This is one of the worst, Mr Clarke. But much of the valley is poor. I think visitors should see the bad parts and understand what we are up against.'

Eventually back in the Durbar Marg, they parked the car and walked into Thamel. It was once an old village outside the walls of Kathmandu but was now a busy suburb near the old town; its cobbled streets were clean and lined with busy little shops. Krishna took Harry to a cafe he said was popular with tourists. Seated there, he refused to join Harry in a meal, explaining he did not take food at that time of the day, but accepted a glass of chan, the rice beer.

'You drive well, Krishna,' Harry said. 'Have you been at it long?'

'Four years, since I left school.'

He was not much more than twenty. 'Have you finished secondary school?'

'Yes, in Kirtipur. Education is very important to us.'

'You'll continue to be a driver?'

'No. But it is better than a cobbler. There is more money.' Why a cobbler, Harry wondered until Krishna said, 'My family have always been cobblers.' He shrugged, 'Very low caste, you could say. I hope it does not worry you.'

Harry had read about the untouchables. 'No it doesn't, Krishna, not at all,' he said

'Cobbling is good for some. It means they have work. But it is not for me. I will start a successful business soon.'

'What sort of business, Krishna?'

'I am a typist. I have become skilled at that and have already bought a modern typewriter and a duplicating machine. I save to get capital. In another year I'll rent a shop and start an office services business, type for people, make copies of their papers for them. There's a demand for that. I will come to employ staff.'

Harry could see the quiet strength in his Krishna's face, his controlled eagerness. He admired the young man's spirit and thought he would supplement the pay he got from the travel agency. 'Good for you, Krishna,' he said.

When next Krishna Sarki came to the Hotel Laxmi he suggested that Harry might like to visit Kirtipur, again saying it was his own town and there were people there who would like to meet him.

Harry agreed. He remembered that Kirtipur, perched on its hill three hundred feet above the valley floor, was where the Gurkha King first attacked in his long campaign to take the Valley of Nepal. He had read of the Kirtipur people's courage then. The punishment for Kirtipur's resistance had been cruel, the disfigurement of their men and boys.

On their way there Krishna drove near the ancient Swayambhunath, the great Buddhist chaitya standing on a hill. The golden rings on its high canopy sparkled in the morning sunlight and flags of many colours fluttered in the breeze. Painted on its toran were the eyes of the Adi Buddha that looked sternly out over the valley;

'It is a holy place,' Krishna said. ' Would you like me to take you there? Buddhists worship there and also many of my Hindu religion. I do sometimes.'

They parked the car and were about to climb the Swayambhunath's hill when two Europeans, a man and a woman, approached Harry. They were dressed in soiled yellow robes; their hair was long and unkempt and the man was bearded; both were barefoot and both wore large silver earrings. The woman held a few faded flowers and held out a begging bowl, her glazed eyes looking into Harry's. The man asked for alms in English, saying they needed food. Harry donated but it was not enough. The man demanded more and threatened, until Krishna sent them off saying he would have the police come and return them to their own country.

'They live near here with others like them,' Krishna explained. 'Hippies you could call them. They are lazy people and drug addicts.'

'Do you have many of them?'

'Not many now. Some years ago many hippies came to Nepal with their drugs and idleness. From England and America, from Europe and also your country, Mr Clarke. After a while our government sent most of them away. There are only a few here now.'

They climbed the track up the Swayambhunath's hill, up the nearly four hundred steps past the playful monkeys to the temple's precincts. Harry and Krishna mingled with the crowd, the worshippers and the tourists. Krishna pointed out to Harry the great bronze Vajra, which was Indra's thunderbolt, and images of the five Divine Buddhas that the Adi Buddha had created at the start of time. They walked around the sub-chaityas, the stone lingams, the vihars and Saraswati's temple. There were many prayer wheels holding their paper prayer, Om Mani Padme Hum, meaning Hail to the Jewel of the Lotus; prayer wheels that rattled as people turned them time and time again praying to the Buddha, beseeching him, perhaps, to spare them future re-births in this world and take them straight to Nirvana when they died.

Then Krishna drove further through the valley to the foot of Kirtipur's hill. 'You will have another climb here, Mr Clarke,' he said. 'But I think you will like to meet some people.'

They climbed the steps to Kirtipur, a town still gathered within the ramparts of its stout walls and the sheer brick sides of its outer houses. They passed through a gateway into the ancient town, now poor and neglected. Krishna led the way along the narrow cobbled streets, broken in many places and dark in the shadow of the old three-storeyed houses of burnt brick as in old Kathmandu, with buttressed eaves overhanging the street below and fine old wood carvings adorning their windows. They walked passed temples, little shops and roadside stalls, and many idle people sitting about, then stopped at a house near Kirtipur's central square.

'Please wait here, Mr Clarke,' Krishna said, hurried into the house and returned saying, 'Yes, they are here waiting for you. Please come in.'

Harry followed Krishna into the house, into a room with a hard earthen floor and a hearth where a fire was burning under black iron pots. A servant was preparing vegetables at a table, and a fowl waiting to be killed was pecking about in a corner. Krishna led Harry up a ladder to the floor above, where he caught a glimpse of two of the house's womenfolk, shy women who kept their faces turned away from him. He followed Krishna up a second ladder to the top storey into a room of creaking wooden floor boards. It was sparsely furnished with long wooden benches, bedding in a corner, a table with bottles and bowls, and a chair. A window, its lattice open, looked out towards Kirtipur's sunlit central square and caught a glimpse of a Himalayan peak, dazzling white with snow. A dozen or so men were waiting, seated on the wooden benches.

Krishna led Harry to the chair and those waiting joined their hands in welcoming namastes. Their eyes appraised him and Harry returned their gaze, wondering who exactly they were and what they might want of his visit. All young men, they were dressed western-style in shirts, warm jumpers and trousers, and some wore topi caps—earnest-looking young men with serious faces. Krishna introduced each of them; several were Sarkis which was Krishna's caste, Harry remembered. Most were university students, and Krishna introduced his cousin, Ari Sarki, who had a doctorate from Cambridge and was a lecturer at Nepal's Tribhuban University.

Ari Sarki, the eldest, tall, thin, the brown skin of his face tight over prominent cheek bones, spoke to Harry. 'Krishna has told us you're a journalist from Australia. We asked Krishna to bring you to visit us. I hope you don't mind.'

Ari Sarki went to the table and poured from a bottle. 'Have some raksi,' he said offering the drink to Harry. 'I hope you like it. We'll all drink with you.' Each young man took a bowl. Harry found the rice spirit strong but pleasant enough.

'You wonder why we wanted Krishna to bring you here, Mr Clarke?' Ari Sarki asked.

'I am a little curious,' Harry said, smiling.

'It's about our trouble with the government, the Panchayat system, and with our King. You should know that we're demanding democracy,' Ari Sarki said, watching for Harry's reaction. Seeing no objection he went on, tapping the table with his fist to emphasise each point. 'Yes, we demand democracy. We'll have free and legal political parties and fair elections, and our own representatives in parliament. We're fighting for it now. Already many hundreds of activists are in prison and many have been killed. But a crisis is coming and we will prevail. I hear you're here to cover it for your paper. A lot of foreign journalists have come here for that.'

'Yes, I will cover it,' Harry told him.

Ari Sarki talked at length about the decades of struggle against King and government, showing his anger that the Nepali Congress Party and the parties of the United Left Front were banned, but praising their leaders like Ganesh Man Singh and Man Mohan Adhikari. He spoke of the recent years of terror and the bombings at many places, mentioning: Pokhara, Birganj, the Bhairahawa Airport, Biratnagar when the King was visiting, the gates of the Royal Palace in Kathmandu, the Hotel Annapurna in Durbar Marg, the Singha Durbar. He told Adam about the army's crushing of activists in the Timure Bhot forest and Khampa activists in their mountain hide-outs. He spoke of sadistic riot police, prisons overflowing and insanitary, torturers busy with their irons, and executioners busy with their swords and ropes.

One of the women of the Sarkis' house came up the ladder and into the room carrying a tin tray with food which she handed to Ari Sarki. She peeped around at Harry for an instant then quickly climbed down the ladder again.

'We have a Nepalese dinner for you, Mr Clarke,' Ari Sarki said, taking the tray to Harry and pouring more raksi for him.

Harry looked at the compartments in the tray, filled with chicken, curried cauliflower, rice, dal, garlic and a few hot chillies. 'Thank you,' he said and waited for the others in the room to be served. But Krishna said, 'You should eat, Mr Clarke. We're not eating now. It is to you we are giving the Nepalese dinner, not to ourselves.'

So Harry ate whilst the others watched.

'Nice and spicy. Just as I like it,' Harry assured them as he finished the meal. Krishna brought a bowl of water for him to wash his hands.

'We brought you here because we need your help, Mr Clarke,' Ari Sarki said.

'What can I do?'

'We want to make a bargain with you, a fair exchange. True, all parties in Nepal are banned, but they are active now. Our party is active and needs help.'

'Is it the Nepali Congress?' Harry asked.

'No, we have our own party to support them.'

'The cobbler's party,' Krishna said.

A smile touched Ari Sarki's lips. 'No, it's not that, it's a secret name. We are more than only Sarkis, many more. We have a thousand members.'

'What do you need from me?' Harry asked, shaking his head doubtfully. 'I could have nothing to do with violence, with killings. No bombs. You must understand that.'

All in the room were agreeing. 'No, no,' Ari Sarki said. 'We use no guns or bombs. There's no violence and killings. None of that, I assure you, Mr Clarke. We are a non-violent party. We educate people and demonstrate peacefully; we mould public opinion.' He pointed to Krishna. 'Krishna helps us. He's a good typist and has a duplicating machine. And we duplicate leaflets urging change, and put these around Kathmandu. But it's little, so very little.'

'What help could I be?' Harry asked again.

'We need a printing press, Mr Clarke. We must reach all the people of Nepal. We can get one from India. In fact it's already at the border, at Roxaul. It's a job press, an old one they no longer use.' Ari Sarki hesitated.

'Do you need money to pay for it then?' Harry asked.

'We do, it's two thousand American dollars.'

'And you want the money from me?'

'We do. We've heard of the gift your cousin is making to Nepal. It's only a small part of it we want, and it's a good cause.'

Harry still looked doubtful.

'I said it's a bargain,' Ari Sarki told him. 'We'll let you know what is happening here, and give you information for your paper. It would be worth much more to you than the two thousand dollars.'

But of course Harry saw the danger, and sat there wondering how to reply.

'I saw your difficulty before we arranged to meet you.' Ari Sarki continued. 'But I assure you it would be done in the greatest secrecy. We have friends in the Rastriya Bank and Customs, who will arrange it for us. No one will connect you with it.'

They talked on and Harry had to admit to himself that he had sympathy with what the young men were trying to do. They did not seem to be violent people. They were teachers and students. 'Perhaps I will', he told them as he left. 'But I won't promise now. I need time to think about it.'

Before leaving Kirtipur, Krishna took Harry to see the shrine of the Goddess Indriana, explaining that she was an Ajima, one of the grandmother goddesses and a representative of the Shakti which is the Supreme Energy. He told Harry that in early times Indriana was a widow so poverty-stricken that she was hardly able to feed and clothe her children. She had rich sister goddesses, who looked down on her, and slighted her by refusing to invite her to their celebration of Pasachare, a day when houses are cleaned and decorated and relatives and friends are invited to a feast. Instead, they had Indriana and her children visit them the following day when the guests had gone, to eat left-over food. Insulted, sad and crying, Indriana refused the food and returned to her poor dwelling with her children to cook a pumpkin which a generous friend had given her. A miracle occurred. The pumpkin in the pot turned into a fabulous treasure of gold and diamonds, pearls and other gems. Indiana became rich and was accepted by her sisters.

As Harry walked down the steep steps back to the car, he thought that the people of Kirtipur might well sympathise with Indriana in her erstwhile poverty. They, too, were poor. They were people who must dream of a treasure like Indriana's for themselves. It was then that Harry decided he would give Ari Sarki and his party the two thousand dollars for the printing press, donate it from his own money, perhaps getting reimbursed when Mary Clarke's five million became available.

Five

When Bruce Singer called at the Hotel Laxmi to advise on the spending of the five million dollars, Harry took him to Pad's Bar which was warm against the cold day. Few other guests were there and Pad served them drinks in a corner of the lounge. Harry was pleased that Bruce had taken up the matter seriously and prepared himself well.

'It's a useful sum, Harry,' Bruce said. 'Five million dollars is about one hundred and fifty million Nepalese rupees. But I'll be frank with you. It's no good wasting the money on some nice idea. It needs to be put where the market will do the most with it, bring the best returns. We must be rational about it, Harry. Let me give you some of the background.'

Bruce gave Harry an account of Nepal's economy, and talked about the need for faster growth, for a greater national product. He lamented the country's lack of investment funds, its trade balance being all shot up, and the big national debt. The rupee was run down to thirty to the US dollar, inflation was on the up and could sky rocket.

'Sounds bad, Bruce,' Harry said. 'So what do you advise? How should the money be spent?'

'I'm coming to that.' Bruce sat thinking for a moment or two. 'It's the manufacturing sector, Harry. It's a factory. I said that before. A modern factory with modern technology. It has to be efficient, one that can compete. They're your criteria, Harry.'

'Producing what?'

'There'll be different things to look at, and we'll have that done. It will take a little time but we'll push ahead, Harry. I want to take you to look at something today. Out to the Industrial Services Centre. The Balaju Industrial Estate, as I promised. It's not far from here.'

They were about to leave Pad's Bar when two men came in, ordered their drinks and came over to Bruce. Bruce introduced them. Mr Brown was past middle-age, overweight and with a whisky nose. The other, Pierre Lamonde, was younger, dressed casually, and smiled back through his heavily rimmed spectacles. 'They're from the Asian and Pacific Bank in Bangkok,' Bruce said. 'An important bank. They come to Nepal often and lend out a good deal of money here.'

'I know Sydney,' Mr Brown said to Harry. 'Nice town. You're on a holiday here, Mr Clarke?'

'He's here for his paper. Harry's a journalist,' Bruce answered for him.

'So you're covering the trouble, Mr Clarke,' Mr Brown said. 'Nasty business developing. Saw an angry demonstration on the Tundikhel this morning. There were a hundred or so in the park with their placards protesting against King and government. I saw it. The police were rough beating up some young men. Took some away in their wagons.'

'Certainly a nasty business,' Bruce agreed. 'I'm all for democracy. Of course I am, make no bones about that. But I don't like to see things hotting up. Keep out of it, myself.'

'They need to get together and talk, the government and the political parties,' Harry said.

'They can't very well,' Mr Brown laughed cynically. 'They've got themselves in a mess, with political parties banned, illegal, and many of their leaders in prison. This confrontation has been going on for years. Activists' bombings and killings, savage reprisals, prison, executions, and torture some say. All that doesn't make talking easy, Mr Clarke.'

'They'll have to talk in the end,' Harry said.

'Maybe they will.'

Mr Brown turned to Bruce. 'We have some business to get around to, Mr Singer. I'm free this afternoon.'

'Afraid I'm not though,' Bruce replied. He looked at his watch and then at Harry. 'In fact we must leave now. We're off to Balaju for an appointment there. They'll be waiting for us.'

Bruce and Harry drove through the cold afternoon to the west of the town, along Naya Bazar, over the bridge spanning the Vishnumati River and across the ring-road the Chinese built.

'Balaju was their first industrial estate,' Bruce said. 'It started with help from USAID, but that was well before my time, thirty years ago. I'm sorry I rushed you off like that, Harry. The truth is I wanted to get away from the Bank people. I don't agree with some of their ideas, and don't want to do business with them.' Bruce looked at his watch again. 'We still have a little time, so come and see the Reclining Vishnu they have here.'

Bruce led the way to the Balaju Gardens, with its ancient two-tiered temple for Shitala, the Goddess of Smallpox, and a score or so of stone dragons which had icy water from the stream pouring from their mouths. The Reclining Vishnu, carved in black stone and larger than life size, lay peacefully in his secluded tank, half-immersed in the dark water and supported by the stone coils of his protector, the enormous cobra Ananta whose hoods formed a halo around the great god's head. The god's stone eyes looked calmly towards the heavens and the hands of his four arms held a discus, a mace, a conch shell and a lotus seed. For centuries Vishnu's image had rested there serenely and in peace. Priests attended to him, washing his face each morning, ringing bells to summon people to come and worship him. Over the centuries multitudes had adored him, prayed to him and attended his festivals. People were lavish with their flowers and many other offerings.

Leaving the Balaju gardens, Bruce drove along the gravel roads of the industrial estate, pointing out to Harry some of its fifty or so factories; almost all were small, many in make-shift buildings. Harry looked over some that manufactured furniture, sheet metal goods, knitwear, textiles, polythene piping and footwear. He passed a dairy, a printing press, a bakery, a biscuit factory and a battery factory, amongst others.

At the office of the Industrial Services Centre, the Chief of Projects—one of Nepal's brightest young engineers Bruce told Harry—welcomed them. 'Would you like tea?' he asked. 'Mr Singer has told me of your cousin's gift to Nepal, Mr Clarke. It is a considerable amount, most generous. We are grateful.'

'I shall need your advice on how to spend the money,' Harry said.

'It's our job to help,' the Chief of Projects assured Harry. He explained that they helped people to set up factories in each of the industrial estates in Nepal.

'They do a thorough job,' Bruce added.

The Chief of Projects shook his head doubtfully. 'It's still just a start, no more. Do you know that we have less than fourteen thousand employed in factories in all Nepal? In all except the smallest factories. It's not much for a country with eighteen million people, is it Mr Clarke?'

Harry agreed.

'Lack of investment funds,' Bruce said. 'That's the main hold-up.'

'It is,' the Chief of Projects confirmed. 'A lot of people with good projects are waiting for money to get them going.' He pointed to a filing cabinet. 'There's a hundred filed away there waiting. It depresses me.'

'Well there's five million dollars that might get a few going,' Bruce said.

The Chief of Projects pointed to the files on his desk. 'I've taken out some you might like to consider, Mr Clarke. They seem to meet the criteria that Mr Singer set.'

Bruce glanced at the files. There was a mechanised foundry to produce small castings, a glass works, a plastic goods factory, a factory making hand tools, one making pesticides, a match factory, a few others. Bruce arranged to take the files back to his Ministry to read and decide on what he would recommend to Harry.

That evening in Pad's Bar for a drink before dinner, Harry found the men from the Asian and Pacific Bank whom he had met earlier that day. They claimed him, seemed most friendly, chatted away for a while and bought a round or two of drinks. Then they invited Harry to dinner. 'We're off to the Annapurna tonight for a meal. Come with us, Mr Clarke. A good hotel the Annapurna. In Durbar Marg. There's a good Chinese restaurant there. Szechuan food. Be our guest,' Mr Brown said.

The Annapurna's commissionaire, his uniform spick-and-span, his medals polished and shining and a sword in its scabbard, welcomed them. He opened the big doors and ushered then inside. They walked through the wide foyer of the five-star hotel, with its marble and tiles, lush pot plants, luxurious lounge chairs and highly polished woodwork, its reception desk with neatly uniformed staff.

'It was terrible for the staff here a few years ago,' Mr Brown told Harry, pointing to the reception desk. 'Terrorists bombed the place, the foyer here. Bad damage. Three of the receptionists were killed.'

'Oh that's tragic,' Harry said.

'Don't worry, Mr Clarke,' Pierre Lamonde reassured. 'Not likely to happen again. It's the only time they attacked a hotel.'

As they seated themselves in the restaurant, its red decor, candles and flowers were multiplied in big mirrors on the wall. Harry thought how well Nepal was doing for its tourists. Attentive waiters hovered about and Mr Brown ordered Star beers, saying it was brewed in Hetauda down on the Terai in Makwanpur, and a beer of good quality. Pierre Lamonde recommended the Szechuan dishes and a French wine.

They talked about trivialities, rather uneasily. The conversation lagged occasionally and the men from the Bank looked at Harry uncertainly. It was not until the meal was nearly finished that Mr Brown said, 'We had news about you this afternoon, Mr Clarke.'

'Did you,' Harry said, wondering.

'The money you have for Nepal from your cousin in England. A most generous gesture.'

'Admirable,' Pierre Lamonde supported.

'I must say news here gets around quickly,' Harry said. Not that it worried him unduly.

'It does. And we have something that will interest you,' Mr Brown said. 'There's a project needing just that sort of money. Five million, isn't it? I think you'll like it.'

'Perhaps,' Harry said.

'We have one of the ministries interested,' Mr Brown said leaning over the table and speaking quietly, nodding his head in confirmation. 'They are very interested, but capital's the trouble. A total of ten million's needed. Our bank would put up half. The ministry people would need to put up the other half. But they are short of funds. Your cousin's gift would help them out nicely.'

'What's the project?' Harry asked.

'To put it simply, a great amusement park.'

'Go on, now. An American Disneyland here?' Harry said, surprised.

The men from the bank were shaking their heads, concern on their faces. Not American, I assure you,' Pierre Lamonde replied. 'True it's a major park that's planned. But it's Nepalese, truly Nepalese. And there's nothing like it yet in the whole of Asia, as far as I know. Nepal will have a first, a remarkable first.'

'A Nepalese Disneyland?' Harry suggested.

'Yes and no,' Mr Brown said. 'Perhaps not quite that scale. Nepal itself would provide the themes. They've got a lot to go on. Just think of it, Mr Clarke. There's the great Mount Everest, all the Himalayas in fact, trekking, mountaineering, yaks, wild animals of the Terai, elephants, tigers, leopards, rhinoceros. There are jungles, folk tales about demons like Ghanta Karna, their wars against the British and Tibet, the old Malla kings, their legends, Manjusri draining the lake to make the Valley of Nepal, and so much more. There's plenty to choose from.'

'There's also the Yeti,' Pierre Lamonde suggested. 'No doubt you've heard of the Yeti, Mr Clarke. The so-called abominable snowman who haunts the Himalayan snows.'

'Who hasn't? It's a nice fairy tale.'

'Not a fairy tale,' Pierre Lamonde said. Pierre Lamonde talked about the hairy ape-like giant. He spoke of reports of its huge but almost human-like footprints found in the Himalayan snows, of loud yelling and whistling and other unexplained noises in the night in the high valleys, and hairy figures hurling great branches and boulders into the camps of travellers as they slept. Yaks had been killed with a single blow and left half-eaten. He claimed that many—Sherpas, Europeans and others—had glimpsed the great monsters' shadows in the moonlight, and their shapes moving across a distant snow-covered valley or along high tracks in the icy mountains. He said several places held the remains of yetis. The bones of a yeti's hand were in the monastery at Pangboche and a yeti's scalp was in the monastery at Namche.

'And the park would have a casino and a new five-star hotel,' Mr Brown added.

Mr Brown lent back in his chair watching Harry's reaction. 'Don't have any doubts, Mr Clarke. Picture the finished park. Buildings in white stucco, halls for mountaineering, for big game hunting, for war, and Manjusri hurrying around the surrounding mountains and making his great cut to release the waters of the lake and create the Kathmandu valley here. We'll put the viewers in the act with plenty of electronics —virtual reality even in some of the halls.'

'And a zoo,' Pierre Lamonde added. 'And a miniature Everest that people would climb; a five-hundred-foot hill of ice and rock. Also a huge fun fair for adults as well as children. Slides, merry-go-rounds, magic tunnels, ghost houses, magic mirrors, much more.'

'We could go on and on,' Mr Brown said.

'Where would they have all this?' Harry asked.

'The Tundikhel. It would be perfect.'

'Could you get the great park?'

'The ministry concerned thinks so, at a price of course, a percentage of the profits.'

'Would ten million be enough?'

'If not, our bank would see it through.'

Harry still had questions. 'And what would happen to the profits?'

The men from the Bank smiled condescendingly. 'Don't worry your head about profits,' Mr Brown said. 'Look, they get more than a third of a million tourists a year here. Say each on average spent a conservative twenty dollars at the park. That's more than six million turnover a year, two-thirds of our capital cost. Then there's the local people. A few Nepalese are earning enough money to spend a bit.'

'What about the running costs?' Harry asked.

'Labour is cheap here, dirt cheap, next to nothing compared with your country or mine. We'd run our own diesel electricity plant. There'd be some imports.'

'And would there be interest to pay your bank?'

'Of course. That is business.'

'Well I'll have to think it over,' Harry said.

'Do that. That's the way,' Mr Brown told him with a satisfied smile. Then as they were leaving the restaurant he said, 'We'll send you a file with all the details, all the figuring, Mr Clarke.'

Six

Next time Harry went into Pad's Bar he found Anne Jackson there with her papers again. She smiled across at him, and when he smiled back she came and sat beside him.

'Do you mind,?' she asked.

'Not at all.'

'Have you news for your paper yet, Mr Clarke?'

'I'm Harry,' he said.

'Well have you any news for your paper, Harry?' she asked again. 'You may call me Anne if you like. It's not a favour that I'd grant everyone.' She smiled, wrinkling her nose.

A nice nose, Harry was thinking.

'You haven't come to see me at the Ministry. I've been waiting for you.'

'I'll come tomorrow.'

'Oh it doesn't matter now. I'm arranging a little dinner party and I'd like you to come. Just a few people, Bhu Vamsi whom you've met and her friend, and Major Bista. I can't cope with many in my small flat. Will you come?'

Harry agreed readily.

'Tomorrow evening at six-thirty. My place is number four.' She took her papers and left.

Pad walked back along the bar. 'A charming young lady, Miss Jackson. She's having a meal sent from here.'

'Isn't her flat one of those over from the hotel?' Harry checked.

Pad gave directions, then asked, 'How did you find the restaurant last night, Mr Clarke? The Annapurna wasn't it?'

'Fine,' Harry told him.

Pad looked at Harry uncertainly. 'And the company, if I might ask about that? The men from the bank, I'd be cautious with them. They're not always popular here. It's said Mr Brown's very pushy, too pushy by far.' Pad went off to serve another customer, then came back and lent over the bar close to Harry. He raised his eyebrows and with a hint of a smile said quietly, 'I hear Mr Brown won a big lottery in Bangkok. He won the first prize.'

'First prize. What a lucky chap. How much?'

Pad grinned. 'You'd never guess. He's won a Thai girl, Mr Clarke. Her and tickets for two for a tour of Asian cities, Calcutta, Manilla, Hong Kong, Tokyo. The best hotels and all paid for.'

'He won a Thai girl?' Harry queried.

'As I said, in the lottery. He has her only for the tour of course.'

'A prostitute?'

'I hear she's a university student.'

Harry shrugged, 'Not a good idea, Pad.'

'Perhaps not, but it happens. A fact of life, Mr Clarke. They're sending the girl up here for him. She'll be here before long.'

When Harry went to Anne's flat for dinner the electricity was off again and he made his way through the dark, the cold night, across the hotel gardens, through a heavy iron gate, past high walls of ancient brick and between flower beds and overhanging trees. In the starlight he could make out the buildings—two-storeyed and finished in white stucco with curving roofs of terracotta tiles. An oil lamp was burning in one of the entrances as he climbed up the stairway to flat four.

'Do come in, Harry,' Anne welcomed him.

He looked at her for a moment or two then said, 'I must say I like it, Anne.'

'What do you like, Harry?'

'Your sari, of course,' Anne was wearing a green silk sari that night. 'You look charming. It suits you. It goes well with your hair.'

'Oh come now, you're being too nice,' she admonished a little. 'Come and I'll pour you a drink.'

The living room was in shadow, except where the light from an oil lamp fell, and candles were on the table set for dinner. A papier-mache face of the elephant-headed God Ganesh looked down from a dark corner of the wall, and a vase of flowers stood on the wide wooden sill of the window that looked out into the night over the gardens below and beyond to a glimpse of the Hotel Laxmi's roofs. In one corner a heating stove managed to warm the flat. Doors led to the other two rooms, which Harry guessed were bedrooms.

Then the other guests came. Bhu Vamsi impressed Harry, her red sari and her turquoise earrings, the tika mark on her forehead, her black hair shining and fixed on top by a golden ornament. She introduced her friend, Jang Pandey, telling Harry he was the principal of the Durbar School which was one of Nepal's important colleges. Anne introduced

Major Bista, now retired from a Gurkha regiment, who ran an accountancy business.

A waiter from the hotel served the entree and attended to the wine and a fruit juice for Jang Pandey.

'French wine, Harry,' Anne said. 'It's Chablis, Calvet & Cie it says on the label. I couldn't find any of your Australian wines. I hope you don't mind.'

'I'll forgive you this time,' Harry said.

'I can take wine in moderation, just a little,' Bhu Vamsi said, glancing at Jang Pandey who was making a play of hiding the contents of his glass of fruit juice by wrapping a serviette around it.

'Fruit juice is healthier,' Jang Pandey said. 'It tastes better. It's less expensive and not imported. It has many advantages, you must agree.'

'They're good points. I do agree rather,' Anne said.

'Not me though,' Major Bista said. 'Give me wine. But I must say I respect Jang Pandey's not taking alcohol. He's orthodox, at least in that regard.'

The meal progressed and the waiter from the hotel brought the next course. He served more wine and they talked. The candles on the table burnt low and Anne replaced them. Then the coffee came.

'Far too many people in Nepal go against their traditions nowadays,' Major Bista said during a lull in the conversation.

'But not yourself, Major,' Jang Pandey replied.

'No, I do not. I'm proud to say that,' the Major affirmed. 'And I never shall. I have my King. I still have the army. I have my country. I pray to my gods.'

Jang Pandey laughed.

Major Bista asked the waiter to refill his glass. 'We must be careful Jang Pandey. To break some traditions must surely amount to treason, no less than treason,' he said, seriously. 'Perhaps you should be reminded of it.'

'What do you mean by that, Major?' Jang Pandey came back.

Bhu Vamsi intervened. 'Perhaps Mr Clarke isn't interested in such matters. I would like him to tell us something about Australia.'

Harry answered questions about Australia. The usual run of questions, the country's size, how many people it had, its climate, the bush, the kangaroos, koala bears and so on.

Then Jang Pandey said, 'I believe your country is a republic now, Mr Clarke.'

'Not yet. One day it will be, no doubt,' Harry replied.

'They still have their queen, 'Major Bista said. 'Queen Elizabeth of England is also Queen of Australia. I know they are loyal to her. Always will be I hope, if I may say so, Mr Clarke.'

Harry shrugged. He was not going to be brought into it.

'They're democratic though. She's a constitutional monarch,' Jang Pandey said. 'That's what we want in Nepal.'

'And how will you get that?' the Major asked. 'By force?'

'Yes, if it comes to that. I hope it doesn't.'

The Major's face set in a frown. 'So you are saying that openly now, Jang Pandey. I've often suspected you. I used the word treason before. It seems it's not too harsh a word.'

'It's far too harsh Major. It's completely unwarranted. And it's foolish. People must have the power to govern themselves. They must have their free political parties. They must elect their representatives to parliament. And it will happen here.'

'Even to say that, Jang Pandey, is a crime against the King.'

Jang Pandey spoke loudly. 'No crime at all, major. The King stays King and a son of the good Lord Vishnu. But the people will govern for him.'

Changing tone, Major Bista spoke sadly. 'What you say is a cruel blow against our King. A King who has done so much for the people.'

'Come now,' Jang Pandey said. 'True some of us are better off. A very few are much better off. But most of the people in Nepal —nearly all—are still poor, miserably poor most of them. Is that doing so much?'

'I repeat that much has been done,' Major Bista said. 'And we are still one country. We are still one people. Your political parties would split us. Nepal would break up, shatter. We would return to the days of many little princedoms before the great Prithvi Shah. It's the King who binds us together, makes a nation of us.'

'The King will still do that, Major.'

'He will do more than that, Jang Pandey. He will still rule. Your people will not rob him of his power.'

'They will take power. The people's time has come.'

The scowl darkened on Major Bista's face. 'I warn you Jang Pandey. Death is a just punishment for traitors.'

Jang Pandey laughed. 'There are millions of your so-called traitors, Major. Death for them? It's ridiculous.'

'The army is strong. It will cope.'

By this time the meal was long finished. The candles on the table had burnt low again and one spluttered and went out. The heating stove was struggling to give enough warmth and the cold night was taking over the room. Both Major Bista and Jang Pandey turned towards Harry, their concern clearly evident on their faces.

'I owe you an apology, Mr Clarke,' Major Bista said. 'We have provoked each other, Jang Pandey and I, and we should not have. We neglected you who are a guest in our country. I'm afraid we have bored you with our argument.'

'We have,' Jang Pandey said. 'I, too, apologise.'

'There is no need at all for apologies,' Harry assured them. 'Your views interested me, and I enjoyed the company.'

The Major took his leave of Anne and soon after Bhu Vamsi and Jang Pandey followed.

'Stay and make yourself comfortable, Harry,' Anne said as she turned up the heating stove. 'There's something I want to tell you. It won't take very long.'

Harry seated himself on the sofa and Anne came back and sat beside him. 'I'm in no hurry, Anne. I assure you of that,' he said, moving closer to her.

'It's about something other than the trouble here. Would you like to hear?'

'Of course, Anne,' Harry replied, leaning over and taking her hand.

She smiled. 'No, it's not that Harry. But tell me, do you always want to hold hands before you get to know a person even a little?'

Harry hesitated. 'Not always, of course not. But you're a very attractive girl, Anne. Very attractive.'

Anne pulled her hand away, frowning. 'Girl, Harry? Girls are children. How old do you think I am?

Harry was about to say she was in her late twenties, when he remembered Bruce Singer had said not to call her a girl. 'I think of young women as girls, Anne, always have. Perhaps I shouldn't.'

'Certainly you should not. You're hardly a modern man, are you Harry? But I won't say any more about that. I want to talk to you about the employment centres I mentioned them the other day at the Sun Kosi. Are you interested?

'Yes, I could be.'

Bhu Vamsi and I are going to the employment centre at Hetauda, down in Makwanpur on the Terai. We'll be away a few days. You could come with us. Have a look and take notes. Write an article for your paper.'

Straight away he liked the idea.

'But there's something else, Harry,' Anne said, a little anxiously. 'It's because of something I've heard about you. You won't be annoyed?'

'You'd better tell me what it is first.'

This time Anne took Harry's hand. 'I've heard about the money you have from your cousin. I must be honest with you: it's not only for an article for your paper. You'll see that our employment centres need more funds. Badly, very badly. Do you mind?'

Harry was not sure. He was beginning to realise the money was an important responsibility and so did not want to rush into a decision. At the same time he did not want to discourage Anne, a young woman he found attractive; he could become very attracted to her he had to admit to himself.

'No, Anne, of course I don't mind,' he said. 'I'd like to see your employment centres. But I can hardly promise anything yet.'

A little later, as Harry was leaving, Anne stretched up and quickly kissed him on the cheek. 'I'm so glad your coming with us Harry. Oh, I do hope you can help,' she said.

On Monday after the mists had risen they left to go down into Makwanpur. It was a pleasant crisp morning with the sun shining on the roofs of the temples and the ice and snow sparkling on the great mountains. Krishna called for Harry at the hotel in a jeep borrowed from the United Nation's office. He assured Harry the four-wheel-drive was well suited for the trip; and it had extra jerrycans of fuel and a second spare tyre on the roof rack. Harry dumped his pack and climbed in beside Krishna. Anne and Bhu Vamsi, who were warmly dressed in woollen jumpers and jeans, welcomed Harry from the back seat. Krishna thanked Harry for the opportunity to drive outside the Kathmandu valley.

They drove out of the hotel grounds, around into the Kanti Path, through the town and past the Tundikhel and the national stadium to the start of the Tribhuban Raj Path. They followed the Raj Path out of Kathmandu past the peasants' fields, some lush with vegetable crops and some ploughed black ready for the new spring sowing, then on past thatch-roofed farm houses to Thankot village at the southern end of the valley. From here the Raj Path led upwards, past a statue of the good King Tribhuban, towards the Chandragiri Mountain and the pass out of the valley.

Anne asked Krishna to stop the jeep at the southern side of the pass and pointed over the Mahabharat Ranges to a panorama of mountains and valleys, a land forested and green except where mountains were tipped with the winter snow and here and there the ochre-coloured rock of landslides. In front of them the ground fell away from the pass down into a deep valley two thousand feet below. Harry could see the road they were to take descending steeply, zigzagging, edging steep precipices or hugging the mountain side, till it became a thin line in the distance and then lost itself amongst the forests.

'It is steep,' Anne said with a laugh. 'I hope Krishna is a careful driver. Does it worry you, Harry?'

'I'll make it if Krishna does.'

'Naubise village is our first stop,' Bhu said.

Krishna drove slowly, carefully down the steep road, honking the horn at every curve. He kept well to the side to leave room for ascending vehicles—the overloaded buses with passengers on the roof, other jeeps, an occasional sedan, and trucks gaily decorated or old and grey and struggling to make the steep grades.

At Naubise village, the four sat in the busy market square drinking Coca Cola. 'We have a choice from here,' Bhu said. 'We can take the road the Chinese built to Mugling and go on to Bharatpur and then the road back east to Hetauda. Or we can keep on the Raj Path which goes directly to Hetauda.'

Harry noticed Krishna grimace.

'The Raj Path is by far the shorter way,' Anne said. 'Hetauda's not fifty miles from here, I'd say.'

'And it's more than a hundred miles the other way, getting on to three times as far,' Bhu said, smiling at Krishna's concern.

Krishna looked to Harry. 'It is not a good road now, the Raj Path, Mr Clarke. Shorter, yes. But it would take much longer to go that way. I would not like to keep on the Raj Path.'

'Why is that, Krishna?' Harry asked.

'I have driven over it, Mr Clarke. It keeps high around the mountains. Round and round them. It's a dangerous road. It skirts deep precipices. The grades are steep. Landslides have broken the surface in many places. There are very many bends, hairpin bends you call them. It is a narrow road with only one lane in most parts of it. There will be snow and ice on some places now, near Daman certainly. There are accidents on this road. No, I say it is not a good road to travel on.'

Anne and Bhu held back their smiles as they listened to Krishna.

'But he's right,' Bhu said. Best we go via Mugling, it takes no longer.'

'And is safer,' Anne said.

They left Naubise for Mugling on the Chinese road, which kept low along the valleys between the mountains that reached upwards on each side, through forests of oaks and conifers, sal and pipal trees, jacarandas and the great rhododendrons which Bhu would point out. They passed Jemire and other villages of mud brick houses limed white and thatched, and watched their people tending the fields and the cows and goats grazing.

For much of the way the road ran beside the Trisuli River. Harry would look out at the river, its waters crystal clear and cold from the Himalayan snows, rushing and swirling over great boulders, and in other places streaming over flat grey river stones and patches of white sand. Sometimes the banks the river had cut were steep, in other places flat and wide and lush and settled with a farm house or two and fields of growing crops.

'It's a very scenic road, Harry. Beautiful, don't you think?' Anne asked. Harry agreed. The scenery, the river, the farms on its banks, the forests, all delighted him.

'It's a good road for an army to take,' Bhu said. 'The Raj Path is different. People say that India built the Raj Path high around the mountains to make it too difficult for a modern army. I think they meant the Chinese army. Difficult for it to get to India.' Bhu laughed. 'The Chinese might have had that in mind when they built this easy road along the valleys.'

'I can't see either road being useful to an army today,' Harry said. 'They're too vulnerable to aircraft. A few bombs would bring the mountain sides tumbling down over them and finish them off.'

'The Chinese wouldn't want to go to India. They must find their own problems quite enough,' Anne said.

It was midday by the time they reached Mugling, a town for travellers tucked away amongst its forested hills—a junction, and a stop-over for a meal or a night's rest. Here cars and buses, trucks with their engines grunting and exhausts fuming were constantly coming and going. Passengers were getting in and out of buses, or up and down from their places on the roofs. Many people crowded around the central area. They were Nepalese, mainly, and some Indians and Westerners, stretching their legs or buying refreshments from the little stalls selling drinks, sweetmeats, bananas, oranges and tea brewed over a little brazier.

A few dogs and cows wandered about and a large black bull had claimed a place on the roadway and was lying there lazily chewing its cud. On one side of the central area a dozen or so little hotels abutted each other, some only twelve feet wide, roughly built and brightly painted, the smallest hotels Harry had ever seen.

'Very inexpensive, Harry. Fifty cents a night about, but not too bad. And the restaurants here are cheap.'

Krishna chose a restaurant run by a friend, who found them a table. Harry looked dubiously into the kitchen, open for all to see. It was black from years of soot and smoky, with old iron pots, water in a forty-four gallon drum, and battered rice bins; one fowl was being plucked and others were waiting in the kitchen to be killed.

It amused Anne. 'Perhaps it's your first experience, Harry. Oh, what shall I call it? Culinary underdevelopment, that will do.'

'I suppose it is.'

Bhu frowned. 'I must say our kitchens do need improving.'

'Oh, you get by,' Anne said. 'You'll be all right, Harry. Eat only cooked food. Drink beer, not the water.'

Harry started the meal with some trepidation but managed the chicken curry and rice and the Star beer well enough.

Through the afternoon they continued south along the Chinese road to Bharatpur, then back eastward over the flatter and more open land below the Mahabharat Ranges into Makwanpur and on to Hetauda.

There Anne, Bhu and Harry booked into the Hotel Rapti, and Krishna went off to stay with one of his cousins. The Rapti, the best hotel in town Bhu assured Harry, was in a wooden building of two storeys that needed a paint and looked generally neglected. It was in Hetauda's main street, which had a general store and other shops, a garage and workshops. Cars and trucks bumped along past children at play and a few cows. Joining Anne and Bhu for a drink, Harry found them sitting near an open window to catch some of the evening breeze.

'Well we're here, Harry,' Anne said. 'Down out of the mountains. Hot weather, isn't it? Back to summer.'

They had changed their woollen jumpers and jeans for cool clothing, Anne into a white frock and Bhu into a silk sari. Harry lingered for a while appreciating the two young women before he said, 'I have two beautiful companions. I'm a lucky man.'

'Oh, come now Harry. Of course you're lucky.' Anne said, 'But we'll get down to business. There's the itinerary I've drawn up for you. It's visits to the training workshop at the employment centre, a Tharu village and then the Mushahar people.'

There was a disturbance in the street outside. Looking out the window they saw twenty or so young men walking along the middle of road, following two who were holding up a banner and another beating a drum.

'It's against the King and his Government,' Bhu said. 'The banner demands a people's government.'

The demonstrators stopped near the Rapti and soon a crowd gathered around them. Someone found a wooden box and a speaker stood on it. For a long time he talked loudly, his face taut, arms flaying the air as he harangued the crowd.

'He puts a good argument,' Bhu said, her approval obvious. 'He touches the people: he's persuasive.'

A second speaker had his turn on the box. Then a third started, and to Harry's surprise it was his driver, Krishna Sarki. But soon that was the end of it. An army van came speeding down the road and pulled up near the demonstrators to let soldiers get out with their batons and guns. The crowd quickly dispersed and the demonstrators ran off. But Harry saw soldiers taking stragglers and moments later he heard shots from further down the street.

'Perhaps Krishna is hurt,' Anne said, concerned.

Bhu, who had hurried out the front door to look along the street, came back. 'Not too bad,' she said, relieved. 'Their shots missed. No one was hit and most got away. The soldiers took two or three, no more.'

'Thank goodness for that,' Anne said. 'You know Bhu's a rebel, Harry.'

'A progressive,' Bhu said. 'There are many like me.'

'Do you demonstrate, Bhu?' Harry asked.

'I do,' she assured him.

'Could be dangerous for you, demonstrating,' Harry said, thinking how small she was, and would have little strength in a street fight; how easily her slim body could be crushed in a crowd out of control.

Bhu waved the danger aside. 'People must demonstrate. They have no other power. I do it for my country, Mr Clarke.'

The following morning Krishna had the jeep waiting for them in front of the Rapti. 'So you got away yesterday, Krishna,' Harry said. 'We saw you demonstrating.'

'I was lucky.'

'Bad luck for us if we'd lost our driver.'

'Do you object to what I did, Mr Clarke?'

Bhu answered for Harry. 'I think you were really brave, Krishna. I admire you for it.'

That day Anne and Bhu took Harry to look over the employment centre's training workshops, where the head instructor welcomed them. Bhu pointed to the buildings, 'Trainee masons and carpenters built them, Mr Clarke,' she said proudly. 'And trainee brickmakers made the bricks. Come and we'll show you the carpentry workshop.'

'You must realise it's basic, Harry.' Anne said. 'It is simple training, but it meets a local need. They have only hand tools and not enough of them, so you won't think it well equipped. But there's very little money.'

The workshop was indeed basic. On the grass outside, trainees were hewing planks from a great sal log with an adze and axes. Inside was dusty and the earthen floor was covered with shavings; it smelt of cut timber. Trainees were smoothing rough planks with planes, sawing them to the lengths required and stacking them in a corner. Harry watched the trainees at work, all young men and most little more than boys, neatly dressed, some in trousers and shirts and others in white loin cloths. Without stopping their work, their fresh brown faces would look up at the visitors, with shy glances from black eyes. As Anne and Bhu looked back at the young trainees, Harry saw proud smiles lighting their faces, and a softness in their eyes. Their maternal feelings at work, he thought, but he saw also professional satisfaction.

'Do they always work so hard?' he asked.

'They're good students, almost without exception.' Bhu replied. 'They pay great attention, and they make the most of the opportunity.'

'Many are from villages and some from the country towns. Some from Tharu villages,' Anne said.

Bhu asked the trainees to stop work and gather around. She interpreted as their instructor talked about the table and chairs they were finishing, the properties of the sal wood and the need for better hand tools. Rustic no doubt, Harry thought, but well enough made, strong too, and adequate.

'There's a good market for the furniture,' Bhu said. 'It's not expensive. It's a comfort for village people to have some proper furniture in their houses.'

The head instructor brought Harry to other training courses that afternoon. There were trainee masons laying bricks to build another workshop and trainees cutting slate for roofing. In the printing workshop trainees were busy with their sets of typeface, working an old treadle job press and using a paper cutter. The job press reminded Harry of the Sarkis in Kirtipur, and he wondered if they had used the two thousand dollars he gave them to get the press up from India.

Finally, they went to the weaving, cutting and stitching courses. Harry watched the trainees at the hand looms, those cutting cloth from patterns, those using the sewing machines, and praised their work—the runs of cotton cloth, the finished children's clothing, saris, shirts and blouses. The young women here were neatly dressed in their saris and protective aprons, all still wore bangles and had tika marks on their foreheads; their black hair was tied back from their faces and away from their work. They were very shy, keeping their eyes turned down and, except for a quick glance or two from the braver ones, away from Harry.

'You must frighten them, Harry,' Anne said, smiling.

'It takes time for women to get used to me.'

'Oh, not all women I hope,' Anne replied, as the instructor made tea for them.

Next day Anne took Harry out of Hetauda westwards for some miles and back part of the way on the road to Bharatpur. They turned into a rough track along a hilly part, through stretches of elephant grass and a thick sal forest, and out into a broad clearing of cultivated fields and a Tharu village. Anne asked Krishna to drive slowly and stop some distance from the village. 'They'll see us,' she said. 'We'll wait. If we're welcome, they'll come to us.'

Harry looked over to a group of about two dozen grey-looking huts, made from bamboo plastered with clay and cow dung; their thatched roofs extended out from the walls on crooked poles to give shade. The openings in the walls served for windows and doorways. A haze of blue smoke from the cooking fires hung low over the village, and crude farm implements, large clay pots for water, and straw baskets were scattered about. A water buffalo grazed in a field nearby, a pig was foraging around the huts, a cow wandered about the village and fowls pecked to find seeds and grain. The villagers stirred when they saw the jeep. People appeared from their huts and those working in the fields came walking back to the village.

Anne watched Harry taking it all in. 'It's a backward village,' she said. 'Most Tharu villages are very poor like this one, very backward. The people barely survive, Harry.'

'But it has charm, Anne. It is picturesque, I'd say.'

'Picturesque, Harry?'

'Yes, I'd say so.'

'Oh yes, picturesque,' Anne said, irritation on the edge of her voice.

A young man from the village walked over to the jeep, joined his hands in a namaste with a welcome smile for Anne. 'I know him,' Anne told Harry. 'He learns carpentry at the employment centre.'

Speaking slowly to allow for his limited English, Anne told the young man she had brought Mr Clarke to meet the village headman and the other elders, to talk about the employment centres. She would like them to come and talk. The young man ran off and before long several village elders came and sat on the ground under the long branches of an old banyan tree not far from the huts. The old weather-beaten men, rugged and with brown wrinkled faces, were dressed in dhotis hanging loosely from the waist and cotton tops, and some wore a jaunty Nepalese topi cap. They welcomed Harry with polite namastes, their manner dignified, and nodded their approval, smiling, many with toothless smiles.

The village elders treated things very seriously that morning under the banyan tree, talking slowly and choosing their words carefully. They told Harry that people in their village needed many things. Their numbers were increasing each year, and now there was not the land to grow enough food. Many were now idle for much of the year and they wanted more work. The elders knew the Hetauda Employment Centre trained people in different skills, and they were sad that only one of their own young men was there.

They wanted skills so they could get jobs in Hetauda and Bharatpur, also to make things to sell in the market. Some talked of using the cane and bamboo they had to make furniture, and making rope from the local babi grass. Some wanted to keep bees for honey, which was almost unheard of in the district. Others talked of such things as making mats and other goods from the rice straw, of making bricks and tiles from the clay they had and using their straw to burn them, or making bamboo walking sticks, as well as cutting the slate they had for roofing. They also talked about joining with other villages to build a school and a health centre, and improve the forest tracks. They told Harry they wanted to build better temples, that many Tharu villages needed better temples.

At length the village headman apologised for their talking so long and invited Harry and Anne to join them in drinking tea. The village had prepared for them and watered the lanes to help lay the dust, and the foraging pig had disappeared. Women stood outside, dressed in colourful blouses and short red saris, the tops pulled up over the back of their heads. They watched timidly, keeping a distance. 'They are dressed for the occasion,' Anne whispered to Harry.

Near the centre of the village they had a crude shrine where they worshipped their ancient animistic gods, as well as the Hindu gods they had adopted; and sacrificed he-goats to Kali Bhagvati and pigs to the ancient spirit Goraiya—a spirit said to bring great evil to the village if his worship were neglected. Inside the village headman's house, Harry really saw the Tharus' poverty, the bare earthen floor and crude furniture, a black iron pot near the hearth, just a few clay pots, a straw basket and bedding rolled up in a corner. At one end of the room, an earthen ball topped with an iron trident and holding a piece of gold represented the family god, Mainyan, and another ball, of plain earth, represented Goraiya.

When the time came to leave, the elders farewelled Anne and Harry with polite namastes. The village headman looked closely at Anne and his old face implied that they had done their bit in telling her of the villagers' needs, that it was now for her to muster help for more of his people.

As they drove back to Hetauda, Anne finished her notes and looked curiously at Harry from her seat in the back of the jeep. 'What do you think of it, Harry?' she asked. 'Could there be an article for your newspaper. At least a start of something about the plight of a Tharu village.'

'Could be, Anne. I'll think it over.' Harry replied.

'A little of the generous gift your cousin is making could be used well here. They need help to make a start, Harry.'

'Perhaps, Anne. But there are also other needs for the money. We'll see.'

Anne bit her lip and her brow wrinkled in a frown before she replied, 'There are other things, Harry. Oh yes there are. Tomorrow I'll show you people who are even more picturesque.'

After breakfast next morning at the Rapti, they left to visit a group of Mushahar people who lived further east along the Terai, in the Mahotari District nearly a hundred miles away. They drove south into the Siwalik Hills as far as Patlaiya and then turned into the road the British had built along the eastern Terai. For many miles the road was shaded by the tall trees of thick sal forests, and Bhu made sure that Krishna took care to avoid the monkeys which would scamper out on the road and the partridges which would fly lazily across the jeep's path.

Out in the open country Harry soon realised that he was in a tropical Nepal in the dry season, hot even in February. The fields stretched away each side of the road, some parched and cracked and waiting for the monsoon rains that would not come for some months. Others were a lush green with irrigated crops and dhoti-clad peasants and grey water buffalos at work. There were farmhouses roughly built of wood and thatch-roofed, with their ploughs and carts and their farm animals about, and here and there an isolated banyan tree or a pipal tree broke the flatness. In some parts the road was busy with stout-wheeled drays lumbering their way, hauled by grey water buffalos or black oxen. They were piled high with fodder or carting other produce from the farms, their drivers slumped in their seats and letting the draft animals go on at their own pace.

'This is a different Nepal,' Harry said.

'It's more like India,' Bhu said. 'You see many people here who are Aryan-looking. They have eyes shaped like yours Mr Clarke, different from mine.' She gave Harry a smile that narrowed her own soft almond-shaped eyes. 'India is only a few miles from here. and people come and go. It's often hard to say just where the border is.'

Anne pointed to the roadside stalls. 'A lot comes from India, Harry. much of what they sell. They're things the people here could make for themselves, and Indian people come and take many of the jobs here, trade jobs, labouring work too. The Nepalese have to sit and watch, poor things. It's a shame.'

Reaching the town of Janakpur, Krishna inched their way along the streets crowded with pedestrians, cars and trucks, rickshaws and slow-moving oxen carts. Janakpur was an ancient, once cultured, town and well planned with many temples; but the years had not been kind to it. They bought fruit at a market square and made a meal of it in a pleasant park. Then Bhu had Krishna drive to the Janaki Temple near the centre of the town.

Harry was pleasantly surprised at the beauty of the temple set in its great square. For a long time he stood gazing at its long marble facade which gleamed in the early afternoon sun. His gaze took in the graceful doors and windows, and roofs picked out in terracotta, its ornate parapets, and four beautiful domed towers like minarets. Magnificent, he thought.

'It was built for a Queen of Tikamagarh who was here once,' Bhu said. 'It's like a building of Moghul India. It's Sita's temple, a very holy place.'

Bhu told Harry about Sita who married Rama, the story from the Ramayana. Long ago, King Janak ruled Janakpur and was preparing one of his fields for a fertility ceremony when he found a baby girl in a furrow. He took her to his palace and called her Sita, and she grew into a lovely princess renowned for her great beauty and purity. King Janak promised her in marriage to the man who could bend a great bow, which Lord Shiva had given him. Suitors came from many places to try their strength—nobles and warriors—but none could bend Lord Shiva's bow. That was not until Rama came.

Bhu went on to tell Harry about Rama. In early times the diabolical King Ravena and his demon followers, spirits of the foulest depravity, ruled and spread evil over heaven and earth. Brahma the Creator, had promised Ravena he would never die at the hand of a god; but he agreed that Ravena could die at the hand of man. Hearing this, Vishnu decided to reincarnate himself in the form of a man who would kill Ravena. For this he chose the three childless queens of King Desaratha who ruled in Ayodhya in northern India, and had them drink a nectar containing his divine essence. Each gave birth to a son. The eldest and chosen one was Rama Chandra who grew into a man with many good qualities: great strength and courage, manly beauty, wisdom and compassion. People came to adore him. Rama Chandra took on the task he was created for and, helped by a band of divine and powerful monkeys under their leader Hanuman the Monkey God son of the Wind God, he waged an epic war against Ravena and his demon hoard.

Bhu told how one time when he had fought Ravena and annihilated a band of his demons near Janakpur, Rama went into the town and took Lord Shiva's bow. Not only did he bend it, he broke it with his powerful arms. And so he claimed the beautiful Sita and married her in a gorgeous wedding ceremony, a splendid procession and beautiful flowers and music which fell to earth from heaven to indicate the pleasure of the gods.

Rama took Sita to his home in Ayodhya, but there was trouble for them there. King Desaratha, to please his youngest queen who was under the spell of a wicked servant named Manthara, exiled Rama to the forest. In Rama's absence the evil Ravena captured Sita and carried her off. Many times he subjected her to his lecherous advances, but each time Sita resisted him. Then when Hanuman found where Ravena was holding Sita, Rama and Hanuman and his monkey warriors resumed the fight against Ravena. Eventually they slew the arch fiend, drove off his horde of demons and regained Sita.

Bhu broke her story to look at Harry. 'You see good triumphed over great evil,' she said happily.

But when Rama inherited the Kingdom of Ayodhya, the people there demanded that he should put his wife aside on the grounds that Ravena's lustful hands had touched her. Even though the gods proclaimed Sita's chastity, the people persisted in this demand. So Sita, anguished and in tears but determined to let nothing touch the honour of her beloved husband, pleaded with him to let her leave him. Eventually Rama agreed and reluctantly let her go into the forest to live.

'People come to Janakpur each year to celebrate Sita's marriage to Rama,' Bhu said, with a touch of pride. 'Many thousands come from far and wide. Sita is a model for all women. She is an example for every wife.'

Harry looked at Anne, but she had turned her face away.

Driving out of Janakpur, Anne directed Krishna past farms and villages towards Khairbani, then off the road and onto tracks over parched and rugged ground until they came to the place of the Mushahar people. It was hardly a village. There were a dozen or so crude dwellings amongst the trees, hovels with sticks holding up a roof of leaves and with walls made of branches dabbed with clay and baked hard in the hot sun. These Mushahar people had very little, a few water pots, some tin ware and baskets lying on the dusty ground, a few hens, a pig, a few scrawny dogs, but nothing much else.

Here the people were lean and wan, and appeared cowered as they stood outside their hovels looking back at Harry. The men wore sparse loin cloths, women were in grey rags, the children naked. Harry glimpsed several elderly people sitting inside a hovel, naked, shrivelled and bony, almost cadavers. Their glassy eyes stared out at him, from their darkness to the hot sunlight. For the first time Harry looked into the face of utter poverty.

Bhu stepped forward and several of the men came up to her, joined their hands in a namaste and bowed low.

'Bhu knows them,' Anne told Harry. 'She can speak a little of their language. She's saying you have come to see them.'

The Mushahar men turned towards Harry, welcoming him.

'Bhu will talk to them about some of their young men being trained,' Anne said. 'They have no land of their own, Harry. Landless labourers, they work for a rich peasant who lets them live on a corner of his land. Their life is terribly hard. Their work is seasonal and their wages are a pittance. They can't grow crops for themselves or keep more than an animal or two, and have little or no schooling so can't read and write. The sick have little help from doctors and hospitals. They have no skills to build their temples. It's sad, Harry. They are amongst the saddest people I've seen.'

Anne looked at Harry, wondering about his reaction, then said mockingly, 'And do you find these people picturesque also, Mr Clarke, the Mushahar people here?'

Harry, uncomfortable, turned from her gaze.

'You could say something about them in your article. I suppose your paper would be interested in them.'

'Yes it could be, Anne.' But Harry was thinking that countless instances of poverty had been written up over the years, and that people had been bombarded with it by all parts of the media. He thought he would need something more for an article, a new slant, something different to capture the readers' interest.

'I'm wondering if there's anything really different about these people,' he said. 'Something to give flesh to a story about them, liven it up a bit.'

'To titillate your readers, Mr Clarke?' Anne asked icily.

'If you want to put it that way, Anne.'

For some moments Anne stared at Harry, then said with a wry smile. 'Oh, the Mushahar people eat rats, Harry. They often have to. They often have nothing else to eat. That is true, only too true. Their name in Nepali means people who eat rats. Would that titillate your readers?' Then her face saddened.

Harry took her hand. 'I shouldn't have asked that. Of course I see the plight of these people, and your great concern for them. I feel sorry for them myself. You and Bhu can tell me all about them and I'll fit them into an article. Publicity might lead to some good for them.'

'And money from your cousin's gift,' Anne asked.

'Perhaps, Anne. I'll see. No one could say they don't need help.'

Back at the Hotel Rapti that evening Harry was left to himself. Bhu told him that Anne had a headache and was staying in her room, and Bhu herself was fasting, and soon went to off to offer her evening prayers to Lord Shiva as she often did. Perhaps he had been thoughtless, Harry told himself, thinking he would need to go carefully with Anne.

But next morning Harry found that Anne had a smile for him when she came down early. 'I'm afraid I was rude to you yesterday,' she said. 'I'm sorry. You're new to all this. I should have understood. So please let me apologise.'

'Not at all,' he said. 'It is I who should make the apology. It was thoughtless of me.'

Waiting for breakfast, Anne stayed talking with Harry. He learnt that she came from Bristol in the west of England, had studied at London University and had lectured there for a while. She had worked with the International Labour Office and then had come to Nepal to work with their Ministry of Development under a grant from the London Institute of Development Studies. A few months ago she had gone on home leave, but was glad to be back in Nepal again. She was very attached to Nepal. She liked the country, its beauty, the scenic grandeur, its climate, and the people and their customs. And above all there was her work, which was of great importance to her.

Harry wondered. He pictured Anne with a partner or a husband settled in a suburb with children, perhaps with a research job or university teaching on the side. 'Don't you find it lonely, your life here?' he asked her.

'Oh not at all, Harry.' She read his thoughts. 'I suppose you think I should be settled down, have a family and all that. Even get married.'

'I didn't say that.'

'But you thought it. I can tell. Well one day, perhaps, I could marry and have a family. But not yet. There's too much to be done here, too much more for me to do.'

They talked on. She asked Harry to tell her something of Australia. Then she talked a good deal about the problems of the village people, suggesting points for the article for his newspaper. As their breakfast came, she lent closely to him and said, 'The money from your cousin could help a lot of village people, Harry. It would be well spent, very well indeed.' She lent and kissed him on the cheek. 'It would make me happy. You're a nice man, Harry, I know that.'

Seven

Back in Kathmandu there was a message for Harry to meet Ram Maske in Pad's Bar. He found the old man in the lounge near the image of the golden peacock with the electric light shining down on his face. Ram Maske joined his hands in a welcoming namaste and ordered a scotch for Harry and a fruit juice for himself. 'From what I hear you have been busy, Mr Clarke.'

'Yes. Moving around a little.'

'I hear that some young people in Kirtipur have a printing press. I also hear that Sarki people and others are busy printing subversive leaflets. Leaflets for a great demonstration. The printing press came from India.' Ram Maske smiled. 'One of my trucks brought it up from Roxaul. It was generous of you to give the two thousand dollars. It was also rash, I would say. You are a visitor to our country.'

'It was done in confidence, Ram Maske.'

'I know that, and I have undone it. The printing press has been paid for from my own funds. It is surely my responsibility, and no one in the Government would dare take any action against me. I am returning your money. I hear the Sarkis have printed pamphlets for Democracy Day, fifty thousand and more.'

'Democracy Day?' Harry queried.

'It goes by that name and is coming soon, the 18th of February. On that day in 1951 the good King Tribhuban promised Nepal democracy. It is celebrated each year with the civil servants and the army marching and bands playing and the politicians and the King there.'

'But there's no democracy in Nepal to celebrate,' Harry pointed out.

Ram Maske's old face broke into a grin. 'It is all an act, Mr Clarke, for forty years an act. But I hear the coming Democracy Day will be different. It is planned that the people of Nepal will rise and confront the King. Hundreds of thousands some say.'

'As many as that?'

The old man shrugged. 'Perhaps not. The people's leaders will not be there. Many activists are in prison, leaders from the United Left Front like Sahana Pradhan and Bishnu Manadhar are under arrest. I hear that the Nepali Congress' three top people are being put under house arrest—the supreme leader Ganesh Man Singh, Krishna Prasad Bhattarai the party president, General Secretary G. P. Koirala.'

Ram Maske changed the subject. 'Have you decided how to spend your cousin's gift to Nepal, Mr Clarke?'

'I would like your views on that,' Harry said.

'I know what is being put to you,' Ram Maske said. 'There is a modern factory at the Balaju Industrial Estate where you went with the American Bruce Singer. And the amusement park Mr Brown and Pierre Lamonde spoke to you about during dinner at the Annapurna restaurant. There is the family planning project that the Director Tej Shamsher mentioned. There are also the employment centres you learnt about when you went down to the Terai with the English young woman, Anne Jackson, and Bhu Vamsi.'

'What would you choose, Ram Maske?

'No, I would not choose for you. It would be wrong. We are different kinds of people, very different I should think. Our Dharmas are different, you might say. The path you must walk is different from the path I must walk. You must keep to your own way.'

Early one morning, when Krishna came with the car to the hotel, he told Harry there were rumours of bad trouble at Pokhara, a town a hundred miles or so to the west of Kathmandu on the beautiful Lake Phewa and overshadowed by the great white Maccha Pucchare Mountain. Krishna told Harry that the day before—the 12th of February Harry remembered—many students had gone to Pokhara from Kathmandu to take part in a march. Some of his cousins had. Bhu Vamsi had. The police had attacked the marchers.

'Was it a demonstration against the government?' Harry asked.

'It was not to demonstrate. They went to rejoice at the release of Mr Nelson Mandela from prison in South Africa. They intended to have a procession, a peaceful march. Do you know of Nelson Mandela, Mr Clarke?'

Harry assured him he did. 'But why go to Pokhara, Krishna?'

'Our King was in Pokhara, I think, staying in his castle near the lake there. Nepal, too, has political prisoners, hundreds of them. Mr Mandela's release should be a lesson to our government, a warning that times are changing.'

'Are you worried about your cousins?'

'I am, none have returned yet.'

'Have you any news of Bhu Vamsi?

'No, Mr Clarke.'

Harry did not have to wait long for more news. Anne joined him at breakfast.' I'm terribly worried about Bhu. Have you heard about it?' she asked.

'Only that there was trouble in Pokhara.'

'People went there to celebrate the release of Nelson Mandela,' Anne said. 'A lot here admire him. Many do everywhere, no doubt. But here he is special because Nepal has had its own political prisoners for a long time.'

'Did the police break up the march?'

'I'm afraid it's much more than that, Harry. Five hundred students marched in Pokhara, mainly men but a hundred young women as well. Many riot police were brought in. Hundreds. The police attacked with batons, only a few at first and the march continued. But towards the markets and further on, riot police were waiting and they attacked viciously. They fired into the students and soon the march was broken up. People were injured, some killed maybe. The marchers dispersed, and the police chased after them with guns and batons, up and down the narrow streets. Pokhara is an old and hilly town, Harry.'

'And Bhu?'

Anne looked through the restaurant window out over the hotel gardens then turned to Harry, her face drawn. She was tense with anger. 'The women students were no match against the police. The police chased them, caught many of them and carried them to a woman's hostel.'

'Was Bhu amongst them?'

'I don't know. It was horrible for them. Some police went wild, quite mad in fact. Armed with guns and sharp kukhries, they stood over the young women. They threatened them, stripped them of their clothing, then laid them on the beds and assaulted them in the vilest of ways. It was a night of rape and terror for them.'

Harry was amazed. 'The police really did that, Anne?' he queried. 'Are you sure?'

'People are saying so. I believe it.'

'The police will be charged, surely. I heard the King was in Pokhara. Action should be taken against the police.'

Anne shook her head. 'Maybe it will, but I don't know.'

Anne's eyes were moist, and Harry's heart went out to her. 'There is my car and Krishna,' he told her. 'We could drive to Pokhara and find Bhu, bring her back with us.'

Anne lent forward and took Harry's hand. 'Thank you, it's very kind of you, but I'm imposing on you.'

Harry assured her she was not.

That morning Harry had Krishna check that the car was in order for the trip. He got a few things together then picked up Anne and set off for Pokhara, through the town, on to the Raj Path, and along the valley to Thankot. But they got no further than there. Police stopped them, turned a deaf ear to their pleadings and directed the car back to Kathmandu.

The next morning, a holiday with the offices closed, Harry decided to call on Anne to see if she had news of Bhu and if there was anything he could do to help. He walked across the hotel grounds, through the iron gate, past the ancient high brick wall and along the brick paths between the flower gardens, to the white stucco and terracotta roofed buildings set amongst the trees. Anne welcomed him and asked him in, saying she was about to make tea.

The flat was bright that morning with the sunlight streaming in through the windows and the open door. The bookcase was full of books, a typewriter and several files covered the table, and a sewing machine stood in a corner. The mask of Ganesh was still looking down from the wall. Vases of flowers decorated the sideboard, the window sill and the top of the bookcase. Harry knew them well, the petunias, stocks, daisies and pansies, fresh and bright with a touch of scent from some.

'Nice flowers,' Harry said as Anne returned with the tea.

'Yes, I like having them. They're from the garden outside. The hotel gardeners bring them to me.'

'Have you heard any news of Bhu?'

Anne shook her head. 'Nothing.'

'How can I help?'

'I don't think there's anything we can do just now. The road to Pokhara is still blocked to us. I checked.'

Anne sipped her tea, staring into space. 'I've been thinking that Bhu might have been more than a match for the police.'

Harry looked doubtful. 'She wouldn't have the strength. She's too little.'

'Bhu is clever. She might have sensed what was coming. The police are dumb, Harry. Or many of them are. Bhu could outsmart them. Get away.'

'How?'

'I don't know, but she could.'

'Well let's hope so.'

Anne sat looking at the sunlight streaming into the flat. 'The days are beautiful this time of the year,' she said. 'I'll leave my files alone today. Would you like to see something more of the valley, Harry. Visit one of the temples? There is the Bodhnath. It's very old, the largest temple in Nepal, where the lamas from Tibet worship. We could go there.'

They drove out east of Kathmandu, with the Himalayas rising high to a blue sky and their snow and ice glittering in the sunlight, then on towards the massive Bodhnath, the ancient stupa dating back at least fifteen hundred years. From a distance Harry saw the Bodnath's spire and, above it, the gilded pinnacle reaching sky-wards, sparkling where the sun touched it, and its prayer flags of many colours waving in the breeze. Drawing closer, he saw the great painted eyes of the Adi Buddha, stern and watchful as they looked out from the sides of the toran. They drove through the township that had grown around the Bodhnath and the Tibetan village. They reached the Bodnath's great garb, a huge white hemisphere, a solid austere mass standing on a huge base of three wide terraces, one rising above the other and set in the pattern of a sacred mandala.

They mingled with the crowd of pilgrims from many places, monks in their robes of dark red or yellow and tourists in western dress. And there were Bhotia people from Nepal's high mountains dressed in colourful coats and aprons, bulky fur-lined boots, their tall ornamented hats, and wearing a profusion of jewellery of red coral, turquoise, necklaces, earrings and bangles.

Anne led Harry around the great stupa, walking with the crowd in the required clockwise direction. They stopped at a stone image of the Amitabha Buddha seated on his stone lotus flower; he was the father of Padma Pani the Buddhisatva who was given the task of creation and then the governing of the world. Anne and Harry turned some of the great prayer wheels as they passed, sending up to the gods many times the paper prayer inside, the mantra Om Mani Padme Hum, Hail to the Jewel of the Lotus.

At his gonpa the Chinya Lama welcomed them and invited them in. He was pleased to explain the paintings of the gonpa's four guardians at the entrance. He told them that two were friendly and welcoming, Kuvera the yellow-faced God of Wealth, who nursed a small animal with coloured jewels coming out of its mouth, and Dhritarashtra the white-faced King of the Incense Eaters. The other two were suspicious and forbidding, the green-faced Virudhaka who was King of the Giant Demons and the red-faced Virupaksha who looked fierce and held a basket of jewels on his knee. The Chinya Lama then displayed some of his sacred implements, the bronze thunderbolt which was the male symbol of power, the bronze bell which was the female symbol, a silver water jug with its sacred peacock feathers, and oil lamps, mirrors, and musical instruments used in worship.

The Chinya Lama then told Anne and Harry a little about the gonpa's large painting of the wheel of life, which symbolised the unending succession of reincarnations. He pointed to the central circle indicating the three basic vices: a red rooster for lust, a green snake for hatred, and a black boar for ignorance. The white half of a sacred ring depicted a god leading people upwards to heaven, and the black half indicated people being dragged down to hell.

He told them of the six sections of the wheel representing the six worlds for reincarnation: there was the pleasant world of the gods; the world of the demi-gods trying to gain the tree of knowledge; the world of men which had a little Buddha pointing out the path to bliss; the benign world of animals; the hot and frigid hells for sinners; and the world for the greedy ones of earth who were doomed to hunger and thirst forever. Yama, the God of the Underworld, was depicted holding up a mirror for a departing soul to look back on its life on earth and judge itself, while a bird-man nearby used white and black balls to add up the good and bad during life: to decide to which world the departing soul should go.

They thanked the Chinya Lama and Harry left a donation. Then they visited a Tibetan silversmith's workshop of fine jewellery, rings and necklaces, pendants, bangles, earrings and amulets and other charms. Many pieces were set with turquoise or other semi-precious stones. Harry noticed Anne take up a little silver figure of a goddess.

'It is Tara,' she said, handing it to him. 'The White Tara. It's nicely done.'

Harry looked closely at the delicately worked face of the little silver goddess, her forehead with a third eye, her crown, necklaces and bangles. Her body was seated on a silver pedestal, her breasts bare; she held lotus flowers and her left hand was extended in the preaching position. 'It is nicely done,' he agreed.

'It's beautiful,' Anne said. 'The White Tara is an important Buddhist goddess, as a redeemer and a protectress she has great power. I believe she represents the Shakti which is the awesome supreme power that is embodied in all that is female.' Anne glanced at Harry and smiled as she continued, 'It's said Tara is reincarnated in all worthy women. She is a good goddess. Good at least some of the time.'

'You seem to like her, Anne.'

'I like the idea.'

'Of women's awesome power?'

'Of a woman's power to attain her goals. What's wrong with that?'

It depends on the goals, Harry was thinking, but he said, 'I want to buy the silver goddess. Give it to you as a present.'

Anne frowned. 'That's patronising, Harry.'

'No. It's to say thanks for your bringing me to the Bodhnath,' he replied as he beckoned to the silversmith.

'If you want to,' Anne condescended. 'I'm making an exception this time.'

Eight

They had taken a table near the fire at the Sun Kosi and ordered a lunch of wonton soup, momos and Star beer. 'I want to talk about your cousin's gift, Harry, the hundred and fifty million rupees,' Bruce Singer said. 'There are hundreds of uses for the money in Nepal. But I have just the project for it.'

'Sounds promising, Bruce. What is it?'

'A glass works, Harry. A modern glass works to make sheet glass mainly, but other glass as well. There's nothing in Nepal just now except a small bottle works down on the Terai. There's a great need for it here. Glass for housing, factories, public buildings, shops, offices, and of course more. It's all imported now, Harry. There'd be significant savings in foreign exchange. And there'd be foreign exchange earnings with exports to Sikkim and Bhutan, across the border to Indian towns and even to Tibet one day. A modern glass works, Harry, with the latest technology, efficient and competitive.'

Harry sipped his beer thoughtfully.

'Come, Harry. I hope you haven't already decided what to do with the money. Not the Bank people's Disneyland, I hope. It couldn't be that.' Bruce laughed. 'Mickey Mouse, Donald Duck and all the rest, Harry.'

'They want to talk again.'

'The family planning, Harry?'

'I'm looking into it. Can see it's badly needed.'

'You rather like it, Harry?'

'I do. But haven't decided yet.'

'What about the employment centres?' Bruce asked with a hint of a smile. 'You've had a look at what they're doing down in Hetauda and round about. No doubt the girls showed you some of the villages, some of the poorest I suppose.'

'Yes they did,' Harry confirmed.

'But money's the catch, Harry. Believe me, there's a vast number of things wanting money in Nepal. Nepal's amongst the ten poorest countries in the world. We've got to get our priorities straight. We've got to spend what money there is where it will do the most good for the economy—get the market going better.'

'That sounds reasonable,' Harry agreed. 'There's a lot in what you say.'

'There certainly is. Look what's happening in South Korea, Taiwan and Thailand. Good planning, I know because I worked in South Korea. You could say it's a rich country now. And all done in two or three decades.'

'Yes, there's a lot in what you say,' Harry reiterated. 'I'm depending on your advice, Bruce. It's not in my line, the economy.'

'Then why not follow my advice, Harry?'

'I'll consider it most seriously.'

As the waiter came with their bill the two sat for some moments looking into the fire glowing in the hearth. 'I suppose you'll want to talk further with Anne about the employment centres,' Bruce said with a knowing glance.

'Yes.'

'She's an attractive young lady, Harry.'

'Most attractive.'

They paid the bill and left the Sun Kosi and walked out into the Durbar Marg on that cold February afternoon.

That evening in the bar Pad came up to Harry smiling and his black eyes glistening. 'Bhu Vamsi is back from Pokhara,' he said. 'Unharmed, I'm told.'

'Great news, Pad. I'm delighted. I am pleased for her.'

'I'm told she sensed bad trouble coming when the police first attacked the marchers. She knew she'd have no chance in a fight so she made a break for it. And she got away. She ran off down along the Pokhara streets to the lake.'

'Good for her.'

'She decided to get well clear of Pokhara, so hired a taxi and went down into Palpa. It's a most dangerous road, Mr Clarke, worse than the Raj Path, a narrow road, the surface broken and badly in need of repair. The grades are steep down the mountains and it winds around deep drops and precipices. I heard she stayed a day or two with relatives who have a farm near Dansing. Then she went on to Tansen—but the telephone was out of order there—then on to Butwal and Mugling, and back to Kathmandu.'

'You said she's unharmed?'

'Yes.'

'Thank God for that.'

Early the next morning Anne telephoned Harry to confirm that Bhu was back in Kathmandu. She also told him that there was to be a sacrifice at Dakshin Kali, an offering to the goddess in thanks for Bhu's safe return. The sacrifice was that day because it was an auspicious day for such things. Bhu's relatives and friends were organising it. Harry was welcome to come and she would like to go with him in his car.

After the morning mist had risen, Anne and Harry left the Hotel Laxmi for Dakshin Kali, fifteen miles away near the southern end of the valley. On the way, Krishna told them that, save for two in gaol, his cousins had returned from Pokhara, although some were knocked about by police batons.

The road to Dakshin Kali went south, past Parechap and on to Pharping, sometimes skirting the Bagmati's banks, sometimes on high ground when Harry would look back to the chain of Himalayan massifs silhouetted sharply against the bluest of skies, dominating the north. Past Pharping they stopped the car at the top of the long stone stairway that led down, between high hills green with forests and grasses and touched by snow on their peaks, to the terracotta colours of Dakshin Kali's ancient temple and sacrificial pit in the hollow below.

'Only some will be sacrificing for Bhu's return,' Krishna said. 'Most will sacrifice to Kali because they want her favour with the great demonstration on Democracy Day.'

'Dakshin Kali is Kali of the South,' Anne said, pointing down the stairway. 'The temple is very old. People say that long ago Kali appeared in person before an old Malla King and ordered him to build it for her. Countless sacrifices have been made there, of cocks, he-goats, rams, and sometimes buffalo.' Anne lent towards Harry and spoke softly, 'And once humans were sacrificed to the goddess at Dakshin Kali. Once it was allowed.'

Krishna overheard. 'That is true, Mr Clarke. And perhaps it still happens. Some people think it does. It is said that sometimes an old man will disappear, sometimes a young girl, with no trace whatsoever. People say the Tantrics have got them. They hide the girl in the forest, train her in their rituals and use her in their orgies. Then one dark night when no one is about, the Tantrics will bring their captives to Dakshin Kali. They will sacrifice them to the goddess. It is said the Tantrics make a powder with the bodies, which they use for incense.'

'Come now, Krishna. That's going a bit far,' Harry said.

'Some believe it,' Krisha replied, his face solemn.

'Bhu's friends have brought two goats to sacrifice,' Anne said. 'Will we go down to the temple? Sacrifices are not my thing really, but it's for Bhu's sake.'

They walked down in the hollow, across the old stone bridge spanning the icy mountain stream, to the sacrificial pit, which was already busy. They watched priests sacrificing the many animals, cutting their throats with their long knives and holding the bodies high for their blood to spurt on Kali's symbol at one end of the pit, then cutting off the heads and placing them there for the goddess. Blood washed the tiled floors of the pit and stained red the priests' white robes and their bare arms, and their legs and feet as they waded through it, then it ran out to colour the nearby stream. To one side of the pit, assistants were working at several little braziers, holding the bodies of the sacrificed animals over the hot coals to burn away any unshaven hair or remnants of plucked feathers, then they washed the carcases in the water of the stream.

Anne led Harry over a small hill to a grassed field where people who had sacrificed had gathered in their groups. They joined Bhu's friends who had two large copper cauldrons set on stone fireplaces. Some of them lit the fires, some cut up the goats and put the pieces in one of the cauldrons with herbs and spices, while some cooked rice in the second cauldron. Others were opening bottles of beer and handing them around, or glasses of raksi for those wanting the strong rice spirit.

'A picnic,' Harry said to Anne.

'They have worshipped Kali. Now they'll enjoy themselves.'

Harry saw Bhu Vamsi talking to others, still looking well in a red and blue sweater warm against the cool air, with large golden earrings, her black hair shining in the sunlight. She came up to Harry, 'Thank you for coming to Dakshin Kali, Mr Clarke. I hope you enjoyed the sacrifice, and now the feast.'

Harry congratulated her on her safe return,

'I was a lucky one,' she said. For a moment her dark eyes flashed sparks of anger. 'Others were not lucky. It was tragic for them, and it was an insult to many. To Mr Mandela far away in South Africa, and to all who marched to celebrate his release from prison. And to all people in Nepal. The world is dismayed with us. We must make amends.'

Harry did not disagree.

'You will have heard of our Democracy Day, our coming demonstration,' she said, looking around for Krishna.

'He's joined his cousins who are also sacrificing here,' Harry told her.

'Yes, they too will be seeking Kali's favour. The goddess will favour us, Mr Clarke. Democracy Day will bring a new Nepal for all of us. The people will confront the Government and the King. The masses will demand democracy. They will not be denied. Then we will make amends for very many things. Please wish us luck, Mr Clarke.'

'Of course I do,' Harry assured her. 'And particularly for you. You're a brave lady, but be careful. Take good care of yourself, Bhu.'

'I have managed to do that so far. I shall take care.' she replied.

It was not long before the meal of goat and spices and rice was ready in the steaming cauldrons. Anne and Harry joined people sitting around on the grass eating from paper plates and enjoying their beer or raksi. When the meal was over, more drink was served and people talked and laughed at the jokes. Some danced in little groups, others picked wild flowers on the grassy slopes.

Anne and Harry walked with others up along a steep track to a pleasant little temple set high on a nearby hill and looking down over forests and green fields. There, the image of a goddess was adorned with flowers and jewellery, who Harry learnt was a mother goddess, the mother of Kali they told him. Anne and Harry watched the others at their worship, then they joined them to make offerings of a little money and have the old temple priest put tika marks on their foreheads and flower petals in their hair.

As they left the temple they met Krishna and his Sarki cousins coming up the hill, one's head was bandaged, another's arm was in a sling, another was limping. Ari Sarki came up to Anne and Harry. 'We have sacrificed to Kali for Democracy Day, Mr Clarke. Today is an auspicious time and we have been very generous with our offerings. We have offered Kali goats and cocks and a lamb. No doubt we will have her favour.'

'The King and government might also have her favour,' Harry said teasingly.

Ari Sarki thought for a while then smiled. 'It is most unlikely, Mr Clarke. We have the greater numbers. I think she will side with us.'

'I see some of you were injured at Pokhara,' Harry pointed to the bandages. 'Not too badly, I hope.'

'Badly enough,' Ari Sarki replied. 'One of us was badly beaten and will be in hospital for a long time. Two are in gaol.'

Ari Sarki turned to Anne. 'I hear that your colleague, Bhu Vamsi, has returned safely. She was lucky, but also clever. Please congratulate her for me. She is a worthy person. I know she is fully on our side.'

He turned back to Harry. 'I suggest you go to New Road a little after midday to cover the demonstration on Democracy Day, Mr Clarke. This time it will be different, very different.' Ari Sarki's black eyes gleamed. 'The people of Nepal will rise; hundreds of thousands will rise. In Kathmandu we will be waiting for the procession, we will confront the King and his ministers. The people of Nepal will have real democracy at last. No more the fraud of forty years,' he said, bitterly.

Nine

Harry would often rise early and take a walk around the Hotel Laxmi's gardens before breakfast. Some mornings the mist would be thick, blanketing everything, and he would have to peer hard through the whiteness to make out the almost hidden shapes of things now familiar to him: the pot plants on the hotel verandahs, the little temple and its god in one corner of the garden, terracotta elephants on the lawns, the stupa on a grassy rise, and the surrounding old brick walls. Other mornings the mist would be thinner, drifting in white shreds over the lawns, shrubs and jacaranda trees, and rising quickly over the brick walls and up above the great oak trees to dissipate in the blue-grey of the early sky.

Generally Harry used the time to think over how best to spend his cousin's gift to Nepal. Now, having seen something of the country's great problems, he was determined to give the best advice he could. The family planning project he was sure was necessary, perhaps the most necessary of all. The bank people with their amusement park had not impressed him all that much, but he was ready to read the papers they had promised. At the thought of the bank people, Harry remembered that Mr Brown had won a Thai girl in a big Bangkok lottery, and he wondered if she had yet come to Kathmandu. Then there were the employment centres, and the great backwardness of the Tharu village and the abject poverty of the Mushahar people worried him. But Harry was most impressed with Bruce Singer's understanding of Nepal's problems, and the idea of a modern glass works seemed sound. No economist himself, he was rather disposed to take Bruce Singer's advice. But he was not yet ready to come to a decision.

Often Harry found himself wondering about Anne, realising that she attracted him strongly, much more than any of his former girl friends. To him her pleasant face and soft fair hair were delightful, and her shapely figure excited him. And he liked the kindness he saw in her. She was obviously a capable person and he liked that, too. But at the same time Harry felt uneasy about Anne. It was not because she was independent, a liberated woman as Bruce Singer had said, although Harry never knew exactly what women's liberation really meant. He felt uneasy, he decided, because Anne seemed inaccessible to him, to any man perhaps, living for her work up in the shadow of the Himalayas with no time to spare for men, as Bruce Singer had said. True, Harry had good memories of the executive kind of girl friends he had friendships with for a while. But now, with Anne, he was thinking of something longer-lasting, permanent perhaps, even marriage. Why not children before the years caught up on him too much?

When Anne joined Harry for breakfast in the hotel restaurant on the morning of Democracy Day she had decided not go to watch the demonstration that afternoon. 'I know the police and army have been beastly, worse than beastly,' she said. 'They've gaoled many good people and have murdered more than a few. But I'm not a demonstrator by nature and it's certainly not my place to demonstrate in Nepal.'

Harry agreed.

'Bhu will go,' Anne said. 'I know she'll take an active part. I've pleaded with her to be careful. I was worried enough about the trouble in Pokhara and so glad she came back safely. I'd hate any harm to come to her now.'

'I'll keep a watch out for her,' Harry said.

Harry left the Hotel Laxmi mid-morning to be early for the demonstration that was to bring democracy to Nepal. Krishna parked the car off the Kanti Path near Ratna Park, saying it would be safe there. They turned through the great white stucco gate into New Road, the modern commercial centre, which was still busy and crowded in spite of the fact that the demonstration was being held in the afternoon.

People went about their business as usual, the shops were open, and there was a stream of cars and trucks and bicycles, and tourists from many countries. They walked on, to a square with a little temple under the shade of a large pipal tree, and Krishna remarked that a number of young people gathered there talking excitedly with each other were students waiting to demonstrate.

Further on, they came to the statue of Juddha Shamsher, the Rana prime minister from 1932 to 1945. Krishna stopped and for a long time stood looking up at it. Harry waited, watching Krishna, surprised to see the contempt and so much hatred in his young face. When they left Juddha Shamsher set in stone, Harry took Krishna to the Hotel Crystal in Shukra Path and into its old bar and restaurant, a room panelled in dark wood and dimly lit. It had the pleasant musty smell some old pubs have. He ordered Star beers and Krishna agreed to join him for a lunch of curry.

'You don't like Juddha Shamsher's statue, Krishna,' Harry said. 'I saw that.'

'I do not. I have no love for the Ranas, especially for the evil Juddha Shamsher.' Krishna pointed in the direction of New Road. 'It was once named Juddha Sadak for him. New Road is a better name.'

Krishna told Harry how Juddha Shamsher had tried the young men of the Praja Parishad—non-violent young men who sought to foster democracy—for high treason. Four of them, Dasarath Chand, Sukra Raj Shastri, Ganga Lal and Dharma Bhakta Mathema, were condemned to death. One winter's night, in the darkest hours and away from watching eyes, Juddha Shamsher's soldiers came to the Kathmandu prison, took Sukra Raj Shastri and hanged him from a tree in nearby Teku. Then they took Dharma Bhakta Mathema and hanged him from a tree on the road to the Pashupatinath. They bound Dasarath Chand and Ganga Lal together on bamboo poles and shot them near the Bhagabati Temple. The four bodies were left exposed for all to see: a warning to those who disputed Juddha Shamsher's rule.

'Yes, Juddha Shamsher was evil,' Krishna repeated. 'We will always remember the four young men of the Praja Parishad and honour them.' Again Krishna pointed in the direction of New Road. 'Four streets just near here are named after the young men. They are streets that lead away from Juddha Shamsher's statue, and will carry their names forever, Mr Clarke.'

When Harry left the Hotel Crystal, the traffic had cleared in New Road and shops had put up shutters. Demonstrators were out in increasing numbers, students most of them, and more kept coming out of the narrow cobbled streets that connected New Road with the old town. As Harry passed the square with the little temple and pipal tree, Ari Sarki came hurrying out to him.

'The time is near. The people are coming. They are about to speak,' Ari Sarki said excitedly, waving his arms and turning his head to point along the street towards the Kanti Path. 'Before long very many thousands will be here to demonstrate. We will be ready for the procession when it comes, ready for the king's ministers and generals. We will get justice. The people will have their rights. Newspapers across the world will proclaim our success. Your newspaper also will do so, Mr Clarke.'

'I'll write up today's happenings.'

'My cousins are here and ready,' Ari Sarki said, pointing back to the square. 'We will be amongst the leaders this afternoon.'

'Be careful,' Harry said.

Krishna hurried off to join his cousins.

Demonstrators continued to come. But not that many, Harry saw, certainly not the very large numbers expected. Harry kept a look out for Bhu Vamsi but saw no sign of her. He joined a group of foreigners not far from the great white gate at the entrance to New Road, and discovered they were mostly journalists and photographers sent to cover events. Talking with some of them, he found they were from many places of the world. He was looking for fellow Australians when two riot police came and moved on the photographers and any journalists they recognised.

Police action against the demonstrators start suddenly. A wagon came along the Kanti Path, its brakes screeched to a halt, riot police dismounted quickly and grouped together with their batons and shields. Another wagon drew up, followed by another, then others until a large police force was ready to confront the demonstrators. A police chief called through his megaphone, ordering the demonstrators to disperse. His voice, loud and harsh, reverberated around the buildings. There was silence for a while, until one demonstrator called back and then another and another and then a whole chorus demanded the end of the Panchayat system, demanded the right to have political parties and to vote in fair elections. They wanted the people's right to govern themselves. The police chief ignored these calls, again ordering the demonstrators to disperse, and repeated the order several times. But there was no response. Police and demonstrators stood confronting each other.

Harry and others withdrew back along New Road and waited for the coming fray, and didn't have to wait long. Masked riot police emerged from everywhere. They shot tear gas into the crowd until the air was filled with stinging and blinding fumes. To escape the pungent gas the demonstrators ran back along New Road and into the narrow streets of old Kathmandu. The police advanced in force, their batons beating, clearing the way of demonstrators.

As the demonstrators were fleeing, the Democracy Day procession made its way full of pomp and colour along the Kanti Path. The Prime Minister and Home Minister led, riding in a carriage and ignoring the riot police attacks on their young countrymen. But each had to hold a damp cloth to his face to ease his eyes from the gas that lingered in the street. Harry watched the army band in their uniforms of red and green and gold and the bandmaster's great shining silver mace topped with crossed kukhries. Well-drilled soldiers marched in their smart brown uniforms, their red and white belts, and caps with a red band and a red pompom on top. Then came men of the royal cavalry mounted on beautifully groomed horses, in red tunics and snow-white breeches and black boots and shining helmets with red plumes. And last the public officials marched in black jackets, round-necked white shirts, jodhpurs and topi caps.

But the demonstrators had not given up. A group of students came running out from the narrow streets of old Kathmandu and hurled stones at the marching soldiers and public officials. The police chased them back, in their turn hurling stones after them. As the procession passed, more students came, hurled more stones at the marchers, only to be chased back by the riot police.

Harry went back to his car which was parked near Ratna Park and waited until there was no sign of remaining demonstrators and the last of the riot police had gone, when the town was quiet again. After a while he saw Krishna walk slowly out from the old town onto the Kanti Path near the Bir Hospital, look cautiously about, then hurry along to the car. A little later Bhu Vamsi followed him.

'You are hurt,' Harry said to Krishna, seeing his bandaged head.

'It is nothing, Mr Clarke. A stone the police threw hit me. The hospital bandaged it for me. They said the cut will heal quickly.'

Bhu Vamsi's black hair was dishevelled, mud covered her jeans and her face showed her strain and dejection. Harry opened the car door for her and she sat there quietly. 'We'll drive you to your home,' Harry said.

'Please,' she said very quietly.

'Are you hurt, Bhu?' Harry asked.

'I am tired. That is all. It is Nepal that was hurt today. The people did not come, only students and people from political parties that are banned. The mass of the people did not come. It is sad, for us, Mr Clarke.'

Nothing more was said that afternoon. Bhu Vamsi and Krishna were silent, lost in their own disappointed thoughts as they drove to Bhu Vamsi's home and then back to the Hotel Laxmi. Later that evening Harry prepared copy for his Sydney newspaper.

Ten

After the demonstration on the 18th of February, Prime Minister Marich Man Shrestha's Government stepped up action against the movement for democracy. It reinforced the curfew to keep people off the streets at night, tightened censorship further and banned newspapers supporting the movement. And it ordered mass arrests of students, teachers, university professors and others, and strengthened the riot police and hired experts in the martial arts—brutes some of them—to take on the movement's activists.

'What is happening yet again in my country horrifies me,' Ram Maske commented. 'The government is reacting brutally. A thousand or more have been arrested, gaoled without trial, most put into makeshift prisons with hardly any food and filthy sanitary conditions. The victim's names are kept secret and their relatives are denied access to them. Many are tortured or beaten, their limbs broken.' He shook his head sorrowfully. 'More activists died recently, Mr Clarke, forty throughout Nepal, I hear. The police in Chitwan shot dead or wounded several people. A dozen or more were shot dead at Bharatpur and Narayan Ghat. Several died near the road to Heta Netaura; six have been killed in Bhaktapur and others wounded.'

'They used dum dum bullets in Bhaktapur, Mr Clarke,' Puskar Maske continued shaking his old head sadly. 'They're terrible bullets that fly apart when they hit and make a horrible wound, a gaping hole in the victim's body. Once the British used them against the Indian people. They made them at Calcutta in their arsenal at Dum Dum. But we are worse,' the old man said bitterly. 'We kill our own people with them. We kill ourselves.'

'Surely it will stop,' Harry said.

Ram Maske shook his head. 'Brutality has its way now in my country, not brotherhood. It is very sad. I am a Mason, Mr Clarke. All the people of Nepal must become brothers. You must come to our temple. I must build many temples for Masons, temples in many places.'

Marich Man Shrestha's Government's persecution of the movement for democracy brought many protests. University teachers went on strike, the Nepal Journalists' Association protested against the ban on newspapers and censorship of the press, and lawyers and doctors condemned the use of dum dum bullets—some lawyers refused to attend the courts and doctors and nurses at the Tribhuban University Teaching Hospital went on a twenty-four hour strike. Even some forty members of Nepal's National Panchayat protested against the use of force and an assistant minister resigned.

And there was world-wide condemnation of happenings in Nepal. The United State's State Department expressed its concern and wanted the repression and violence stopped. Some aid donor countries indicated their disapproval, with their ambassadors telling the government that aid would be cut if repression did not stop. The Asia Watch Organisation condemned the occurrences in Nepal and published details of some of the atrocities against human rights.

Then in early March there was a lull in the struggle for democracy, less violence and not so many soldiers in the streets. The police were less provocative, although their secret agents and informers were still there, and the curfew was relaxed a little. There were no more strikes and many of the activists who were still free kept to their houses. With this lull most of the foreign journalists left Nepal, returning to their home countries or going to other places that their editors thought more newsworthy. Harry was one of the very few foreign journalists left in Kathmandu.

When Krishna told Harry that Ari Sarki was not well and was confined to his house, he suggested a visit. Harry agreed, wanting to wish him a quick recovery, and hoping to get more information for his paper. Carrying a block of Swiss chocolate which he found in a shop in the Durbar Marg and a bottle of scotch, Harry followed Krishna up the steep path to Kirtipur, through the town gate, along the narrow cobbled streets to the central square. He waited for Krishna to announce his arrival, then went into the house, into the room with the earthen floor and the hearth and pots and the shy women who stole a glance at him, and then up the ladder to the top floor. Ari Sarki got up from his chair, joined his hands in a namaste and welcomed Harry as he appeared in the room.

'I hear you are not well,' Harry said, giving him the gifts.

Ari Sarki thanked him. 'Not seriously ill. I'm told to rest up for a while.'

'Were you injured on Democracy Day?'

'Only bruised where the riot police hit, stiff and sore though. I'd best keep out of action for a while, out of sight of the police.'

'Things have calmed down,' Harry said.

'For a while only.'

'Foreign journalists have left Nepal.'

'They misjudge things. You stay here and you'll get a good scoop before long, Mr Clarke.'

'When?'

Ari Sarki pointed through the open window out towards the snow-capped mountain in the distance under the blue sky, to the sun shining down on the square below. 'Your wait will not be that long. The winter is going, the days are getting warmer. Our New Year is not far off. It comes in your mid-April, in our month of Baisakh. The New Year will bring a new Nepal.'

'A new government?'

'Yes.' Ari Sarki's face was serious as he continued, 'We have a legend, Mr Clarke, about a beautiful princess who lived in Tokha village in the hills to the north-west of Kathmandu. She fell in love with an old man who was riddled with leprosy. She married him. For this, she lost favour; her father disowned her and her people made her an outcast. It all seemed hopeless for the princess. But then she was told in a dream that her husband's leprosy would go if she bathed him on the day of the New Year in a nearby pond, the Sapena Tirtha which means the pond of dreams. She bathed her husband there. The water washed his leprosy away and he became a handsome young man. Then the princess was accepted again by her father and her people.'

'Are the people of Nepal dreaming, Ari Sarki?' Harry asked.

'They are. They are dreaming of their rights, the right to have political parties, the right to vote. Things will not remain calm for long. The people will rise and realise their dream. The masses of the people of Nepal will rise. The New Year will bring a new Nepal, Mr Clarke.'

At that time Harry had a telephone call from Mary Clarke's solicitor in London to say that she was very ill with a serious heart problem and her life was threatened. He told Harry that she had read in the London papers about the trouble in Nepal, the riots and the killings, and it disturbed her. She had not yet made final arrangements with the money for Nepal, and was now doubtful about going on with a gift to people who rioted against their King and government. Harry's letters were not enough. She wanted him to come and talk with her. The solicitor advised Harry to come immediately, because she might not last much longer, so he had put airline tickets at Harry's disposal. Harry made a booking to leave the following day, then rang Anne and invited her to dinner that evening in the Hotel Yak and Yeti's Chimney Room.

The Yak and Yeti, one of Kathmandu's fine hotels and five-star by almost any standard, is in a street off the Durbar Marg not far from the royal palace. It is a converted old Rana palace, the Lal Durbar or Red House, which the Rana prime minister, Bir Shamsher, built after he murdered his uncle, Prime Minister Rana Udip Singh, and assumed power in 1885.

Harry welcomed Anne when she arrived at the Yak and Yeti and led her to seats in the lounge near the hotel foyer and ordered drinks. A waiter took her cloak, and Harry saw that she had taken trouble for the night out, noticing the mauve Indian silk of her frock, her fair hair thick and glossy, the gold bangle and earrings, and her touch of perfume. She smiled happily as she settled into the lounge chair with her drink.

'You're beautiful tonight, Anne,' Harry said.

Anne smiled again. 'Thank you. It's nice of you to ask me out. And I like the Yak and Yeti best of the restaurants here. I'm sure you'll like it too, Harry.'

Harry felt his pulse quicken as he looked at her. There and then, he told himself that he wanted her, wanted to take her back to Sydney, set up house with her, to marry her. But he said, 'I must tell you I'm off to London, Anne.'

'Oh, to London. When?' Anne tensed, surprised. She looked at Harry, waiting for an explanation.

'Tomorrow.'

Anne's lip dropped. 'So you're leaving us, Harry. It's a little farewell dinner tonight. I suppose you've written up the troubles here for your paper. You've decided how your cousin's gift is to be spent.' Anne's throat caught a little as she said, 'There was the article on our employment centres, Harry, the poverty you saw. The village people are still there.'

Harry felt her relief when he told her he would be away only a week or less perhaps, that he would be back.

They left the lounge and walked along the narrow corridor and down an old passage with its steep stairs. On their way Anne showed Harry the banquet room, not in use that night, still with its Rana extravagance of marble and tiles, and great crystal chandeliers. 'It was a Rana palace once,' Anne said. 'Bir Shamsher's palace. He lived in luxury. Imagine the great parties he gave here.'

'And the ladies of his harem,' Harry said. 'Wives, concubines, dancing girls. A hundred of them or more.'

Harry saw Ann's nose pucker. 'These walls would have heard a lot.' She touched the old brick.

'Bir Shamsher's parties, his gala evenings?'

'No, the women's suffering, Harry, imprisoned in the harems, the Ranas' slaves. It was wrong. It ought not have happened. And ought not still be happening.'

'Is it?'

'Of course it is. Even in England and your own country. The home can be a prison for a woman and often is.'

Harry did not agree, but said nothing.

Down the stairs in the Chimney Room, its old brick whitewashed in places, once a place for dungeons perhaps, the head waiter welcomed them. He showed them to a table not far from the fire which was blazing in its hearth, a great round hearth half as wide as the old room and open to all sides, its big metal chimney gleaming, its wide throat hanging over the fire to take the leaping flames, the round flue going high up through the roof.

Harry was impressed. 'Just the thing on a cold night, Anne.'

'Cozy,' Anne said. 'And atmosphere. May I ask why you're going to London?'

'I'm afraid there's a problem with my cousin's gift to Nepal. Her solicitor rang saying there's some doubt about her going ahead with it. She's read the London papers about the riots and killings here. And she's worried. She doubts if she should make a gift to a country that rebels against its King and government. She's also ill, Anne, near her end very likely. Her solicitor advised me to come quickly and talk to her.'

'Poor thing. I'm sorry to hear she's so ill. Her idea of a gift is marvellous, very generous. But I don't think she understands.'

The Chimney Room was almost full when Harry noticed a waiter seat a couple at a table over on the opposite side of the fireplace, a young woman with a stout man past middle-age and florid-faced in a blue suit. Harry recognised Mr Brown from the Asian and Pacific Bank. The young woman he could not see properly, because of the chimney flue.

'Have you met Brown from the Asian and Pacific Bank, Anne?' Harry asked, indicating the table. 'He's just come in.'

Anne looked over. 'The man with the Thai girl? I've heard of him doing business here for his bank, but I've never met him. Doesn't interest me much. His bank would have nothing to do with the employment centres.'

'He won her in a lottery,' Harry said, laughing.

Anne was puzzled. 'How do you mean?'

'Won her in a lottery in Bangkok, and tickets for the two of them around Asian cities, the best hotels, all expenses paid.'

Anne froze as she sat there and Harry quickly smothered his laugh and sat looking at her.

At last she spoke. 'Oh, I don't believe it. I've never heard of such a thing. What a disgusting man this Mr Brown must be even to buy such a ticket. Where are his morals? What would his bank say?'

'Don't blame me, Anne. I'm dead against that sort of thing.'

'Of course you are, Harry. Every decent man would be. The girl's a prostitute of course?'

'A university student, I'm told.'

Anne shook her head vigorously in dismay, her hair brushing around her cheeks. 'An intelligent girl, or supposedly so, selling her body for money? It's disgusting.'

'I shouldn't have mentioned her. It's spoilt your evening.'

'No, you should have, Harry. I'm glad you did. I should know about such things. And it hasn't spoilt my evening at all.'

The wine waiter refilled their glasses and their main course came.

'Let's forget Mr Brown and his Thai girl.' Harry said. 'How is Bhu Vamsi keeping?'

'Oh, she's well, recovered from the demonstration on Democracy Day and not so depressed about it now. In fact she's talking about another attempt, one where the masses of people will really come out of their houses and confront the government and the King.'

Later when they had almost finished the meal, a waiter carried in logs to replenish the fire. They watched him stoking it, sending sparks racing up into the flue, the flames burning high and free again. On the other side of the fireplace Mr Brown also watched the waiter attending to the fire, then he looked across in Harry's direction. A few minutes later he came over to their table and stood looking down at them.

'Thought I recognised you, Mr Clarke,' he said. He looked at Anne, 'With your charming companion.'

Harry introduced her.

'Tell you what, Mr Clarke, we'll come over and join you for coffee.' He glanced back towards his own table. 'My friend and I. You don't mind, do you?'

Harry was hardly pleased, but he checked with Anne and agreed. A waiter moved up two more chairs and brought coffee for the four of them.

'Miss Siam,' Mr Brown introduced his friend, winking at Harry.

Harry glanced at her, curious, taking her in. A pleasant face, he thought, dark eyes, olive skin, full lips, long black hair, in her early twenties and wearing a dark red dress, a turquoise necklace and earrings.

'I hope you don't mind,' she said with hardly any accent. She looked at Anne. 'My name is really Miss Pramoj.'

Anne nodded, a little stiffly Harry thought. 'I hope you enjoy your stay here, Miss Pramoj.'

'Thank you. Well stay in Kathmandu a little while because Mr Brown has work to do here. Then we're going on an Asian tour.'

'I'm sure that will be nice for you. I suppose you and Mr Brown are old friends,' Anne said smiling.

'No, not old friends. Only a few days. Mr Brown bought this for me,' she said touching her turquoise necklace. 'He's a nice man, a charming man.'

Anne looked quickly at Mr Brown then turned away.

'She's a university student,' Mr Brown said. 'In her final year.'

'A degree is important,' Anne said. 'And very practical at times, Miss Pramoj.'

'I want to talk to you about your cousin's gift to Nepal,' Mr Brown said to Harry. 'You remember the bank's proposal.'

'Yes, I read the files you sent me.'

'Much to be said for it, Mr Clarke. Big profits, no doubt about that. Have you come to a decision?'

Anne turned to Harry with a questioning look.

Harry told her briefly about the amusement park, then Mr Brown added a lot. He spoke of the idea of halls covering mountaineering and big game hunting, Nepal's wars, the country's history and so on, with plenty of electronics, virtual reality even. Anne listened attentively, too attentively Harry thought.

When Mr Brown mentioned merry-go-rounds, magic mirrors, haunted tunnels and a ghost house, Anne showed her annoyance. 'You can't be serious, Mr Brown,' she said, shaking her head. 'You can't be serious about wasting money on such frivolity, on such trivia. Such a waste of money in a country as poor as Nepal. And what an affront to centuries of Nepalese culture. I'm afraid I find the idea objectionable, most repugnant.'

Mr Brown was taken aback, but only for a second or two. 'It would be very profitable, Miss Jackson. But perhaps you cannot understand that.'

'I understand very well, Mr Brown.'

'Perhaps profits don't matter to you, Miss Jackson. Money just doesn't matter.'

'You are also insulting, Mr Brown. It's one of your charms apparently,' Anne said icily.

Her anger surprised Harry.

'Come now, Miss Jackson,' Mr Brown persisted, 'Think how. an amusement park would attract tourists and bring money into Nepal. And we would build a miniature Mount Everest.'

'Where?'

'Here in Kathmandu, on the Tundikhel. The whole project would be there.'

'Good God! So much of their history is there.' Anne said.

The Thai girl intervened. 'Mr Brown is a very good business man. I'm sure of that already, Miss Jackson. I don't think you should disagree with him.'

Anne looked back at her for a few moments before she replied. 'And you, Miss Siam as your winner calls you, you too seem to be good at business. Oh yes, you are good at business, Miss Siam.'

Harry saw Anne holding back her tears.

Miss Pramoj stood up, glared at Anne, took her cup with the dregs from the coffee and tossed it over the table cloth. 'That was cruel of you,' she said. 'But I suppose you can't help that. You are only an English snob.' She turned and flounced off with Mr Brown following her.

Anne sat in silence for a minute or two, crest-fallen. She looked at Harry. 'It was really cruel of me. I was wrong. I should not have hurt her. Mr Brown is to blame. He's a hateful man.'

When they left the Yak and Yeti, Anne and Harry walked through the cold night back to the Hotel Laxmi past the high walls of the royal palace and into the Kanti Path under the rows of tall oak trees. Bats were hanging high in their branches, some were gliding from tree to tree. Anne was still upset. She said little and Harry did not try to make conversation.

At length Anne said, 'I'm sorry, Harry. I spoilt your evening, and it was so nice until that nasty Mr Brown came over to us. I should have behaved better.' She reached for his hand. 'And you didn't finish your coffee. Come and I'll make you some.'

They went over to Anne's place, she switched on the lights, turned up the heating stove and went into the kitchen to make coffee. When she came back with the coffee she sat beside him. 'I hope I'm forgiven,' she said softly with a touch of a smile.

'There's nothing to forgive, Anne. Everyone gets annoyed at times.'

'You don't like that Thai lottery either, do you Harry?'

'No.'

'Do you like Mr Brown? I think he's hateful.'

'Not much,' Harry replied.

'Do you like his amusement park?'

Harry was well aware how badly Anne thought of the idea, and, sitting there with her that night, he certainly was not going to speak well of it. At the same time he could not dismiss it altogether. He was wondering how to reply when the lights in the flat flickered and the electricity went off.

For a minute or two they sat there. Then Harry said, 'It's nice sometimes, the dark.'

'I could light some candles.'

'No, don't spoil it,' he replied. 'Just the two of us, Anne. The dark locks everything else out.'

Harry lent towards Anne and put his arm around her. He felt her body stiffen at first, but soon she relaxed and let him draw her close to him. Harry's hand stroked her hair, felt for her face and caressed her cheeks. He told her how beautiful he thought she was, how nice her soft hair felt. And he told her how much he admired her for the work she was doing. Before long he sought Anne's lips and she turned her face up to be kissed.

When the electricity came on again and the darkness gave way to the light flooding the flat, Anne stirred and took herself out of Harry's arms. She got up from the sofa and turned the heater up. 'The nights are still cold in Kathmandu,' she said.

Harry waited for her to come back to him, but she did not. At the door Anne wished Harry a safe trip to England the next day, and a quick return. 'The winter is finishing now', she told him. 'But spring will be here when you come back and the weather will be warmer.'

Eleven

In London, Harry telephoned his cousin's solicitor to say he had arrived, then wasted no time in going down to Kent, to the Connor Street house in Hollybrook. A housekeeper opened the door to him, showed him into the room looking out onto the garden where Mary Clarke had served him afternoon tea a few weeks earlier, then went to tell his cousin he had arrived. As Harry waited he noticed that the painting of Christ of the Sacred heart was missing from over the mantelpiece, but the portraits of the Clarke baronets were still hanging on the wall. He could now clearly recognise the Nepalese half of the seventh baronet, his ancestor Francis Clarke.

A nurse in a starched, white uniform told Harry his cousin was sleeping, but would want to see him when she woke. When Harry asked about his cousin's condition, the nurse shook her head slowly, told him it was not good and suggested he talk with the doctor when he called the next day. She also told Harry his cousin expected him to stay in the house and a room had been prepared for him.

It was dusk when Mary Clarke woke and asked that Harry talk with her. The nurse took him upstairs along the darkening hall to his cousin's bedroom, lit by only the last of the grey dusk coming through the windows. Harry saw that this room, too, belonged to the past, with its faded carpet, the french-polished furniture, an engraved commode and an embossed metal ceiling painted in pastel colours. A strong perfume pervaded the room, eau-de-Cologne, Harry recognised it. Mary Clarke was propped up on pillows in a great old bed, with its four posts and a canopy, holding her rosary beads. Harry followed her gaze to the far wall where the Christ of the Sacred Heart now hung with a tiny red lamp glowing on a table beneath it.

The nurse led Harry to a chair beside the bed, Mary Clarke looked up at him and he saw the change. Her face had almost lost its life—in just a few weeks—her bones pressed on her skin, she was deathly pale and her eyes large and staring.

She moved her lips slowly in a smile and thanked him for coming. 'You see I am sick, Henry. Very sick perhaps, and I might not have long before I go to be with Christ and his Father and the Holy Ghost. I hope

I am prepared for them, I have always tried.' She was silent for a while, looking at Harry until her breathing steadied. 'We all should be prepared, Henry, all our lives. You should be prepared. I think that you have lost your religion. You should go back to it.'

Harry nodded.

'Now I have said that to you. It is the most important thing and I hope you will take notice of an old woman. There is also something else I want to talk to you about.'

She fingered her rosary beads and her gaze went back to the painting. Harry waited for some time, then said, 'I think you want to talk about Nepal, about the gift you are making.'

'Yes, thank you for reminding me. I was reading about Nepal in the papers before I became sick. It did not please me, Henry. I read that the people there are arguing amongst themselves, fighting, torturing each other, killing one another. I do not like it.'

Harry started to explain.

'No, Henry, it is bad. They live in sin. It is mortal sin and it offends God terribly. It's sin that will be punished in the fires of Hell.'

'Some do commit sins as you say,' Harry told her. 'But those are few. Most people there, almost all, are suffering. They're not sinners, they're sinned against.'

'No, Henry. It is the good and merciful God who is sinned against. The question is, ought I make a gift to such people?'

Henry tried to explain something of the cause of the trouble in Nepal. Mary Clarke listened for a while then interrupted saying, 'What you tell me is all very well, Henry. But people in Nepal are against their King. That, too, troubles me. In England we are fortunate to have a queen. Likewise they are fortunate to have a King.'

Harry started to tell her how the monarchies in England and Nepal differed from each other, that people in Nepal still wanted a monarchy, one with less power, like in England. But before long Mary Clarke's head lent forward and she fell asleep. The nurse settled her in the bed and told Harry that he could come the next day and talk further with her.

But the next day Mary Clarke was not able to talk, and for several days after. Her doctor told Harry that her heart, greatly weakened by the first attack and too far gone to even think of an operation, had now been weakened further by a second attack which she might not survive for long.

The parish priest also spoke with Harry. He praised Mary Clarke for the devoted life she had led, her years of work with the church, her gifts of flowers and altar cloths, the many vestments she had given to priests over the years, and her generous contributions to parish finances. He knew of the Clarkes' ruby pendant and was not against her idea of making a gift to Nepal, even though it was not a Christian country. The priest's face was sad as he told Harry that for years he had looked on Mary Clarke as a dear friend as well as one of his precious flock. He was hoping that the good Lord would spare her for some time yet.

Mary Clarke was spared for just a little longer and she improved enough for Harry to talk to her again. This time when he went to her bed, he found her with the letters he had written about ways her gift might benefit Nepal: the glass works, the amusement park, the employment centres and the family planning project. He congratulated her on her recovery, slight as it might be, and, when she asked, he assured her he was being well looked after in her house. He started to talk about her gift to Nepal, when she stopped him.

'No Henry, I will say it now, I could not agree to the family planning you mentioned in your letter. You spoke well of it, I'm afraid. But it is disgusting. It's very, very wrong. It would be a terrible insult to our good Pope. How could I face our dear Lord and the immaculate Virgin Mary if I gave money for that? What would they think of me? Her old hand tightened its clutch on Harry's letters. 'No, I could never support a thing so evil.'

Harry started to reply, but stopped. He saw it was no use.

'I am thinking of still making the gift to Nepal,' she told him. 'But I do not know. You said that not all the people there live in mortal sin. And you said that they want to keep their King. Is that right, Henry?'

She thought it over for a while. 'Yes, an amusement park could be nice. People need fun in their lives. Poor people, as you say they are, in particular need some fun to brighten their lives. I think the idea appeals to me. But you used the word Disneyland in your letter, Henry. I would not like it called a Disneyland. Not at all. It's far too American. Something like a village fair would be nice. What do you think, Henry?'

'Perhaps, and what about the others?'

There is the glass works. I would say that a country must have glass. It has all sorts of uses. I find it hard to imagine how they manage without making glass for themselves. They need it for windows for their houses, shop windows, mirrors even apart from anything else. A glass works also appeals to me, Henry.'

'What about the employment centres?' Harry asked.

She thought for a while. 'They are harder for me to understand. I gather from your letter that the centres would help village people there. You wrote about how poor they are, uneducated and illiterate, some with only little farms or no land at all.'

'Many are like that, desperately poor.'

'I feel very sorry for them.'

'Then the employment centres also appeal to you,' Harry prompted.

Mary Clarke shook her head. 'No, I really don't think so, Henry. It's too big a job to help people like that, too hard. The money would be wasted. We will always have the poor, Henry. We always have had them. We can only do a little for them. It is the good Lord who will care for them when they eventually go to him.'

Her attitude surprised and worried Harry. He did not want her to put the employment centres out of consideration, certainly not on the grounds she mentioned. So he spoke about the landless Mushahar people he had seen near Janakpur, in abject poverty, with few possessions, the leanness of their bodies, and that they had to eat rats. He mentioned the naked, shrivelled aged people who had looked out at him from inside the hovels staring at him with their glassy eyes.

'You seem to favour the employment centres, Henry.'

'I don't want them dismissed too quickly.'

'They are unfortunate people, Henry, those you speak of. I shall pray for them. I hope you, too, will pray for them.'

Then the doctor came to check on Mary Clarke's progress and Harry left his cousin. She asked him to call on her again next day when she would tell him of her decision about the money from the sale of the ruby pendant.

But Harry did not talk with his cousin again. Next day she had a third heart attack, one that proved fatal, and she lingered on unconscious for only a few days. Harry waited on and attended his cousin's funeral. On an autumn afternoon, in the company of her heirs who came over from America, grandsons of Sir Anthony Clarke, and some of her friends, Harry attended the old parish church in Hollybrook for a service that commemorated her life and recommended her soul to her god. Her burial was not in the churchyard, where the earlier Clarkes had been laid to rest—which had now given way to a housing estate—but in the public cemetery.

After the funeral, back in the Clarke house where the mourners had gathered for a few drinks and cake and solace, Mary Clarke's solicitor came up to Harry, saying, 'I spoke with your cousin in one of her last lucid periods before she died. I had several matters to discuss. What concerns you are her instructions about the money from the ruby pendant.'

'It wasn't clear what she wanted when she spoke to me,' Harry said.

'Well the money is to go to Nepal, that is in order. All arrangements here in England, which I attended to some time ago, will stand. I shall hold the money and will transfer it to the Nepalese Government when I hear from you. That pleases you, I think?'

'It does,' Harry told him, 'And there is the question of how the money is to be spent. She told me the family planning project was definitely out. That worries me. I think Nepal is in a bad way with population pressures.'

'Yes, family planning is out. You cousin was adamant on that,'

'The others?'

'Mary Clarke instructed me on them. She prefers the glass works project. She said that no country should be without a glass works. I wonder if you agree with that, Mr Clarke?'

'Perhaps.'

'There is the amusement park. She told me she was sure people of a country like Nepal needed the pleasure it would bring. It was her second preference. But it must on no account be called a Disneyland.'

'And the employment centres?'

'She wasn't at all sure about those. She found the idea hard to accept, but did not put them out of account altogether. I hope you don't mind me saying this, Mr Clarke.'

'No, please go on.'

'It embarrasses me to say it, but I must tell you that your cousin believed you have lost your faith in God. She lamented it at some length. Then she asked me to pass on to you her strong recommendation that you yourself should pray for the backward people you told her about. She was sure that prayer was the best thing for them. But she said that if, after another month's research, you came to favour the employment centres, and favoured them strongly, they could have the money. Then she made a condition regarding that, an essential condition she said. One quarter of the money she is giving, that is about three quarters of a million pounds, would have to be used for prayers for the backward people. No doubt that could be arranged if necessary. I hope it is all clear, Mr Clarke.'

The condition surprised Harry but he did not question it. It was part of his dead cousin's instructions and that was that. He thanked the solicitor. 'It is clear,' he said.

'Then I shall wish you a safe return to Kathmandu,' the solicitor said. 'Please let me have your proposal.'

Twelve

Back in Kathmandu, Bruce Singer offered Harry his condolences on Mary Clarke's death, then spoke about the glass works. 'There's been some luck, Harry. One of the big internationals has been here looking around. AGP, do you know it?'

'Heard the name. That's all.'

'AGP is big, Harry. It's in Europe, the States, China, South America, your country too I should think. Fingers in many pies. It's into plastics, chemicals, oil and gas, and so on. And glass, Harry. AGP would start a glass works here. Thinks it would be profitable. A modern glass works, modern in every way. Efficient machinery doing most of the work; not depending so much on a large labour force. Very productive and able to compete. AGP agrees to a joint project with the government. They'll put in five million. The government wants to put in five million and a bit, it wants 51 percent, to have control. That's about your cousin's money isn't it?'

'That's it. But ten million's not a big project for an international, Bruce. They usually deal in hundreds of millions, billions I'd think.'

'You're right Harry. It would be just a start in Nepal for AGP. They'd get a toe in. Get on the learning curve here. Would start up other things here too.'

'Sounds good.'

'Better than good, Harry. It's rational. What a prospect for GNP growth, savings on imports, a foreign exchange earner later, keep the foreign debt in check a bit.'

'Yes.'

'You want to go ahead with it, Harry?'

Harry knew a glass works was his late cousin's preference, but he only said, 'Most likely, Bruce. I'll need think it over.'

'Why on earth think it over, Harry? You won't do better, that's for sure. Don't delay.'

'Just give me a little time, Bruce.'

That evening, Harry walked over to Anne's flat to join her and Bhu for a meal; Anne had invited him, saying she owed him hospitality in return for their evening at the Yak and Yeti. Of course Harry accepted readily. He had missed Anne during his visit to England and was delighted to have her company again.

They offered Harry their condolences for his old cousin's death, then seated him at the table. Anne served the curry and Bhu poured the wine.

'Spring is nice in Kathmandu,' Bhu said.

'It's beautiful weather now,' Harry agreed, looking towards the open window that let in the last of the dusk and a soft breeze. 'You always have flowers, Anne,' he said looking at the vase on the window sill.

'They are nice. The hotel's gardeners still keep me well supplied,' Anne said.

'So you think there will be another demonstration, Bhu?' Harry asked, not anxious for them to raise the matter of his cousin's gift.

'I know there will be, Mr Clarke. And it will be much better than last time. It will be a success. I think it will be soon.'

'The world press doesn't expect it, not soon anyhow. The foreign journalists aren't back.'

'You are back though, Mr Clarke. You will see.' Bhu lent towards him. 'Kathmandu might seem quiet nowadays, on the surface. But things you do not know of are happening. The movement for democracy is still very much alive. One of its leaders, Dr Bhattarai, is very active. All will be ready soon.'

But Anne changed the subject. 'You cousin's gift to Nepal, I've been wondering about it, Harry,' she said anxiously.

'It's all right, Anne. The five million is available.'

'Have you decided how to spend it?' Anne asked, still anxious.

'There's the family planning project,' Bhu said. 'It needs more money badly.'

'Sorry, Bhu. That one is out, definitely out. It's against my cousin's religion. At least the way she looked at her religion.'

'It's a shame', Bhu said. 'Nothing can be done?'

'Afraid not.'

'What about the employment centres?' Anne asked.

'Yes, I want to talk about them,' Harry said uneasily.

'Did your cousin favour them for her gift to Nepal?'

'She preferred the glass works.'

Anne became tense. 'And what about the amusement park?'

'She gave it her next preference.'

Anne winced. 'Not that, surely not Mr Brown's amusement park. How could your cousin do that?' she asked, puzzled.

'My cousin thought the park would provide pleasure for the people, make them happy. She said she thought that poor people in particular need to have some fun.'

'She didn't understand what poverty is.'

'She had no idea, Anne.'

Anne sat there, concerned, shaking her head. 'So your cousin didn't support the employment centres?'

'She didn't rule them out completely.'

'But it is the glass works?'

'We've heard talk about a glass works and the AGP,' Bhu said. 'And Bruce Singer wants it. But the AGP's rich. It's worth not millions, not tens of millions, not even hundreds of millions, it's worth billions—many billions no doubt. What's your cousin's few million to the AGP? Why can't it go ahead with the glass works using only its own money?'

'I suppose the AGP would,' Anne said. 'But I think Mr Singer's Ministry wants to have control for itself.'

'Control an international like AGP?' Bhu laughed. 'Not likely Anne, not even if it were all the Ministry's own money.'

'At least some control,' Anne corrected herself.

'The Ministry shouldn't put money in. The Ministry shouldn't be given the money for that, Mr Clarke. I don't think it would be right.' Bhu said.

Anne looked at Harry, 'I think Bhu's right. AGP wants the profits. The AGP would start the glass works in any case. Why put your cousin's money into it?'

'You might be right,' Harry said. 'I'll talk to Bruce, and I'll think it over.'

'If we're right,' Anne said, 'then the money would go to either the amusement park or the employment centres. There's nothing else, is there Harry?'

'No, but don't go too quickly, Anne,' he cautioned.

'So the employment centres are not out altogether?'

'I said that.'

Anne and Bhu sat there in silence, their eyes firmly fixed on Harry waiting for more of an explanation. For some moments he looked back at them, then, uncomfortable, he turned away from their gaze. 'My cousin instructed that the money could go to the employment centres should I come to favour them after further research—if I favoured them strongly.'

Harry looked back at the two young women and caught the relief on their faces. 'So we still have a chance.' Anne said.

'There's something else. My cousin set a condition to apply if the money were to go to the centres.'

'Oh did she? Of course we'd meet it,' Anne assured him.

'It will surprise you.' Harry hesitated. 'A quarter of the money would have to go for prayers for the village people.'

Both of the young women caught their breath and sat there wide-eyed. 'More than a million dollars worth of prayer. It's too much.' Bhu said.

'Why on earth prayer?' Anne asked. 'So much money, and the village people are so poor. There's so much that needs to be done for them.'

'My cousin thought prayer was best for them. She thought prayer was really the only way to help them, that only God could help people so poor, and that the job was far too big for man.'

'No!' Anne cried, shaking her head regretfully, 'It's wrong. It's very wrong. It's man who has to help. It's the responsibility of man. There is no one else.'

Harry looked at Bhu for her opinion.

'I think that prayer can help,' she said, and Harry heard the sincerity in her voice. 'I often pray to my gods. Sometimes I ask them favours, sometimes I thank them for their help. But I think it is wrong, fully wrong, to expect too much of the gods. It might anger them. There are things for us to do. There is our Dharma, a righteous order for our lives.'

'My cousin's instructions would need be met,' Harry said.

Anne had been listening attentively to Bhu and turned to Harry, 'We'll help you with more research on the employment centres, Harry. We'd be only too happy to. Wouldn't we Bhu?'

'Of course.'

'You could come on another visit with us. We would go to Jomosom, up in the high mountains near the border with Tibet, so you can see the need for an employment centre in the Mustang District. There's none there now.'

Looking at Anne, her comeliness, her now warm smile, her pretty face turned to him expectantly, Harry decided he needed to do more research on the employment centres. Any decisions on the glass works and the amusement park could wait. He had no hesitation in accepting Anne's invitation.

Thirteen

The aircraft, a Twin Otter, left Kathmandu's Domestic Airport for Jomosom early on a cool morning in late March, gaining altitude quickly up into a cloudless sky, leaving the wisps of mist in the valley below. Soon it was flying smoothly alongside the majestic Himalayas. The fasten-seat-belts sign went off and a stewardess served tea or coffee and biscuits. Harry looked along from his seat at the back of the aircraft, past the passengers towards the two Nepalese pilots. Anne and Bhu Vamsi in the seat in front of him were dressed in woollen jumpers and jeans, and there were trekkers, a government official and a shaven-headed lama in his dark red robe; and also Bhotia people, the men in reddish brown long-sleeved cloaks, the women in flowing dresses and big aprons with brightly coloured stripes, their black hair parted and plaited, wearing heavy jewellery, bangles, earrings, nose rings and necklaces of silver coins.

Harry's gaze fixed on the great mountains which now towered above as the aircraft flew westward, their huge expanses of ice and cold grey rock and immense white peaks shone in the morning sunlight and were silhouetted by the deepest of blue skies. It was the vastness of the Lantang-Jugal Himal with its towering Gasain Than across the border in Tibet, of the Ganesh Himal and Mansalu which reached almost twenty seven thousand feet, then Himal Chuli and Kang Gulu. Further to the west came the Annapurnas, named for the Mother Goddess Annapurna who was one of the earth goddesses, and a protectress of the peasants' harvests.

The aircraft touched down at Pokhara to let people off, then pick up more passengers bound for Jomosom. One of the pilots clicked the intercom and announced an immediate take-off and that seat belts must be fastened during the whole flight. Aircraft had to leave early of a morning for Jomosom, before the fierce wind blew, a gale-force from the south which could take an aircraft like the Twin Otter and smash it against a mountain side. As the aircraft gained height again, Harry's attention was taken by the mass of the Annapurnas, the beautiful Maccha Pucchare where his gaze lingered. For him, and no doubt many others, it had to be one of the most beautiful of all the world's great mountains.

Then there were the Annapurna's other peaks, Annapurna South, Annapurna I, the mighty Fang and more. They flew close to huge precipices of ice and rock, cold and hard, that went deep down to black depths far below. Upwards, high above the aircraft's path the peaks were drenched by the morning sunlight.

Soon the aircraft was flying over the valley of the Kali Gandaki and woodlands with profusions of rhododendrons and azaleas, over the high Ghorepani Pass and the country of the Thakali people and their little inns which provide inexpensive beds and meals and are popular with trekkers. It flew over the world's deepest gorge, it's sheer walls more than five thousand feet. The beautiful Nilgiri Mountain to the east of the valley rose above a collar of cloud, and to the west the majestic Dhaulagiri I broke through the clouds at twenty seven thousand feet.

Soon the aircraft descended ready to land at Jomosom, where the country had changed markedly. It had became progressively more dry and barren in the high altitudes and the rain-shadow of the Himalayas, until it took on the features of the stony wilderness of the high Tibetan plateau. Turbulence buffeted the aircraft strongly as it flew between the mountains down to land and passengers gripped the arms of their seats tightly.

Once out of the aircraft under the cold blue-grey sky and in the chill wind, Harry pulled up the collar of the down-filled jacket he had bought on Anne's advice. He looked around at the rugged valley, almost treeless, snow on the ground, surrounded by mountains and rocky cliffs. A few black yaks nosed amongst the snow to graze. A little caravan trundled along with its train of sturdy mules, their bells clanging and red cloths and yak tails fixed to their bridles. 'They are setting out down the Kali Gandaki,' Bhu said. 'With salt from Tibet, and wool, and turquoise I would think.'

Bhu pointed to buildings not far from the airstrip. 'The District Office is there,' she said. 'We could stay at the Nilgiri View Hotel. There is another place in the village, not so comfortable, but it is how the people live. You might prefer that, Mr Clarke.'

Harry agreed to that one and followed Anne and Bhu over the snow and across a bridge spanning the Thak Kola, its banks wide and strewn with boulders and little black stones. The river was waiting for summer and the monsoon when the Himalaya's winter snow would melt. They walked into the town along the cold, windy alleys between the long rows of small flat-roofed houses which huddled closely together, houses of mud brick and grey wood, where snow covered the firewood stacked on their roofs.

'This is Chan's house. They take guests,' Bhu said. 'I've been here before. They have little but they are nice friendly people.'

Chan, a small wiry man with high cheekbones and a flat nose, dressed in his brown cloak against the cold, came out into the alley to meet them. He joined his hands in a namaste, bowed low and thanked Bhu for choosing his house again. He led them out of the snow through a covered courtyard with a few farm implements and sheltering fowls, and into the main room of the house. Smiling and obviously pleased to have guests, he introduced his wife and daughter who were waiting there in their aprons of red and blue stripes.

Harry was glad to be out of the cold and in the room which drew some warmth from a fire smouldering in a pit. It was a smoky room and dark, with light only from a little window up near the roof. Its walls were plastered with a mixture of clay and cow dung and its low wooden beams were blackened by years of smoke. A poor room, it had little: an old carpet, a table and benches and chests made from roughly hewn wood, a spindle and a heap of wool waiting to be spun rested in one corner. The kitchen had black iron pots, a cooking tripod, plates and bowls, a heavy pestle and a mortar, and a bundle of herbs hanging from the rafters. Chan asked his daughter to show his guests to the sleeping area in an annexe on the other side of the pit, then his wife served the meal of dal, chicken and potatoes, and tea she had prepared for them.

They were busy all the next week. Anne and Bhu set up in the District Office and people came to talk—from Jomosom, from the town of Mustang near the Tibetan border, from Morpha, Tange, Kabang, Kagabeni and other high mountain villages. Harry learnt of the poverty of the Panchguang and the Bhotia people of the Mustang District. He sat in to listen whilst Anne and Bhu explored the people's needs, their many suggestions: small irrigation projects for better farming, upgrading their roads and tracks, schools and health centres. They suggested a small factory to process wool, a cheese factory, a tannery for yak hides, little plants for generating hydroelectricity, better facilities for trekkers and other tourists, and improved weaving, dressmaking and carpet-making facilities, better houses and temples. People thought they had the small amounts of money needed to set up some of these things. What they lacked were the skills.

During the cold, windy evenings, the three would return to the Chan's house for a meal and then sit at a table with blankets around them and a nearby pot of glowing embers for warmth. Harry would listen as Anne and Bhu considered an employment centre in Jomosom, the practical opportunities, its potential for employment, the finance needed, the trainers and the skills to be taught. Many of them were simple skills such as basic carpentry, building with river stones and rock, stone-breaking and laying for roads and tracks, earth digging and levelling for irrigation channels, hand loom weaving, cutting and stitching.

By the last evening of their stay in Jomosom, sitting around the table with the blankets and the pot of glowing embers, Anne and Bhu felt pleased they had completed their investigations. The two young women looked to Harry for his favourable opinion, expecting him to agree that his late cousin's money should go to the employment centres.

'You must see the need for more employment centres, for a centre here in Jomosom, Mr Clarke,' Bhu said. 'It's so obvious. So much needs to be done. They are simple things and take so little money. Don't you agree?'

'Could be,' Harry said.

'It is really that or nothing for these poor people.' Bhu continued. 'They cannot wait for industry to modernise the cities and then reach out to them. They would all be dead before that, long dead.'

'Perhaps,' Harry replied. 'But hasn't modern industry done well for some countries? There's Singapore, Taiwan, South Korea, the Asian tigers. They're rich countries now.'

'They are different,' Bhu assured him.

'What about Indonesia and Thailand?' Harry persisted.

'No,' Bhu said. 'In many of the poorer countries, in most I'd say, many village people alive today, hundreds of millions—billions no doubt in total—will die a natural death long before modern industry could hope to touch them.'

Anne nodded her agreement. 'Another thing, Harry. Neglect the villages and many of their people go to the cities. They build up shanty towns there, poverty-stricken places. Horrible places with filth and disease, and unemployment, crime too, Harry. I've seen shanty towns with millions of people living in them in Manilla, Calcutta, other places too.'

'Not so much in Nepal, though,' Harry suggested. 'There are too many mountains blocking the way to Kathmandu, and too few roads.'

'It is happening here already,' Bhu said. 'It must be stopped.

Harry did not disagree, but he was still unsure, and still not going to commit himself to the employment centres. So he said, 'A quarter of the money would have to go on prayer. Don't forget that.'

'Oh, would it really have to?' Anne asked.

'My cousin made it a condition so I'd have no option. Her solicitor would require it.'

The two young women sat in silence, troubled. Chan came in with another pot of glowing embers, and eventually Bhu spoke. 'There is a way, which I think would suit the solicitor and not take money from the employment centres. And I don't think the gods would object.'

'What is it, Bhu?' Anne asked.

'Temples,' she said. 'Village people we've met want better temples. They need people with skills to build them, like trained carpenters, masons, painters, brick makers, workers in stone. What is really meant by a quarter of the money being used for prayer? Have priests to be paid to pray, monks paid to turn their prayer wheels?'

Harry thought so.

'Temples are used for prayer,' Bhu said. 'We could spend some of the money on training people to build temples. That would do it,' Bhu said with authority in her voice.

Harry and Anne were in no position to disagree.

'But would they actually build temples?' Harry asked.

'We would see they did,' Bhu assured him. 'After that, the skilled could work on the other things the village people need.'

Harry looked at Anne to see her agreeing strongly.

The next morning the three left Jomosom in the Twin Otter and flew back over the Kali Gandeki Valley to Pokhara. On landing, they were told of a minor fault in the engine and that the aircraft would not be going on to Kathmandu that day. There was a message for Bhu Vamsi saying that she was wanted in Kathmandu and that a seat had been booked for her on another aircraft, which was leaving immediately. The airline had booked Anne and Harry into the Fishtail Lodge Hotel overnight.

On the landing platform on the shore of Pokhara's Phewa Lake, Anne watched Harry's surprise as he looked over the water to the Fishtail Lodge Hotel set on its promontory on the far bank. Out on the lake, a flat wooden raft was floating towards them with a man standing on it and pulling it forward with a long rope secured at one end to the landing and at the other near the hotel steps.

'We go on the raft,' Anne said. 'An unusual way to get to a hotel, but a nice way, Harry.'

He agreed, watching the raft draw close.

On the raft Anne pointed back to the Annapernas, the Maccha

Pucchare dominating the skyline. She told Harry that the Fishtail Lodge Hotel was named for the Maccha Pucchare, which means fishtail in Nepali. 'Viewed from the west, the mountain's twin central peaks were in the shape of a great fishtail,' she said.

'A beautiful mountain, and quite a lake,' Harry said, looking across the water.

They climbed off the raft and walked up the steps leading from the water's edge, and Harry looked around approvingly at the hotel's well-kept grounds, the expanse of green lawns, shrubs and colourful garden beds. There were neat thatched-roofed bungalows for guests and a larger building for a restaurant and reception.

The receptionist welcomed them and checked the hotel register. 'You are together,' she said uncertainly. 'The airline has booked a double room for you. Is that correct?' She held up a key. 'I've given you number five. It's in one of our nicest bungalows with a lovely view of the lake and mountains.'

Harry looked at Anne enquiringly, his eyebrows raised a little, a hint of a smile.

Anne returned his gaze, smiled and shook her head. She turned to the receptionist. 'I don't know why the airline did that. No, we need single rooms.'

'All our rooms are double,' the receptionist told her.

'We want separate rooms.' Anne's tone was definite enough. 'Don't we, Harry?'

The receptionist went to change the key. For some moments Harry looked at Anne, into her face, her blue eyes looking back up at him. 'Do we really, Anne?' he asked.

'Of course we do.' Then she took Harry's hand, saying, 'You can come and get me later and I'll show you around Pokhara.'

That afternoon they went on the raft back over the lake. On the bank there, people from Mustang were selling jewellery, carvings in bone and ivory, and yak tails and other Tibetan artefacts, their wares spread out on carpets on the grass. Harry bought turquoise earrings for Anne and a little brass Buddha for himself. They explored that part of the lake shore, then hired a car and drove to see the deep Seti River gorge, the Tibetan village and Pokhara's museum, and spent time in Pokhara's old town.

At the Fishtail Lodge late that afternoon Anne and Harry watched the sunset from a bench in the gardens overlooking Lake Phewa. They saw the great white Maccha Pucchare being dressed in its evening colours, first the shades of pink, then the pastel reds and violets as the sun went lower. And close in front of them they could see it again, all reflected in the mirror of the lake's waters, clearly, every detail of the mountain and each change of colour. 'The lake is so blue and clear isn't it Harry?' Anne said. 'It's the Goddess Annapurna's looking glass.'

For some time they watched in silence, absorbing the glory of the scene, and they were unstinting in their praise. Harry was sure the Maccha Pucchare had no equal anywhere in the world, and Anne knew of nothing like it—in Europe or elsewhere in Nepal.

After a while Anne looked at Harry and asked, 'I've been wondering if you've thought more about Jomosom, Harry. About having an employment centre there.'

'You've broken the spell, Anne,' he said, laughing.

'Yes, but what do you think?'

'I still haven't decided what's to be done with my cousin's money. I must talk again with Bruce Singer. And there's Mr Brown.'

Anne made a wry face. 'You shouldn't mention Mr Brown in a place like this. Such a nice place. So romantic.' She moved along the bench a little, close to him.

'It is romantic,' he agreed.

'You'll have to decide soon about your cousin's gift, Harry. I suppose you'll be leaving Nepal before too long.'

'Yes, back to Sydney. My paper will be getting impatient. I will miss you, Anne. Very much.' He put his arm around her shoulders.

Anne accepted his embrace. 'Would you, Harry?'

'Have you ever thought of going to Australia, Anne?'

'For a holiday?'

'To live. Settle there. Continue your career there. Have a partner or even a husband, a family perhaps.'

'I've never thought of Australia.'

'What about a family?'

'One day, perhaps. I said that when you asked me in Hetauda.'

For some time Harry sat watching the Maccha Pucchare, acutely aware of Anne sitting beside him, wondering what she thought of him, what affection she might have for him. Then at length he decided it was time to make his play. 'You've become very dear to me Anne,' he said, turning towards her.

'Have I, Harry?'

'Very dear indeed. More than any young woman I've ever known.'

Anne lent and kissed him on the cheek. 'You're a very nice man.'

Harry hesitated again for a while before he said, 'Why not come to Sydney with me, Anne, when I return?'

'Live together, you mean?'

'Yes, that's what I want. I've a flat there. You'd like it. It's roomy enough and comfortable. Harbour views, the Opera House, Harbour Bridge. The block has a swimming pool.'

She smiled. 'You sound like an estate agent.'

'What about it, Anne?'

It was some moments before she answered. 'It is nice of you to ask me, Harry. And I appreciate it very much. But apart from anything else there's my work here. You've seen how important it is, and important for so many people. People who must have a little help so they can do a lot for themselves. How could I leave it?'

'I know it would be difficult for you.'

'And we haven't known each other very long. Weeks only.'

'Does that matter?'

'I don't know. Not always, perhaps.'

'I have no doubts about you, Anne. None at all,' Harry said sincerely.

Anne looked up towards the Maccha Pucchare and then at its reflection in the lake. The sun had now gone down, and the colours of the great mountain had changed to mauves and darker purples, and to nearly black where the last rays of the sun had left.

'I don't know,' she said again. 'Not yet. But I do like you, Harry. I might. Let's wait a while and see.'

The restaurant in the Fishtail Lodge had a great round open hearth with its central chimney, like the Chimney Room in the Yak and Yeti Hotel, Harry thought, only much larger and surrounded by seats for guests to sit on. After dinner Anne and Harry joined others there to sip an after-dinner drink and watch the fire, its big logs glowing and crackling and the flames licking upwards. There was little talk between them as Harry turned over in his mind Anne's responses late that afternoon.

Before long they left the restaurant and walked out into the cool night. The waters of the lake were dark except where they were touched by the few lights from the opposite bank; and the beautiful Maccha Pucchare loomed through the night's blackness, now a purple giant of a ghost. They soon reached Anne's bungalow, Harry lingered with her for a while. Then she slipped out of his arms and disappeared inside, closing the door after her.

Back in his own room, Harry thought again of the events of the afternoon. Anne's warmth delighted him, for itself and for the possibilities it might perhaps promise him. She had not ruled out coming to Sydney with him, and he pictured his Sydney flat with her there. He let his thoughts run further, to being married to her, and the father of her children. But Harry soon felt that was going too far. He knew full well that Anne badly wanted Mary Clarke's five million for the employment centres. He also knew she was a well-qualified career woman who valued her career very highly, probably above anything else.

Then Harry began to think if he could possibly give his late cousin's money for the employment centres. The family planning project was out, no matter how necessary he himself thought it, because Mary Clarke had decided that before she died. And he had serious doubts about Mr Brown and his amusement park. But he still saw the glass works as a very good project, and that it was a good idea to get the AGP into Nepal. Bruce Singer's advice to take the glassworks counted heavily with him.

Harry was still thinking about the glass works when there was a knock on the door to his room, softly at first and then a little louder. Wondering, he got out of bed, switched on the light and opened the door. It amazed him, it was totally unexpected. Standing there in the cold night was Anne, with only a blanket around her and in her slippers, looking up at him, looking at him anxiously.

'I'll come in if you like, Harry,' she said shyly. 'Do you want me to? Do you want me?'

Harry hid his surprise but made no attempt to contain his delight. 'Want you to, Anne? Of course I want you. I couldn't want anything more,' he replied.

She came in. For a little time she stood there. Then Harry took her in his arms and drew her to him. They stayed together, closely, Harry seeking her lips and Anne not denying him. After a while Harry took the blanket from around her, lifted her and carried her over to the bed. He laid her there on the white sheet, her head supported by the pillow, her eyes looking up at him.

'You are very beautiful, Anne,' he said to her.

'Thank you,' she said and turned her head away.

'Do I embarrass you? I don't want to do that.'

'It's not that,' she told him. 'But we really shouldn't do it, Harry. Should we? I shouldn't.'

Harry lent over and kissed her gently. Anne responded. Then again she looked away.

'Come on,' Harry said. 'There's nothing to worry about. Nothing to blame yourself for.'

'Are you sure, Harry? Really sure?' she asked.

'Of course, I'm sure. I'm certain of it. You are a darling, Anne.'

Anne relaxed back into the blankets. 'The dark can be nice,' she said. 'You said that once, Harry.'

Harry got up and switched off the light. Back in bed, he drew Anne closely to him and lovingly he caressed her. After a while, he felt her relax and her body soften and grow warm. Then Harry took Anne to him, and soon she had responded eagerly, passionately. Later they fell asleep in each other's arms.

Next morning Harry rose early, and, out in the hotel gardens, stood watching the sunrise in the clear morning air. He saw the first of the sunlight touch the beautiful Maccha Pucchare, and the great mountain's colours of the night give way to the pinks and sparkling silver of the morning. And, close by, he watched it all reflected in the crystal waters of Lake Phewa. Harry thought of Anne who was still asleep in his bed. It was then that he decided what the ruby pendant could do for Nepal. It would go to the employment centres.

Fourteen

Back in Kathmandu, Harry found that action against the movement for democracy had intensified; it was often brutal action. People were very worried. They talked constantly about the demonstrations and the killings, expecting a major confrontation to come soon—a showdown between the movement for democracy and the King.

In his Bar Pad spoke of the trouble. First, smiling, he told Harry that the men from the Asian and Pacific Bank had taken themselves away from it all. They had left Nepal. Mr Lamonde had flown back to Bangkok and Mr Brown had gone on his tour of Asian cities.

'With the Thai girl?' Harry asked.

'Of course. She was the prize.'

Well that was that for the amusement park, Harry thought.

Then Pad's mood changed and he spoke angrily of trouble in nearby Patan. Riot police had shot three demonstrators. And the people there had dug trenches, set up barricades in the streets and declared themselves a republic. In his anger, Pad was sure the police killers and torturers would come to have a terrible price to pay. Surely one day people would seek them out, hang them, cut their bodies to pieces. Pad took care to remind Harry that he himself had been a Gurkha soldier and never a policeman. Pad was against Patan's declaring itself a republic, saying it was disloyal to the King, and that Patan was far too small—only a few square miles—to be a separate country.

When Harry met Krishna Sarki, he, also, spoke of killings. Four were killed when police fired into a peaceful demonstration on the Tribhuban University campus near Kirtipur. Krishna did not hide his anger and cursed the police, swearing vengeance on King and the government—the vengeance of both the people and the gods, which, he assured Harry, would come soon.

Ari Sarki also brought bad news. Over morning tea with Harry in Pad's Bar he spoke of two of his cousins. 'The last time my cousins took the bus for Biratnagar to deliver our pamphlets,' he told Harry, 'the police got them at Thankot, even before they left the valley. They pulled my cousins off the bus and took the bags of pamphlets.' His anger rose. 'They threw my cousins into a disused warehouse in Patan, not far from the Ganesh Temple, Mr Clarke. They dragged them down into the dark basement that they'd made a dungeon of, and chained them to iron rings they'd put in the old stone wall. For days they left them, no food, just a little water.'

Harry remembered the earnest young men he had met in the house in Kirtipur.

'A police inquisitor got at them,' Ari Sarki said sourly. 'He asked them where we kept the printing press. Only Krishna and myself knew that; my two cousins only delivered the pamphlets. When the inquisitor asked who their leader was, they refused to tell.'

Sadness mingled with Ari Sarki's anger as he went on. 'I owe them much, Mr Clarke. Each time my cousins refused to give me away, the police had a brute who laid into them, bashing them with his heavy baton, bruising their bodies and damaging their bones. When they still refused to tell, the police had their torturer light the brazier they had in that dark basement and heat his iron in the hot coals. Each time they didn't answer the brute would burn into their flesh.'

To make sure he would not to be overheard, Ari Sarki looked around to see Pad busy tidying up behind the counter and no other early customers in the bar. He lent close to Harry. 'The torturer is dead now, Mr Clarke,' he whispered. 'We, too, have our informers. Others of my cousins have sharp kukhries. Last night they despatched the torturer and brought our two cousins back to Kirtipur.'

It horrified Harry. 'How tragic, Ari Sarki,' he said. 'But it is murder.'

Ari Sarki shrugged.

'The police will go to Kirtipur and charge your cousins with murder,' Harry said, very concerned.

'The police do not make charges. They just take people away.' Harry saw the grimness in Ari Sarki's face. 'But they will not take my cousins, Mr Clarke. If the police come up the hill to Kirtipur, we will never let them down again.'

'And the movement for democracy is non-violent,' Harry said, remonstrating.

'Sometimes there are limits.'

'When will this trouble stop?' Harry asked.

'I will tell you. The people are nearly ready this time, they are organised. Parties banned for a long time are active—the Nepali Congress and the United Left Front. Even now Ganesh Man Singh, who is the supreme leader, Sahana Pradhan and others are drawing up an eight-point charter of demands. The people will confront the Government and the King. We will have our democracy, we will have it soon. It is then that the trouble will stop, Mr Clarke.'

Harry found Ram Maske highly critical of the Marich Man Shrestha Government. He blamed it for much of the brutality, and condemned the prime minister for bringing more hardliners into his cabinet. 'The prime minister has gone too far this time,' he told Harry. 'Opposition is building up strongly and very quickly. The banned Nepali Congress and the United Left Front have been organising widely; they have been pressing for action.'

'So things will happen?'

Harry could see the tiredness in Ram Maske's old face as he thought for some time before he answered. 'Perhaps. We shall see. But my way is no longer the way of Nepal, neither the way of the people nor the way of the government. I have said, so often said, that we must all be brothers. My way is through Freemasonry. That is the way I hope my country will go one day. That way, we shall all be brothers.'

Some days later, the 6th of April as Harry remembered, Krishna Sarki came early to the Hotel Laxmi, with the car, and found Harry in his room. He was obviously excited and was talking quickly.

'The car must stay in the hotel grounds today,' he told Harry. 'It is safe there. And you must stay in the hotel, Mr Clarke. I have come early to warn you. The streets will not be safe for you today.'

'Is it another demonstration, Krishna?'

'More than that, much more. It is the day of reckoning. The greatest of all days in the history of my country. The people are awake. They are coming out. The people will confront the King himself. The mass of the people will assemble on the Tundikhel today. Then they will march on the palace.'

'Then why shouldn't I be safe? Why should I stay in the hotel?' Harry wanted copy for his paper.

'There are the riot police, Mr Clarke, and the King's royal guard. Bullets can kill foreigners as well as us—foreign journalists like you.'

'Will it come to bloodshed?'

'I hope not. There has already been much blood spilt.'

'I'll look after myself, Krishna.'

'Yes, but take care. I must go now.'

'To demonstrate?'

'Of course, and to hand out pamphlets on the Tundikhel. And to march on the palace with the people. I'll be amongst the leaders,' Krishna replied proudly as he left.

That morning Harry sensed the tension in the hotel staff. The clerks at the reception counter offered no welcoming smiles, the maids who cleaned the rooms and always spoke to him now looked away. At breakfast the usually friendly faces of the waiters were serious, and the head waiter cast anxious looks at Harry. Then the hotel manager came up to him.

'Have you heard the news?' he asked with a worried frown.

'The demonstration, you mean? I've heard the people will march on the palace.'

'Perhaps, Mr Clarke. We do not know. But I'm sure there will be nothing to worry about. Nothing at all.'

'No, I hope not.'

The manager attempted a smile. 'But we must take care,' he said, glancing around the room. 'We have many tourists with us and we are advising them to stay in the hotel today, to keep off the streets. Of course we are apologising for any inconvenience.'

'Would it be dangerous for them?'

'I don't think so. But the tourists should not take chances. Nor should you, Mr Clarke.'

Ram Maske came into the dining room and went over to Harry's table, asking if he could join him that morning. Harry welcomed the old man, expecting news of the coming events of the day. But for a long time he was silent, looking out the window to the hotel garden. It was a fine morning, a blue sky, the garden bright in the sunlight. Harry followed his gaze over the lawns, the flower beds full of colour, the little white stupa on the grassed hill, and the ancient brick walls on the boundary and the curved terracotta roofs of the buildings beyond. One was the roof of Anne's flat, and the thought pleased Harry.

'A fine morning, Mr Clarke,' Ram Maske said at length. 'It is beautiful. The sun is shining. There is no mist today, no trace of mist.'

'Will the people really rise and march on the palace today, Ram Maske? I've seen no journalists back at the hotel.'

'I hear a few have come back to Nepal, not many and not to my hotel. Our Democracy Day was not encouraging for them.'

'Will the people march, Ram Maske?'

'Yes.'

'Is it an auspicious day, do you think?'

Ram Maske shrugged. 'Perhaps. It depends on what is done today. What the people do and what the King and his ministers do. But the morning is beautiful.'

'Will you march with them, Ram Maske?'

'I am past marching. But I will be asking my gods to help bring democracy to my country, to guide the King and his ministers. And to guide the people and their parties, the men of the Nepali Congress and the United Left Front, and the other parties. I will pray that they guide all of them to a peaceful solution. We should all be brothers, Mr Clarke. I am a Mason; we should all act like brothers.'

'Perhaps some Masons will kill each other, Ram Maske, 'Harry said.

Ram Maske shook his old head several times before he replied, 'No, I hope not. And I am sure that the gods hope not. Too much blood has been spilt already in my country. I hope it will be a peaceful confrontation.'

Later Harry left the Hotel Laxmi to go to the Tundikhel. He walked out into Lekhnath Marg and found the street deserted. There were no men with their rickshaws, no young boys asking for money, no traffic, only a cow or two. Walking past the great iron gates of the western entrance to the royal palace, he saw the guard was doubled, and looking through the gates into the palace grounds he saw many more soldiers about. He turned towards the Durbar Marg, past the statue of the late King Mahendra which was near the main entrance to the palace; that wide street, too, was deserted. When he went back towards Thamel he saw a few people hurrying in his direction towards the Tundikhel. In Thamel itself the shops were closed, many with iron shutters secured or with their windows boarded up; and the street vendors with their carts and barrows had gone.

In Anson Tole, the cobbled streets of the old town were also deserted except for a few elderly people and children. Here a long-haired, bearded saddhu, his thin body naked except for a loincloth, emerged from a laneway and accosted Harry. He spoke excitedly, and too quickly for Harry who had only a smattering of the language, and kept pointing up to the sky and the roof tops of houses, yelling, jerking his head to emphasise what he was saying. Harry looked up but saw nothing he thought out of place. The saddhu kept throwing his arms upwards and began to yell even more loudly, but then stopped, lowered his gaze and stared at Harry. Harry looked back into the saddhu's face, the traces of white paint on his skin, the blackened teeth, his dark eyes wide and full of fear.

Harry began to walk away but the saddhu ran in front of him, persisting and still pointing upwards. Again Harry looked up, and this time he saw the birds, a dozen or so black birds perched on one roof-top, more on other roof-tops; and he saw even more come flying down black against the blue sky, circling, looking for places to perch.

Harry realised what was troubling the saddhu. They were crows, the messengers from Yama the God of the Underworld, and, he had heard, often messengers of death. Harry shrugged and hurried off quickly, looking away from the saddhu who was still yelling, and gesticulating wildly.

Harry joined other late-comers who had now spilt over from the Tundikhel onto the Kanti Path not far from the Royal Nepalese Airlines office. The size of the crowd surprised him; about three hundred thousand, he learnt later, and very many times more than the turn-out for the recent Democracy Day demonstration. From where he stood, Harry saw people he guessed were from all walks of life: officials, farmers, priests and lamas, students, and other groups, and women and children. And Harry also saw the riot police standing in groups a little away from his part of the crowd, watching.

Over the heads of the mass of people, Harry could see the leaders of the movement for democracy haranguing the crowd out in the open-air theatre of the Tundikhel. They condemned the Panchayat system, the absolute power of the King, the brutal police. They demanded democracy, political parties and representative government, fair elections and a constitutional monarchy. And they called for a peaceful demonstration. As each speaker made his point, the crowd roared its approval, a great roar from a third of a million throats. When the last speaker urged the people to march on the palace, the crowd thundered its agreement.

People moved out of the Tundikhel onto the Kanti Path, a few at first, and Harry stood near the junction with New Road and watched. Soon great crowds of people were surging out, massing along the Kanti Path, calling excitedly and urging each other on to the royal palace. Here and there in the crowd someone would yell the Gurkhas' war-cry, "Ayo gurkha, ayo gurkha!". Many marched with banners held high proclaiming against the King, the Panchayat system and ministers, and demanding democratic government, political parties and human rights. Amongst those leading, Harry saw Ari Sarki and Krishna and other Sarki cousins. As thousands hurried along the Kanti Path, many thousands more kept coming from the Tundikhel and followed them.

Harry joined in and marched with them, past Ratna park and the Rani Pokhari and on past the travel and trekking agencies which were closed and shuttered that day, then past hotels where tourists stayed well inside, until they came to the walls of the palace. Those in front stopped and others joined them until thousands of people massed there, many near the main palace gate at the end of Durbar Marg. People pressed on each other, some held up banners for democracy and all it meant. Leaders called for the King and his ministers to leave the palace and come and face the people. But Harry could see soldiers of the royal guard positioned at the palace gate and still others standing by inside.

Harry was watching when several young men approached the statue of the late King Mahendra near the main gate of the palace. It was King Mahendra who had put an end to Nepal's brief period of democratic government and started the Panchayat system. The young men vented their anger on the statue, hammered at it, thrusting, and tried to push it over. But a shot rang out, then more shots, cracking, reverberating sharply above the noise of the crowd. The young men fell and their blood spilt on the roadway.

At first the people were quiet, then they realised what had happened. Enraged at the killing, they yelled for vengeance. As people surged foreword and pressed towards the gate there was a volley of fire, indiscriminate fire, then volley after volley into the crowd. Many people fell, lay dead or wounded on the road. The crowd pushed back and people panicked, seeking to escape the bullets, and horrified, confused at the unexpected slaughter. The firing continued and many more fell, until the crowd broke up as people scattered, running from the bullets to safety back along the Durbar Marg and further off.

Harry, too, retreated, and hurried back to the Kanti Path. But here he met another mass of people surging towards the palace, aiming to approach the western gate. For them, too, the security forces were waiting. From some distance back, Harry heard the firing—heavy firing and many volleys—and he heard the yelling and screaming from the crowd. But people pushed still further on to approach the western gate, only to come under fire again. Again the security forces fired into the crowd, slaughtering indiscriminately as their bullets thudded into flesh. And many more people fell wounded or dead.

The crowds dispersed. People hurried back into Thamel, into the old town, back along the Kanti Path, and along the Durbar Marg and the other streets, some to collect vehicles they had parked, or to board trucks or buses they had hired to return to their towns or villages. Others went away slowly, some supporting the walking wounded, some carrying those who could no longer walk. Others stayed to search amongst the bodies for relatives and friends. They went to take up their dead and carry them away, but the riot police drove them off. The police seized the cameras of two photographers there and sent them away.

Harry was horrified and shocked at the tragedy, and full of pity for the people who had died and those who were wounded. Furious with a government that could let it happen, he walked quickly away towards the Hotel Laxmi. But he walked only some way then turned back to the scene of slaughter, to watch more closely and get copy for his paper.

That afternoon riot police brought in dozens of their trucks and ambulances and lined them up along the roadside. They moved amongst the hundreds of bodies now strewn over the roadways. The dead lay where they had fallen, the wounded lay still or tried to crawl through the blood that had been spilt. And Harry watched as the police started to clear away the carnage. They threw dead bodies into the trucks, and carried the wounded to waiting ambulances.

The massacre shocked everyone. The Hotel Laxmi was quiet again that evening, very gloomy; the reception staff said little. In the dining room waiters went about their work silently, avoiding any eye-contact with their guests. Pad's Bar was almost empty, and Pad had lost his happy grin. Tourists talked amongst themselves in hushed tones about the massacre. Hearing that the curfew had been tightened, they expected more trouble and stayed off the streets that evening. Harry shared in the dejection. He walked over to see Anne and found that Bhu Vamsi had already called on her and told her of the killings. Anne was horrified, depressed with what she had heard.

Ram Maske also was depressed, mortified that so much slaughter could still happen in his country. He looked older, Harry thought, his face drawn and his black eyes subdued. 'It was to be a peaceful demonstration,' he said. 'The leaders emphasised that, in fact demanded that it be. I understand people took no guns, no weapons. No kukhries or knives even. You were there, Mr Clarke. Did you notice people with weapons?'

Harry told him he had not.

Ram Maske shook his head sorrowfully, 'It was a great offence. A great offence against humanity. And it was an offence against our gods.'

'Police threw the dead bodies into trucks,' Harry said. 'Carted them away.'

Ram Maske's face was indeed sad. 'People are being denied their rights in death as well as life,' he said. 'The dead are being denied their priests. Denied their families. Denied the proper rites for the passage of their souls. Families are not being told of their own dead. The bodies are not being given to them. I hear that the police are taking the truck-loads of bodies to a military cremation place. Heaped together, they will be burnt in great fires.'

'Why would they do that?' Harry asked.

'To stop family funerals which could draw sympathy. And to hide the number they killed. It will never be known how many were killed, Mr Clarke.'

Fifteen

'The killings were tragic, greatly so,' Ram Maske said, when Harry met him some days later. 'But it has turned out that the dead are not without their victory, and I thank the gods for that.' Harry noticed that the sadness had lifted from his old face and his black eyes had regained their vigour.

'The King was shocked. He was deeply disturbed at the killings,' Ram Maske said. 'He lifted the ban on political parties and Ganesh Man Singh took the eight-point charter to him for his agreement.'

'There are to be many reforms, Mr Clarke. Political parties will be legal, political prisoners released, and those guilty of atrocities will be punished. The families of those killed and those who were wounded will be compensated. And a commission, with people from the Nepali Congress and the United Left Front on it, is being be set up to consider a democratic constitution. The movement for democracy has won the day. They are wonderful improvements, are they not, Mr Clarke? You must write them up for your Sydney newspaper.'

'Of course, Ram Maske. My copy covers the killings, but not only that,' Harry said. 'I will certainly claim a great victory for those who died. I will report what they have won. People will know of it. And the world press will also do so, I'm sure of that.'

In the days that followed, people in Kathmandu waited happily for the democracy they were to gain. Not so many police were on the streets, and already people started to sense the warm glow of a free society. In other ways life started to returned to normal for most people, except of course for those mourning for their loved ones and those suffering from wounds. There was a change of mood in the Hotel Laxmi. Staff at the reception counter became relaxed and friendly again, waiters were even more attentive than usual and were pleasant and smiling. The hotel manager stopped at Harry's table near the window and remarked on the pleasant weather. 'Our troubles in Nepal are over', he told Harry. 'Tourists are back to normal. We are busy again with people taking tours around the valley, people going on treks, and mountaineers going to climb in the high Himalayas.'

When Harry visited Anne, he found her as happy as anyone with the arrangements to lead to a democratic government. He felt a surge of pleasure when he looked at her.

'I'll make morning tea,' she said, as Harry sat on one of the old easy chairs.

The flat was bright again that morning, the sunlight streaming in the open windows, and the door at the entrance showing a glimpse of the blue sky, and the trees and flower garden outside. The garden seemed to be repeated in Anne's flowers in vases on the window sill and on the top of the bookcase. And the God Ganesh appeared happy as he looked down from his place on the wall, the sunlight touching his papier-mache face, his little eyes and long elephant trunk.

Anne came in with a pot of tea and teacups and pulled up a chair beside Harry. 'April is a delightful month in Kathmandu,' she said. 'Such beautiful weather. And the hotel gardens are lovely just now. Have you looked at them, Harry?'

He told her he had.

'I have something to show you,' she said, taking one of the files from the table. 'You'll be interested. I've been working hard since we got back from Pokhara.'

Anne had drawn up a plan for an employment centre at Jomosom. Harry saw it set out there: the buildings, a research officer to get information about jobs and training needs, an employment placement officer, types of training courses, instructors, estimated costs, follow-ups, a timetable.

'Of course it's still a draft,' she said. 'It will need the Ministry's approval.'

'You have been working hard,' Harry commented.

Bhu Vamsi came to the door and joined them for tea. She had been as pleased as Anne to hear Harry had decided that his late cousin's gift was to go to the employment centres, and she told him that the money could not be spent in a better way.

And Bhu brought news that a great celebration for the new democracy was to be held in Kathmandu. There would be dancing and singing in the streets. People would bring chan beer and raksi. Party leaders would be there. Bhu herself was going to celebrate, and she suggested that Anne and Harry also might like to go.

'Is it allowed? There is still a curfew,' Anne said.

Bhu shook her head. 'It does not matter. We are a democracy now, Anne.' She arranged to meet them near the Rani Pokhari.

That evening, of the 16th of April, the weather was a delight in

Kathmandu, the sky was starry and cloudless. A soft breeze came along the streets, fanning the temples, tinkling the little metal leaves on the pagodas. Not far to the north, the great white mountains were bathed in starlight tinged with purple.

Anne and Harry walked to the Durbar Marg and then on to Thamel and Anson Tole, and through the old town to New Road to join in the celebrations where many people were already celebrating. Bells were ringing, people were blowing conch shells, and somewhere a band was playing. Masked and colourfully costumed dancers pranced about, cavorting along the narrow cobbled streets, and people held flaming torches to light the way for them.

In the squares and market places, temples were lit up by many oil lamps burning in little clay bowls; temples people had adorned with flowers and red sindar powder, and where they had made other offerings of gratitude to the gods. Friends and relatives met and congratulated one another, some joining each other in drinking beer and raksi. It was all very convivial. Harry met Krishna and Ari Sarki who were there with some of their cousins. Ari Sarki offered them raksi, which he had in good supply.

'The raksi is good and strong,' Krishna said as Harry drank and Anne made a show by sipping hers. 'Raksi should be strong on a night like this, Mr Clarke. It's a glorious night for us.'

Laughing happily, Ari Sarki refilled Harry's glass. 'You see our dreams have come true, Mr Clarke. Nepal is cured. Also my father's dreams have come true, and his father's and further back over the generations. The long struggle is finished. We are free now. We are a free people at last. We will steer our own way ahead.'

'And you and your cousins have played a most important part in that struggle,' Harry said. 'Please let me congratulate you. We both congratulate you,' he repeated, glancing at Anne who was nodding her head in agreement. They left them and walked on towards the Rani Pokhari to meet Bhu Vamsi.

It was then that Harry heard the firing. Rifle shots barked out, harsh above the din of the celebrations, cracking and shattering the night. People listened and became hushed. More shots broke the night. Then more shots. Then Harry heard firing in several directions.

The celebrations stopped, the bells and conch shells were silent, the masked dancers were still and torches were put out. People, no doubt with the massacre of the 6th of April in mind, showed great concern and stood still and listened as the noise of the firing continued. Then, greatly disturbed, most hurried back to their homes, and before long the streets were empty except for the stragglers, the wounded who could not walk and had no others to carry them away, and the dead.

As Anne and Harry hurried on to meet Bhu, they saw a party of police and heard them call to the stragglers, ordering them back to their homes and threatening to shoot any who continued to break the curfew.

'They are the riot police,' Anne said quietly, moving closer to Harry. He heard the anger in her voice. 'It is so cruel,' she said. 'So unnecessary. The curfew should have been stopped. It is cruel and useless murder, Harry.'

Gloom now hung heavily over the night in Kathmandu, the pleasantness was gone. The breeze now carried the groans of the wounded, and by morning would carry the smell of death. The stars had paled and the great mountains to the north were great purple ghosts. In the Kanti Path near the Rani Pokhari, Anne and Harry found the streets deserted. They searched for Bhu but found no sign of her. Then the riot police saw them and ordered them back to the Hotel Laxmi.

'Perhaps Bhu is safe,' Anne said, worried. 'We know she escaped in Pokhara that time. Perhaps she went to her house.'

Harry doubted it but said nothing.

Back at the hotel, Harry saw Anne to her flat. 'It is tragic,' she said as she kissed him goodnight. 'But it is the last act of a shameful government, I am sure of that. The very last act I'd think. Nepal will have a new and better government now. It will end the killings here. Let's hope so, Harry.'

Harry met Ram Maske next morning, and the old man lamented the slaughter again. 'The police killed many during the celebrations,' he said. 'A hundred at least. Many were wounded. It was a terrible mistake. The curfew was not lifted and the police acted on their orders.'

'They should not have opened fire,' Harry said.

'Yes, their leaders should have stopped them, and ordered them to hold their fire.' Ram Maske agreed. 'Some police will pay dearly for this and their other brutalities. Lynching parties are going around looking for the police they want. It is not the act of brothers.'

Ram Maske brightened a little. 'But it's not all bad news, Mr Clarke. Some of it is good. Very good news indeed. News people have wanted for many years, for generations.'

Ram Maske went on to tell Harry that the King was sacking his cabinet and dissolving the National Panchayat. On Ganesh Man Singh's recommendation, he was making the Nepali Congress President, Krishna

Prasad Bhattarai, the new prime minister of Nepal. There would be an eleven-member cabinet, with three ministers from the Nepali Congress, three from the United Left Front, two human-rights activists, two nominees of the King, and one from the pro-Soviet Communist Party.

Ram Maske brightened further as he continued. 'Political prisoners have been released, and some activists guilty of even serious offences have been pardoned. The senior justice of our supreme court has been given ninety days to draft a democratic constitution for Nepal for the commission to consider. Soon there will be an election. All that is good, Mr Clarke.'

Certainly, Ram Maske. I agree wholeheartedly,' Harry said.

For some moments Ram Maske sat there thinking and his old head nodded slowly. 'Of course there was a price to pay, a heavy price for us. In just the last year or so, six hundred and more brave activists have died. We owe much to them. I trust the gods will look on them with favour.'

Ram Maske looked keenly at Harry. 'Ari Sarki was killed yesterday. You have had dealings with him, Mr Clarke.'

It surprised Harry. 'I met him there last night. Are you sure, Ram Maske?'

'I am. He was an outstanding young man. A scholar and a teacher.'

'Such a tragedy for his family. And your country badly needs those like him.'

'It does, Mr Clarke. He would be a great loss to any country. I hear the police deliberately sought him out. Revenge, I'm told. You will know why, I think.'

Yes, Harry knew.

'Another person you know was shot last night. You worked with her. She's Bhu Vamsi.'

'Shot! Is she dead then?' Harry asked, shocked.

'Wounded. She is in hospital, the Teaching Hospital in Maharajganj. It's not far away, and a good hospital.'

'We were to meet Bhu last night. We looked for her but couldn't find her.'

'I think the riot police also might have looked for her—and found her first. She was very much the activist.'

Half an hour later Harry and Anne drove out to the Teaching Hospital at Maharajganj. They found Bhu under emergency care, not long out of the operating theatre, still unconscious, wan, an ashen face above the white sheets. The surgeon, a specialist from Japan, spoke to them softly and in grave tones. Two bullets had damaged a lung, damaged it badly. They had to operate and take part of it out.

'What will happen?' Anne asked, with a tremor in her voice. 'What hope does she have? Is there any?'

'There is hope,' the surgeon said. 'There is some hope. We have done what we can. Now her gods will need to favour her.'

Sixteen

Now that his cousin's gift to Nepal had been attended to and the movement for democracy successful, those reasons for Harry's stay in Kathmandu came to an end. People from the ministries were generous in thanking Harry for his cousin's money. Tej Shamsher had arranged a dinner for him at the five-star Soaltee-Oberoi Hotel. Senior staff of the ministries attended, including, of course, Bruce Singer. As Mary Clarke was dead, there was no question of a letter of thanks from the King, so, in its place, Tej Shamsher suggested that one of the employment centres, perhaps one of the new ones which would be set up, be named after her.

Harry's Sydney newspaper was expecting him back, impatient after his protracted stay away, so when he next went to Anne's flat, his coming departure from Nepal—his leaving Anne—was very much on his mind.

Anne welcomed him warmly and he held her in his arms for a long time. As she made morning tea, Harry stood looking up at the papier-mache mask of Ganesh on the wall. It would be good, he thought, to have the pot-bellied god's favour now.

Anne's brought the teapot and cups and put them on the table and looked at him searchingly. 'It seems that your work here has finished, Harry,' she said.

'Yes it has, Anne.'

'What will you do?'

'There's no job for me here, no income, no permit for a longer stay I expect.'

'Will you return to Australia?'

'I'll have to, it seems.'

Anne turned away and stood looking out the open window. 'Do you want me to go with you?'

'Of course I do.' He walked over and stood beside her.

Anne turned and kissed him on the cheek. 'It would be nice. You're a lovely man, Harry.'

'There's the flat in Sydney, harbour views and all that,' Harry said with a casualness he did not feel.

'Oh yes, you told me that in Pokhara.'

'You'd like it there, Anne.'

'Yes, I think I would.'

'Will you come with me?' Harry asked.

For some time Anne stayed there looking out the window. Then she took the teapot from the table. 'I'll make fresh tea,' she said as she went back to the kitchen. And it was a long time before she returned. Harry waited for her to speak.

'I can't, Harry,' she said. And he saw traces of tears on her cheeks. 'It's so difficult for me, too difficult. I would like to but I can't.'

'Is it your work here?' Harry asked.

'Of course it is.'

'You could come back to it sometimes, for part of each year perhaps.'

'Yes, I could. I might one day. But not now, Harry. It's a shame for you. A shame for me too. But there's even more for me to do here now.'

'Because of my cousin's money for the employment centres?'

'Yes. And with Bhu out of action,'

'How long will it take you, Anne ?'

'A year, perhaps.'

'What then? I could wait. Then I'd come back for you.'

Anne poured the tea. She looked at Harry—a long look, her eyes soft— her concern showing clearly on her face. 'You would do that? You would wait?'

'Yes,' Harry assured her.

Anne thought for a while. 'It's really not so long,' she said. 'The time will help me. Help me to be sure. And it would help you too, Harry. I should like you to come back.'

A few days later a Royal Nepal Airline's Boeing 727 took off from Kathmandu and rose high into the early morning sky. Harry looked down at the valley, at the ochres and terracottas of the towns, the brown fields waiting for the monsoon rains, the rivers, the great temples. Soon the Boeing 727 would turn south on its flight to Bangkok, where Harry would board his Sydney plane.

Harry had made his farewells. He had offered Krishna his sincere condolences for his cousin's death and both had lamented the loss of Ari Sarki, to both his family and to his country. Then Krishna's mood had changed to one of optimism, with his high expectations for a democratic Nepal, and his praise for the King and the political parties for their agreement. Harry had wished Krishna well for the offices services business he proposed to start, and he had been generous in supplementing the driver's pay that Krishna had from the Himalayan Tourist Agency in the Durbar Marg.

Harry had lunched with Bruce Singer at the Sun Kosi, on wonton soup and momos and Star beer as he had first done not long after coming to Kathmandu. He had been apprehensive about telling Bruce that he was giving his late cousin's gift—the money from the ruby pendant which two centuries before had been taken from the treasury of Shuja-ud-daula the defeated Nawab of Bengal—not for the glass works but for the employment centres.

But Bruce had treated the matter pleasantly enough. 'It's your decision, Harry,' he had said, his tone serious and not mentioning Anne Jackson. 'I would have preferred the glass works. But there are many things to be taken into account in such matters. I admit that.'

Harry had agreed, thankful to be getting off so lightly.

'Perhaps it is best for the money to go to the employment centres,' Bruce had mused. He thought for a while, then shrugged, saying, 'Industrialisation or the villages? What's the balance? How do you decide? Yes, it is your decision, Harry,' Bruce had repeated. 'Of course, it had to be—one way or the other.' And that time Harry noticed him hiding a smile.

In Pad's Bar the afternoon before he left Nepal, Harry had taken a long time saying goodbye to Ram Maske. The old man's tone had saddened as he spoke of the recent killings, particularly those of the 6th and 16th of April. But he brightened when he spoke of the democratic constitution that was being drawn up, and of the new government with Prime Minister Krishna Prasad Bhattarai and a cabinet including ministers from the political parties.

'At last the people will rule themselves,' he had said. 'The bad years have gone. They were long years, Mr Clarke. They were years of confrontation and bloodshed. In those years, that was the only way. But no longer. Now, the people will vote. They will vote in the parties they want in power, and vote out those they do not want.'

'It is the best way, Ram Maske,' Harry had agreed.

Ram Maske thought for a while. 'I have decided I will have a temple built, a temple for more Masons to come to. It will be large, for many Masons to use. That would be good, Mr Clarke.'

Pad had come to refill their glasses but Ram Maske had to leave, having business to attend to. They had made their farewells, with Harry saying that he intended to return to Kathmandu. Then Harry had taken his leave of Pad, telling him, also, that he wanted to return.

Late that afternoon Harry had visited Bhu Vamsi in the Teaching Hospital, and found her sleeping, still very ill and not yet well enough to have visitors. Jang Pandey by her bedside told Harry that her doctor had said she was doing well and was expected to make a good recovery. Harry left a card for her with his best wishes and a promise to write to her, and flowers he had brought from the Hotel Laxmi.

That last evening Harry had taken Anne to the Yak and Yeti for dinner, to the Chimney Room. The April evening was still cool and the fire there was burning in the great round hearth. Anne, yet again, told him how grateful she was for the gift for the employment centres; and she talked enthusiastically about the Mushahar people and the Tharu people and Jomosom and ways in which the money would be spent. But she also asked Harry to tell her about Australia and his Sydney flat with its harbour views. Harry described the Opera House, the great Harbour Bridge, the deep blue waters and blue skies, the busy ferries and the multitude of white-sailed yachts. And they talked of Harry's return to Kathmandu. They lingered over the dinner that evening at the Yak and Yeti. Then back at the Hotel Laxmi, through the iron gates, past the old brick wall and across the gardens at Anne's flat they lingered longer.

From his seat in the Royal Nepal Airline's Boeing 727, Harry looked down on Kathmandu and found the royal palace, the nearby Hotel Laxmi, and beside it Anne's flat. Then the aircraft turned away. Harry thought of his ancestors, so long ago. He thought of Hume Clarke and Maneka and their infant son leaving the Valley of Nepal one misty morning more than two centuries ago with the Capuchin priests and their flock including some of the noseless and lipless ones from Kirtipur. He thought of Adam Clarke leaving Kathmandu last century, after the tragedy of the Kot, and receiving Lalit's ashes from the burning ghats near the Pashupatinath, ashes he had cast on the Bagmati's holy waters.

Harry took a last look at the great Himalayan mountains, immense, the roof of the world, their great grey rock faces shining, their snows glistening in the sunlight. The air was very clear that morning, no mist at all—crystal clear. Then the aircraft turned south for Bangkok against the great mountains, now close and silhouetted against the dark blue sky.

APPENDICES

APPENDIX ONE

FACT AND FICTION

In each of the three books the characters, some of whom are historical and some fictional, act in a broad factual setting.

In Book One, the main historical characters are: the Gurkha King and his brother Surpratap, the three Malla kings, the Satbahalyas, the Pradhans, Robert Clive and other officials and soldiers of the British East India Company. The main fictional characters are: Hume and Alexander Clarke, Maneka, Puskar Maske, Atal Thapa, the peasant Dongol, the Raj Guru, the old priest Vajracrya, the Dewar and General Josi. The Capuchins are based on priests who lived in Nepal at the time. All the main events actually happened, including the execution of the sepoys before the Battle of Buxar; the Gurkha King's blockade of the Valley of Nepal and his atrocity in Kirtipur; his victory over Major Kinloch; his taking of Kathmandu on the night of the Indra Jatra when people were intoxicated; his taking of Lalitpatan and his execution of the Pradhans; his taking of Bhaktapur; his treatment of the Malla Kings; and his exiling of the Christians. Descriptions of temples and festivals and various events, such as the minting of debased coins for Tibet, the search for treasure and the stone-throwing, are based on fact.

In Book Two, the main historical characters are: the Thapas, the Pandeys, King Rajendra Shah, the Heir Apparent, the Senior Queen, Queen Laxmi Devi, Gagan Singh, the British Residents and the Governors General. The main fictional characters are: Adam Clarke, Lalit, Dor Maske, the St Clairs, Dr Jones and Captain O'Keefe. All major events are based on fact including: the murders and executions; Rajendra Shah's visit to the British Residency after the death of his Senior Queen; the Heir Apparent's mocking and cruelties; the army mutiny; the threat to the British Residency; Laxmi Devi's reaction to the murder of Gagan Singh; the massacre at the Kot; and Rana Jung Bahadur's appointments. Rajendra Shah's statement to the army and the army's reply are from Dr H. A. Oldfield's Sketches from Nepal which was first published in 1880 by W.H. Allen & Co. of London.

In Book Three, some reference is made to actual Kings, ministers and leading activists; however all the characters are fictional. Events relating to the movement for democracy are factual, including the trouble in Pokhara on the 12th of February 1990; the demonstration on the 18th of February; the march on the palace on the 6th of April and the killings there; and the tragic celebrations on the 16th of April. Almost all the killings, bombings and other atrocities are based on fact. The poor villages, the Tharu and Mushahar people, Jomosom, the employment centres, the Balaju Industrial Estate, the temples, the Hotel Yak and Yeti and the Fishtail Lodge Hotel are all real.

Appendix Two

WAR WITH THE BRITISH

War, or preparations for war, did not end with the victory of the Gurkha King over the Valley of Nepal in 1769, but continued for some fifty years. Prithvi Shah himself did not rest. Before he died in 1775, and his body was burnt with twelve of his wives and concubines as satis, he had brought more of the Chaubisi princedoms in the west of Nepal under control, and had taken the eastern mountains and Terai right to the Sikkim border. He left his Dibya Upadesh to guide the warrior leaders who were to follow him.

A most important warrior leader was one of Prithvi Shah's brothers, Bahadur Shah. He extended the nation further to the west, taking the rest of the Chaubisi and the Baisi princedoms, and Jumla, Doti, and the Kingdom of Kumaon; he also entered the Kingdom of Garhwal.

Bahadur Shah also attacked Tibet, then a Chinese Dependency. In 1791 the Gurkhas made a quick entry there and sacked the great treasure of the Panchen Lama. But the Chinese Emperor called a halt and sent his General Fu-kang-an to Tibet's defence with some twelve thousand men, including Daghor horsemen from Mongolia, Chin-ch'uan mountaineers from Szechuan, and Kodonor cavalry. After fierce fighting the Gurkha's force had to withdraw.

Just after the turn of the nineteenth century, Bhim Sen Thapa, one of Nepal's greatest sons, became prime minister and commander-in-chief of the army. He soon consolidated and extended his power by acting against those who might pose a threat. He executed or banished members of the Pandey family, murdered the Raja of Palpa, and had the Senior Queen, Rajeswari Devi, burnt as a sati on the river bank near Sanku village, along with her fourteen maids whom he claimed were her late husband's concubines. He had no trouble from the throne itself, with King Girbana Bikram Shah a boy just ten-years-old and the full support of the Regent Queen Lalit Tripura Devi, who was his lover.

Bhim Sen Thapa was the most ambitious of all Nepal's warrior leaders. For ten years he waged war, with much success, against other mountain princedoms, and greatly expanded Nepal's territory. His General Amar

Singh Thapa fought to consolidate the position in Kumaon, then took Garhwal and brought it under firm control. He moved into the territory of the Sikhs to take many princedoms there, and crossed the Sutlej River to take Tehra and put the fort of Kangra under siege. Kangra was the gate to Kashmir; and with Kashmir the Gurkhas would have much of the north of the Indian sub-continent.

But Amar Singh Thapa was never to take Kangra, nor to advance further west. The British East India Company called a halt to expansion. The Governor General in Calcutta, the Marquis of Hastings, had long been wary of Nepal's expansions and was now ready to put a stop to them; not only in the west but also on the Indian border where the Gurkhas had taken a score or more Districts and hundreds of villages, including some in the domain of the Raja of Hindoor in the territory of the Sikhs.

In May 1813, Hastings wrote to Kathmandu saying that he had adopted a "Principle of Limitations", whereby the Company would not interfere with Nepalese expansion in the hills, but Nepal must not take lands below the hills. Bhim Sen Thapa's reply rejected this outright, pointing out that the British East India Company had established its dominion over India by the power of the sword, and, likewise, Nepal had acquired lands both in and below the hills by the sword.

In April 1814, Hastings reacted by putting a force into lands long occupied by Nepal in the Butwal and Rautahat areas near the Indian border. The Kathmandu Durbar was shocked, and Bhim Sen Thapa sent a force that drove the British out. This time Hasting's reaction was by no means confined to Butwal and Rautahat. He started war with Nepal, planning a campaign that would extend along much of the eight hundred kilometres of Nepal's south, a campaign into which he was to put nearly fifty thousand men.

At first the British met with defeat after defeat from Amar Singh Thapa's forces. In late 1814, in the far west near Dehra Dun, Major General Gillespie—with his three thousand five hundred men, including two companies of the 53rd British Regiment and a hundred dismounted dragoons of the Royal Irish Regiment, his ten pieces of bronze ordnance, howitzers, twelve-pounder guns, mortars, horse artillery and six-pounders— attacked Kalanga, a small fort on a hill of about six hundred feet, which was built of rock and with breastworks of logs and barricades of sharply pointed bamboo stakes. He met disaster. The Gurkhas opened up the gate of the fort, brought their cannon there, and held their fire till the time was right. Then, with all the Gurkha fury, their fire rained down on the British charge: their small cannon with grapeshot enfilading, muskets firing continuous volleys, and arrows streaming from the walls. Confusion broke the British ranks, their charge shattered. Then Gurkhas left their fort with shields and kukhries to fight hand-to-hand. The Irish Dragoons in the forefront of the charge fared worst, with more than half of them falling. Gillespie, frantic, tried to rally his men, urged them on, and with sword and pistol in hand led them up towards the fort. But it was the end for the gallant major general. A Gurkha marksman aimed his musket and a bullet pierced Gillespie's heart; he died in the arms of Lieutenant Frederick Young. The British army retreated and returned to the town of Dehra Dun.

On Gillespie's death, Major Mawbey took command, waited in Dehra Dun for heavy cannon to come from Delhi, and in late November renewed the attack. His big guns breached Kalanga's walls, and again the British stormed the fort. For a second time the Gurkhas drove them off, with British casualties of some five hundred.

In December, Major General Martindell attacked the fort of Jythak near Nathan. Yet again the Gurkha defence was furious, costing the British force three hundred in dead and wounded, and much of its morale. Martindell, fearing the annihilation of his force, ordered its retreat, and, back in Nahan, refused to take further action against the Gurkhas.

Further east, Major General John Sullivan Wood moved into Palpa. Here, too, the Gurkhas attacked fiercely, and Wood retreated after suffering serious casualties including the loss of senior officers. His two further attempts to enter Palpa also failed under the ferocity of Gurkha resistance. General Wood took no further action, being demoralised by news of losses at Kalanga and Jythak and believing he could not match the Gurkhas in the hills.

In the central Terai, Major General Marley with the main British force prepared to climb the Mahabharat Mountains to attack Kathmandu itself. But in January 1815 the Gurkhas attacked his advance posts at Parsa and at Sumanpur, caught them unprepared, and routed them, with hundreds of casualties including the commander of each post killed in action. Major General Marley was to proceed no further. In the darkness before dawn one February morning, completely demoralised he gathered his belongings together, left his tent and mounted his horse; he abandoned his army of some twenty thousand men, his ample ordnance, his eighteen-pounder guns, his large bore mortars and howitzers. He left his command without permission, without appointing a commander to take his place. Leaving Nepal to the Gurkhas, he returned to India.

But about that time the tide turned for the British. Hastings sent a force into Kumaon, which took the Timely Pass, advanced along the Kali River, entered the town of Champawat and laid siege to the nearby fort of Kutalgarh, then took the Gananath Ridge. In April Colonel Nicoll went on to attack the Almora Fort. There he worked his big bore mortars hard, his howitzers and his big cannon belching eight-inch shells. For two days and nights the Gurkhas defended bravely. They came out from the fort, in the smoke of the guns by day and by night in the red glow of the burning, to strike the British with their swords and kukhries. British soldiers fell but Gurkha losses were great. Eventually the Gurkhas flew a flag of truce, and the Governor Bum Shah wrote to Amar Singh Thapa telling him that Kumaon was lost.

Bhim Sen Thapa now had serious doubts about continuing the war. With the British in Kumaon, supplies and reinforcements for Amar Singh Thapa's army in the far west were blocked. He had learnt of the great power of the Company's army; the fifty thousand men it had in the field against Nepal, its large guns which in time they could haul up into the higher mountains, even up to Kathmandu, guns which his mountain forts could never withstand for long. Moreover, Bhim Sen Thapa's dream of an alliance with the Marathas and other Indian States had faded. He wrote to his General Amar Singh Thapa in the western hills expressing his great concern, wanting to end the war and restore good relations with the British. He was willing to give up the disputed areas, and more of the Terai and even some of the lower hills. He told Amar Singh Thapa to retire with his commanders to that part of the country, the higher hills and the mountains, which they were able to defend.

Amar Singh Thapa rejected the ending of the war. He feared that the British would want all of Nepal in the way they had taken Indian States. He told Kathmandu that, if he succeeded against the British, Ranjit Singh would bring the Sikhs in with him. They would fight their way into India and, when they reached Lucknow, the Nawab there would surely join them; then, further south, the rajas on the Deccan would come in. The British could not cope with such a force. They would be driven out of India. So Amar Singh Thapa consolidated his army in the western hills, in the rugged almost impregnable ranges cut by the Gambar River.

Major General Ochterlony, who was now given charge of operations against Nepal, attacked Amar Singh Thapa's outer positions with some six thousand men and sixteen large guns, and took several small forts.

He then obtained four thousand five hundred reinforcements, added to his artillery, and built roads that could take his big guns. Ochterlony moved further into the hills and occupied the Ramgarh Ridge, taking the forts of Jorjori, Taragarh and Chamba. He advanced further through the mountains, carefully, taking fort by fort, and taking the two Deonthal hills to attack Amar Singh Thapa's main stronghold in the fort at Malaon. He worked his heavy cannon hard on Malaon, by day and night, their projectiles screaming through the cold mountain air, their roar reverberating amongst the hills and valleys. Eventually, stout as they were, Malaon's stone walls were badly broken. But more than the stonework of the fort was broken: it was the end of Amar Singh Thapa's hopes, and the end of Nepal's expansion.

On the 15th of May, Amar Singh Thapa surrendered, sadly and with great reluctance. He met Ochterlony and, proud soldier that he was, could do nothing but accept the major general's terms. He gave up to the British all of Garwhal, all of the Bahra Thakurai and the Athara Thakurai. With Kumaon already gone, this was all the country from the Kali to the Sutlej, all the mountains and lowlands there with all their towns and villages, and all the Gurkha forts and other strongholds. Ochterlony treated Amar Singh Thapa, his commanders and the surviving Gurkha soldiers with all the respect and consideration due to such brave fighting men, allowing them to return east with their private possessions and provisions.

In Kathmandu, Bhim Sen Thapa sought an end to the war, and Hastings had the Treaty of Sagauli drawn up. The Treaty's first article provided for perpetual peace and friendship between the Honourable British East India Company and the Kingdom of Nepal. Then it required Nepal to give up more than a third of its territory: the disputed Terai lands in the Butwal and Rautahat areas; all of Kumaon and Garwhal and all other lands to the west of the River Kali with almost all of the lowlands. Added to that, Nepal was never again to molest the Sikkim Raja, and the King of Nepal was never to take or retain in his employment any British subject or the subject of any European or Asian State without the consent of the British Government. Furthermore, Nepal was to accept a British Representative in Kathmandu.

Hastings ratified the treaty within a week or so, but ratification from Kathmandu did not come for many months—not until December 1815. That was only after Major General Ochterlony brought an army of twenty thousand below the Makwanpur hills. There, in spite of the fierce Gurkha defence, he took villages then hauled his cannon up and put Makwanpur fort under siege to threaten the very heartland of Nepal, Kathmandu itself.

The year the war finished, Rajendra Bikram Shah came to the throne of Nepal as a boy aged two, and Queen Lalit Tripura Devi again became regent. Bhim Sen Thapa continued as prime minister and commander-in-chief of the army, with not only Lalit Tripura's protection and support but also her continued affection. The Honourable Edward Gardner became the first British Resident in Nepal under the Treaty of Sagauli.

For the next twenty years Bhim Sen Thapa continued as the undisputed ruler of Nepal. They were years of peace. He posed no further threat against the British, and they posed no threat against him, with the less ambitious governors-general, Amherst and Bentick, following the expansionist Hastings.

Nevertheless they were also years of vigilance. Bhim Sen Thapa ensured the Gurkha army was well manned and well supplied, and always ready to defend Nepal if the need should arise. He guarded Nepal's independence with the greatest of care and was jealous of its right to rule itself without outside interference. To this end he closed Nepal's borders to almost all, except the pilgrims coming to visit the holy temples, the trading caravans and, of course the British Resident and his staff.

A British Resident in Kathmandu was a continuing embarrassment to the Gurkhas, a symbol of Nepal's defeat and a threat to be watched carefully. Bhim Sen kept Edward Gardner, and his successor Mr Brian Hodgson, and their staffs virtually confined to the grounds of the British Residency, allowing them to visit only designated places in the valley and to enter and leave Nepal only by a specified route. He forbade everyone in the Durbar—almost every Nepalese in fact—any contact with the British Residency. He alone was to communicate with the Resident, and he did this seldom. Bhim Sen Thapa did his best to ensure that none of the secrets, none of the politics and little of even the ordinary business at the Durbar reached British ears.

Under Bhim Sen Thapa's guidance, Nepal survived as an independent State, a rare thing then on the Indian sub-continent. Nepal remained free to follow its own way of life, free to govern itself, free—for good or evil—to carve out its own destiny.

Appendix Three

THE RANA CENTURY

On the night of the 14th of September 1846, before the sun rose on the massacre at the Military Headquarters of the Kot and all the dead were piled up on the parade ground, and before the vultures flew down out of the mist to feed on the carrion, Queen Laxmi Devi appointed a new prime minister and commander-in-chief of the army. It was Jung Bahadur Rana who had slain his way to power that night of bloodshed, had slain all who might compete with him.

It was the start of the Rana Century when Rana despots ruled Nepal. Despots who hogged the country's meagre wealth and amassed great fortunes for themselves, lived in luxury in their great houses, ate off golden plates, indulged in great harems. It was the Rana's Century: not the people's. For the people of Nepal time stood still. For most of that one hundred years Nepal remained in its dark ages, a land of arbitrary and corrupt justice and devoid of human rights, where widows could still be burnt as satis and where slavery persisted. People lacked even the crudest schools and hospitals, and were cut off from any progress, cut off from the outer world. Even by the middle of the twentieth century, Nepal was very much a land of unenlightened peasants who were backward and poor, tied down by their struggle for subsistence.

After the massacre of the Kot, Jung Bahadur extended and secured his power. He put his seven loyal brothers—Bharkta Bir, Bom Bahadur, Badri Nar Singh, Krishna Bahadur, Rana Udip, Jagats Shamsher and Dhir Shamsher—in the country's most important jobs; and he kept King Rajendra Shah and his sons confined to the palace. He crushed the powerful Queen Laxmi Devi forever as a force in Nepal. First he refused her order to murder the King's sons and make way to the throne for her own son. Next he uncovered her plots to kill him and, at the Bhandarkhal Gardens near the palace, he murdered her co-conspirators including Bir Basnet and also twenty three others. Then he stripped her of her powers and banished her to India; and finally, at Alau, he routed the force of dissidents and Indian mercenaries she sent against him.

From that time, Jung Bahadur was the absolute ruler of Nepal. He had King Surendra Shah formalise this by issuing proclamations vesting in him all important royal powers: power over life and death, power to declare war or peace, power to codify the law, and power to appoint and dismiss those in the service of the government. And, gilding the lily, he had Surendra Shah confer on him the hereditary title of Maharaja of Kaski and Lamjung, two provinces in west Nepal. The title, the powers and the prime-ministership were to pass down to his Rana successors.

Having secured the future of Rana rule, Jung Bahadur drew up a Roll of Succession providing for his brothers in order of age, and then his sons and his grandson—Juddha Jung whom he made a general as a baby—to succeed as prime minister of Nepal and Maharaja of Kaski and Lamjung. He put Surendra Shah's proclamations in a copper box which was covered in red velvet—the "red box" as it was called—and he always kept it near him with his Maharaja headgear and the sword he used during the massacre at the Kot.

Jung Bahadur ruled Nepal for three decades and laid down the way of Rana rule for his successors. Most important was the safeguarding of Rana power. To that end, the kings were stripped of any real authority and kept confined to the palace; the police and secret agents were vigilant and pervasive; liberal ideas at home were crushed and their perpetrators cruelly punished; and Nepal was closed to progress from abroad. Plotters against the Ranas could be tried either in public or in secret, and the prime minister could decide on death or blinding, exile or prison, or some other punishment for them.

Besides guarding their own powers, the Ranas guarded well the country's independence, wanting Nepal for themselves and not for the British. They kept the army strong to deter attack. They brooked no interference from the Governor-General in Calcutta and later the Viceroy in Delhi. They held the British Resident in Kathmandu and his staff very much at arm's length and kept them out of Nepal's affairs, restricting their movement and keeping guards near the Residency to watch them.

But at the same time, the Ranas reversed the years of war or the threat of war with British India; they wanted the British as friends, not enemies, seeing this friendship as a boost to Rana power. Jung Bahadur made war on Tibet, where, after ferocious fighting and heavy loss of life in the ice and snows of the rocky heights of the Himalayas, it came to very little. But he made no attempt to expand into India. Shortly after coming to power, Jung Bahadur offered Lord Hardinge, the Governor-General of the British East India Company in Calcutta, eight regiments, with himself at their head, to help fight the Sikhs in the Punjab where the Second Sikh War was looming. His offer was not taken up, but a little later Lord Hardinge invited him to make a State visit to Britain.

Jung Bahadur visited Britain in 1853, the first at the head of a State or near it on the Indian sub-continent to do so. It was a grand affair, the hospitality showered on him was boundless. Queen Victoria accepted his gifts, granted him an audience, and had him attend the christening of her new-born son. Prime Minister Lord Russell, the Duke of Wellington and other dignities indulged him. He was entertained at the theatre, lavishly at restaurants and at the best of country houses. He reviewed artillery at Woolwich, visited Plymouth Dockyards and inspected the 2nd Life Guards. He was shown the basis of Britain's might on visits to mining and industrial centres, naval ship-building establishments and munition factories. Then during a short stay in France, Jung Bahadur was well received by President Louis Napoleon.

Within a week of Jung Bahadur's return to Kathmandu his brother Bom Bahadur called on him one night at the Thapathali Durbar and confessed that there was a plot against him. Their brother Badri Nar Singh, their cousin General Jai Kunwar Rana, and the prince Mihla Sahib had come to him saying that Jung Bahadur was no longer fit to govern Nepal and had to be disposed of. They said that Karbar Khatri, one of the ministers who went with him to England, had told them that he had ignored the religious duties required of him, by eating beef and drinking wine and taking food from forbidden hands. They also suggested he had sold out Nepal to Britain. Bom Bahadur told Jung Bahadur that the plotters were to have him assassinated, shot by a hired assassin next morning on his way to the Kathmandu Dubar. Then their brother Badri Nar Singh would cut the head from his dead body and hold it high before the army assembled on the Tundikhel, proclaiming it the head of a traitor.

Jung Bahadur acted immediately. He hurried through the night to the Military headquarters of the Kot and changed the guard at all posts throughout Kathmandu. He sent large detachments to the homes of his brother and cousin and the prince, with orders to take them dead or alive. He also sent for the rumour-monger, Kabar Khatri. Within the hour, the four were taken from their beds and put in irons in the Kot. The three plotters were brought before a council which first ordered their execution; but at his mother's pleading Jung Bahadur refused this. Next the council ordered their blinding, but again the mother's pleading saved them. Finally the plotters were imprisoned at Allahabad in India, at Nepal's expense, in foul cells and on rations limited to a rupee per day. Karbar Khatri, an offender with his tongue, was taken by two low caste musicians who urinated in his mouth, and then, losing caste, he was confined to his house.

When the Sepoy War broke out in India in May 1857, Jung Bahadur threw in Nepal's lot with the British East India Company. By June, a British Gurkha battalion from the Sirmoor Rifles' headquarters at Dehra Dun had established itself in the cantonments on the outskirts of Delhi. Now reinforced, in August the Gurkhas took the sepoys' guns at Ludlow castle. In September they were amongst the first to mount the breach near the Kashmir Bastion to take possession of the ramparts. Then they drove the sepoys from Korwali and the Chandni Chauk, stormed through the Kashmir Gate and fought in the Delhi streets until the city was retaken.

In December, responding to Governor-General Lord Canning's request, Jung Bahadur joined General Sir Colin Campbell to take part in the battle for the town of Lucknow, proud to be leading his army of some eleven thousand, with his brother General Rana Udip Singh second in command and his brother General Dhir Shamsher as his assistant. The Gurkhas fought hard at Lucknow, at the Kundoo Nadi, in the suburbs of the town and at Alambagh. They did well out of the Sepoy War. In March 1858, they returned to Kathmandu with booty that filled thousands of wagons, forming a long baggage train which the British helped escort to the border of Nepal. On their way, at Allahabad, Lord Canning thanked Jung Bahadur for the part the Gurkhas played; and Britain gave back to Nepal parts of the Terai taken in 1815 under the Treaty of Sagauli.

After the Sepoy War, Jung Bahadur was to lead a lavish and self-indulgent life. He was well established, rich and powerful. He had royal status and his children were married into the Shah royal family. Jung Bahadur was a dictator with absolute power which no one dared dispute, and rich with revenues from lands and his unlimited and unimpeded access to the country's treasury. There was the treasure he obtained from defeated sepoy leaders seeking refuge in Nepal, including the Nau Lakha Har, the million rupee necklace, from the wives of the Nana Sahib, with its priceless gems, its great diamonds, emeralds and pearls. He had his valuable hoard of precious stones, diamond rings and emerald necklaces, and British decorations on his gorgeous uniforms included the Great Commander of the Bath and the Great Commander of the Star of India; and he had the Chinese Emperor's honorific of "Commander-in-Chief of the Forces Truly Valiant Prince". His house, the Thapathali

Durbar, of more than a hundred rooms, was furnished at great expense. In his large harem he had a dozen or so wives, scores of concubines, and a hundred or more maids and female slaves. After the Sepoy War, he gave refuge to the Begum of Lucknow and to the womenfolk of the Nana Sahib, including the beautiful young Kashi Bai whom he installed in a house near his own in Thapathali. Eunuchs and female police guarded the women of the harem, and excluded all men except Jung Bahadur. There was much competition for his attention, much waiting by his favourites at night in their huge beds of many mattresses, quilts and pillows. They had a lot to gain. A maid who pleased him might be raised to a concubine; a concubine to the status of a wife; a wife given the rank of maharani with the wealth and privilege it entailed. Jung Bahadur kept his favourites in luxury, their tables bearing the richest foods, their jewellery encrusted with precious stones. In return they gave him hundreds of children, amongst whom he recognised twelve sons as Ranas.

In 1877 Jung Bahadur died suddenly at his camp on the Terai during a hunting expedition. A detachment of the prime minister's guard brought the red box, the maharaja's headgear and the sword he used at the massacre at the Kot, to his brother, Rana Udip Singh who was aged fifty-two and next on the Roll of Succession. Rana Udip Singh appointed his next brother, Jagats Shamsher, commander-in-chief, and the last surviving brother, Dhir Shamsher, senior commanding general.

Before long, however, the Ranas were to fight amongst themselves. Rana Udip Singh and Jagats Shamsher were without children; but Dhir Shamsher had many, including seventeen sons whom he recognised as legitimate heirs. All of Jung Bahadur's twelve legitimate sons and grandson, the Jung Ranas, were ahead of Dir Shamsher's sons on the Roll of Succession—and the Jungs were rich having inherited Jung Bahadur's great fortune. In particular the eldest, Jagat Jung, flaunted his wealth; he maintained a great house at Manohara and held lavish parties with much liquor, concubines and dancing girls. In the streets of Kathmandu, Jagat Jung drove in a carriage with four horses and a pair of ostriches strutting out in front, and he flew his own flag which was an image of the Monkey God Hanuman on a red background. He paraded with his band, which had dozens of sterling silver instruments imported from England and an English bandmaster.

For a time the Shamsher Ranas watched all this with envy. Then Dir Shamsher acted and several Jung Rana supporters died, including the

Crown Prince Trailokya of poisoning. Next Dhir Shamsher alleged that Jung Rana supporters were plotting to murder the prime minister, and he used hot irons and racks to get evidence against them. Jagat Jung escaped to India and his name was taken from the Roll of Succession, other Jung Ranas were imprisoned. Twenty one Jung Rana supporters were chained together and dragged through the streets of Kathmandu to the bank of the Bhackakhusi River near the holy Bhagawati Temple, and there the executioners cut deeply with their kukhries to hack the life from their bodies, and they left their corpses for the wild dogs and the vultures.

When Dhir Shamsher died of an illness, Prime Minister Rana Udip Singh let Jagat Jung return to Nepal and restored him to the Roll of Succession as next in line to the prime ministership. It was the dead Dhir Shamsher's sons who acted then. Under the eldest, Bir Shamsher, they decided to kill the prime minister and Jagat Jung, and, once and for all put an end to the Jung Ranas.

On the night of 22 November 1885, Bir Shamsher deployed his regiments to advantage around Kathmandu. Towards midnight four Shamsher brothers—Chandra, Bhim, Damber and Khadga—arrived at Rana Udip Singh's house dressed in black great coats against the cold and to conceal their guns, and asked to see their uncle saying they had an important message from the British Resident. In his bedroom, dimly lit by an oil lamp, Rana Udip Singh was lying on his bed praying to the gods, with a maid massaging his feet with oil. At the doorway, bunched together, the four brothers took their guns from their black coats, and without a word fired at their uncle. Screaming, the maid sought refuge near a gilded image of Lord Shiva. Rana Udip Singh raised himself and called to the gods for mercy. As more bullets riddled his body he fell back dead.

Also towards midnight, Bir Shamsher's soldiers arrived at Jagat Jung's house at Manohara. Jagat Jung, awoken, wondering what was wanted at such a late hour, rose from his bed and went down the stairway towards the courtyard. Bullets hit his chest and killed him, his body rolling down to the bottom of the stairway.

News of the murders spread quickly in Kathmandu. The Jungs and their supporters gathered up their gold, silver and jewellery, left their houses and—having no where else to go—sought protection in the British Residency. Jung Bahadur's grandson, the boy General Juddha Jung, forgot to bring his treasure with him and was sent back to his house to get it. It was unfortunate for him. At his house he gathered up his treasure and changed into the dress of a peasant, but he neglected to take the diamond rings from his fingers and to change his English silver-buckled shoes. On his way back to the British Residency he was accosted by a group of Shamsher soldiers who saw his shoes and rings and realised he was the Rana, Juddha Jung. They shot him and cut off his head which the commander brought to Bir Shamsher.

The day after Rana Udip Singh's murder, Bir Shamsher succeeded as prime minister and he ruled Nepal for sixteen years, up to the beginning of the twentieth century. Bir Shamsher stayed on friendly terms with the British, providing Gurkhas for the British army in return for rifles. Visiting India, he was received by the Viceroy with full honours and later decorated with the Great Commander of the Star of India. He entertained lavishly the Commander-in-Chief in India, General Sir Frederick Roberts, and his wife in Kathmandu, with a march-past on the Tundikhel. Some twenty thousand Gurkha soldiers were dressed especially for the occasion in uniforms bought at great expense, generals wore uniforms tailored in England, and officers wore imported uniforms including plumed headgear, long boots, Sam Brown belts and epaulets.

Bir Shamsher loved luxury and with access to the nation's treasury he could well indulge himself. He built several great mansions, each with a hundred or more rooms, including the Seto Durbar (White House) and the Lal Durbar (Red House). They were designed by Indian architects, and took years to build by many thousands of slaves and labourers who were paid a pittance. Bir Shamsher spared no expense on decoration and furnishings. Nor did he spare the backs of the porters who had to carry everything up the mountains, up the rough often almost precipitous tracks and into the valley: Italian marble and tiles, carpets from Persia and Belgium, pianos, furniture, chandeliers from England, glassware from Rome and Venice, silverware, gas lamps, generators to light lamps in the gardens, plumbing and modern toilets.

Bir Shamsher's great houses and high living were his absorbing interests. An epicure, he employed trained chefs to cook the best game and other dishes. He spent heavily on his harem, on his many wives, concubines and maids. He had his girl musicians who played on traditional instruments and on pianos and violins from Europe. He gave great parties in the Lal Durbar under dazzling chandeliers, with music and drama and the dancing of his Talimay girls. Bir Shamsher died of natural causes in the Lal Durbar on the 3rd of March 1901, and his brother Dev Shamsher succeeded him.

Dev Shamsher also lived a life of luxury with his wives, concubines and scores of maids. He loved pomp. Dressed in gorgeous robes and seated in a howdah on a favourite elephant, he would go on great processions through Kathmandu with massed bands, elite infantry regiments, and masked men who performed traditional dances. Crowds would line the streets to watch and applaud.

Rana power meant less to Dev Shamsher; and so in this he broke the Rana mould. He was a kind man, a liberal by nature, and deplored the people's backwardness. He called a meeting in the great hall of his Thapathali Durbar, bringing together people from all walks of life to discuss measures to improve their lot. Then Dev Shamsher went further, much too far for his brother Chandra Shamsher who was next in line to be prime minister. He decided to draw up a constitution for Nepal, with a parliament of the people and the king at its head.

Chandra Shamsher struck. Late one night he had Dev Shamsher seized, put in a carriage covered in dark cloth and guarded by a strong detachment, and in secret taken to Dhankuta, a remote village high on a hill in far eastern Nepal. Later Dev Shamsher managed to escape to India, where the British gave him refuge.

Chandra Shamsher was to rule Nepal for twenty eight years, from 1901 until 1929. It was a time when India was awakening and moving towards independence, with early meetings of the Indian Congress Party and with leaders like Barindra Ghose and Bal Tilak, and then Jinnah and Jawaharlal Nehru and the great Mahatma Gandhi. From his mountains, Chandra Shamsher saw the Indian awakening as the gravest of threats to Rana power. To safeguard it, he ruthlessly suppressed any spilling over from the awakening in India, any political reform whatsoever. His spy network had secret agents in many places. He imposed the tightest curfew on Kathmandu, denying much of the night streets to all except his patrolling police. He closed the valley of Kathmandu to Nepalese citizens from other areas, as well as to foreigners, and admitted none without passports. He set up a board of censors which suppressed anti-Rana writings, and in fact almost all literature in Nepal. He had the British suppress anti-Rana newspapers which Nepalese dissenters had started in India: the Gorkhali in 1903 and the *Tarun Gorkha* and the *Gorkha Sansa* in 1927.

Chandra Shamsher's prisons were crowded and his torturers were busy. Krishna Lal, who criticised the Ranas in a book, was publicly whipped and sentenced to prison, where he died under torture. Many political dissidents received life imprisonment and some, like Krishna

Prasad Koirala and Krishna Vir Kami, died in gaol. Chandra Shamsher's vigilance was also directed at his own Rana relatives. He excluded from the Roll of Succession those he thought might oppose him, and graded the Rana families, nominating sons from high caste wives as A Class Ranas; those from wives of a lower caste as B Class; and illegitimate sons as C Class Ranas with few privileges.

Believing that if India threw off British rule, Nepal would throw off Rana rule, Chandra Shamsher was very much in support of the British in their struggle in India. He visited the Viceroy, Lord Curzon, in Delhi; lavishly entertained Lord Kitchener, the commander-in-chief in British India, in Kathmandu; and visited Britain where he was well received by King Edward VII. He entertained the young King George V on a great hunting party on the Terai, when hundreds of animals were shot; the King, himself, said to have taken twenty one tigers and ten rhinoceros. King George presented Nepal with some two thousand Lee Metford rifles and a million rounds of ammunition, and made Chandra Shamsher a Great Commander of the Victorian Order, to add to his orders of the Star of India and the Bath.

In 1914 Chandra Shamsher brought Nepal into the First World War on the side of the Allies; but he did so with some difficulty. Many in Nepal, including the Regent Queen Mother, strongly opposed such an intervention, were against having Gurkha soldiers killed on battlefields in Europe, so far away. Chandra Shamsher assembled army regiments on the Tundikhel, then called on the Queen Mother at the palace and held his revolver closely at her head until she agreed to send the boy King Tribhuban to address the regiments and announce that Nepal was at war. Chandra Shamsher sent ten of his own regiments, sixteen thousand men, to help the British in the north-west frontier as well as for garrison duties in India. He recruited Gurkhas to join the British Indian Army; and some two hundred thousand fought in the trenches in France and Flanders, on the sands of Egypt, the battlefields of Persia and Palestine and on the rocky cliffs of Gallipoli. They proved to be amongst the very best of soldiers: loyal, disciplined and brave; ferocious in their attacks on the enemy; skilled riflemen and machine gunners; and deadly and much feared wielders of their sharp kukhries in hand-to-hand combat. In a treaty of friendship, a grateful Britain recognised the full sovereignty of Nepal and replaced the British Resident in Kathmandu with an Envoy Extraordinary and Minister Plenipotentiary.

In November 1929, Chandra Shamsher was succeeded by his sixty five year-old brother Bhim Shamsher. He ruled ruthlessly for three years, suppressing any political awakening in Nepal. His son, Ram Shamsher, was the chief of police and brought in a reign of terror. People with liberal views were arrested, sometimes tortured, imprisoned or exiled and had their property confiscated. False charges were made to settle old scores, and innocent men were punished. The prisons became even more overcrowded. A disciple of Mahatma Gandhi, Tulsi Mehr, who tried to start a village spinning movement, was imprisoned for life. Several youths, who started the Prachanda Gorkha movement aimed at replacing the Ranas with King Tribhuban and an elected parliament, were arrested, tortured and sentenced to life imprisonment. One of them, the King's relative Umesh Shah, was sent to Palpa in chains and in a cage, while others were chained in the foul cells of the Kathmandu gaol.

Bhim Shamsher died in September 1932, to be followed by his brother Juddha Shamsher aged fifty eight, who ruled Nepal until 1945. A quick-tempered and overbearing man, he was very much the tyrant. He tried hard to stop liberal ideas coming from India. He censored Indian newspapers and books coming into Nepal, banned radios that would pick up Indian news; and his police checked all travellers and informed the British of Nepalese with liberal ideas who were moving into India.

Mahatma Gandhi horrified Juddha Shamsher. When the British arrested several Nepalese young men in India for their part in the Mahatma's Quit India Movement, Juddha Shamsher applauded. When several Indian disciples of the Mahatma sought refuge in Nepal, Juddha Shamsher arrested them and clapped them in gaol. And when hundreds of Nepalese youths stormed the gaol and released the Indians, Juddha Shamsher took the youths' leaders, imprisoned them and tortured them so brutally that some, including Abdul Miya, died in the torture chamber.

Juddha's crushing of liberal ideas which were arising in Nepal itself was vicious. In 1936, five young men started the Praja Parishad Party which wanted a democratic system for Nepal with an elected parliament and a constitutional king. Working in secret for several years, the Praja Parishad became a rallying point for other liberal thinkers and met with King Tribhuban's approval. Young men of the Praja Parishad smuggled a duplicating machine up from India, hid it from Juddha Shamsher's secret police and printed pamphlets encouraging people to raise arms against the Rana despots. Then in September 1940 on the night of the Bhoto Jatra day, when gambling was allowed and Juddha Shamsher had lifted curfew to let gamblers return home, the young men went cautiously along the narrow streets of Kathmandu and Lalitpatan leaving their pamphlets on street corners.

There was no revolt against the Ranas—not then. Juddha Shamsher's agents hunted out some five hundred men of the Praja Parishad, held them in guardrooms at the Singha Durbar, whipped them to wring confessions out of them, then burnt their bodies with hot irons to discover the names of their leaders. Juddha Shamsher made much of the trial of the leaders, which was held on the Singha Durbar football ground before a military court, with tents set up and refreshments for notables invited to attend. The leaders, in heavy chains, were charged with high treason; they were not allowed to deny the charge and not allowed lawyers, and were whipped before the court when they tried to deny the prosecutor's evidence. All were found guilty.

Four young men—Sukra Raj Shastri, Dasarath Chand, Ganga Lal and Dharma Bhakta Mathema—were sentenced to death. In the following January, late one winter's night, a Rana general came to the gaol in Kathmandu with a military detachment. They took Sukra Raj Shastri from his cell, dragged him to a waiting wagon and took him to Teku where they hanged him from a tree near the roadway. They hanged Dharma Bhakta Mathema beside the road near the Pashupatinath. They also took Dasarath Chand and Ganga Lal from their cells, tied them together on bamboo poles, took them to the bank of the Bagmati near the Bhagabati Temple, to be shot by an army firing squad. All four dead bodies were left exposed in death with placards pinned to them to warn of the fate for all who rebelled against the Ranas.

When the Second World War broke out in 1939, Juddha Shamsher made eight regiments available to help the British suppress unrest in India. As the War progressed, the Gurkha Brigade in the British Army was increased from twenty to forty five battalions, with ten training centres and various support units, to a total of more than two hundred thousand men; this from a backward country with a population of barely six million. Again the Gurkhas distinguished themselves on far-flung battlefields. They fought in many places: in Greece and Cyprus, Iraq and Persia, North Africa and in Italy where on the road to Rome they were conspicuous in the attack on the German stronghold on Monte Casino. They also fought in Malaya and Burma. Again the Gurkhas won many medals and were praised highly by their British officers. The Gurkhas became renowned throughout the world as brave and skilful fighting men.

In November 1945 Juddha Shamsher gave up office, and Padma

Shamsher succeeded him to rule Nepal for two and a half years. An intelligent man, from the very start he saw the time for the liberalisation of Rana rule had come. He announced himself as, "the servant of the people". He had good reason to. An interim government had been set up in India, a democratic government with Jawaharlal Nehru as prime minister. Revolt against the Ranas was brewing in Nepal and at Biratnagar the police shot several strikers and gaoled activists including the brothers B.P. Koirala and G.P. Koirala.

Padma Shamsher moved to give the people of Nepal a measure of self-government, and a constitution of sorts with the people having the rights of freedom of speech, freedom of religion and freedom of assembly. But his reforms came to nothing. Even at that late stage, the Ranas' hardliners, led by Mohan Shamsher, were strongly against reforms. Warned that Mohan Shamsher's men would murder him, Padma Shamsher fled to India where Mohan Shamsher's agents threatened him and he signed a letter of resignation after.

Mohan Shamsher came to power in April 1948, receiving the red box, the Maharaja headgear and the sword which Jung Bahadur had used at the massacre of the Kot a little more than a century earlier. During that long century, very little had been done to raise the people of Nepal from their poverty and backwardness. True, a few improvements had been made, mainly by Dev Shamsher out of the kindness of his heart, and by Chandra Shamsher reacting to the pressure of changing times. Some moves had been taken against the burning of widows, slavery and the extensive use of the death penalty. A few schools and a small degree-conferring college in Kathmandu had been set up, and the weekly newspaper, the *Gorkhapatra*, started. There were also a small hospital and a library. There had been a few public works—mainly minor drains and water services—but notably an overhead ropeway from Bhimphedi up the steep and rugged slopes into the Kathmandu valley, and a narrow-gauge railway for some twenty miles along the Terai. After the Second World War, the Nepal Bank, the Nepal Trading Company and a small telephone service were established, and consulates in Delhi and Lhasa were set up.

But by the middle of the twentieth century Nepal was still very much imprisoned in its dark ages, a land where the people had no voice in parliament and where human rights were few. There were hardly any schools and people were denied education, and there were no health services to speak of and people suffered and often died young. Farms were backward and there was virtually no industry. There were no roads, only tracks connecting up the country. Nepal was a poverty-stricken country, very nearly the poorest of all the countries in the world.

From the start of his reign, Mohan Shamsher faced growing pressure from students and from Nepalese organised in India. At first he reacted in the traditional Rana way, abrogating the people's rights which had been given by Padma Shamsher in 1948, banning political parties, arresting their leaders and again filling the gaols. But the pressures on him for reform increased. He set up a parliament, but let it be a mock-parliament that was never used. This enraged Nepal's liberal-minded men, and in April 1950 they formed the Nepali Congress, under men like B.P. Koirala, G.P. Kiorala, Ganesh Man Singh and K.P. Bhattarai. The Nepali Congress set out to overthrow Rana power and give Nepal a constitutional government under King Tribhuban. With the support from many in India, it formed a Liberation Army.

The Liberation Army's first foray failed. Agents sent to Kathmandu to assassinate Mohan Shamsher were caught with bombs and confessions were forced from them. Condemning them to death, Mohan Shamsher called for the King's warrant for their execution (always a mere formality under Rana rule). But this time King Tribhuban refused, openly challenging Mohan Shamsher and putting his own life in danger. Under threat, King Tribhuban left the palace with his family for the Indian Embassy, then fled to India where the Indian President met him and welcomed him as a guest of the State. Then Mohan Shamsher put his grandson, the young boy Gyanendra Shah, on the throne.

At this time the Liberation Army escalated its operations. At dawn on the 11th of November 1950 it attacked Birganj, then moved northwards further into Nepal. Within a week it had taken Biratnagar and Jhapa on the eastern Terai and had put Bhiarahawa in the west under attack. The people welcomed it, and fighting broke out in many places throughout the country. The people fought bravely—the Limbu and Kiranti people, those on the Terai, in Lumbini and many other places. Fighting continued during December and into January 1951, and the Liberation Army overran Nepal, taking Biratnagar, Dhankutta, Bhojpur, Malangwa, Palpa and many other towns and villages. In Kathmandu, people demanded the restoration of King Tribhuban and held mass demonstrations under fire from Mohan Shamsher's guns.

Cornered and searching for a way out, Mohan Shamsher turned to India. On advice from there, he agreed to reinstate King Tribhuban and set up an interim government which included representation from popular opinion. He reinstated the laws relating to people's rights introduced by Padma Shamsher in 1948, granted an amnesty for most political prisoners and allowed political parties which were compliant with the law.

On the 16th of February 1951, King Tribhuban returned to Nepal to a rousing welcome from the people and the next day the Liberation Army put down its arms. King Tribhuban issued a proclamation annulling all powers and privileges given to the Ranas by his great grandfather King Surendra Shah in 1856; and annulling the Ranas' hereditary right to the prime-ministership of Nepal and to Kaski and Lamjung. Mohan Shamsher handed over to the King the red box which held King Surendra Shah's proclamations.

On the 18th of February 1951, King Tribhuban issued a second proclamation establishing an interim government, a coalition cabinet made up of five Ranas including one B Class and one C Class Rana, and four members and one nominee of the Nepali Congress. Mohan Shamsher was made prime minister and B.P. Koirala leader of the Nepali Congress faction. Cabinet members were to be collectively responsible to the King and hold office at his pleasure.

Thus the Rana century had ended. The road was now open to travel to a democratic Nepal, for the Nepalese people to come to rule themselves. In 1951, people looking along that road could see—not too far in the future, they hoped—a new Nepal, at last a country of the twentieth century, a free and open country, and a member of the community of nations, having a democracy with an elected parliament, political parties and a constitutional monarchy. There were high hopes then. And the high hopes lasted. But the road turned out to be a long one, with many twists and turns, a road still to be coloured by the blood of many martyrs.